THE
REGRESSION
STRAIN

THE
REGRESSION
STRAIN

A THRILLER

KEVIN HWANG

NORMAL
RANGE
PRESS

ISBN: 979-8-9927270-0-5 (eBook)
ISBN: 979-8-9927270-1-2 (paperback)
ISBN: 979-8-9927270-2-9 (hardcover)
ISBN: 979-8-9927270-3-6 (audio)

To mom

1

As THE CAB rounded the corner behind the service buildings, the full bulk of the ship rose into view, a floating city gleaming white and blue against the gray Baltic sky. The *Paradise* would be Peter's home and workplace for the next month.

His shoulders tightened. Had he forgotten to pack anything? It was too late now.

The taxi ejected him into the cool summer of Copenhagen—heaven compared to the stifling heat of Texas. He checked in at the terminal counter, cleared security, and joined the stream of chattering passengers traversing the covered gangway to board the vessel. Most of them spoke in English and a few in Spanish. Others conversed in German, French, or Scandinavian tongues. They seemed affluent and confident, not at all like his impoverished patients in Houston's Fifth Ward. That guy in front—his Rolex probably cost more than Peter's Outback.

Peter wheeled his suitcase through a colonnade of clapping crew members and across the threshold of the grand atrium. Its rich wood paneling and glittering chandeliers were as opulent as the brochures promised. He fused with the crush of passengers piling up in front of the diagrams posted near the elevators. Living quarters for the medical crew were on the lowest deck, conveniently adjacent to the clinic.

Amid the throng, a woman was fussing over a teenage boy in a wheelchair. She leaned in and whispered something in his ear, then tousled his thick mop of brown hair. With one hand cranked tight against his chest, he lolled his head back and rewarded her with a crooked smile. Her haggard face lit up. Now that was one tired mama.

"I like his shirt." Peter pointed to the graphic of Thor wielding his massive hammer.

"You hear that, Calvin? He likes it."

Calvin's nose crinkled above the sparse stubble dotting his chin. She retrieved a ChapStick from her floral fanny pack and slathered Calvin's lips first, then her own.

She offered the tube to Peter with a glistening smile. "Want some?"

He cringed. That was weird. "Uh, no thanks."

"Want him?"

Peter's eyes snapped up to hers. "Excuse me?"

"You can take him for a while." She smiled and tipped her head. "He doesn't eat much."

"Ah…"

"Ha ha, it's a joke." She licked her moistened lips. "I've been on this boat too long. Cabin fever." She gave him a little nod and wheeled the kid into the elevator.

The adjacent elevator dinged open, revealing a family that looked right at home, mom admiring the decor, two school kids horsing around. Sipping coffee in his striped polo, dad looked a bit like Peter's microbiology professor—placid and plump.

Peter pulled his suitcase to the side with a smile. It was nice to see people relaxed and carefree. And if they needed medical attention—well, he could offer it. It would be a relief to simply treat patients. No rationing medications against their rent. No fighting through nettles of bureaucracy just to get a CT scan. He wasn't built for that fight, and the last few rounds had left him bruised.

The younger child in the elevator darted out. Mom lunged and grabbed his collar, jostling dad into Peter. Coffee sloshed out of the man's cup and down his jeans.

An animal snarl flashed over the man's pale, doughy face. "Watch it, prick."

"Sorry, I didn't expect…"

The man leaned in, eyes glowing hot behind round bifocals. Peter jerked back. "Whoa, are you okay?"

As the man cocked his fist back, Peter watched the sleeve of his polo shirt ride up his bicep, almost in slow motion. Peter quickly raised his open palms.

"Honey," mom hissed. She tugged her little one back, and he huddled under her frail wings.

The man lowered his fist, the stench of coffee hot on his breath.

Peter nodded. "It was an accident. I'll buy you another coffee. Or jeans."

The heat in the man's eyes dissipated and he blinked a few times, looking at Peter's face yet his attention was directed elsewhere. "Ah, shoot."

Sorry, mom mouthed and hustled the whole family away.

Peter stepped into the elevator among passengers who seemed oblivious to the encounter. His heart hammered in his chest, and his mouth soured with adrenaline. Microbiology professor? Scratch that—this guy was more like that assistant principal caught in a minivan with the high school girl. And here he'd nearly gotten into a fistfight on his first day.

But hey, he'd defused the situation. He was still supposed to be here. This was going to work out. He closed his eyes as the last passengers got off and the elevator continued to the bottom level.

The doors opened onto a hallway with plush burgundy carpet and polished handrails. Colorful abstract prints enlivened the walls. This was where everything could begin again, even at age thirty-two. He would be a healer on the high seas, applying his hard-earned expertise to help people on vacation.

But the aura disintegrated when he opened his cabin door. Inside was a single bed, a nightstand no larger than a magazine, and a built-in desk with a swivel chair. The sheets lay twisted in a lump at the foot of the bed, exposing a mattress with stains the color of dirty bathwater. A smudged TV hung crookedly from the ceiling, and a stale scent lingered in the air. The only feature that distinguished the cabin from a hospital on-call room was the round porthole window giving view to rusty shipping containers on the dock.

Well, he wasn't on vacation, after all, even if everyone else was. Peter heaved his suitcase onto the lumpy mattress and began stowing his clothes. Luckily he'd packed light for this trial run. The tiny closet contained a white uniform, starched and waiting like a suit of armor, as well as an orange life vest and a safe the size of a cigar box.

The only real valuable he'd brought was his new 3M Littmann Cardiology IV, an upgrade from the battered stethoscope from residency. He fished around in the side compartment of the suitcase but came up empty. It should've been right there.

He checked every zippered pocket, then rummaged

through his backpack. Nada. How could he have forgotten his freaking stethoscope, of all things? He'd followed his packing list. He loved lists, for heaven's sake, loved checking off each item. Little good it had done. He drew a deep breath in then out, trying to clear his mind by counting to ten like the therapist said.

Ten seconds was a long time to think about nothing. Maybe he needed a higher dose of Lexapro. He'd been reluctant to accept his diagnosis, one he himself had given to so many patients, but the antidepressant seemed to help with his mood, concentration, and sleep.

The ambiance of the bathroom matched that of the bedroom, with black spots of mildew mottling the lower edge of the shower curtain. The sink offered little space for personal items.

He opened his bottle of Lexapro, shook a tablet into his palm, and swallowed it dry as he stared into the dingy mirror. Working aboard a cruise ship would be a huge change, and he needed to bring his best. He set the bottle on the narrow counter, but it clipped the edge, flipped out of his hand, and plopped into the toilet with an insulting splash.

His stomach clenched and he squeezed his eyes shut. Maybe, by some miracle, the bottle had landed upright with the tablets safe and dry inside, like a lifeboat. A tiny boat in a tiny toilet on a gargantuan ship.

He peered down. Nothing doing—the bottle floated on its side, surrounded by white tablets bobbing in the murky water like pearls of pasta in chicken broth. Why did the water have to look like that? Was it just reflecting the grimy inner surface of the toilet bowl?

Didn't matter. His mental health was officially soaking in shit.

The half-life of Lexapro was around thirty hours, and he'd taken one yesterday back in Houston. He could just retrieve the tablets, wash them off, and dunk them in rubbing alcohol. Without more doses, the effects would diminish over the next few days. He could picture his exit interview: *I'm sorry, Dr. Palma, you came ill-prepared.*

One hand drifted to his pocket. At least he'd remembered to pack his favorite metallic pen. Even in the age of digital everything, a quality pen remained one of his favorite tools— that and old-fashioned index cards. His fingers closed around the pen, clicking the top: *Ta-tick, ta-tack. Ta-tick, ta-tack.*

Someone knocked on the door, but the bolt clicked open before he could reach it. The slight, olive-skinned man turned back to the hall almost as quickly as he'd come in. White shirt and charcoal vest—must be a steward.

"I'm sorry, I come back later," he said with a duck of his bald head.

Peter waved him in. "It's all right. I just got here."

"Nobody clean your room yet?"

"I guess not."

"You the doctor, no?"

"One of them." He propped the door open for the man's cart.

The steward glanced around the tiny room. "It will be my pleasure to serve you. I come later when you have gone out."

Peter suspected the man's cheerful acceptance hid the same bone-deep fatigue that had weighed down his own mother. She used to clean offices, back before Felipe joined the army, and she was always exhausted. Chemical fumes permeated her clothes and hair, and her knuckles cracked and bled until he bought her the non-latex gloves that her cheap-ass boss wouldn't pay for.

Before Peter could return to the bathroom, somebody else came knocking: a petite woman in blue scrubs, probably late thirties. A tight ponytail held back her glossy chestnut hair. Her sharp cheekbones and jawline were all business.

"Luisa Calderone, nurse on staff." The strength in her bony handshake matched the intensity of her hazel eyes. "They said this is your first gig."

Yep, a fresh start, a sorely needed one. "Sorry. I'll try to learn quick."

"We can do a proper tour later, but let's just walk and talk for now." She nodded back at the hallway. "I can give you some time to get changed, but we have patients—so not too long, please."

Right back into it, then. He was a kid on a roller coaster cresting the first big incline—the moment before the bottom fell out. He opened the closet and confronted his uniform. Sure, he'd paid for the ride, but that didn't make it any less stomach-churning.

Peter followed Luisa down a wide corridor bustling with crew members in charcoal vests and the occasional white-clad officer.

"This is I-95," she said, "the quickest way to get anywhere on the ship. The clinic is just around the corner. Shortest commute in the world."

His uniform felt as stiff as it looked. He fiddled with the black and yellow bands on each shoulder signifying his rank as a junior officer. "So it's busy even on these port days?"

"Absolutely. New passengers are boarding, and continuing passengers are heading out on excursions, although a lot of them just laze around the ship." She shot a frown in his direction. "Yet somehow they get sick."

"I see. Alcohol?"

"That and then some."

The demonic dad in the elevator must have had a few too many, although Peter hadn't detected alcohol on his breath.

"Dr. Hartley did the morning shift," Luisa continued. "She'll be glad you're here. Some of us have been on board since Athens."

A placard on the steel door indicated that the clinic was open from 8 a.m. to 11 a.m. and then from 3 p.m. to 6 p.m. Banker's hours—perfect for coughs and colds, ankle sprains, and heartburn. This low-key atmosphere was exactly what he needed to get back into the game.

In the boxy waiting area outside the entrance, a well-dressed passenger in her fifties filled out paperwork on a clipboard, while a younger man sat cradling his head in his hands. Peter and Luisa slipped past.

The clinic bore only a passing resemblance to the expansive facility featured on the orientation video. Here, gray tiles and overhead fluorescent panels reminded him of the rural clinic where he'd moonlighted as a resident, treating teenagers for gonorrhea and farmers for gout.

An exam room door opened, disgorging a woman maybe three decades his senior wearing a white uniform and a stethoscope with green tubing. She leveled a stern gaze at him through round glasses. "You must be..."

"Peter Palma."

"Elizabeth Hartley, chief physician," she replied in a light Scottish accent. Her eyes flicked down to his neck. "Where's your stethoscope?"

Of course she'd notice. Suddenly he was back in med

school on the first day of the brutal internal medicine rotation, before he'd gained the knowledge and experience that he wanted to wield now. "I haven't finished unpacking yet."

"I suppose you could pick one up in Scotland." She shot Luisa a quick look. "For now, she can dig up an extra one we have lying around, but I can't vouch for the quality."

Luisa gave a tight-lipped nod.

"Well," Hartley continued in the clipped tone of someone taking great pains to move past an egregious offense. "You're American."

"Yes."

"Board-certified?"

"In family medicine."

"How many years in practice?"

"Three," he said.

She shook her head and muttered, "Lord have mercy."

He clamped his mouth shut. So much for making a good first impression.

"I suppose this is your first go-round on a cruise."

"It is." Hell, it was his first time on a boat with an actual engine. His salary at the community clinic left no room for the yachts and other toys his cardiology buddies enjoyed. Oh, well. To each their own.

"You won't last long by treating this like a vacation."

"Understood."

He had no intention of loafing. The edge in her voice was jarring, especially compared to the warmth of Dr. Nora Wetzel, the medical director of the cruise line. During the interview in Miami, he'd harbored the irrational fear that Wetzel somehow knew about Felipe's death, like a dream where you realized you'd been walking around naked and everyone was staring at you. But she'd called after all: They had an immediate need in Europe, and was he ready? He cleaned out his condo the next day—unloaded all his crates of Dr Pepper onto Nali, scrubbed the hell out of his kitchen and bathroom. He didn't want to come back to roaches. He sold his discus fish back to the pet store with much regret. The iridescent creatures had just started breeding in the pH-calibrated aquarium he'd painstakingly set up on his free days.

"At least we're back up to a full team now." Hartley began wiping her glasses with an alcohol pad. "I've been the only doctor since Barcelona."

This probably wasn't the time to ask what had happened. He followed Hartley to the office area, with Luisa pointing out the laboratory and supply closet on the way. The office looked like any other medical charting room, cluttered and cramped, except the porthole window offered a glimpse of sparkling, sunlit waves.

Hartley plopped down in a rolling chair with a huff. "It was hectic this morning, but I've got them all tucked away. A little bit of asthma, lumps and bumps. One fellow had nausea—but fortunately, no diarrhea." She swiveled to face him. "That would have been a disaster."

"Norovirus?" A good chunk of his orientation in Miami had been dedicated to infection control.

She put her glasses back on and shook her head. "Doesn't matter. Everything shuts down. Covid had its day, but it's not the only bully on the playground. I was going to step off for a few hours. One of my cousins lives outside of Copenhagen, and I haven't seen her in ages."

"Okay." A few hours off seemed reasonable—that was the point of having two doctors on board—but a smoother hand-off would've been nice.

"Unless you'd prefer me to stay?" She slipped her fingers under the arms of her glasses and rubbed her temples.

The *Paradise* was a new environment with new colleagues. This was clearly a test, but he didn't know the right answer. Was she sounding out his confidence or his humility? Both attributes were necessary for success in this job. "Dr. Hartley, please enjoy your afternoon. I can—"

She held up a hand. "All things considered, I'll stick around."

His ears burned; he'd failed the test. "Right."

After Hartley left to see the next patient, Luisa had him download the SeaText app on his phone for onboard messaging. "The Wi-Fi's good all over the ship." She demonstrated how to join the medical team group, which included another nurse named Mandy. The tour continued through three exam rooms and a critical care bay.

She paused at the pharmacy closet, one hand resting on the handle. "You know, Dr. Hartley's under a lot of stress."

So it wasn't just him. He cracked a careful smile. "Have you all worked together a while?"

"For years. Usually she's pretty steady."

"If I may ask, what happened with the other doctor?" Wetzel had been vague about the sudden vacancy and he hadn't pressed her on it, eager as he was to leave the ghosts of Houston behind.

"It's a long story." Luisa seemed like the type who wouldn't get into juicy details. Instead, she slapped a cheap plastic stethoscope into his hand and raised her eyebrows. "Ready for your first patient?"

After months of wondering if he'd ever practice medicine again, the moment was finally here. It wasn't perfect. He'd already screwed up—how could he have forgotten his stethoscope, of all things?—and he'd have to find time to call the hotel. But he'd graduated from med school with honors. Aced the boards. This was a cruise ship with happy, smiling passengers.

He squared his shoulders. "Let's do it."

———

She wasn't exactly happy or smiling, his first patient, the 54-year-old lady who'd been filling out the questionnaire in the waiting room. Claudia Stevenson's hands pressed down on the padded exam table where she sat, bunching her shoulders under her thick blond curls. She wrinkled her nose and surveyed the puny exam room. "No offense, but does this place smell a little bit?"

Peter detected nothing but a whiff of chemicals. "They must've just cleaned in here. Maybe they got overzealous."

"It's more like rotten eggs."

He gave a tiny shrug. "How can I help you?"

After a long breath in and out, she placed her palm on her chest. "I have this funny feeling here. I'm a bit winded."

"Does it hurt when you breathe?"

"Not really." She squinted. "But it's tight."

Her only other symptoms were a mild headache and fever a few days ago. A violent, dry cough erupted from her chest, engorging the veins on her forehead. Her eyes went blank and her mouth gaped—just for a second—and then she was back.

"Are you okay?"

She puffed out her cheeks. "Sorry, I'm just stressed."

"I understand." Something was eating at her.

He put on a mask and listened to her lungs with the plastic stethoscope, but her breaths sounded hollow and too loud.

The cheap instrument was amplifying layers and frequencies without discrimination. He slipped outside and found Luisa taking vitals on a young man in the triage area. He motioned to her and held up the stethoscope. "Is there another one I can try? I need to get a good listen to her lungs."

"You could ask Dr. Hartley."

Eh, he'd already gotten off on the wrong foot with Hartley. "I'd prefer not to. Could I use yours?"

She gave him a sour look.

"Just for a minute."

She stepped over to the steel counter and plucked an alcohol pad from a box, wiped down the diaphragm, bell, and earpieces of her own stethoscope, and handed it to him without a word. Her initials were etched on the gray circular ID tag attached to the tubing. He nodded his thanks.

Back with Stevenson, he now heard a high-pitched wheeze with each breath. Her lungs were pulling and squeezing against constricted airways. He swabbed her for Covid and flu, but both were negative. He suggested an albuterol treatment. "That'll open up those tight airways, make it easier to breathe."

Within minutes, she was inhaling a fine mist amid the hum of the nebulizer machine Luisa set up. Stevenson gave him a thumbs-up. "I feel better."

So did he. What a relief to help her in such a straightforward way. This was exactly what he was looking for, even better than the primal satisfaction of weed-whacking the overgrown patch of grass at his condo. In the darkest days before he'd started Lexapro, he'd taken to watching lawn guys on YouTube mowing down urban jungles. Cheap, mind-numbing thrills.

Ouch. No more Lexapro.

As if on cue, Luisa pulled him out of the exam room to show him how to retrieve medications from the pharmacy closet. She pointed to a clipboard on the cabinet. "Document every prescription here. It all gets reconciled, and it has to match what you enter in the chart."

He scanned the boxes on the metal shelves: scopolamine patches for seasickness, and antibiotics like ciprofloxacin. Vials of insulin and bags of sterile saline. He didn't see a section for antidepressants, but maybe they were tucked away somewhere. He grabbed an albuterol inhaler and wrote all the info on the next blank row, Luisa peering over his shoulder. He signed his name in the last column beneath his colleagues', some with flowing handwriting, others blocky and condensed.

Stevenson was breathing easy when he returned, her eyes closed. Listening to her lungs, he noticed the wheezing was almost gone. "Let's watch you here for a while. Assuming everything stays good, I'll send you out with this inhaler."

Now that her lungs were expanding smoothly again, out came her story: She worked as a sales rep for a distributor of commercial kitchen appliances. Her boss had gifted her this cruise as a bonus for achieving the highest sales in Michigan last year. "But I feel guilty for being here. It's so extravagant. Many other people never get anything like this."

"But you deserve it, right? It's a nice way to celebrate."

"Our son." She blinked back tears. "He blows all his money on sports gambling. He doesn't even like sports. He just goes online and uses his credit card. Can you believe it? He found this site that takes credit cards. He bets money that he doesn't even have."

"I see." He sat on a rolling stool next to her.

"And I just put my mother in a nursing home. Dementia."

"I'm sorry." Apparently even people on a cruise reeled from the same uppercuts and jabs as everybody else. Nobody escaped the flurry. We all ended up on the mat someday.

"You're such a nice man." She glanced at his unadorned ring finger. "What's your girlfriend's name?"

Wow, that came out of nowhere. "Ah, well, we broke up before—"

She cut him off with a wave of her hand. "Whatever. When's the last time you got laid?"

Oh yeah, she was feeling better for sure—a little too good. He stood up. "I'll get the nurse and we'll get you checked out of here. You can keep the inhaler."

"Okay, cutie-pie." She winked. "I'm only here for the view."

His cheeks burned hot. Was she really doing this?

"Thanks for listening to me. I mean, not just my lungs. The other stuff." She sat up, pushing her chest out. "Do you do house calls? I'm in room 592, and you can come check on me anytime."

What was her deal? Peter had never considered himself particularly good-looking or charming, and he was certainly no regular target for propositions. If anything, the past few months of enchiladas and scallion pancakes had aged him a few years. He shook his head. Maybe vacation mode, or alcohol, or the long distance from home had lowered her inhibitions. At any rate, her advance was even stranger than that demon-dad's eruption in the elevator.

He returned the stethoscope to Luisa on the way out. "What'd you give her anyway, laughing gas?"

Luisa gave him a puzzled look and draped her stethoscope back around her neck.

Peter retreated to the office to regroup. He jotted Stevenson's name on an index card along with reminders of her presentation: *respiratory, mental.* An old habit, keeping notes like this in the age of electronic records.

He really needed to find his own stethoscope so he wouldn't have to keep begging off others. Since they still had decent cell signal here at port, he googled the hotel. Maybe his stethoscope had fallen out of his luggage last night. He explained his problem to the receptionist and waited through a prolonged hold and a transfer. Finally, they connected him with the concierge, who understood his request but put him on hold again.

The ship's overhead speaker emitted seven short blasts followed by a long one.

A terse male voice said, "All assigned personnel, report to your stations for the assembly drill."

"Come on." Luisa strode toward the front of the clinic.

Peter tightened his jaw. If he hung up now, he might not have a chance to call back before they departed. "What is it?"

"Assembly drill. It's all hands on deck, except for Dr. Hartley. She'll stay." Luisa held the door. "You coming?"

"Actually, I was trying to..." It wasn't really a question, coming from her. "Sure."

They dove into traffic on I-95, Luisa leading the way toward midships.

A series of three chimes heralded an announcement: "Attention all guests, this is your captain speaking." His baritone voice dripped with easy confidence. "As part of our commitment to your well-being, we will now conduct the assembly drill."

A knot of kids jostled their way past Peter and Luisa.

"Please proceed to your assigned muster station, as indicated on your key card. Make sure to bring your life jacket from your cabin. Your welfare is our top priority, and this drill ensures we are prepared in the unlikely event of an emergency." The captain chuckled. "In other words, don't screw up my safety record."

Several crew members ahead of Peter snickered.

He caught up with Luisa. "Why do they call it a muster station?" He'd meant to google the term after hearing it at orientation. "What do we actually do?"

She stopped at a large, open stairwell. "Help them find their stations."

The fourth level teemed with multitudes from all nations, sharing the common bond of the summer's hottest accessory: orange life vests identical to Peter's. The scent of sunscreen and floral perfumes swirled in briny air. The drill appeared to be old hat for some passengers, who headed directly for the decks, while others swarmed and murmured in confusion.

An older couple approached Luisa. "So sorry to bother you," the man said, "but where's B26?"

She pointed them toward a set of sliding glass doors. "Out those doors to the left and all the way down. You'll see them holding up signs."

The lady gave her a kind smile and grasped her husband's elbow as they shuffled off.

"It's as easy as that," Luisa said. "Check their key cards for their station number. *A* through *J* is over there"—she signaled left—"and *K* through *T* is that way"—she pointed right.

Peter's uniform seemed to attract the lost and confused, but he got the hang of the shepherding business soon enough, checking their cards and directing them to the appropriate sides of the ship. Following Luisa's lead, he reminded those without life vests to fetch them and return quickly. Most complied with embarrassed looks.

One thick-necked guy scowled under his gray mustache. "They don't have any extra out there?"

"They want everybody to practice with their own," Peter said.

The guy trudged off, muttering under his breath.

After the last stragglers had made it to their respective sides, Peter joined Luisa at the *K* through *T* stations. Half the roster of the *Paradise* amassed before them. Yellow-vested crew members issued instructions through megaphones, cajoling and pointing until the throng gradually resembled an army of boot camp rejects, packed shoulder to shoulder, ten rows deep, facing the sea. An impressive sight—such density of flesh had been forbidden during Covid.

Above the passengers, orange and white lifeboats the size of school buses swung from steel rafters. As big as they were, the dimensions didn't square up in Peter's estimation. It was hard to imagine everybody here cramming inside. How would the older or disabled passengers manage in the chaos?

"Do they do this for every stop?" he asked.

Luisa shook her head. "Just the major ones where a lot of new passengers get on."

The assembly leaders were young and perky, that one there with killer cheekbones and waves of lustrous hair. "They look like cheerleaders."

She rolled her eyes. "They're mostly singers and dancers."

The horn blasted the muster signal again, seven short tones and one long. Assembly leaders scanned each passenger's key card with clunky handheld devices. The most important message, as far as Peter could tell, was that if the signal sounded for real, all passengers should report to these very stations with their life jackets. The passengers now donned their life jackets and secured them with thick Velcro straps. Attached to each jacket was a whistle and water-activated light should they find themselves bobbing in the ocean in the dark.

Peter crossed back through the width of the ship to the other side, stations *A* through *J*. The scene was identical: passengers, cute assembly leaders, and massive yet seemingly inadequate lifeboats.

Tightness cinched the base of his neck. It was one thing to know that he was one of two doctors responsible for the health of four thousand passengers and crew. It was another to see them all together. Back in Houston, the office manager had tallied his panel at 1,877 patients, a figure that stuck in his brain because it was one digit off from his street address. But he saw those patients a few times a year at most, depending on their conditions, and never all at once.

He closed his eyes, half wishing and half praying for the collective good health of all aboard. The first thing he saw when he opened his eyes was a pair of sneakers protruding from the front row at station *D*—that teenager in the wheelchair he'd seen earlier by the elevators. Calvin, if he remembered correctly. The boy was smiling and enjoying the sea breeze ruffling his hair. Fanny Pack Mom seemed distracted, irritated by something on her phone.

2

LUISA'S PONYTAIL SWUNG like a pendulum as she raced ahead of him, taking the carpeted steps two at a time.

"You still owe me a real tour," Peter huffed between breaths. Damn those extra pounds.

"This doesn't count?"

Not an hour after the muster drill, the Alpha Alpha Alpha had sounded overhead, and Hartley shoved the red canvas crash bag at Peter. She urged him and Luisa to move their asses and said she'd be up later when the elevators cleared.

Who decided to put the clinic on the lowest deck? The burning in his lungs sharpened flight after flight. It didn't help that the crash bag bounced off his hip with each step. Still, it felt good to rush into the fray again with the slim but real possibility of saving a life.

Luisa scowled as they reached the balcony above the main pool deck. She nodded at the crowd below. "We're too high."

He tried to slow his breathing as they descended the spiral stairs. Nobody was splashing around when they arrived, just a hat floating in the center of the pool. Vacationers, wrapped in towels and glistening with sunscreen, elbowed each other for a better look at the victim, some even standing on lounge chairs to record with their phones.

They pushed through the onlookers to where a broad-shouldered security officer kneeled beside someone on the concrete.

Peter recoiled. God, it was just a kid, maybe sixteen or seventeen, in green swim trunks, his gangly, tan limbs splayed out. His smooth chin jutted up at a grotesque angle, and his caved-in forehead resembled a dropped watermelon. Strands of reddish-brown hair lay matted in a slowly widening puddle of blood.

Peter checked for a carotid pulse under the still-warm skin of the boy's neck. Nothing. He used Luisa's stethoscope but heard no breath sounds. The teenager's eyes stared into space, and a penlight examination revealed blown pupils. Luisa leaned over to rub the victim's sternum. No reaction.

"Did anybody move him?" Peter asked. The boy's neck had probably snapped on impact, but still.

"If they did, it was before I got here," the security officer said.

Peter unzipped the crash bag. Typical emergency supplies: endotracheal tubes, syringes, and an Ambu bag. Why bother? The bag might as well have been filled with rocks. There was no magic wand here. Nothing on earth could save this boy.

It was one thing to call time of death after CPR in the hospital, or to watch a patient with terminal cancer pass with dignity surrounded by loved ones. It was another thing entirely to see this—this boy, crumpled amid a cluster of whispering sunbathers framed by azure skies and the North Atlantic sun. He met Luisa's eyes and shook his head.

Unlike hospital patients, he had no identification, no

wristband with his name and medical record number. Peter found a key card in the pocket of his trunks, but that did little good. The card had no room number for security purposes.

"He fell offa there!" An old guy in a wide-brimmed hat pointed up at the balcony. "Looked like he mighta slipped."

The passengers mumbled other theories: The kid jumped. Someone pushed him. He lost his footing.

It looked like a twelve-foot drop, fifteen from the top of the railing. A fall from that height would net you a broken ankle and a couple of bruises if you got lucky—or you could land on your head and die instantly. One of the wrists was broken, but there was no sign of trauma below his knees, other than a few scrapes. That didn't make sense unless he'd gone headfirst, and—

Sour acid shot up Peter's chest. How do you just land on your head? He opened his mouth to ask witnesses for details but then shut it. This wasn't the time. These people were drunk, shell-shocked, or both. Besides, he hadn't signed on to play Sherlock Holmes. That was security's job.

Luisa asked if anybody knew the victim's family. Nobody came forward. The security officer had taken a wide stance with hands on hips and his head on a swivel, but there was no violent energy in this crowd. Parents shepherded their children away, and the inner ring started to break up. Luisa retreated to a deck chair and buried her face in her hands.

Hartley finally hobbled into the circle, out of breath but with enough reserve to spit out "Dear Jesus." She kneeled gingerly beside the body and repeated many of Peter's maneuvers with the same negative results. As she struggled to rise, Peter stepped over and helped her to her feet.

A commotion rippled through the crowd as they parted to let someone through. A middle-aged woman dropped to her knees in front of the boy, hands fluttering helplessly above his shattered body. "My baby, my baby, oh my God, nooo…" She grabbed her hair as if to rip it from her scalp, eyes bulging and wild. Her anguished wail tore through the sky.

Peter crouched and reached for her heaving shoulders, just a feather touch. She didn't collapse or pull away. Her ragged sobbing gave way to incoherent mumbling. He'd comforted family members of the deceased before, walking the line between the chasms of sympathy and detachment. Leaning too far in either direction meant a long fall.

Maybe his own mother had reacted like this when she heard Felipe was dead. He didn't know because he hadn't been there. He'd disappeared, avoiding everyone for weeks, including his own sister. Poor Nali. All he could remember was the dark, muffled sensation of grief mixed with guilt.

A fresh breeze swept across the pool deck and lifted the hair from Peter's sweaty forehead. Above the balcony, behind the silhouettes of the onlookers, the steel cranes of the cruise terminal pointed to the sky like bony fingers clawing out of a freshly dug grave.

Peter rode the elevator down in a daze. He didn't even know the boy's name. This could *not* be a normal first day. His first shift as an intern at the hospital had been a disaster too, but at least he'd shown up with his stethoscope. And nobody had died.

He came to an intersection in the corridor. The clinic was to the left. To the right was I-95, and beyond that, his little cabin. He ought to go back to the clinic, check in with Hartley, see if—

Screw it. Raging dads, creepy come-ons from patients,

teenage boys swan-diving to their death—not what he'd
signed up for. He turned toward the staff cabins. They were
still docked in Copenhagen. He could pack his stuff and leave,
get a cab to the airport.

His neck seized, and he rolled his head until the tightness
eased. What was he thinking, really? It was too early to quit.
He'd just begun. Might as well see some more patients, do
what he came here for.

Back in the clinic, a young Asian woman in a face mask
was wrapping an elastic bandage around the wrist of a middle-
aged man. She encouraged him to come back anytime, her
voice smooth and light, and walked him out.

She introduced herself as Mandy Chin. "I'm the other
nurse."

Yes indeed, it might actually be fun with her around.
"Peter Palma."

A small rectangular bottle dangled from a lanyard around
her neck. "Dr. Hartley called me in while you all were at the
pool. Rough way to start, huh?"

What an understatement. "Well, I did not expect *that*."

"Not to sound callous, but accidents happen. I've seen it
all." She crossed her arms. "Still, it's terrible."

More than terrible. The kid's skull had been crushed with
no significant trauma below the knees. The physics didn't
make sense. Peter shook his head and looked away.

"What?" Mandy asked.

"Nah, it's nothing."

"What?"

He leaned against the edge of the counter. "Sounds weird,
but I'm not sure it was an accident."

Her eyebrows flew up.

"Never mind. I'm the newbie here." He massaged the lingering cramp in his neck. "What are they doing with him?"

She shrugged. "The family has to decide. We can keep his body on the ship until New York, or they can get off at one of the ports of call."

"I see. So it's no big deal, then."

"That's not what I mean," she replied crisply. "I'm just telling you so we can function—not so we can move on, because you don't just brush this aside, but so we can continue working, or... or being." Her forehead creased. "That's not the right word."

"I know what you're saying." He was in no position to lecture anybody about coping.

"By the way, your patient with the cough, Stevenson? I gave her some more albuterol and sent her off."

"She was okay?"

She laughed and tilted her head. "You don't trust me, Dr. Palma?"

He grinned back. "Just asking."

"Since we just met, I'll give you a pass." She narrowed her eyes, but he could tell she was smiling under her mask. "I was an ICU nurse for six years. I know how to assess respiratory status."

"I get it, sorry. Where at?"

"Portland."

"Was she behaving funny?"

"Who?"

"Stevenson. The patient."

"Oh. No, just annoying. She said I speak good English."

"You have no accent." He could listen to her buttery voice all day.

"I was born in California. But whatever—you can't let that

stuff bother you. Life's too short." She squirted a dollop of gel from the lanyard bottle onto her palm. Rubbed her hands together and worked the gel into the webs between her fingers. "Want some? It's non-alcoholic. It's the only brand that doesn't flare up my eczema."

He held up both hands in a warding gesture. "Don't waste it on me."

She shrugged. "I've got a whole case in my cabin. Here." She caught one of his hands and squeezed a blob onto his palm.

He rubbed the gel into his hands. It was thick and fruity, silkier than the typical industrial-strength hand sanitizer. Interesting. Like Mandy Chin.

The next patients were straightforward. A Turkish man with a strained back from lifting his son into the bunk bed. A young woman with an ear infection. Stomach pain, high blood sugar, more bread-and-butter stuff. Peter got into a groove. This was what he was here for.

But Mandy warned him about the next one. "It's... strange. You'll see."

He scanned the intake form. A facialist from the spa was concerned about her own blemished skin. Forty-seven-year-old Thai woman named Intira Lamai.

She held out her arms for inspection, her eyes bouncing between them: left, right, left, right. "I keep scratching, Doc, but I can't get it off."

Deep scratches crisscrossed her forearms, some congealed with blood and others already crusted with brown-black scabs matching the flecks under what must've once been a pristine manicure.

"Can't get what off?" he asked.

Lamai's eyes widened. "The paint! You don't see it? I don't like the color."

Oh boy. "What color is it?"

With a huff, she thrust her left wrist toward his face. "All that green and blue—it's hideous."

He bent in for a closer look. There was no paint or foreign substance on her skin, only ragged excoriations and scattered red pustules.

"I try washing with soap and one of those pumice stones at the spa, but it doesn't come off. So I scratch."

He checked behind her ears for a scopolamine patch—great for motion sickness but capable of causing hallucinations. Nothing. "I'd recommend that you stop scratching, or you'll get an infection. Does it itch?"

"No, but that's not the issue."

"Oh? What's the—"

"What can you do about the paint?"

He tried to redirect her with standard questions, and she admitted to sniffles, a mild sore throat, and occasional constipation. Nothing serious. "Let's try an antibiotic ointment, bandage everything up, and I'll see you back here tomorrow."

She mumbled and grimaced.

Mandy smoothed things over as she applied antibiotics and gauze. She handed him a clipboard with a work form. "Check one of the boxes and sign."

This patient was in no condition to provide beauty and hygiene services to passengers. He checked *Not Fit for Duty* and wrote that she had an active infection with risk for exposure to other persons on board, follow up in one to three days, signature.

"You and I are going to get along just fine," Mandy said with a smile. "Good job standing up to corporate. All they want to do is rush people back to work."

She returned to Lamai to go over the form and her discharge

instructions, and the two women exchanged contact info on their phones. That was weird. Afterward, he asked Mandy, "Just curious, do you normally give out your cell to patients?"

"It's not a big deal, it's just the app. Sometimes they don't want to come back to clinic, or their bosses won't let them. It's a tough life."

Mandy going the extra mile. She was a keeper, for sure. "Well, maybe if she doesn't see the wounds, she'll stop this thing about the paint. Out of sight, out of mind."

In the office, he created an index card for Lamai: *skin, mental.* He logged on to the electronic health record system and opened her chart. He entered her symptoms, physical exam, diagnosis of impetigo, and treatment with mupirocin. The artificial intelligence agent in the right-hand panel offered suggestions. He experimented with the parameters, watching the list of recommendations expand and collapse. At the highest sensitivity setting, the AI returned a list of exotic illnesses that would have been impossible to confirm, problematic to treat on the ship, and extraordinarily unlikely.

She had a skin infection, no big deal.

But there was something about the *Paradise.* Duty aboard a cruise ship was supposed to be easy-breezy, not fodder for case studies in a medical journal. He fired off a query: *hallucinations.* The AI returned *delirium associated with acute infection,* as well as *schizophrenia.* He snorted. Of course it would suggest those two diagnoses; they were textbook. He poked around in Lamai's chart but found no prior visits and nothing listed as chronic medical problems. Not much help there—so much for the AI.

He moved on to Claudia Stevenson, the first patient. The negative Covid and flu tests were already in her chart. Thinking about her sudden advances, he added *disinhibition.*

Dialed to the maximum sensitivity, the AI served up alcohol, illicit drugs, prescription meds, and acute mental illnesses.

Next, the teenager at the pool. He popped open the search field but dropped his hands into his lap. He didn't have his name. Besides, he wasn't technically a patient—they hadn't even attempted resuscitation. Peter pulled his metallic pen from his breast pocket and clicked it: *ta-tick, ta-tack, ta-tick.* The mechanism was smooth and solid, and the heft felt good in his hand. He jotted a reminder on an index card to check on the boy's records later.

The overhead speakers chimed three times. "Good evening, travelers. This is the one and only Captain Forster speaking. It's my pleasure to welcome you aboard the *Paradise.* I apologize for the unavoidable delay, but we'll depart as soon as we can."

The captain made no mention of the nature of the delay. Probably half the ship had already heard about the boy who jumped. He sketched out the itinerary: a day at sea followed by a brief stop in Mioven in Norway, then Scotland, across the Atlantic for a few days, and arrival in New York. The entertainment director came on next, hyping the shows, movies, and casino offerings in a friendly Australian accent.

Mandy popped in and glanced at the digital clock on the wall. "It's almost closing time, and nobody's waiting. I'm going to start shutting everything down."

End of the day, a long day, and Peter should've been relaxing. He should've been appreciating this fresh start to his career and making use of amenities the passengers paid a lot of money to enjoy.

Yet the cruise had not been kind to all passengers. That kid had died by suicide, maybe? It was Felipe all over again. Felipe hadn't jumped, but—

"You okay?" Mandy was leaning on the door jamb, eyebrows furrowed.

"Sorry, I just zoned out."

"Is all this"—she traced a circle overhead with her index finger—"something you've thought about for a while?"

She couldn't mean Felipe. "All this?"

"Working on a cruise ship. Like, was it a goal? No offense."

"Should I be? Offended, I mean?" He cracked a tiny smile. He liked the way her ears stuck out, just enough to be cute.

"Absolutely not. I was just curious."

"I like to travel." He hardly ever traveled.

She smiled and nodded. "I remember feeling that way when I started."

"And?"

"I'm still here."

"You've seen it all," he said.

"Each cruise is a little different. There's always surprises."

"Hopefully not more surprises like today."

"Fingers crossed. You need anything?"

Yeah, but she couldn't provide it. He needed to sort out his brain. Damn, that Lexapro had sure picked a good time to take a dive. Might as well get used to this place, this little office in this little clinic. "I'm just gonna hang out here, get settled in."

She said goodbye and shut the door behind her.

Peter rocked back in his seat and swept his gaze around the humble space. The walls, ceiling, floor, and even the desk were all neutral shades. What had he expected, dark wood paneling accented with brass lamps? This wasn't a pirate ship from the movies. The only pop of color was a small vase of fake flowers next to the computer. Beside it sat a framed photo of Dr. Hartley with a bearded gentleman in a pub. She was laughing, hoisting a massive tankard of ale, looking so carefree, so—

A rustling drew his attention to the front of the clinic, followed by soft voices. Mandy was explaining to a visitor that they were closed, and if it wasn't urgent, we could see her tomorrow. But moments later, she poked her head back into the office with a grin. "There's someone out here for you."

Another head popped around the corner. "And surprise!"

Peter jerked back and did a double take. For some reason, his little sister stood a mere five feet in front of him—five feet, not five thousand miles. Acid streaked up his chest and pooled in the back of his mouth. What in the world was she doing here?

"It's me!" Nali flashed a wicked smile. "And I missed you at graduation."

Peter's face burned. "I was busy."

She breezed straight to Hartley's desk, where she snatched up the framed photo for examination. "Doing what? Not working." Her brown hair streaked with auburn highlights was gathered up in a loose bun that accentuated her plump cheeks. Still the baby of the family—but given her presence here, too clever for her own good and too clever for his own tastes.

"In fact, I was. I had orientation for this."

"Graduation was at one. Your flight wasn't until six."

She'd always been a stickler for details. "What are you even doing here?"

"Good to see you too. I'm in the chorus line."

He blinked.

"What do you think, Peter? Vacation." Nali's gray T-shirt boasted an anime hero with enormous eyes and spiky blue hair. His favorite Rockets and Astros shirts hadn't even made his packing list. Looking at her now, he missed them. During his losing battle with futility, he'd found comfort in cheap T-shirts from Academy. All grays and navy blues. Solid. Predictable.

He scoffed and shook his head. "Right. Your first cruise ever, and you chose this one?"

"A girl's gotta have fun once in a while. Lord knows I deserve it. So are you going to let me into your fancy office here?" She plonked Hartley's picture back onto the desk and flopped into a chair without waiting for an answer.

"How did you pay for this? Don't say credit card."

"Okay, I won't. Who do you think I am?" She swiveled the chair left and right.

"Someone with student loans and no job."

"I started babysitting."

"Enough to afford this?" He gestured at the immensity of the ship above them.

"Ever heard of a friends-and-family discount?" She stabbed a finger at him. "Of course not. You basically ghosted us."

That stung. He couldn't blame her though. He fixated on a little coffee stain that marred the otherwise neatly arranged desk. "But you'd have to sign up through me."

Silence.

"Nali…"

She hummed innocently.

Aw, hell. He should've known. "So you hacked in. Is that what your degree was—hacking?"

"Comp sci. And I have a job."

"Where?"

"NASA."

"Congratulations, then." He figured they looked ridiculous, glaring at each other with their chins lifted like a pair of bulldogs.

"Anyway, they have a ping pong table. I mean on the ship,

by the pool. You wanna?" She flicked her wrist as if using a paddle. Back in the day, they would play at the community center on that chipped and cracked table. Half the balls were dented but they made it work.

"I'm gonna be busy. I already am."

She shrugged. "Lame."

Mandy popped her head in. "I don't know what's going on here—don't really want to—but it's trivia night at the bar. Everything's buttoned down here. Just turn out the lights when you leave. The door locks automatically."

When she'd left, Nali sat up. "She's cute."

"Geez, I just started. I'm here to work."

"Cuter than Elena."

Elena had dumped him when he wouldn't commit to the RV lifestyle. Their trip to Huntsville State Park had convinced him to never empty another black tank again. He may be a doctor, but shit was still shit, no matter how many Porta-Pak pods you dropped down the toilet. The similar fate of his Lexapro tablets made him laugh in spite of himself.

Nali stood up, looking annoyed. "Don't worry, I can take care of myself. But we should get dinner—you know, if you can find the time." She gave him an awkward half hug over the desk before leaving.

He stared at the computer, wondering why she was really here. She'd somehow stayed focused on her studies through the long months of grief. She'd always been one to persevere. He could've handled things better. He should've at least gone to her graduation.

The sun slanted low through the window, casting harsh shadows across the gray tile. It was 8:30 p.m. local time. He hadn't eaten since breakfast in Copenhagen, although his stomach didn't seem to mind.

It was quiet. He made for the front of the clinic, passing green and amber equipment-status lights that glowed from the dark corners like the eyes of alien critters. There was a ventilator on a rolling stand and a defibrillator on the red crash cart—neither of which would've saved the kid with his brains smashed in. What a way to go.

He paused near the pharmacy. Abrupt withdrawal from Lexapro was a setup for failure. Maybe… He shook his head and continued forward, then pivoted and opened the pharmacy closet. It wouldn't hurt to check.

No Lexapro, but he spotted some Paxil. Both medications worked by raising the levels of serotonin in the brain, addressing a deficiency that Big Pharma would have you believe was the key to eternal happiness. There was only one way to see if Paxil would work for him.

He snatched the box of tablets and froze, his pulse racing. He needed help and he needed this job. He could open it and take a few, or he could take the whole box, which would leave nothing for the passengers. As he deliberated, the box somehow found its way into his pocket, where the hem of his shirt softened its angular bulge just a little.

He scanned the scripts log. Handwritten entries filled the upper half of the top sheet, including his own entries for the meds he'd dispensed today. The documentation from Luisa, Mandy, and Dr. Hartley stretched back weeks: albuterol, antibiotics, topical steroids, and—

There was an entry for Paxil, from Mandy, dispensed to a patient three weeks ago. Would another entry stand out? Would anybody cross-check this log against the patient charts? Maybe Luisa spent the end of every shift doing exactly that, or maybe Hartley ran a second sweep. He could definitely see it. There had to be accountability.

He could make up a patient name or just scrawl illegibly, like the jokes about doctors' handwriting. Hmm. Using his own name as the patient and prescriber would be a middle finger to the establishment. *Yeah, so I stole drugs on my first day—what are you gonna do about it?* He fingered the box of Paxil in his pocket. He could leave a fiver in the tip jar, heh. Geez, he had no practice with this sort of thing. He'd always been one to follow the rules. Nali, not so much, growing up under the lenience afforded to a little sister of two brothers.

The air in the pharmacy was thick and heavy. The weight of the massive ship—how many tons, how many levels?—pressed through the ceiling and onto Peter's shoulders. The walls squeezed in. Every expansion of his chest met with subtle resistance. He scrubbed a hand over his face. It sucked that he had to choose between mental health and honesty. He needed to get out of here.

He returned the Paxil to the shelf. He wouldn't go down that road, not yet. He squared away the other meds to make it look like nothing had been disturbed.

As he left the pharmacy, the floor shifted beneath him with a soft thunk. He peered out the window. The cranes and buildings were now easing by. The low rumble of engines siphoned through the soles of his shoes and into his bones.

Prepared or not, he was officially sailing the ocean.

3

HE WAS SUPPOSED to alternate with Hartley, one day on, the next day off. But yesterday's mayhem—and her contempt for his abilities—hadn't exactly set the stage for a regular schedule. He needed caffeine and a good workout to clear his mind. He would jog a few laps around the deck encircling the *Paradise* and hoist some dumbbells at the gym.

Fortunately, there'd been welcome evidence of the cabin steward's work when Peter had trudged back to his cabin last night. The bed had been made. The staleness still lingered, but it wasn't coming from the trash can. Maybe it was baked into the walls. The steward had also paid dutiful attention to the bathroom, which now smelled lemon-fresh. The toilet bowl gleamed with water clear as bottled Ozarka, devoid of happy pills and shit.

In shorts and a T-shirt, Peter found a breakfast kiosk wedged into a nook off I-95. The other crew members in line for morning coffee looked exhausted. Peter opted for a banana to go with his brew.

The map at midships showed the jogging deck on the

fourth level. Before the elevator arrived, a sharp voice rang out behind him.

"The captain wants to see you," Luisa said.

His stomach lurched, but he played it cool. "Sure."

"His boardroom is on Deck 9." She looked him up and down.

He shifted his weight from one foot to the other. "Right now?"

"Better get a move on. He doesn't like to be kept waiting."

What was it about Luisa? She always seemed to be steering him like a sled dog: *Do this, go there.*

He scarfed down the banana on the way back to his cabin. There, he changed into scrubs, whose breast pocket was embossed with a ship against the backdrop of a rising sun. New scrubs for his new job. Day two had to be better than yesterday.

The captain's boardroom gleamed with burnished brass and inlaid mahogany. An antique world map hung over a sideboard loaded with crystal tumblers and decanters of liquor. An expansive window with maroon drapes gave view to the turbulent ocean. Tropical fish swimming infinite loops in an octagonal tank reminded him of the discus he'd relinquished back home.

Captain Forster presided at the head of a massive oval table. His commanding presence matched the rich voice from last night's announcements. With a sculpted jaw and thick, dark hair sweeping back past a dab of gray at each temple, he looked the part of a CEO who'd risen through the ranks with charisma and ruthless drive.

To the captain's right, Dr. Hartley acknowledged Peter with a stiff nod. And to his left sat Chief Security Officer Tom Harrington. Peter recognized him with his crew cut and sturdy shoulders from the pool deck where the teenager had died.

He slid into a wooden chair along the wall, the coffee still warm in his hands.

"Dr. Palma," Captain Forster said with a small smile, "you're welcome to sit at my table. We don't bite."

"Yes sir." He shifted to a high-backed leather chair at the far end of the table.

A large screen displayed a navigation map, with a little triangle leaving a dotted trail from Copenhagen. Overnight, the ship had rounded the tip of Denmark and was heading west into the North Sea.

"As you might guess, we're talking about the boy," Forster added.

"Rickey Turner," Hartley said. "That's his name. His mother intends to bring him back to Michigan."

With this new info, Peter recorded the name on an index card. No labels were necessary; just a stick figure of a body, supine and broken. At orientation, they'd said the ship had a morgue with three refrigerated drawers, an industry standard for vessels of this size.

The Copenhagen police had secured the upper pool deck for a full two hours yesterday for forensics, Harrington explained. "If we hadn't given them this video, they would've shut us down for a whole day." He tapped on a laptop to display footage on the wall screen.

Peter groaned at the bird's-eye view of the balcony over the pool deck. The color video was sharp but thankfully silent.

"That's him." Harrington paused the clip and pointed at Rickey entering the frame.

Rickey was shuffling along listlessly. He stopped for a few seconds, then turned toward the waist-high railing. Nobody was interacting with him, at least not from the camera's vantage point. He leaned on the railing and looked down at the pool deck like any people-watcher. But then he swung one leg over the railing, hands gripping the top bar, followed by the other leg. It was a careful and deliberate maneuver. He moved with intention.

"Now they see him," Harrington said.

A bystander on the balcony was pointing at Rickey, while another inched toward him.

Rickey repositioned himself to face out into open space, one hand on the top bar and feet planted on the lip of the balcony, outside the railing. He launched into a swan dive, his back arched and arms extended sideways as he sailed through the air. The hair on the back of Peter's neck rose as the boy brought his arms together above his head. His hands and forearms folded like toothpicks upon impact. His head smashed into the concrete and snapped back, the momentum rotating his body in an arc to settle in the position in which Peter found him. Dead on arrival.

The only sound in the room was the bubbling fish tank. The polished wood paneling abruptly felt centuries old—a relic of bygone eras. Lifeless remnants. Even the ocean outside seemed cold, dark, and ancient.

"Jesus." The captain leaned back in his chair and turned toward the window. He examined his reflection with narrowed eyes before giving himself a small nod.

Harrington replayed the clip. It was worse the second time. Peter could almost hear the watermelon thud of Rickey's skull striking the concrete. A wave of nausea roiled his stomach. The replay continued as the mother broke through the crowd and collapsed on her son's wrecked body. And then Peter's tentative reach toward her.

The captain turned to face them. "I brought you all here to answer this question. I've seen the video a dozen times, and it still makes me sick. Could we have prevented this?"

"Depends on who you mean by 'we,'" Hartley said.

"I'm not assigning blame." Forster tapped the table with manicured fingernails. "We need to have this conversation."

"My question is whether he was under the influence." Harrington folded his arms and leaned them on the table.

"Of course we can't do it on the ship, but a postmortem tox will take weeks or even months," Hartley said.

Harrington grimaced. "I'm asking if his behavior suggests anything. It does, if you ask me."

"He was too young to be drinking," she insisted.

"We'd better hope so." Forster clenched his jaw. "My safety record is second best in the entire fleet. That's huge."

"I wouldn't rule out anything at this point." Hartley rubbed her temples. "Psychedelic drugs, mental illness."

Forster turned to Peter. "What do you think?"

Peter swallowed hard. What did they expect? He'd been the first medical professional to examine Rickey, but it's not like he knew anything the video didn't show. The frozen screen continued to display the victim's ghastly sprawl. "He looked purposeful when he jumped, to me, like… he was performing."

Hartley cocked her head like he was talking nonsense. "What did the mother say?"

"Nothing."

"She said nothing to you?"

He shook his head.

Captain Forster looked at Harrington. "What do we know about them?"

"He was sixteen, mother forty-three, VP of marketing in Chicago. They're first-time guests. They embarked in Athens. She favors the comedy clubs and the spa, and she visited the blackjack table last week. Most of their activities involved something physical—wind surfing, scuba diving, hiking."

"Where's dad?" Peter asked.

"Not in the picture. They divorced a few years back. He's a CPA in Seattle."

All that seemed like a lot of background at Harrington's fingertips, yet none of it gave a clue about the kid's motive.

Peter asked, "If he was trying to— Why wouldn't he just jump overboard?"

"The railing is much higher on the perimeter, and it angles inward," Harrington said. "It would take a heroic leap to clear the hull and hit the water. If that's what he was trying to do. He was also seen in clinic three days ago." He looked at Hartley. "What was he there for?"

She slammed her fist on the table. "Bloody hell, how am I supposed to remember? Do you know how many patients we see every day?"

Forster's eyes narrowed, his voice low. "Elizabeth."

Peter glanced away. The man from the elevator, and now her. Everyone was on edge around here.

Hartley smirked. "The nurses are wonderful, but they don't make the decisions. Doctors do. I've been toiling alone. Then they send this kid." She jinked her head toward Peter.

His jaw dropped. Her dismissive greeting yesterday paled in comparison to this outright insult. Public lashings were supposed to be over after residency. He twisted his cup on the table, feeling the coffee sloshing inside. He shouldn't have been surprised. Hartley was on to him, and she was dragging him into the light for all to see. They might not know why Felipe's death had been the worst possible thing at the worst possible time—but they saw something.

It took every shred of strength not to get up and leave.

All eyes were locked on Hartley, who'd flushed deep red. "Dear me," she whispered, her head trembling. "I'm so sorry. If you'll excuse me." She stood up and tottered out of the room. Her dry coughs followed her out the door.

"Shit," Harrington said. "She needs to get back on her meds."

Peter winced—too close to home. He fixed his gaze on a corner of the antique map.

"Palma?"

Peter snapped back to attention. "Captain?"

Forster gave him a stern look. "Are you ready?"

"For what?" Great job projecting confidence.

"For anything."

"Yes sir." He raised his coffee cup to his lips to hide the muscles twitching in his neck. The brew had gone cold, but he swallowed it anyway.

"Good," Forster said with a curt laugh. He turned to the window again and ran a hand through his mane of hair. "With Hartley questionable, you'll need to be ready. For anything."

––––––––––

To be fair, Dr. Hartley hadn't exactly chosen Peter. He was the one standing after all the other kids had been picked for teams on the playground. She was stuck with him as much as he was stuck with her. Still, her belittling comments bit deep. The captain and Harrington had noticed, and that made it worse.

And of course, Luisa wanted him back in the clinic today because Hartley was suddenly AWOL. So much for a workout.

Then there was Nali, a reminder of all he wanted to escape from. It was impossible to fathom that she was even here. She kept messaging him on SeaText. *Wanna get breakfast?* He didn't recall setting her up as a contact.

These women were making his life very complicated.

Mandy was the exception. She looked pleased when he reported to work. Behind that mask, she probably had a great smile.

His pocket buzzed with another message from Nali. *How much does a pirate pay for corn?*

"Heard you met with the captain," Mandy said.

"Don't ask. How was trivia?"

She flexed her biceps and grinned. "We just missed second place. You should join us sometime. We could always use another brain."

"Sounds like fun." He'd loved history in college, blasting through thick tomes on ancient civilizations with ease, although his consumption these days was limited to five-minute YouTubes.

She fiddled with the bottle of hand sanitizer on her lanyard. "Everybody was talking about the kid. It's all over social media."

"Already?" The idea left a rancid taste in his mouth.

"There's a dedicated group for each itinerary. They start posting even before they get on the ship. They ask questions about food, excursions, that sort of stuff." She shook her head. "First place was a bunch of cheaters though. They kept looking up the answers."

"No one stopped them?"

"They tried, but it got kinda rowdy. As in punches thrown. This one guy might need stitches. We'll see if he shows up today."

"All that over trivia. That's intense. Is there a prize?"

"Just some lame coffee mugs." She shrugged and handed him a stethoscope with heavy violet tubing.

It was the real thing, similar in quality and heft to his own missing instrument.

He draped it around his neck and gave her a thumbs-up. "Nice. This an extra?"

"Martina's." She grabbed a paper towel from the dispenser and dabbed her moist eyes.

Nothing on the surface was weird about using the former doctor's stethoscope, but had she left the position? Maybe she didn't like working with Hartley. Any reasonable doctor would chafe under that kind of disparagement. Hell, maybe Hartley ran her off. "What happened?"

Mandy's gaze drifted downward. "It's complicated."

Another text came in from Nali. *A buccaneer.*

A buck an ear: That's how much pirates paid for corn. It was a thing they shared, the corny jokes. He couldn't suppress a tiny smile and responded with a laughing emoji.

He and Mandy worked together to get patients in and out. She was neither pushy nor tentative, and she seemed to lack the world-weariness that came with a long career in health care. Maybe switching out of the ICU had been exactly the right move for her.

A stagehand came in with a headache, and a young woman brought her toddler in for a rash. A Peruvian sociology professor had a wheezy cough. Reading their body language, riding the back and forth, Peter sussed out their personalities and forged brief connections. Knowing when to affirm their concerns, when to offer another perspective—it was good to get back into the flow. This new venture might just pan out if he could focus on these moments.

Just as he finished splinting a maintenance worker's sprained ankle, his phone buzzed. Nali again, with *Shits goin down. Look out for strangling victim.*

That was odd. *Stay out of trouble,* he typed.

He showed the text to the nurses. Luisa crossed herself

and Mandy got busy tidying the boxes of gauze and tape in one of the cabinets.

Within minutes a security guard and a teenage boy were helping an older Indian man inside by his elbows with such haste they nearly lifted his sandals off the tile. His forehead glistened under tangles of white hair. Angry bruises encircled his scrawny neck, and burst vessels painted the corners of his eyes red.

Peter and Mandy guided him to a stretcher in the crash room, but he refused to lie down. They cranked the head of the stretcher up so he could remain somewhat upright. His hands fluttered around his neck and low moans escaped his swollen lips.

The wiry security guard gave report to Peter. "Mr. Harpreet Sharma here and his family, they're all at breakfast up at the buffet. The whole family. This is his grandson." He nodded to the shell-shocked boy. "Things get a little heated, they're arguing about something. Then the niece jumps out of her chair and grabs him, like—" The guard curled his hands around an imaginary neck.

"I don't know what happened," the grandson muttered through tears. He had a thick tousle of black hair and wore a soccer jersey. Couldn't have been more than thirteen or fourteen.

Sharma's heart rate was high and his oxygen low. The sinews in his neck pulled taut with each breath. "I can't," he croaked. "I can't."

Peter gripped the railing of the bed and leaned toward Mandy. "How far offshore are we?"

"I don't know. Too far." She strapped an oxygen mask on Sharma's face and cranked up the flow.

Each labored breath was accompanied by a high-pitched

whistle, all stridor from his traumatized larynx. Peter slipped Sharma's oxygen mask off long enough to examine his mouth as far as the penlight would illuminate. His oral mucosal lining was beefy red but not swollen. This could go either way.

Luisa focused on the vital signs on the monitor above the gurney. "I'll get the crash cart."

Peter turned to the grandson. "What's your name?"

"Rahul."

"Rahul, how long was this going on?" He pointed to Sharma's neck. The woman must've been very strong or enraged to leave bruises like that.

"I don't know, like ten or fifteen seconds."

"Did he pass out?"

"No, but his eyes got really big when she—" Rahul broke off in a choking sob.

Luisa wheeled in the red metal cabinet. Sharma's stridor was growing louder. With each breath, his ribcage expanded and contracted with exaggerated effort, and his eyes rolled around like those of a snake-spooked horse.

"Hartley's not answering," Mandy reported.

"Where is she?" he demanded.

"I don't *know*." Her eyes flared wide. "Do you want to tube him?"

"I will if I have to."

The last time he'd intubated anybody was four years ago, when he was a resident in the ER—four years since he'd controlled another human being's breathing. Intubating under ideal conditions was stressful enough, but on a cruise ship with the patient's airway shrinking? If it didn't work, he'd have to cut a hole in Sharma's neck to establish an airway. He'd done that exactly zero times before.

Mandy reclined the stretcher a few degrees and started

an IV. She handed Peter a syringe of milky fluid. "Here's the propofol."

Sharma's oxygen saturation was bouncing around in the low nineties. Not much of a buffer there. If it dropped much farther, he'd have to intubate.

Peter's mouth turned to cotton, and everything faded to the background as he scrutinized the patient's face and the monitor. The clear plastic mask over his face fogged and cleared with each breath. Peter held the propofol in one hand, ready to push, and the laryngoscope in the other. He could do this. He was ready.

But he didn't want to. Not here, not on this ship.

Dammit, where was Hartley?

Five seconds followed by five more seconds, with no significant change. Then five more. A minute passed that felt like an eon. Was the man breathing easier now, or was he just getting fatigued? Peter nudged him. "You with me?"

Sharma nodded. The creases around his eyes smoothed, and his breathing eased. When he began looking around, scanning the ceiling and all the equipment, Peter's grip on the laryngoscope relaxed. Curiosity meant that the patient had moved beyond the survival-only phase, at least for now.

Peter showed him the plastic endotracheal tube. "I really don't want to put this into your lungs and hook you up to a machine, but if it's necessary—"

Sharma wagged his finger and shook his head.

Peter released a long sigh. In the doorway, Rahul was now flanked by family members staring wide-eyed at the scene. The security guard talked with them in hushed tones. Mandy joined them with an update while Luisa secured the IV tubing to the patient's skin with tape.

Movement in one corner caught Peter's eye. Dr. Hartley

had materialized like a wraith, hovering where the edge of the steel cabinet blocked the overhead light. Her gray hair was disheveled and her face drawn. She made no eye contact with anyone and said nothing.

He leaned forward to catch her attention. He wasn't looking for credit, but some kind of acknowledgment would be nice. Maybe a *well done* or a thumbs-up. But there was nothing from Hartley. With her hands behind her back, her dead-eyed gaze lingered on Sharma before drifting sideways. She shuffled off, muttering and shaking her head.

Lord have mercy, indeed.

———————

"Everything okay?" Mandy was checking the seal on a vial of epinephrine from the crash cart. "You seem troubled."

Peter leaned on the steel counter on the other side of the critical care bay where Sharma was hooked up to all the monitors. "Is this a typical day, or am I a black cloud?"

"You're definitely a black cloud." She paused with a serious look before cracking a grin that lifted her cheeks. "I'm kidding. Well, maybe not."

Peter had earned the black cloud label during his second year of residency due to his proclivity for attracting the toughest cases. His fellow residents would jokingly groan when they found they were on call with him. The curse had lifted in his third year, like a ghost seeking other houses to haunt, but now it seemed determined to reclaim him.

"Feels like Hartley has it in for me."

"Sorry to take you down a peg, but maybe it's not all about you."

Mandy was right. He needed to pull his head out of his ass. "I'm listening."

"She hasn't been herself lately."

"How so?"

She shut the drawer of the crash cart. "It's hard to describe. At first, I thought she was just under a lot of stress."

Who wasn't? He checked on Sharma. The bruises around his neck had deepened, even during the past hour. His oxygen saturation hovered in a barely acceptable range, and he was at twenty-four breaths per minute, a respiratory effort above normal.

"I don't like this."

Mandy nodded. "It's tragic."

"He's on the edge." He squeezed Sharma's thin forearm, and the man's eyelids fluttered. "Not bad enough to intubate, but he could go south any minute."

"We'll keep a close eye on him."

"I almost wish I'd just done it. He'd be on the ventilator and we wouldn't have to continually reassess. Now we're in no-man's-land. We need to transfer him to a hospital as soon as we dock in Norway tomorrow."

"The captain will have to sign off on the transfer. I can start the paperwork."

"Hold down the fort. I'm gonna check on a few things." He went to the back office and logged in to the system. A search for Harpreet Sharma or the date of birth supplied by his family returned nothing, so he created a record. Documenting the sordid details was surreal, describing the alleged incident, physical exam findings, and treatment. The AI agent offered a warning with an exclamation point inside a red triangle: *Monitor respiratory status.*

No shit, Sherlock.

But even if they transferred him without incident and he made a full recovery, there was no ignoring the spark that had started this fire in the first place. The man's niece had tried to kill him—kind of a low point for a family vacation.

Peter backed out of the record and entered a search for the attacker. Nothing. Either the Sharma family didn't frequent the ship's clinic, or the niece had a different last name.

He called Harrington in the security office. "What do you know about the Sharmas?"

"It's a shit show in here," Harrington groused. "I've got his niece in the brig, and she's almost catatonic. Totally zoned out. His wife's about to have a breakdown."

"Why did she do it?"

"Beats me. 'Cause it's a Tuesday? Seems like people need no reason to act like animals these days."

The hairs lifted on the back of his neck. "What do you mean?"

There was a shout and a crash in the background, then several voices talking heatedly. "It means we're busy. Anything else? Sorry, Doc."

He asked for the niece's name and date of birth.

Papers shuffled on the other end of the line. "Badakar. Neha Badakar."

"Is she intoxicated?"

"She passed the Breathalyzer."

"How about drugs?"

"That's not the sense I'm getting. But feel free to test when I'm done processing her."

Back on the computer, Peter pulled up records for Neha Badakar. She'd come into the clinic last week for a headache and fever, which Hartley diagnosed as sinusitis and treated with a course of antibiotics. No mention of unusual mental status, nor were there labs, X-rays, or drug tests.

His chest tightened. This could be anything, and now Nali was out there—a smart kid, but just a kid. He texted her: *He came in. It's bad. Be careful.*

Her reply was a line of question marks.

People acting erratic, he typed.

She sent a thumbs-up emoji, as if confirming an outing for burgers. If only life were that simple again.

The system showed that the dead boy, Rickey Turner, had been seen five days ago. Hartley's note described a healthy teenager, accompanied by his mother, complaining of nausea and runny nose. She sent him out with some Tums. No mention of mental status, no drug tests. There was no apparent reason for it.

He checked on Sharma again and discovered that Hartley had returned. She hovered at the patient's bedside, listening to his lungs, examining his extremities, and fingering the IV tubing. Her movements were slow and languid, like a spirit lingering over her earthly charge.

She looked up as Peter approached. "You did well." Her voice was thin and hollow.

"Thanks." He braced for a follow-up insult, but it never came.

He looked at Sharma's swollen necklace of trauma. Saw Rickey's head caved in. Those two were the worst, but even the patient who'd propositioned him and the one who believed her arms were drenched in paint made his stomach turn. Something was off, and he needed answers.

"It's been interesting, to say the least."

She sighed. "Come, let's sit for a moment."

He followed her back to the office, where she slumped into a chair with a tired sigh. "I'll talk to the captain about evac."

Maybe she was coming back to herself. "That would be good."

The cold fluorescent lights washed out the weak sunlight from the window, casting shadows across her pallid face. She looked a hundred years old now. Despite her unpredictability and her recent barbs, any insight from her would be better than nothing.

"I'm not sure how to describe it," he continued, "and I don't want to complain. But something's strange here."

Hartley cleared her throat. "How so?"

"Maybe I'm just new at this…"

She went silent for a long interval. "No, you're right."

"So I'm not imagining things. All the incidents."

She shook her head.

"And the violence," he added. Harrington had called them animals.

Somewhere deep under the floor, the ship creaked, sounding more like a wooden fishing boat instead of a steel-hulled cruise ship.

"I don't have a cousin in Copenhagen," she confessed. "They're all dead."

He willed himself to stay silent, to let this new tangent make itself clear.

"I just wanted to go shoreside." She seemed fixated on the porthole window. "It's nice to get off once in a while."

Weird that she didn't just say she wanted a break. "I guess it starts to drag."

"Even a ship this size can feel confining."

"I can see that."

"It's the people." She spread her veiny, gnarled hands and

looked at the ceiling. "All told, thirty-two hundred passengers and eleven hundred crew."

"That's a lot of bodies crammed in here." He gave her a sympathetic smile.

"Why did you sign up for this anyway? Why give up your practice in America? My impression is that doctors there can make a tidy sum."

"I like to help people. I thought it would be easier to do that here than back home."

"Well, is it?"

"So far, no. Maybe it'll get better. I'm not just looking for an easy gig. I'd like to make a difference."

A small laugh escaped from her lips. "You're curious and you ask a lot of questions. And for a young doctor, you listen well."

A compliment, finally, but one that also exposed his problem: Everybody told him too much, so he always felt compelled to help. That's what kept getting him into trouble. That's what had happened with Felipe.

"If you want to keep pressing forward," she continued, "you'd best get used to a certain…"

He craned his neck, bracing for the truth.

"…a certain level of reality."

Huh. What a bizarre thing to say. "I want to do well here."

She studied him for a long moment. "I'm going to apologize in advance. I might say and do regretful things. I fear I've already done so. Yes?"

He gave a tiny shrug. She was coming clean, so no use making a big deal out of it. She was still his boss, and he needed this job. He looked out the window. From this angle, the horizon wasn't visible, only the churning sea.

She chuckled. "Good boy."

His scalp prickled, not just at the words but at her tone, like a mother talking to a toddler, although maybe he was being too sensitive.

"Heh, heh, you— Oh, dear. Hmm, here it comes." Her cheeks flushed a deep red. Her face scrunched up, and her head dropped to her chest. She took in a heaving breath then exhaled.

He slid forward in his seat. "Are you okay?"

She sat bolt upright, lifted her head, and stared bug-eyed at the ceiling with her lips parted, revealing crooked teeth. The cords in her neck stretched taut and her jaw thrust forward. "Uhhhh…"

He moved to rise from his chair.

Hartley's deep-throated belch would've made any frat boy proud. She then unleashed a whistling howl from the depths of her gut.

He jerked back, grabbing his armrests. What the hell had gotten into her? Something on this ship… The same thing that was making every other person here act up.

Mandy stuck her head in, staring at Hartley, then him. "Everything okay back here?"

He mouthed, *WTF?*

Hartley rubbed her thighs, panting with her tongue lolling out. She smiled at nobody in particular. "We'll get those little buggers. They must eat someday." She clapped sharply and dropped her voice to a thin whisper. "Yes, then we shall have a grand old time."

Bile rose from the pit of Peter's stomach. He needed distance. He made a quick exit to the check-in counter and grabbed a paper cup at the water dispenser, flipped the lever down, and filled the cone.

Mandy swung around in front of him, but he could only

shake his head. He couldn't answer anything for her. Didn't know what to ask either.

He swirled the icy water around in his mouth and let it slide down his throat. The coldness spread through his abdomen, but the bitterness persisted like a stain that couldn't be scrubbed out.

4

PETER EMERGED FOR air on Deck 4, where a crew member in overalls was scrubbing the deck where they'd held the muster drill. The man worked his mop over the wooden planks, glancing at Peter with dark, sunken eyes. The sunlight and salty breeze should have been a balm for any troubles, but the pervasive scent of excrement soured the effect. Hence, the swabbing. Maybe somebody'd dropped a soiled diaper.

Peter found a spot upwind, away from the stench, and leaned on the thick steel railing to scan the frothing waters. Joggers and walkers fanned the air behind him.

A tap on his shoulder. It was Nali in a T-shirt with a band of skeletal cartoon warriors wearing serrated armor. "So I was right."

He turned back to the ocean. He still hadn't reconciled her presence on the ship, but there was nothing he could do about it. No use wishing that she would disappear.

"About the strangled guy," she added.

"Yep."

"How is he?"

"Not good. We have to evacuate him at the next port."

She scowled and shook her head.

"You saw it happen?" he asked.

"With my own two eyes. Even better, I got video. Wanna see?"

The clip on her phone began in the middle of the action. There it was, as clear as day: Sharma being strangled by a younger woman. He didn't seem to know how to defend himself, and others were jumping in to save him. The scene was chaotic and desperate. Chairs and people tumbled to the floor. Nali's voiceover—"Oh my God, oh my God!"—punctuated the chorus of shouting.

Peter couldn't look away. Amazing, the primal intensity of her assault. She was not only choking him with both hands but shaking him as if to pop his head off and—

His breath caught. "Hold it. Pause."

Nali tapped the screen.

"Go back a sec, back, no… yeah, right there."

"What're you looking at?"

He pointed. "Them."

A guy in a maroon sweatshirt wore a huge smile. A girl in a denim vest next to him was pumping her fist and chanting in rhythm. No doubt they were seeing the same horrific struggle as everybody else. But what planet were they from? They exchanged an exuberant high-five and broke into laughter. Disgusting.

"Cheese and crackers." Nali winced. "I didn't notice that. What's with them?"

"Having a good time. Maybe they were placing bets."

"Like one of those dog fights."

Back in the day, the uncle of one of Felipe's friends had kept pit bulls and trucked them around southeast Texas for fights. Rumor was he'd dab cocaine on their gums and inject them with horse steroids.

"But this was spontaneous, right? Doesn't make sense." Peter took a deep breath and blew it out slowly through his nostrils. Nali had been way too close to that monstrous scene. He leaned back against the railing. "What's your plan?"

She shrugged. "I'm on vacation. I'll just explore the ship."

It sounded so benign. "What do you think so far? I haven't had time to look around."

"Let's go," she said. "But I want to do a lap first."

They walked along the jogging path in the same direction the ship was moving. At the end, they entered a covered tunnel that curved around the front of the ship. The dull hum of engines echoed off the steel panels.

Steeped in shadow, the opposite deck was cool and dark. Now they were moving against the ship's progress, like walking down the up escalator. A small placard indicated one lap was a third of a mile.

At the far end of the deck, a boy in a wheelchair sat alone, facing out to sea. Joggers and walkers slowed their pace to move around him, but nobody stopped. It was that boy he'd met in the elevator lobby—Calvin. He was wearing the same Thor shirt, now smudged with food stains. Shoulder straps kept him from slumping too far down in the wheelchair.

So where was his mom? Peter slowed and stopped at the rail.

Nali studied the boy. "Are you okay?"

Calvin whipped his head away from her and flapped his right hand.

"I saw him and his mom yesterday." Peter searched the waves below. There was nobody floating in the water. He crouched to face Calvin, eye to eye. A handful of patients back home had cerebral palsy, and it took a few visits to fully grasp their physical and mental capacities. Some were profoundly disabled, while others were more functional. They usually came in with their moms, but sometimes dads or grandmas too. "Hey bud, I'm Peter. Remember me?"

Calvin rolled his head in a slow circle that was neither yes nor no.

"Is he alone?" Nali looked confused. "What do we do?"

Peter stood up and looked around, half expecting to see Calvin's mom rushing back with a coffee in hand, thankful and apologetic. But the only people around were strangers lost in their headphones. "Let's wait a minute. Maybe his mom will come back."

They waited, Peter on his tiptoes, searching.

Then a woman in a wide-brimmed pink hat caught his eye, walking briskly away from them with a glance back that lingered a beat too long. Their eyes met, and she picked up her pace. He recognized the floral fanny pack bouncing on her hip as she broke out into a quick trot.

"Hey!" He watched her slip through a set of sliding glass doors to re-enter the ship. He turned to Nali. "You got him?"

"What am I supposed to do?"

"Stay here, come along. I don't know. I'm going after that woman."

Peter took off running, and Nali grabbed the foam handles of the wheelchair and pushed with all her might, her sandals clomping on the wooden deck. He jammed the green button on the wall, bouncing on his heels, waiting. Nali caught up as the glass doors finally slid open, and they entered the ship proper.

The crowd inside erased any hope of a rapid resolution. Families, couples, and singles filled every inch around the lounge, relaxing on plush couches, mingling at the bar, hovering around slender glass pedestals.

"Where is she?" Nali asked, panting.

"Damn, I lost her. Stay with him."

"No duh!"

He skirted a knot of passengers and apologetically shot the gap between a server and a smartly dressed couple. He weaved through traffic and edged around the perimeter of the lounge. No sign of Calvin's mother.

Dashing through a gallery of jewelry and clothes boutiques, he emerged at a balcony encircling the cavernous grand atrium. The balcony was wide enough for clusters of seating, all occupied. A middle-aged couple was making out on a couch like teenagers, his thick hands raking at her breasts.

No inhibitions around here.

Mom could've gone any direction. If she'd taken an elevator, she could be on any level by now.

He bombed down the spiral staircase to the floor of the atrium. A jazz trio was playing on the stage—or least trying to, as the drummer exchanged loud words with a crew member while maintaining his rhythm on the snare.

"Did you see a lady with a pink hat come through here?" Peter asked a dude shuffling by in a tank top and cargo shorts who merely blinked his dull, tear-filled eyes.

Something about this ship. Something raw on full display.

He checked the elevator lobby, then doubled back and searched in the alcoves lining the atrium. She probably got rid of that hat; it's what he would have done had he been trying to make a quick getaway. With each passing second, the possibilities of her escape route multiplied exponentially.

He trudged back up the staircase. Nali was on the balcony

with a hand on Calvin's shoulder. The boy was rocking back and forth against his straps, getting agitated.

She searched behind Peter, then dropped her shoulders. "She's gone?"

Peter's gut twisted. They were stuck in a bizarre carnival in another dimension. He plucked the metallic pen from his breast pocket and began clicking it.

"Son of a biscuit," Nali muttered.

His phone buzzed with a message from Luisa. *Need you back in clinic ASAP.*

It must be about Sharma. "I have to go."

"What about us?"

He couldn't just ditch them here. Calvin was probably only four or five years younger than Nali, but they were worlds apart. The boy whined and tapped his jaw with the back of his right hand. It didn't look intentional, more like involuntary spasms. Peter grasped his thin wrist to restrain him. Calvin rolled his head to the left and homed in on Peter's pen clicking open and closed. *Ta-tick, ta-tack.* The boy watched intently.

"You like this?" Peter brought the pen closer to Calvin's face.

The boy grunted. Was that a yes? Hard to tell. He appeared to have more voluntary control and muscular development in his left arm compared to the right.

Peter held the pen out. "Go ahead. My brother gave it to me."

Nali opened her mouth but Peter nodded at her, and she pressed her lips closed in a pout.

He helped Calvin take the pen with his left hand. He got the hang of it after a few clumsy attempts, then he clicked away in an uneven rhythm, his tongue flicking in and out of his crooked smile in time with the up and down of the button.

"Keep it," Peter said. Anything to soothe him.

Nali bunched her shoulders up in an exaggerated shrug. "What do I do with him?"

They had no playbook. Back home, his clinic had a social worker for these types of situations. She was overwhelmed, for sure, but at least she had protocols to follow, steps to take. Calvin didn't appear to be sick, so there was no point in bringing him to the clinic. "Take him to security."

"Where is that?" she asked, her voice shrill.

"Ugh, okay, let's check this map."

He scanned the diagram posted between the elevators. An orange dot indicated they were a little to the rear of midships on the fourth level. The decks were shaped like elongated bullets. The clinic was on the lowest of the ship's twelve levels near the back. Most of the space surrounding it was grayed out. Somewhere within that expanse of gray were his cabin and the wide I-95 corridor. He guessed the crew member quarters were there too. Decks 2, 3, and 4 were dedicated to dining and entertainment—the grand atrium, bars, lounges, shops, and theaters. Passenger cabins were depicted as colored rectangles on various decks.

Dammit, he didn't see the security office on the map. Precious minutes were passing, and Sharma might be crashing. "Come down with me. The nurses will know where it is."

"I don't think that's necessary. I'll just follow him." She jerked her head over her shoulder.

A security officer in a black uniform was escorting a captive along the edge of the elevator lobby, a young male crew member, spitting and cursing with his hands zip-tied behind his back. The officer rapped the top of his head with a baton like a cartoon scene.

Nali patted Calvin's shoulder. "C'mon. We're going for a ride."

Peter pointed to the pen, which Calvin was still clicking in a sporadic tempo with his thumb. "Make sure he doesn't poke his eye out with that thing."

He couldn't make out her reply because he was already storming down the stairs to the clinic.

———

Luisa's mouth twitched when Peter arrived out of breath.

"How is he?" He rushed to Sharma's bedside in the critical care bay. One look told him that the strangling victim was stable. He even gave Peter a quick thumbs-up. Peter released a long sigh and looked up at Luisa. "It wasn't about him?"

"I'm sorry to put you in this position." She looked stressed but not sorry, nodding at one of the exam rooms. "Dr. Hartley saw this patient a few days ago. He's back, and he's not very happy."

"What is it?"

She was mum.

"Luisa."

"Just talk with him. He said she coughed all over him."

Dismay caught in his throat. "What am I supposed to do? Is he going to file a complaint or something?"

"I tried to calm him down, but he insisted on talking with you." She nudged him toward the exam room.

The forty-something man acknowledged Peter with a stiff nod. His hand was wrapped up in an elastic bandage. "I know this is weird, but I had to say something. That other one—Dr. Hartley, is it? I couldn't believe it. I'm watching a soccer game at a bar in Barcelona. The defender scores on his own goal. The ball just flies off his foot, straight in there. Bam! I slam my hand down on the bar. Thought I must've broken a few bones. My insurance is supposed to cover medical on the ship, so I come back here. She totally ignores my hand but says I remind her of her husband, and she starts going off about tractors and rain and why did I have to go out that night."

Peter's neck knotted up. This did not sound good at all. How long had Hartley been acting like this? No wonder the previous doctor left.

The guy continued. "I wasn't gonna say anything. But now I'm sick because she was coughing all over me."

Peter nodded resignedly. "I can see why you'd be upset."

"She didn't even cover her mouth or turn her head. She just hacked all over me." His jaw bulged, and he shook his head.

"That's bizarre. I don't know how to explain it. I'm sorry." Peter fought down a wave of nausea—after all, she'd confessed to doing regretful things.

It wasn't like the man was very sick—his symptoms were minor, just a cold—but Peter had to do something to make it right, so he ordered a battery of tests. Covid and flu came back negative, and a chest X-ray was normal.

"So what is it, Doc? Just a cold?"

"Most likely."

"But I don't feel right." The guy rubbed his forehead.

Hartley had done that a few times, taken off her glasses to rub her temples. It was a common gesture that meant nothing more than a headache. Peter was getting one right now. Everyone got headaches.

But not everybody howled.

He ended up prescribing a course of antibiotics. They

probably would do neither good nor harm, but it might appease the patient and make up for Hartley's behavior.

Luisa ushered the patient out and met Peter back in the office. "Thanks for seeing him."

"Did I have a choice? You said she's under stress." He put air quotes around that last word. "Is there anything more you can tell me?"

She blinked rapidly and looked out the porthole at the slate-gray sea.

"Is it just that I'm the new guy? Or what are you not telling me? It's not just Dr. Hartley but that kid who jumped. And Sharma out there." He told her about Calvin, abandoned on the jogging deck.

She finally shrugged. "It's not you, Dr. Palma. It's just... I can't put my finger on it. Like we're in the twilight zone."

"So this isn't normal."

"I started way back—what, three years ago? This has to be the most peculiar chain of events I've seen."

"I'm glad I'm not the only one." He reached for his pen but came up empty. Oops, Calvin had it. Hopefully Nali had shuttled him to the security office without incident. "What did you do before?"

"A bit of everything." Luisa perched on the desk next to the computer and ticked off gigs on her fingers. "Motorcycle mechanic, hiking guide, dog walker, you name it. I even sold houses in New Jersey—and let me just say this: I wouldn't recommend it."

"Nice. Then you went to nursing school?"

"That was all *after* I became a nurse. I never sit still, always have a lot of things going on."

He almost asked about her family. But what kind of

connections could somebody maintain while living on a ship for months at a time?

Sharma moaned from the critical care bay, which brought them running to his bedside. He mimed the act of drinking from a cup. "Water? Water?" he said in a scratchy whisper.

Peter's shoulders slumped in relief. Asking for a drink was a good sign. It meant the patient was alert and not focused solely on breathing.

Luisa brought him a plastic cup of water with a straw. She coached him in taking small, cautious sips. "Take it easy. We don't want you to choke. Your tissues are still going to be swollen."

No point in jinxing him by saying it out loud, but it looked like he was turning the corner. His face was calm.

Peter pulled up a stool. "Sir, if I may take a moment. Do you remember what happened?"

Sharma's eyes drifted away. The beeping monitor counted out his heart rate at a steady eighty beats per minute.

"It's okay if you don't." Peter patted his arm. "I was just curious."

A dark look passed over Sharma's face. The beeping quickened for few seconds and then settled down.

Mandy arrived bearing gifts of pastries on a tray. "Look what I scored!" Her eyes were little rainbows above her mask.

They congregated in the office as she doled out the goodies. Peter munched down on a baklava, flaky and sweetened with honey. The logical part of his brain said it was top-notch, but that was sterile book knowledge. It tasted like a nervous smile frozen on your face when you don't get the joke. The Lexapro was definitely wearing off, taking his appetite with it.

"This one's for Hartley." Mandy tucked a puffy bun into a coffee cup and set it on the desk. "Her fave."

He set his baklava down after the one bite. "When do we dock tomorrow?"

"You don't like it?" Mandy asked.

"A little motion sickness. Thanks though."

Mandy finished her fruit tart, replaced her mask, and pulled up the interactive map on the computer. The next stop on the itinerary was Mioven, a small town in Norway. The little triangle representing the ship inched along the North Sea every time the screen refreshed. "At 7:45. The paperwork's all done for the transfer. I'll watch over him, and before you know it, he'll be off the ship." She made the motion of washing her hands of the matter.

"You're going to stay up with him?"

"I was an ICU nurse, remember?"

He crossed his arms. The ship's engines hummed underneath. Maybe things would be okay. Mandy and Luisa were solid veterans of this strange life. He didn't have to be everything; he could just take it one step at a time and get ready for the next day.

The vilest curse borne by humankind was that those who needed sleep the most got the least. The Lexapro was supposed to help with that, but his stash had dissolved in the ship's sewage system. Hey, maybe the countless bacteria therein were feeling a little happier now.

Nali had sent an update about Calvin. *They're gonna keep him there till they find his mom. All the cells are full so they had to clear one out for him.* Frowny face.

Like a jail? He'd replied.

Yah.

He imagined Harrington wheeling the kid into a cinder-block cell with a steel toilet-sink combo. It probably wasn't that at all, but he had no frame of reference for what jail on a cruise ship would look like.

Harrington had called it a shit show.

Sometime around midnight, an idea had slithered into Peter's mind. He buried his face in his pillow, pulled the blanket over his head, and sank into the mattress. The gentle rocking of the ship should've been soothing, but the thought lingered, waiting. Probing. Like that night in New Mexico when he and Elena had lain wide awake in the RV as *something* scratched around in the dirt outside. They'd seen the jagged footprints the next morning.

There was a pattern here. Stevenson, his first patient, had come in with wheezing and a cough then invited him back to her room. Rickey Turner came in for a runny nose and nausea before swan-diving into concrete. That last guy said Hartley coughed all over him.

Peter sat up and swung his legs over the side of the bed. It was probably nothing. The waning effect of Lexapro, the new environment, and the stress of caring for sick patients were getting to him. He just needed sleep.

He rummaged through his toiletries and found a battered box of Benadryl. It was 1 a.m., way too late to take it. But he could pop just a single tablet, get up at seven, and pound some coffee. Then he'd get Sharma to a real hospital.

He swallowed the Benadryl and set the alarm on his phone.

5

SOMETHING WAS OUT there. Probably a possum.

Peter rolled onto his side and smashed the extra pillow over his head.

The dull thudding continued.

That was no possum. Maybe it was a bear. That was okay. They were safe in the RV. *Go away, bear, let me sleep.*

More pounding.

He groaned and nestled into the blankets. *You have your den, Mr. Bear, and I have mine. Leave me alone.*

A voice.

You can talk? Smart bear.

"Peter!"

Hmm. Okay.

"Dr. Palma!"

What was that buzzing? Were bees inside?

More pounding.

Oh, no—that buzzing, that was his phone. And somebody was pounding on the door. The door of the cabin. He was in his cabin, not an RV. On the *Paradise*.

A deep voice: "Sir! Sir!"

A female voice: "Peter! Are you there?"

He sat up in slow motion through the murky gloom. This must be day three on the ship. But unlike Jesus, he didn't feel like rising from the dead.

The door of his cabin burst open, revealing a male security guard with Mandy close behind. Her face was unmasked and flushed. "Sharma's crumping!"

"Wha you talking about?" Peter's tongue was thick and fuzzy.

"He's crashing! You need to intubate him!"

"Who?"

"Mr. Sharma!" Mandy put her hands around her neck. "The strangling victim."

Peter slapped his face and snorted through his nostrils. Anything to clear the fog.

She grabbed his arm and leaned back, using her weight to lever his butt off the bed. "Come on!"

He threw himself together—scrubs from yesterday, phone, shoes—and scrambled out the door, stumbling straight into the solid chest of the security guard. He half expected the man to pummel him like the elevator dad had threatened to do.

"Oh my God," Mandy said, "you didn't hear me calling?"

That damn Benadryl had done him in. "What time is it?"

"Six something."

In the clinic, Sharma was sitting bolt upright on the gurney, eyes wild and neck cords straining. Luisa was holding the oxygen mask over his face. "Down to eighty-three."

The man was in extremis, starving for oxygen. The red crash cart brooded nearby, top drawer already open.

"How long has he been like this?" He hated the tinge of

accusation in his voice. He'd failed Mandy also. Whatever answer she gave would implicate him equally.

"About five minutes. I couldn't find Hartley anywhere." Mandy held up a syringe. "Propofol."

Peter grabbed the bed railing to steady himself. Was it the ship moving or the Benadryl?

Luisa snapped her fingers, a surprisingly loud and sharp sound from her slender hand. "Are you with us?"

"Yeah."

"Can you do it?"

Peter took the syringe of propofol from Mandy and made eye contact with Sharma. "I need to put in a breathing tube, okay?"

Sharma grabbed the front of Peter's scrubs, nodding and panting, then let go. Peter injected the anesthetic into the IV while eyeing the man's vitals and breathing. Sharma slumped back onto the stretcher in a drug-induced stupor.

Peter eased open Sharma's jaws, bent down close, and used the smooth blade of the laryngoscope to pull the tongue up and to the side. He searched for the tiny space between the white vocal cords, an upside-down *V*, but Sharma's tongue kept flopping back into place like a troll guarding a cave.

"Bigger blade," Peter demanded.

"That's all we have," Mandy said.

He swiped his forehead with the back of his hand and tried twisting the blade this way and that, searching for the *V* amid the swollen tissues.

"O2 sat is seventy-nine," Mandy reported.

Shit. Where was that space? He couldn't do this. He wasn't up to the task. But just as he was preparing to pull back, he caught a glimpse of white.

He shot the gap.

In a flash, Luisa attached the pineapple-shaped Ambu bag to the endotracheal tube and squeezed it to push oxygen into Sharma's lungs. Peter rocked back on his heels and let her take care of Sharma's breathing for a moment so he could manage his own.

He leaned in and listened to Sharma's chest. His spirits lifted: Air moving in both lungs with each push from the bag. "Sounds good."

As the nurses connected the tube to the ventilator, a riptide of adrenaline washed over Peter, sending his heart rate through the roof. He was definitely awake now. He leaned on the counter with his forearms. "What time is it?"

"6:34." Mandy slipped her mask back on. It seemed like she was avoiding eye contact with him. "Everything was fine one minute, then he started going downhill."

"Okay."

"I swear."

"I believe you," said Peter. No sense making her feel bad, but he was still on edge. "It can happen with strangulation."

"We couldn't have prevented this, right?" Her voice was small and shaky.

Good question. A long moment passed, after which it was too late for him to say anything comforting.

Thankfully, Luisa wedged in and broke the silence with "Let's get rolling."

Peter helped her prepare the patient for transport, securing lines and tubes with tape and connecting the monitor and ventilator to a battery pack. There was nothing left for Sharma here. His niece had made sure of that.

"We should tell his family," Luisa said.

"I'll do it." Mandy wiped away tears.

"Are you sure?" Luisa asked.

"I have to."

"Then afterward, you go ahead and get some sleep."

Peter nodded in agreement. "We got it."

Judging by the creases in her forehead, Mandy didn't look reassured at all. She took a deep breath and went off to deliver the bad news.

While Peter was tweaking the settings on Sharma's ventilator, Hartley shuffled in. "I believe you all were looking for me."

He glanced at Luisa. "We took care of it."

Hartley's gaze roamed all corners of the bay before landing on Sharma's face. "What's the point? Why bother?"

"Excuse me?"

It would've made sense if Peter smelled alcohol on her breath, but he didn't. Her face was smudged with something dark.

"He deserves it. He must've done something horrible to her. Why else would she have strangled him?"

"We don't know what happened."

"That's the whole thing, young sir." She wagged an arthritic finger at him. "Everything happens for a reason."

The clinic was silent except for the puffing ventilator and beeping monitor.

After guiding Hartley to a rolling stool, Luisa asked, "Where were you?"

Hartley scanned the floor, lips set in a hard line. It was no use talking with her. Peter turned away in disgust.

Their approach into Mioven couldn't come quickly enough. He itched to check their progress on the computer but didn't want to leave Sharma even for a minute, although he was now intubated and supported by the ventilator. What else could happen? Nevertheless, he was grateful when Luisa showed him how to pull up the map on his phone with the SeaText app.

He studied the graphic. Denmark was a peninsula, with Copenhagen occupying an eastern island on the right. The dotted trail behind the triangle showed how they'd arched over the tip of Denmark to reach the North Sea. Now they were almost at Mioven, a white square on the southwest coast of Norway. He clicked on Mioven, which pulled up a montage: excursions to the famous fjords, deep-blue inlets surrounded by steeply forested hills.

Each refresh of the map brought them incrementally closer to port, but time was crawling. His bed was calling to him. He had to hang on, get Sharma off the ship. Then there would be time for sleep.

Finally, against the backdrop of Hartley's senseless muttering, a bumping and rocking signaled their arrival at port. The office window showed calm waters outside. Peter imagined men in blue jumpsuits heaving thick coils of rope to their counterparts on the dock, who would loop them around massive iron fixtures.

"The ambulance should be here soon." Luisa tugged on his arm. "Let's go."

She pulled the gurney while he pushed, and they rolled Sharma out of the clinic in a hurry. The crew and officers gave them a wide berth as they trucked down I-95. Luisa turned them into a loading bay filled with supply pallets and stopped at the top of a wide ramp connecting the ship to the dock. They waited there for minutes that seemed eternal.

Movement under the sheet caught Peter's attention. Sharma had raised his hands off the gurney. Luisa made to hold them down.

"Don't touch him," Peter said. "Let's see what happens."

Sharma curled his hands under his chin like he was fist-bumping himself. He looked like a dead man praying. Peter used the flashlight on his phone to check his pupils: large and dilated. The only patient he'd seen in residency who displayed these signs of brain herniation had spent weeks on a ventilator until the family pulled the plug. "He's decorticate. From brain swelling."

"We were too late?" Luisa searched his face.

He shouldn't have taken the Benadryl. How much time had Mandy wasted trying to find Hartley? Trying to rouse him? Had he intubated Sharma reflexively, without making a thorough assessment? It was a knee-jerk decision made in the fog of sedation, an attempt to compensate for being unavailable. And it might've done more harm than good, because intubation may have raised Sharma's already precarious intracranial pressure.

He struggled to formulate an apology to Luisa. Neither he nor Hartley had been shining paragons of leadership.

But before he opened his mouth, a yellow Mercedes ambulance pulled up near the end of the ramp. Peter leaped into position. They rolled the gurney down the ramp and onto the dock, where a pair of EMTs in red jumpsuits came to meet them.

The stout woman donned gloves and gave Sharma a cursory exam.

The scrawny guy with bangs scribbled notes on an electronic tablet as Peter summarized recent events. "It's quite a shame, yes?" the male EMT said. "This is no good at all."

They each grabbed corners of the sheet to transfer Sharma to the ambulance gurney. His lean frame felt like nothing, as if his organs were already atrophying.

Peter stepped back, hands limp at his waist. Sharma's

survival was in doubt. At a minimum, he would need surgery to relieve the pressure on his brain and repair his crushed larynx, a long stint in ICU, and months of rehab—all in a foreign country. He'd be lucky to wake up and regain any function.

Peter stared idly at the bustle of activity on the surrounding dock. Seagulls wheeled overhead, casting flickering shadows on the ground. None of this was in the job description. What had happened to the prospect of happy passengers, grateful for medical care that allowed them to enjoy their vacations? He was supposed to treat their illnesses and injuries, not become engulfed by their sorrows. Yet even here, there was always something beneath it all—a need he couldn't meet. A ruined life he couldn't restore.

Even before Felipe's despondent plea, the yoke had been tightening around his neck.

Once Sharma was settled on the gurney, they switched over the monitor and ventilator connections to the ambulance.

"Where are you taking him?" Peter asked.

"The hospital is thirty-three kilometers," the male EMT said.

The ambulance sped off with its blue bar flashing and siren blaring, *wee-oo, wee-oo, wee-oo*. It was too early for passengers to disembark. He and Luisa were surrounded by an orchestra of dockworkers in their forklifts carrying goods to and fro. A crane hoisted massive metal cages full of crates onto the bays of the ship.

The morning should've felt clean, promising, but exhaustion had prevailed.

Luisa pushed the empty gurney up the ramp, then paused and looked back. "Are you coming?"

He took one step and stopped. "Just give me a minute."

She disappeared into the gaping maw of the vessel.

Perhaps it was the light knifing through the trees, but the *Paradise* looked different today. Back in Copenhagen, the ship had seemed shiny and modern. Now it seemed to have aged decades. Its windows were caked with salty grime, and the paint was chipped and faded in a dozen spots. Abrasions crisscrossed the hull like wounds from unseen assailants. The sight reminded him of that trip to Galveston with Elena before the RV bug had bitten her. A whale the size of an airliner had beached itself. Its skin had looked sleek from a distance, but up close they saw ragged scars and festering sores. Peter had wondered how such an enormous creature could've come there to die on the sand when it should've been gliding through the great blue expanse. Another bystander said it happened when the whales got sick and disoriented.

Sick and disoriented. Too much of that going around.

———————

Peter sought shelter in the glass enclosure of the taxi stand at the far end of the dock. It did little good. A bitter wind lashed from the bay like a vaporous demon of the deep. The ground swayed under his feet, his equilibrium disrupted by a mere three days at sea.

The only steady element here was the public Wi-Fi. He scrolled through his social media, skipping past posts about politics and business.

There was an update from Jared, his former co-resident who'd quit clinical practice to write medical education modules for an agency supported by "unrestricted" grants from Big Pharma. He looked happy in that way of public posts, lounging on a beach with his laptop and a tropical drink. Peter had considered doing something similar, but it seemed heretical to step away from patient care given the sacrifices he'd made. Better to take an alternate route than wander completely off the map.

This cruise was supposed to be that kind of detour. Some people found their pathways early in life. So what if it took him a bit longer.

But the *Paradise* was no haven. The primordial stench penetrated here as much as anywhere—that dad in the elevator, the boy who jumped, poor Sharma on a ventilator. And what was going on with Calvin's mom? Had she truly abandoned him?

It was a load, with or without the warm embrace of Lexapro. Maybe he could've handled it if his "mentor" wasn't off in her own bizarre world, on the edge of a full-blown mental crisis. He was next. This job would shove him over the edge of the abyss, no matter how hard he dug his heels in. He could almost feel his leg bones snapping in two.

Screw that.

Above the ship, seagulls continued screaming and dove for their prey. They were killers, like everything else in nature. He rubbed his hands together against the chill. So now what? He could ride a keyboard like Jared, read some journal articles, and jump on a call once in a while. The hours would be regular and the paycheck decent. Nothing would keep him up at night—except maybe Felipe's face.

He dialed the taxi number on the wall of the enclosure and keyed in the pickup location. Done. He shoved his phone into his pocket and parked himself on the wooden bench.

He couldn't shake the image of Sharma's bruised neck and swollen tongue. *Let me take the night shift*, Mandy had said.

True, she was an ICU nurse at one time, but he should've been there, even with little chance of saving the man.

But soon, it wouldn't be his problem. Soon, he'd be back home.

An off-white taxi pulled up, and the driver rolled down the window. "Where to?"

Peter slipped into the back seat. "Airport."

"Your bags?"

He shook his head. "I'm good."

The taxi eased off the dock and onto the main road. Traffic was minimal, and progress was steady. With each passing minute, a bit more tension melted from Peter's shoulders. Each mile separated him from whatever misery infested that ship.

Apparently this little town considered Wi-Fi an essential service, because he still had a strong signal in the cab. He checked his email. His old practice partner, a crusty guy with no filter, had sent a nastygram about a patient he'd inherited from Peter. *Why were you chasing down all those little ditzels on the CT? It won't make any difference. She's drinking herself to death. Hope you're enjoying your new life.*

On some type of masochistic autopilot, Peter's finger hovered over the bookmark for his online reviews. He shouldn't click it. What was the point?

He clicked it.

His stomach sank at the latest comments, made just two months ago. One patient rated him two out of five stars: *Dr. Palma kept me waiting for an hour and then he was in and out. He barely listened. He used to spend more time with me.* Another patient dinged him for sluggish follow-up: *I got all the tests done but I'm still waiting on the ultrasound results.* He remembered that one. He'd called twice but only reached the patient's full voicemail. The nurse was supposed to send out a letter.

He understood their grievances. There was a clear trend, with his steady stream of five-star reviews bumped down the page by the more recent negative ones. He'd slipped, in ways he couldn't prevent, and it showed.

Was there really anything to go back to? He'd just get sucked into the machine again, only to be ground up and spit out in pieces.

He looked over his shoulder and caught sight of the ship across the crescent bay, dominating the view even at this distance. More than a mere ship, it was an entire city of its own—a vulnerable city like Pompeii, buried under the ash of Mount Vesuvius, or New Orleans, decimated by Hurricane Katrina. But those had been natural disasters. The *Paradise* was different, as if it carried the seed of its own destruction. He'd only glimpsed a shadow of the menace, but something was there. The echoes of Hartley's howl made his skin prickle. The ship wouldn't be safe in her hands if he left.

His neck tightened as another realization struck: Nali. While he was escaping, his little sister was still back there. Dammit, why didn't she just stay home?

He cleared his throat. "Turn around, please. Sorry."

"Turn around?" the cabbie said.

"Take me back to the ship."

The cabbie met his eyes in the rearview mirror. "Did you forget something?"

Peter settled back into the seat with a bitter smile. He sure had—and it wasn't just his sister. He'd almost forgotten why he'd gone into medicine in the first place. Yes, the dream had burned down to cinders, but maybe there was a live ember somewhere under the ashes. If there was any hope of rekindling the fire, he couldn't walk away now. The people of the *Paradise* needed him.

Fifteen minutes later, he stepped up the ramp and into the loading bay of the ship, where a bedraggled security officer scanned his badge and beeped him back into the belly of the whale.

6

PETER CRADLED A tall black coffee on the fourth-level deck. Across the bay, the town of Mioven looked straight out of a fairy tale. Gable-roofed cottages dotted verdant hills and a church steeple rose from the town square. Little fishing boats bobbed next to wooden docks. Somewhere beyond this postcard scene, doctors in a *real* hospital would be tending to Sharma. That knowledge plus the crisp wind skimming off the Nordic water should have offered some comfort, but the knots in Peter's neck wouldn't loosen.

The search for Calvin's mother had kept the ship at port for an unplanned overnight stay. Despite no evidence she had gone overboard, it could not be ruled out. The Danish and Norwegian coast guards dedicated helicopters and rigid inflatable boats to the search, and authorities in Mioven issued an alert and disseminated her photo. All passengers getting on and off the ship were double-verified. After twenty-four hours with no sign of Mrs. Amanda Burchins, the captain made the call to move on. The Law of the Sea dictated that without a legal guardian, Calvin would remain on the ship until they reached New York.

Nali's text didn't make things any better. *Where are you? He's acting up.*

Jogging deck, Peter replied. Maybe the kid was just hungry. Easy to fix that on a cruise ship.

She showed up a few minutes later with Calvin. Strands of hair dangled from under her baseball cap, and her face was drawn.

"I thought you dropped him off at security," Peter said.

"I just picked him up. I had to get him out of there."

Calvin closed his eyes and made a long humming noise. A crooked smile lifted his cheek. He still had Peter's metallic pen, which he clicked open and closed repeatedly.

"What happened?"

She smoothed down a cowlick of Calvin's. "He was all agitated. I thought he was having a seizure, but then it stopped in the elevator."

"Okay. We'll just watch him."

"It was creepy down there." She shuddered. "They have a real jail with padded cells. It's a bunch of freakin' Neanderthals. I couldn't stand the thought of him staying there last night, but what else was I supposed to do?"

She hadn't signed up for this bizarro marathon either. No sense in mentioning that he'd been *this close* to catching a flight back to Houston.

"At least we have some help now." She nodded over her shoulder at a young male crew member just behind her. "This is Agus."

Agus Bambang, Indonesia read his tag. He stood with hands behind his back, a posture Peter had noticed among many of the crew. He seemed friendly with a round, smiling face.

"Are you child care?" Peter asked.

Agus shook his head. "I manage a maintenance crew. But they need me to help you guys, so I help."

"Maybe they can watch him in day care," said Peter. "That'd be better than security."

Nali rolled her eyes. "Duh, we tried that already. But since I'm not registered as his family, they wouldn't accept him. The security guy said he'll tell the captain." She patted Calvin's shoulder and continued in a whisper. "I am so exhausted."

Back in Houston, Peter would've called Child Protective Services. Here, on the cruise from hell, he could only offer his coffee.

She took a sip and sputtered. "Ugh, don't you put anything in it?"

He held out his hand to take it back, but apparently it wasn't quite bad enough.

"What kind of mom would do this?" she murmured.

"We don't know her situation." He had treated a few kids with special needs. Their parents were saints, putting their careers and dreams in deep storage to take care of their kids. But saints could be sinners too. Nobody was perfect. "We have no idea what support she has."

Agus shuffled his feet and gave Calvin a sad smile.

"I still say she jumped overboard." Nali gazed out at the bustling dock. The passengers who'd taken advantage of their extra time at port were returning to the ship. "But I guess they can't search forever."

One man and woman argued all the way up the ramp. He stopped and raised an open hand in a threatening manner. She jerked into a sidestep, tripped, and went sprawling. When he reached down to help her up, she spurned his hand and clambered up herself. They advanced up the ramp in silence.

Peter glanced away. It would be a long vacation for them.

"Did you see that?" She returned the coffee cup, empty and smudged with pink lip gloss.

"Gee, thanks."

"You like the coffee?" Agus asked.

He shrugged. "It's okay."

"I bring you good coffee sometime," Agus said with a shy smile.

Sure, but he'd need a lot more than coffee to get this ship to New York. "What do you think is going on here? These people are so…"

"Maybe they're all on drugs." She said it so softly that he barely heard it.

Oh, but it hurt like an ice pick in the brain. They hadn't talked much about Felipe. "They're snorting coke in their rooms? Meth? It doesn't add up."

"What else, then? Prescription meds?"

It was hard to draw a straight line between bizarre behavior on this ship and prescription meds like Xanax or hydrocodone. Still, they'd both seen Felipe's outbursts. It was impossible to disentangle all the demons that had tormented their brother. PTSD, chronic pain, drugs. "I don't— This guy almost decked me in the elevator when I boarded the ship. He was with his wife and kids." He turned to Agus. "What about the crew? Are drugs a big problem?"

Agus's eyes grew large. "Oh no, Doctor. If anybody use drugs they will be fired."

"What about the passengers?" Or the officers, for that matter—that inhuman howl from Dr. Hartley.

"They behave good," Agus insisted. "This is high-class cruise, sir."

"Then what's that?" Nali pointed to a pair of men in black jumpsuits disembarking, each with a dog on a leash.

"They come on ship and check the rooms," Agus said.

Peter raised his eyebrows. "Sounds like that would take all day."

"I think they check on random basis."

The sleek canines trotted alongside their handlers with confidence and vigilance. Peter knew these dogs were trained to detect illegal drugs. Foreign substances. Harmful things that didn't belong. There might be something to that. "I wonder…"

"Hmm?"

"Maybe it's something else," Peter muttered.

"Like what?" Nali glanced at Calvin then Agus.

Peter eyed the sticky, pink rim of his coffee cup. He didn't want to say it. "A virus."

"Dagnabbit, not again," she said. "No way I'm getting another vaccine."

He couldn't blame her; the world was weary from Covid, flu, and the long list of other infections. "This could be viral. Something that affects the brain."

"What, like brain fog? My old roommate insists she has long Covid."

He stuffed his theory in a sack and cinched it tight because there was no point worrying about something he couldn't control. "Forget it. I'm just spitballing." He suppressed a cough and cleared his throat. "Anyway, I think Calvin likes you."

"He's a trooper." She used a tissue to wipe a bead of snot dangling from Calvin's nose. "Oh, no."

Calvin's face scrunched up and reddened. A small grunt escaped his lips.

Nali clutched Peter's arm. "It's happening again."

The kid contorted in pain, his right arm and leg drawn up tight. Peter tried to straighten his limbs with gentle tugs. No success. The boy's muscles were cramped and quivering.

"He's spasming," he said. "It's common with cerebral palsy."

Nali shared a look of concern with Agus.

Peter crouched and rubbed Calvin's elbows. "Hey boss, do you know what meds you're taking?" There was little chance he could complete the loop of comprehension and reply, but it felt better to try.

Calvin moaned as his right arm and leg twitched and jerked. Peter rubbed his belly, a move he'd seen some parents do. Maybe a bubble of gas in his bowels was triggering the spasms.

It didn't work.

"Let's take him to the clinic." Peter got up and grabbed the handles of the wheelchair. This would be a real test, to see if the little pharmacy had a suitable antispasmodic medication in stock. Time to check out their stores of ammunition.

Dr. Hartley wasn't ready for anything whatsoever. Luisa dispensed an update in an irritated whisper. "She's just wandering around, ranting."

So this was why Mandy hadn't been able to find her when Sharma was crashing. Peter and Luisa started rummaging through the meds in the pharmacy. He truly was the only functioning physician on the ship. "There's nothing here."

"What about this?" Luisa tapped a box of cyclobenzaprine. "A muscle relaxant?"

"It's okay for your garden-variety back strain but not cerebral palsy." Calvin needed baclofen or dantrolene. Diazepam was a poor substitute, but it was all they had—a single box of two-milligram tablets. "If he's already on diazepam, he probably needs a higher dose. But if he's not, it's safer to start with a low dose."

He entered Calvin's name and date of birth from his wristband into the computer. The search came up blank.

"So he's never been in the clinic before," Luisa said.

"I was hoping it would pull stuff from the ship's registers, or whatever you call it."

"It's called a manifest. Sounds Big Brotherish."

"You never know with AI." But the AI agent offered nothing, silent in their time of need. A dull pressure gathered in his forehead.

He asked Luisa to get the diazepam and returned to the exam room where Nali was massaging Calvin's muscles, trying to ease the spasms.

"Let's try this out, buddy." He offered Calvin a diazepam tablet with a cup of water.

The boy screwed his lips up tight and jerked his head away. He was no dummy. No way he was going to take this strange pill from this non-Mommy person. The self-preservation and awareness Peter might've praised at another time were working against him here.

"Can we crush it, mix it in juice?" Peter asked Luisa.

"I don't think you're supposed to crush it, but let me check. Go see the next patient."

A fifty-four-year-old New Zealander with earrings and a goatee had come in with a case of the sniffles. "Sorry to bother you, mate. We usually just get the little packets from that vending machine out there, you know? But they're out, so my wife made me come in."

The skin around Peter's nose and mouth buzzed. He was exposed and vulnerable. They both should've been wearing masks. Or was that an overreaction? The patient's physical exam was normal. He wasn't howling, exposing himself, or threatening to punch anybody. He was just a guy with a cold, right? A cold.

Just like everybody else.

"Do you want a Covid test?" Peter asked.

"Nah, I'm good."

Peter dismissed him with a supply of cough-and-cold meds. As he scrubbed his hands in the steel sink, the hairs on the back of his neck prickled. By all rights, the patient had nothing more than a routine upper respiratory infection.

Just like everybody else.

In the other exam room, spasms still wracked Calvin's right arm and leg. He kept clicking that pen with his other hand.

Luisa was shaking her head. "Micromedex says we can't crush diazepam. The absorption is unpredictable." She was a dutiful nurse, going by the rules. But the rules were written for a normal world, not for right here, right now.

She followed him back to the office, looking annoyed when he settled at the computer. "You don't believe me?"

"I'm just checking something."

He opened the EHR and queried the AI. The response appeared instantly:

Crushing diazepam can lead to a dangerous and rapid release of the medication. Crushing diazepam is strongly discouraged. If you must crush diazepam tablets, use a pill crusher or a mortar and pestle to ensure even crushing. Consider mixing the crushed medication with a small amount of soft food to make it easier to swallow.

Luisa read it over his shoulder. "I'm not doing it. If you want to snocker him, it's on you. You want to intubate another patient?"

"He's going to keep having these spasms. How about half a tablet? One milligram, mix it in some juice." The suggestion sounded worse when he said it out loud. The danger wasn't in the total amount but how fast it would be absorbed into Calvin's bloodstream.

He imagined Felipe crushing a hydrocodone with the bottom of a coffee mug on Mom's cutting board at the kitchen table, snorting the fine powder, and slumping back in his chair with a stupid smile. It was a manufactured memory, one of many that his conscience served up since the overdose.

A sharp metallic clang from outside the porthole window made him jump.

"That's just the ramp," Luisa said. "They're pulling up to leave port."

Back with Calvin, he squatted and tapped the boy's knee. "I'm gonna try something else. Don't worry, buddy, I'll get you taken care of."

Calvin murmured and rolled his head in a slow circle.

"Where are you going?" Nali asked as he rose to leave.

"Security."

They would have Calvin's room number. Hopefully his meds were in there—unless his mom had absconded with them.

"What about me?"

Something about the tone of her voice bothered him more than it should have. "Luisa's got him for now."

"Fine. You go off, then." She crossed her arms, looking like a pouty little girl.

"Sorry, I can't hang out."

"Whatever. Avoiding things, as usual."

"I have to do this and then get back here and see all these patients."

"Yeah, you're a big shot."

He turned again to leave. The dull pressure in his head intensified as he climbed the stairs to the second level. So that's why she was here. But he didn't want to talk about their brother. The tide of Lexapro had receded, leaving him exposed in the sand like flotsam covered in rotting seaweed.

A text from an Officer Kinnard interrupted Peter's trip to security, asking him to report to her office on the bridge for an urgent discussion about the abandoned boy. Maybe they found Mrs. Burchins. Back to the clinic to collect Nali, a trek along I-95 to the fore elevator, and a ride all the way to the top.

"Why do I have to come?" Nali whined.

"We're in this together. Maybe they're on to you. They still toss stowaways overboard these days."

She punched his shoulder.

"What did you end up doing with your lizard thing anyway?" he asked as they neared Kinnard's door.

Her face darkened. "He was a bearded dragon. A hawk scooped him up in the commons right outside my dorm."

Kinnard—First Officer Kinnard, according to the plaque on her desk—was an avian-looking woman with hard eyes. Her office matched her outfit: drab, sterile, and devoid of natural light. She motioned them toward a cluster of padded chairs, two of which were occupied by a young couple. Her gaze slid off Peter and landed on Nali.

"And you are?"

Nali hooked her thumb at him. "His sister."

"Your key card."

Nali handed her the plastic rectangle.

Kinnard scanned it with a handheld device and read from the screen. "Natalia Palma."

"That's me."

"And you're with the boy too?"

Nali and Peter nodded in unison as they sat down.

Kinnard gestured to the other couple. "These Americans claim to be the boy's aunt and uncle."

Peter studied them. They looked fit and trim, she with tawny hair tied back and he with thick curls. "I didn't know he had other family on board."

"Where is he?" Aunt asked.

"Getting treatment in the clinic."

"Do you know what meds he's on?" Nali asked.

The couple looked at each other with concern. "Calvin's mother? I'm her sister. We don't have kids of our own, but we babysit him sometimes back home. This is our first vacation together."

"Do you have any idea where she might've gone?" Kinnard's lips barely moved when she talked.

"I don't know, but…" She frowned and looked at Uncle again. "My key card is missing."

"She took it?" Kinnard asked.

"We're thinking she used it to get off the boat without attracting attention," Uncle said. "When they scanned it, she would've passed."

"We look a lot alike, almost like twins," the woman said. "But we're not."

"You haven't heard—"

The deep bellow of the ship's horn cut Peter off. More than a sound, its low-frequency pulsation shook the walls of the office. Kinnard merely tightened her mouth, but he covered his ears until the last percussions faded. Then the PA system announced their departure from Mioven. Next stop, Scotland.

Peter continued. "You haven't heard from her?"

Aunt shook her head. "It's totally out of character for her to do this."

"My theory is that she finally said screw it and left," Uncle said.

"But why now?" Peter asked. "Why bother booking this cruise and choosing now to do it?"

Uncle shrugged. "No idea."

"Just so you know," Aunt said, "she's never used drugs. We heard about the search, and I know people are talking. I wish it were that simple. It would make some kind of sense, at least."

"Is *she* on meds?" Nali asked. "Like psych meds?"

"It would be news to me. She's rock solid. I mean, she heads a food bank."

Something didn't add up here.

Kinnard looked agitated in her birdlike way, her head snapping back and forth between Nali and Aunt. "Miss."

Nali jerked straight up. "Don't 'miss' me. I was the one who brought him down to that zoo you call security. I covered him with blankets last night. I kept him fed and took him to the bathroom." She turned to mutter to Aunt: "Hope you have some clean underwear for him." And then was indignant again: "So why did it take so long to find you two anyway? I hear all these announcements about spa packages and shows. But what about one for this poor boy?"

Aunt's eyes were now wet. "Please, you have to understand. We didn't know what was happening. We went on an excursion and thought they were on another one. When we got back and heard they were looking for her, we reached out.

But she"—nodding at Kinnard—"wanted us to wait until this morning."

Uncle turned to Kinnard, his jaw jutting forward. "What I want to know is who else tried to pick him up."

Kinnard sat perfectly still.

Nali reddened. "You all better wake up. There's something seriously wacko here. If it isn't drugs or whatever, then—"

"Hold on," Peter said. "You babysit him?"

Aunt nodded.

"So you can handle the tube feeds."

Her eyes pinched for second then relaxed. "Of course. We might need a refresher, but yeah."

Uncle smiled broadly. "It's been a while."

Peter smelled a rat. Time to spring the trap. "His G-tube site looks good. We've been hanging Jevity three times a day, but I wasn't sure if he gets another bolus."

"Three times a day is right," Aunt said.

Nali nudged Peter's shoe with her furry brown Ugg, but he held his tongue. He'd give them one more chance.

"You all manage the tube feeds?" he asked, giving them one more chance.

The couple glanced at each other in the awkward silence.

Peter glared at them, heart pounding in his throat. "Actually, Calvin doesn't have a G-tube, and he doesn't get tube feeds." Confrontation wasn't his thing—but damn.

"Calvin? Did you say *Calvin*?" Uncle shot up, scraping his chair on the floor. "Excuse us, we've made a terrible mistake. We thought you were talking about *Kelvin*, not Calvin."

The interlopers made a quick exit, leaving Peter and Nali to gape at one another across the little office. The ship swayed hard to one side then the other, like a metronome, forcing Peter to shift his weight in countermeasure.

Kinnard lifted her chin at his discomfort. "The yaw is exaggerated at this height."

He rubbed his face, trying not to think about whatever those strangers had wanted with Calvin.

She tilted her hand back and forth. "The ship sways from side to side. We feel it more up here."

That didn't fully explain the sickened feeling in his stomach. "Huh. Well… didn't your team verify those people? What was that all about?"

"Of course we verified them," Kinnard said. "We found no link between this woman and Calvin's mother. But I only thought it fair to solicit your input."

Nali clutched herself and shuddered.

Yet they'd still tried. It was both creepy and stupid. Even worse was the prospect that creepiness had overcome stupid.

———————

Harrington clenched his square jaw and drummed the steel desk with thick fingers. "Why do you need their room number?"

"I need to find her." Peter sat on the other side of the desk in the low-ceilinged, windowless security office. "Her son needs his meds."

"We checked her room," Harrington said. "You don't think we take this seriously? I'm wound up tighter than a wallaby's sphincter."

"Let me search the room. Or send somebody."

"What's your angle?"

Peter gripped his knees. "I'm concerned that the same thing happened to her that's going around the ship."

"And what's that?"

He needed to get better at explaining this to people, fast. "You said people were behaving like animals."

Harrington rocked his chair back. "Hear that?"

"What?" A smell akin to old, wet socks reached Peter's nose, but he couldn't hear anything beyond the distant growl of the engines.

"Exactly. Silence—first time in days, because we just unloaded a half dozen scumbags to local police."

"Okay, so why were they detained?"

"Pretty much the seven deadlies—lust, greed, gluttony, you name it. Maybe the only one missing is sloth." Harrington snorted. "But your kid's mom has that one covered."

"I don't think she's being lazy."

"None of these detainees were drunk. We tested them."

"How about drugs?"

"I called the clinic to see if you had test kits, but nobody answered. Doesn't matter. Drugs or not, I'm kicking them off the ship."

Peter reached for his pen before remembering it was with Calvin. He rubbed his aching forehead and gestured to the adjacent holding cells. "So it could be drugs."

"Can't rule it out."

That was the problem. He didn't have enough evidence to rule anything in or out.

"I don't like asking this." Harrington flattened his palms on the desk. "If I tested you, what would the result be?"

"What are you getting at?" He knew what Harrington meant.

"The nurse couldn't wake you. My guy had to access your cabin."

Heat rushed up his neck. "I was tired." He shouldn't need to defend this. Benadryl was just an antihistamine, but he'd taken it too late in the day. It was an embarrassing mistake, and only by a minor miracle had he been able to intubate Sharma. He wasn't so different from Felipe, was he? Felipe, groggy and barely breathing in his final minutes, until respirations ceased completely. He snapped back to attention. "But the passengers, I think maybe they're all sick."

"Make up your mind, Doc. Is it drugs or are they sick?"

Peter raked his fingers through his hair. "I'm working on that."

"If they are sick, you got the cure?"

A cold sweat slicked his palms. "Not yet."

"Back on the farm, if we can't help the sick animals, we put them down."

He envisioned a younger Harrington pointing a shotgun at the head of an ailing cow. What pathway would lead him to take a position as head of security on a cruise ship? Behind Harrington hung a framed picture of him giving a piggyback ride to a pretty woman on an old stone bridge. Her mouth was caught in a huge laugh. A plaque next to it boasted a US government seal acknowledging twenty years of meritorious service.

If not substances, something else causing such acute behavioral changes. A viral infection had to be considered. He didn't want to pursue that avenue, but there was no way to avoid it. "I wonder if it's encephalitis."

"Say what now?"

"*Encephalo* means brain and *itis* means inflammation, so it's inflammation of the brain." Giving voice to his theory released a pressure that had been building up inside. Now that the idea was out in the world, he could turn it over and examine it.

"Theory or fact?"

"Very much a theory," Peter said.

"Run this by Hartley. No offense."

"I think she has it herself."

"No shit." Harrington's eyes narrowed. "She *has* been off."

His stomach churned as the ship jolted to the side. First Officer Kinnard had claimed the yawing was worse on the higher levels, but to Peter it felt plenty intense down here. The same Kinnard who had almost let that couple scoop up Calvin. They were no better than kidnappers cruising the streets in a white van. Outside of the nurses, Harrington might be his only ally.

Peter explained to him a principle from med school: Occam's razor, which compelled physicians to look for a single explanation for patients who had a variety of symptoms.

"What the hell does that have to do with a razor?"

"I don't know."

Harrington made an *X* with his meaty fingers. "You gonna get me sick?"

Peter suppressed a cough. Back in med school, several of his classmates had suffered the classic psychosomatic response to learning about diseases. After the lecture on Guillain-Barré syndrome, no fewer than a dozen students turned up complaining about weakness in their legs. The smirking neurologist said it happened every year.

"If I'm right about this," Peter said, "the first symptoms are upper respiratory—cough, congestion, sore throat, that kind of stuff. It's not Covid or the flu. Then it travels to the brain. The inflammation affects how people behave."

"But you don't know for sure."

"We need to start drug testing."

Harrington studied the ceiling, nodding. "But if you *are* right, then don't you have to—"

"Isolation. I know." Hartley should have been the one making that call, but...

"You won't win any popularity contests," Harrington said. "In fact, you might need your own personal bodyguard. And I've got nobody to spare."

No use worrying about that now. He needed to focus, get back to why he came down here in the first place. "Can you just send someone to Calvin's room?"

A loud knock on the door cut off Harrington's answer. A ruddy-faced guard with mutton chops stuck his head into the office. "Zulu," he blurted and promptly disappeared.

Harrington sprung out of his chair. "Time's up."

Peter rose as well. "Wait, at least tell me who the prisoners were. I want to check them in the system."

Harrington snatched a sheet of paper from the top drawer and slid it across the desk. "Hurry up, take a pic."

Perfect—a list of names and details. Peter snapped a photo with his phone.

"Don't pull any shit and post it online." Harrington jammed the sheet back into the drawer and hustled Peter out the door.

"What's Zulu?" he asked over his shoulder.

Harrington jostled him forward and shut the door behind them with a click. "Assault."

7

PETER ATTEMPTED BREAKFAST on the starboard deck outside the main buffet. He diced up his truffle omelet and mashed the fluffy eggs between the fork tines, adding salt and a dash of hot sauce. He took a bite—still blah. It was day five since Copenhagen, and he still hadn't truly enjoyed a meal. He dropped the fork in defeat.

He needed a break from this place. Might as well check his socials.

Everyone was living the dream. Jared had scored a lucrative gig with an elite education publisher. One of Elena's besties looked fantastic cavorting on the beach with a bunch of other carefree RVers. Peter flicked to the news. US and Indian defense agencies were both claiming credit for pulverizing an incoming asteroid, a debate on the provenance of laser beams.

The dregs of lukewarm coffee sat at the bottom of his mug. Last night had been brutal, thanks to a surge of patients after his visit with Harrington. Between that and watching over Calvin, he'd had no chance to dive into the list of former prisoners. After passing the baton to Luisa at 2 a.m., he'd flopped onto a stretcher in a pitiful imitation of slumber. This throbbing in the middle of his forehead wasn't helping things. Each cough hammered the inside of his skull. He'd have to take something when he got back to clinic—oh wait, the vending machine was out of stock.

He wasn't the only one ailing up here. The whole dining area was a waiting room. Every other table had somebody sniffling or blowing their nose in linen napkins. Women in summer dresses, men in baseball caps, sullen teenagers enslaved to their earbuds. All nationalities mingled here. Houston was diverse, but not quite integrated, with neighborhoods adjacent but separate, like cupcakes in a tin. This ship was more like a giant cake. Everybody mixed, sharing greetings. And germs.

A server stopped by to refill his mug. With one hand she poured coffee, and with the other she swept her blond ponytail over her shoulder. He jerked back when coffee overflowed and splashed onto his eggs.

The server gasped. "Oh, so sorry!" She plunked the carafe down, grabbed a napkin from her vest pocket, and started cleaning up the glass tabletop. "Did it get on your clothes?" Her accent sounded Eastern European.

He couldn't have cared less about the food, and his scrubs were dry. "Don't worry about it. I'm done anyway." He set his plate aside so she could wipe underneath it.

Her energy shifted from nervous apology to quiet anxiety. "Excuse me, are you the doctor? The new one?"

He squinted upward. Her lips were dry and cracked, and puffy bags had set under her eyes. "Mm-hmm." He wasn't thrilled about engaging in a medical conversation right here, right now, but in scrubs and a borrowed stethoscope around his neck, he had it coming.

She shifted her weight from one foot to the other. "I'm sorry to bother you, but I don't know. I don't feel good."

"Come down to the clinic." He checked his watch. "We open at eight."

She glanced over her shoulder, still holding his plate. "Can you do private consultation?"

"The clinic's on the bottom level. I'd be glad to see you there."

"Please, can we meet somewhere else? I'm so sorry I ruined your breakfast, and now I ask this, but I was just making sure you are him. I was nervous when I pour coffee."

Her twitchy eyes didn't make for easy conversation. Maybe she was just overworked and didn't have time to seek care.

"Is it an emergency?"

A thin film of sweat slicked her high forehead, but that could've been anxiety rather than fever. She checked the indoor dining area behind her, pivoting to scan the horizon as if Godzilla might rise from the North Sea. "Not emergency for me, but…" Her voice dropped to a harsh whisper. "It's important what I must tell you. What you see, it's worse than you can imagine."

That didn't sound good. With his foot he pushed out the spare chair and motioned for her to sit. "Just tell me now."

Her face darkened. "I cannot stay. They're watching. I find you later." She left with his plate, disappearing into the throng of diners and waitstaff.

Poor girl, of course someone was watching. There were cameras everywhere. But what was she hiding? Maybe she was paranoid, certainly a bit bizarre. He shook his head. Bizarre. That was the new normal around here.

———————

Calvin was the only one who'd had a good night's sleep. The diazepam mixed in orange juice did the trick—maybe too well. Mandy was tending to him in one of the exam rooms, her hands on his shoulders as his head drooped. His spasms had abated, but full sedation was no long-term plan.

"He's okay for now," she said. "But won't it just keep happening?"

Peter nudged him. "Wake up."

Calvin grunted and sputtered.

"Ironic," Mandy muttered.

Peter gave her a puzzled look.

"You telling him to wake up."

Ouch. He hadn't talked with her since early yesterday morning, when she and the security guard had roused him from bed. She had the right to be sore about it.

Nali bustled in with good news: The day care facility had agreed watch over Calvin during their regular hours. "I'll take him up there in a sec. But breakfast first." She guided the boy's hand into a paper bag of donut holes. He rallied and took to the treats with gusto.

Mandy smiled. "Girl, you sure got into a big mess, didn't you?"

Nali nodded and popped a donut hole in her mouth. Calvin smiled with flakes of glazed sugar in his stubble.

"Yeah, right?" Nali ate another one. "They're good."

"Mmm… Mum-um-um."

"Sounds like he's saying 'Mom,'" Nali said.

Peter was grateful when Luisa stuck her head in to say a thirty-six-year-old American woman was ready to be seen, but his heart sank when she added, "Assault victim." The Zulu code from last night perhaps.

The patient sat banging the heels of her sneakers against

the metal drawer of the exam table. She braced her arms to her sides. Through wisps of her sandy hair, he saw a bruise the size and color of a plum on her left cheek. The natural landing spot of a punch from a right-handed assailant.

He'd seen this woman before. She was the wife of the guy who'd almost KO'ed him in the elevator, the one who looked like a teacher but snarled like a fiend. He glanced at her record: Allison Muller.

"I didn't know you were the doctor," she said in a small voice.

"Did your husband do this?" he blurted.

Her face darkened, and Luisa's eyebrows flew up. He'd known that man was trouble. "So I wasn't imagining things."

"I couldn't come in till today because I have the girls." Her voice was barely audible.

Luisa was hovering, and Peter realized she was making sure the patient was not alone with another man—even a doctor. She enlisted Mandy to set the woman's children up with a card game, which they played in silence.

Muller also had an abrasion on her right forearm and a tender spot on the lower left side of her chest. "He knocked me over and I landed pretty hard, right on the edge of a table."

The X-ray showed two rib fractures, marked up by the AI with white arrows. He would've noted them regardless, but the joke was that AI had flooded the market with boats and vacation homes once owned by laid-off radiologists.

"Do I need surgery?" she asked.

"No, but you're going to be sore for a few weeks." He retrieved a box of lidocaine patches from the pharmacy. "Stick one of these over your broken ribs every day. Leave it on for up to twelve hours at a time."

Luisa applied antibiotic ointment to the patient's forearm

and bandaged it up, but there was no hiding the enormous bruise on her face.

"What happened?" Peter asked quietly.

Some victims were silent, paralyzed by guilt and fear. Not Muller. Once she got going, she let it all out in a raspy account. Her husband had been ogling other women on the walking deck. "Like really undressing them with his eyes, not even trying to hide it. It's been getting worse and worse; even our girls are asking questions. So I confronted him about it later. Maybe I was too pushy."

"Is he prone to this kind of behavior?"

Her eyes reddened with tears. "Not at all. I don't know what's gotten into him. We have some spats, but... That's normal, right? He's under a lot of stress."

"What does he do? Not that it's an excuse."

She screwed up her face. "I'm embarrassed to say it, but he's an assistant principal."

Any sense of victory from pegging the guy from the beginning was swept away by her torment.

"He's never hit me before." She fell silent. Luisa offered an ice pack for her cheek, which she accepted with a cheerless smile.

"How can we help?" Peter asked.

A moan tremored in her throat.

"Do you feel unsafe around him? Should we get security?"

Still no answer. She'd retreated into the cave after lighting the signal fire. He'd seen this before. How would she and her girls go on from here? Would she press charges? So many questions that shouldn't come up on a cruise. Sharma's clan was dealing with it too—families torn apart. Families were made of people, after all, and people were the problem. Houston somehow didn't seem so far away.

"I'm sorry for all the questions," Peter said. "Was he drinking? On drugs?"

She laughed bitterly. "I wish."

"Does he have anything like anxiety or depression?"

"A few years ago, he was depressed after his dad died. But he never went to see anybody, and I thought he got through it okay."

Time to test his theory. "Did he have a cold, like with a cough, sore throat, headache?"

She scowled. "Why are you so concerned about him? I'm the victim here."

"You're right." He held up a conciliatory hand. "I only ask because others have been assaulted too. We're trying to figure out why."

"Men are assholes."

"It's not only men." That came out wrong. He wasn't defending the male species, just thinking about the niece who strangled her uncle.

"Well, I'm scared of what brought me here." She looked to the floor. "I'm scared of being here. And I'm scared I don't know what to do next."

In the hallway, Peter heard quiet murmurs as Muller did her best to create a bubble around her children. In the elevator, she'd been quick to throw her arms over them when their father's temper flared. Whatever had gotten into the man hadn't begun today.

Hartley's primitive howl had burrowed into his brain. He couldn't unsee the taut cords on her neck when she reared her head back to unleash it. "Where's Dr. Hartley?" he asked Luisa.

Her mouth twisted. "I don't know. I texted her."

It was a stretch to blame Hartley's behavior on drugs, but the possibility of substance-induced delirium wasn't completely dead yet. He ducked into the bay where Mandy sat with Calvin and opened the lower cabinet. The first carton of drug test kits was as light as air. He peeled back the seal and opened the lid. There were no kits inside. He checked the next carton, then the next. They were sealed but empty.

Mandy's jaw dropped. "What the— I stocked these myself. They were full."

"When?"

"In Lisbon," she said in a shaky voice. "They should've lasted us all the way to New York."

"Why are they all empty? And what's the point of keeping empty boxes anyway?"

"If this is some kind of joke— Hold on. There was a lady here."

"Near this cabinet? When?"

"I thought she was housekeeping, but it was weird, because they usually come at night. She looked surprised when I bumped into her."

"They wouldn't come in between the morning and afternoon shifts?" Peter asked.

"Not that I'm aware of."

He puffed out his cheeks. Here went nothing. "So the lady was housekeeping or she snuck in here for other reasons. She wanted to shut down drug testing. No tests, no results—positive or negative." Mandy opened her mouth but he held up a hand. "Hold on though. My other thought is that this is all caused by encephalitis."

"Hmm." She nodded with pursed lips.

"It can cause erratic and destructive behavior." He made a circle with his finger, implicating the whole ship above them. "Make you do stupid things."

He watched the hypothesis take root in her mind, saw her eyes narrow.

"I had a patient with that at the VA," she said. "He tested positive for herpes. Back then I didn't know it could infect the brain. But still, an outbreak of encephalitis. Can you prove it?"

"Not yet. Maybe it's all just drugs. But we can't test for that because the kits are gone." He searched the ceiling and noticed the dark orb of a security camera in the back corner. "Is that thing on?"

"I assume so. I've never had to ask."

A deep cough erupted from his chest, splitting his head open.

She recoiled. "Whoa there."

"It's just allergies." He turned away and leaned on the countertop. "I'm okay. But what's up with the vending machine?"

"What do you mean?"

"It's all out," he said.

"Wait, what?"

"It's out of meds. It's supposed to have regular stuff for cough and colds, right?"

"Huh." She tapped her fingers together, and an adorable little crease formed between her eyebrows. "I guess we need to restock it in Scotland. They don't restock everywhere. Only at certain ports."

The drug test kits were missing and the medication vending machine was empty. They were running a third-rate operation here. What everybody needed was a real city with real medical facilities. Edinburgh couldn't come soon enough.

"Tell you what, Doc," said Harrington, "I'll let you interview him if you can drop some Xanax in the drinking water."

A sedated, peaceful ship. Not a bad aspiration. No wonder nobody picked up the phone when Peter had called ahead. It was mayhem with the groaning and banging in the adjacent cells. Smelled like a sewer too.

"Didn't you clear them out yesterday?"

Deep furrows etched Harrington's forehead. "They filled up quick. All three cells are double-booked."

"I know the feeling." Moonlighting in the ER back home, Peter would scramble to clear out the bays only to have them repopulate in minutes. "Let me run something by you."

"Shoot."

"Drugs."

Harrington gave him a puzzled smile. "I thought you were homing in on elephantitis."

"Encephalitis."

"Whatever. What happened to that theory?"

It was still alive, but some monsters were easier to face than others. "We still need to rule out drugs. How big of a problem is it?"

"Anytime you got people..."

"But here? On the ship?"

"We see it. Would be worse without the random testing. But we have zero tolerance. The crew have duties in case of an emergency, so if we go all *Titanic*, they're the ones loading passengers into lifeboats. They can't be compromised. One strike, and you're out."

"What about passengers?"

"It happens."

Peter shook his head. "Why am I even asking about it? We can't even test."

"Why not?"

He updated Harrington on the empty drug test kits.

Harrington chuckled. "Well, today's your lucky day, boss." He pulled open his drawer and plunked a plastic cylinder on his desk. "I forgot I had one here. I was about to use it."

Peter examined the kit. "You're kidding."

"It's close to the expiration date, but it should be good enough for government work."

For the first time in a while, something was going Peter's way. "Who were you going to test?"

"I've got my eye on this asshole who—"

"Hold on. You said I could talk with Raymond Muller. I want to test him."

"You playing white knight?"

Peter glared at him. Sure, Allison Muller was attractive and vulnerable, but justice would come later. "C'mon, give me some credit. I just need to see if drugs are behind the chaos. That's what I keep saying."

Harrington tilted his chair back and examined the ceiling.

"I saw him when I first got on the ship," said Peter. "It was strange. Like he was a family man, with a wife and kids, but on the edge of exploding. Something didn't fit."

"Fine." Harrington got up, brought in Raymond Muller, and plunked him down in a metal chair. "You all good?" he said to Peter, who nodded, and Harrington left them alone in the office.

Muller was a disaster: sparse hair curling up from his pale crown, bloodshot eyes bouncing around, and chin stubble caked with dried blood from a wound on his lower lip.

Peter didn't know how to start a conversation like this. Must've missed the criminal interrogation lecture in med school. "Do you remember me?"

There was no light of recognition. Muller looked utterly confused. "No."

"We met in the elevator a few days ago."

Still nothing.

"Your wife is seriously hurt."

Muller's face twisted in anguish. "I don't know, I hope— Wait, how do you know that?"

"I'm the doctor. She's beat up pretty bad."

Muller buried his head in his hands. The knuckles on his right hand were red and swollen.

Peter clenched his teeth. This asshole was so guilty. "Why'd you do it?"

A low moan escaped from Muller's throat, followed by incoherent mumbling.

"Were you drinking? Using drugs?" He set the cylindrical test kit on the desk.

Muller lifted his head, his eyes wild and searching. "I don't know what's going on. You gotta believe me."

The guy looked lost, *almost* deserving of pity, but time was running low. Muller stared at his hands, turning palms up and palms down, and rubbed his bruised knuckles absently. He was psychotic or high as a kite. Peter held his breath, waiting for more signs to emerge.

After a span of silence, Muller grunted and sputtered. The rictus smile from the elevator spread across his face, lips pulled back to reveal way too many teeth and lots of gum. "She deserved it."

An itch radiated up Peter's neck. "I need to test you."

"All she does is hold me back. Why does she care what I do?"

"She's your wife. The mother of your children."

"They're leeches." He shot up and made a move for the door.

Peter raised an arm to stop him. "Wait, we're not done."

Muller batted away his arm and swung a knee hard into his abdomen.

Peter crumpled. Breathing was futile. His chest had seized up; he couldn't even groan. Muller swiped the test kit off the desk and crushed it under his boot, shattering the cylinder into pieces.

Funny how someone's definition of a big deal could shift. This was no big deal, getting the wind knocked out of him on a cruise ship. He'd suffered worse on the soccer field back in the day. His stunned diaphragm would recover within a minute, and air would begin to flow.

Losing the test kit hurt a little more. There was no getting back the opportunity to test his drug use theory. And it was definitely a big deal when Muller kicked him in the face next. Peter's nose crunched and splintered—bizarre to hear that inside your own skull. Yeah, that was something else.

"But that's not the worst part," Peter said, his voice sounding thick in his own ears.

Mandy's bottle of hand sanitizer dangled from her neck as she leaned closer and dabbed at the gash along the bridge of his nose with saline-soaked gauze. She had ushered him past the gawking patients and into the rearmost room, where he now sat on the exam table.

"I can't imagine what could be worse." She used a cotton swab to dab bacitracin ointment on the wound. "It's already starting to swell."

"That I didn't get to test him." He hissed as she applied one end of a pair of Steri-Strips. "I can't believe he destroyed the last kit."

She tugged together the edges of the gash and stuck the strips down. "Sorry, I know it hurts, but otherwise it won't stay."

He tried a few tentative sniffs.

"Everything working?" She laughed and held the back of her hand close to his face. "Try again."

He sniffed longer this time, letting the delicate, fruity scent of her skin fill his lungs and diffuse through his entire body. Yep, that part of him still worked.

"You sure you're good to see patients?" she asked.

No time to process what had just happened. The clinic was hopping, and Hartley was still in the wind. Luisa was rooming patients as fast as she could.

"We don't have a choice."

Hydrocodone might take the edge off the throbbing pain, but that was a slippery slope. Look how far Felipe—

Peter helped himself to an extra-strength ibuprofen, the same pill he'd given the abused wife of the man who'd just broken his nose.

The nurses started him off with a seventy-two-year-old Black man who looked ten years younger. His rectangular glasses and salt-and-pepper beard painted a picture of gravitas.

"I'm easy. All I need is a refill on my heartburn medicine," Gordon Burkett said in a deep Southern accent, sounded like Tennessee. "Omeprazole or any appropriate substitute will do. With the food on this ship, I've used more of it than I expected."

"Happy to check on that," Peter said. His exam found nothing concerning, just a little tenderness in his upper abdomen. He fetched a box of the medication from the pharmacy. "Here you go, fourteen tablets. That should last you a while."

"Thank you, Doctor. I'm in your debt."

"Anything else?"

Burkett had a kind, even gaze. "Yeah. How are *you* doing?"

The question caught him off guard. Most patients just wanted to get in and out. They rarely asked after him—nor should they. He was supposed to help them.

Burkett motioned at Peter's nose.

Oh, sure. He must look awful. "I'm, ah, I'm okay."

"Where you from?"

"Houston."

"I was down there, back in the eighties. My uncle had pancreatic cancer, so he was at MD Anderson."

"I'm sorry."

Burkett smiled sadly. "I got to take him to the NBA All-Star game. He wanted to go for a last hurrah. It was at the old Astrodome in the nosebleed seats. You all had Olajuwon. He was quite the firecracker."

Peter laughed. "That was before my time, but I've seen the YouTubes." They talked about sports and argued about which state had the best barbecue. Peter even mentioned how Felipe had played tight end in high school, earning all-district. For some reason, it didn't hurt to say his brother's name. "I don't know why I'm telling you this stuff. You're easy to talk to."

"Thanks, young man. That's a requirement in my vocation."

"What are you, a counselor?"

"That's part of it. I'm a pastor." He raised an eyebrow. "And this is when most people get real quiet."

"I bet."

"But don't worry, my lips are sealed. What happens here, stays here."

He needed to move on to other patients, but he felt drawn to the pastor. Having a good guy like him on the ship somehow made it feel less macabre. "No offense, but do you believe in the supernatural?"

"God created everything that we call nature." Burkett pointed out the window. "The sea, the earth, the heavens." He pointed to Peter. "You and me. Is God part of nature or external to it? That's an important question to wrestle with."

"I mean things like angels and demons."

"There we go. Have I seen one with these eyes? No. But he who believes only in what he can see is either overconfident or needs new glasses."

Peter smiled. "You're pretty confident yourself."

"Ha ha." Burkett pointed to his temple. "You're clever."

It was stupid to even articulate it, but what if this man had an answer? "Reason I'm asking, seems weird to even say it, but—"

"You think something strange is going on."

Peter blinked.

"We all see it. People are talking."

"Yes, they are. I mean, it's hard to miss. And it's just that people seem so…"

Burkett tipped his head. "You're wondering if these people are possessed."

Peter sighed. "I'm willing to consider just about anything now."

Burkett rubbed his hands together slowly. "Have you heard that story about the demons in the pigs?"

"Remind me."

Burkett recounted the parable: Jesus confronts a man

possessed by a legion of demons. The spirits beg to be allowed to enter a nearby herd of pigs, and Jesus agrees. The demons enter the pigs, and the entire herd rushes down a steep bank and drowns in the waters below.

If only it were that simple. Peter grinned. "So let's toss all the pork chops and bacon overboard."

"Then you'd have a real riot on your hands." Burkett laughed from deep in his belly. "In all seriousness, whoever did that to you"—he pointed to Peter's nose again—"deserves all the justice of the law. But for your own sake, don't take eye for an eye, nose for a nose. Don't fall into that. To paraphrase: Forgive them, for they know not what they do."

It stung—both his nose and the fact that he'd been attacked. "Easier said than done."

Burkett held his hands up. "I know, it's a bitter pill to swallow. End of sermon. I'm retired anyway." He gathered his belongings to leave. "You know where to find me. If you ever get a day off, I'll buy you a beer. I promise, no more preaching."

8

THE IDEA CAME in the shower on the morning of day six. Peter toweled off in a hurry and wiped the fog from the mirror. His nose was a disaster and it would get worse before it got better. Good thing he'd had a tetanus booster last year. Who knew what kind of filth had encrusted Muller's boot?

Today's stop in Scotland would be his only chance to nail things down.

Luisa was fixated on processes, and Mandy—what a peach!—followed her compassionate heart. But neither were in a position to call the shots. Hartley was unreliable at best and a liability at worst. That put the burden on Peter to get people to a real hospital for diagnostic tests. An MRI of the brain, basic bloodwork, and drug tests would sort things out.

So, Scotland.

His first order of business was to pay another visit to the perilous domain of Mr. Harrington.

"I need to see Muller again," Peter demanded upon arrival in the brig.

"Why?" Harrington eyed his busted nose. "You trying to

be some kind of martyr? You don't need to press charges. We got it all on tape." He nodded at the security camera in the upper corner of his office. "You look like shit, by the way." He didn't look like he'd gotten much sleep either.

"Thanks."

Harrington adjusted his collar. "Maybe I shouldn't have left him alone with you."

"Apology accepted. But I still need to talk with him."

"First, I want you to see something."

Peter had no choice but to comply. Harrington brought him back to the row of cells and motioned to the small window in the first door. Two men sat on a metal cot, leaning forward with their hands zip-tied behind them. Another man, also with bound hands, was slumped against the padded wall.

"That one right there." Harrington pointed to the fifty-something guy on the cot. "He smashed a blackjack table when he lost. His wife's scared shitless. The other guy stole a bunch of fancy purses from duty-free."

So it wasn't just Muller. Peter pushed against the door. Solid steel. "What about the last one?"

Harrington's voice went low and guttural. "He tried to toss a kid off the water slide. Racist prick isn't even denying it."

The second cell held three men, including Raymond Muller, and the last had three women. All looked clean cut—no scabby or pocked faces, good teeth. No meth heads. A mix of passengers and crew, all irritable and exhausted.

"We're handing them to Edinburgh police, and it couldn't be soon enough."

Back in the office, Peter collapsed into the guest chair. This was making less and less sense.

"I don't think we're dealing with bozos strung out on heroin," Harrington continued.

"Nine of them? And all this since Norway?"

Harrington nodded. "Never seen it before."

"Muller needs an extensive evaluation. More than I can do on the ship."

"Let the police handle it. You and I have our hands full."

"Getting him tested might tell us what's going on with everybody else. Are the police going to just toss him in jail? Are there procedures for medical testing?"

"If it's anything like the US," Harrington said, "they have to see clear signs of distress to initiate it."

"Let me talk with him."

Harrington's eyes narrowed. "Five minutes, and this time I stay here."

It was crowded in the office with Harrington behind his desk and Muller slouched in a chair in the corner avoiding eye contact. Peter could've asked *Do you remember me now?* but that wasn't his angle.

"I want to help you, and I have a favor to ask."

Muller looked ashamed and puzzled. "What?"

"We think your feelings and behavior are being caused by something contagious on the ship. Tell the police you're sick and you need to get checked out. If they bring you to the hospital, don't resist."

Muller picked at the peeling vinyl on the arm of his chair.

Peter couldn't tell whether he didn't understand, didn't believe, or simply didn't care. "What do you think?"

Muller groaned. "I don't know, I don't know."

Peter pressed him again, but Muller continued to dodge and parry. Muller would do it or not, and Peter had no control. Muller himself had no control over his own behavior; that was the matter at hand. Whatever had compelled him to act out was still clouding his brain.

Peter pulled a fresh index card and pen from the chest pocket of his scrubs and wrote down the tests he wanted Muller to get. Muller gave it a mere passing glance. Maybe he could staple it to Muller's shirt or tape it to his forehead—or better yet, tattoo the instructions on his body, like that patient back home with *DNR* on his chest—*Do Not Resuscitate*. Except Muller's would say *Do MRI*.

Harrington called time and sent Muller back to his cell.

"Did you get what you needed?" he asked Peter.

He blew out a puff of air. "Not sure. I have to work on a few things." Like getting a handle on Hartley. He could no longer imagine how she could continue serving as a physician, but she might contribute as a patient. If, and only if, he could get her off the ship for testing.

Harrington plunked a white plastic bottle on his desk. "You might be interested in these."

Peter shook the bottle: ten-milligram tablets of baclofen from a pharmacy in Lakewood, Colorado, for one Calvin Burchins, with a label that read *Take one tablet three times daily as needed for spasticity.* "Thank you. Thank you."

"You can't do everything yourself," Harrington said. A dull thunk shook the walls of the office. "Right on time, 8:25. You better get going. We just landed in Edinburgh, and we're leaving at four."

Peter took a deep breath before knocking on Hartley's door. Maybe she was fine, just having a bad week.

She let him inside and shuffled back toward the bed in her pajamas. Her hair hung in limp, greasy strands. Flakes of dead skin and food crumbs encrusted her lips. Without a word, she flopped onto the mattress and turned to face the balcony.

Pushing dirty clothes aside, he made room for himself on the love seat by the window and surveyed the room. Her cabin was palatial: a queen bed with walk around space, a large TV, and a sliding glass door leading to an actual balcony. Outside, dock workers with their machines crawled over the ship like lamprey on a whale. The sun struggled to pierce the fog hovering over port. There was supposed to be a famous castle out there in the ancient highlands and a giant lake with a famous monster.

Monsters, indeed.

His phone hung from his neck in a clear plastic case that he'd bummed off Nali—labeled in her loopy script as belonging to one *Natalia Palma*. He needed video evidence to support his preliminary diagnosis. He pressed the record button and angled his torso toward Hartley.

He began a difficult conversation, trying to convince her that she was incompetent and needed medical evaluation. She was supposed to be guiding him, but they'd never established that relationship, and his resentment of her public insults had given way to pity.

He appealed to her concern for the greater good. "You could be the key. We can find out what's going on with everybody and get to the root cause."

"I don't know what you're talking about."

"We have to help them."

"Pfft." Her hand rose shakily to a lock of hair.

Inflammation of the brain leading to sensory and behavioral aberrations—but he needed confirmation. "An MRI will tell us if you have encephalitis. That's what I'm concerned about. It all fits together."

Her eyes closed, and she shrugged.

"They can treat you." He wasn't so sure about that.

"What's the point?"

He glanced at the sea birds flashing past the window. He'd had these conversations before, in Houston, trying to persuade elderly patients to allow home health nurses to check on them. They seemed so tired, some with deep regrets.

"You said you've done things you'd regret."

Her eyes fluttered. "I've done things…"

"Don't you want to find out why?"

She said nothing. Leaning forward, he urged her to disembark, knowing that if she did, she might not come back and he would continue to be the only doctor on board for all these people. Well worth the gamble. He had little faith that Raymond Muller would undergo an evaluation given all the conversations, approvals, and logistical steps it would require. Hartley, as a physician, should understand what he was asking of her now. Yet the adage was true—doctors made the worst patients.

Nothing seemed to register with her. He rubbed the back of his neck and stared at a stain on the carpet. The cabinet in front of the TV was cluttered with used tissues and a wine glass with a purple smear at the bottom.

"Don't you have family here?" he asked. "It would be nice to see them."

Grunting, she crooked her limbs this way and that until she managed to flip over in bed and face the other direction. A quaking fart set her flank undulating like a seal flopping in the sand.

He stood up. This was useless. She was too far gone.

At the door, he turned back for one last look. She was

peering back over her shoulder, her face screwed up tight and her eyes watery red. "I don't want to die."

He couldn't leave her like this. He returned, sat on the bed, and laid a hand on her arm. She was trembling. Her forehead was warm but not feverish. He used the former doctor's stethoscope to listen to her heart and lungs, checked her pupils with the light on his phone. She was unkempt, but her physical exam was normal.

Patients in their lowest moments often asked "Am I going to die?" The technical answer, which he never gave, was *We all die at some point.* To the patient writhing in pain from a kidney stone, he would say "No, but it's gonna hurt like hell when that stone passes." To the grandmother with breast cancer, it was more like "They have good treatments now." But for Hartley and the others here who were out of their minds, for the detainees now handed over to the Scottish police, for others still harboring the inscrutable potential for violence, he hadn't yet found the right reply.

He draped the stethoscope around his neck. "What happened to the other doctor?"

"She's a sweet little birdie. You shouldn't have come to this house… All cheese…" Spittle gathered along her lips. Her eyes closed. He tried to rouse her with a nudge, but she drifted off.

He retrieved the Narcan device from his pocket, inserted the blunt nozzle into her nose, and depressed the red plunger. Despite the opioid-reversing medication, she failed to perk up. Instead, her breathing became softer, quieter. She was wandering in some alien country now, one he was still mapping out.

———————

The file took forever to upload, despite the strong Wi-Fi on the jogging deck. Peter pressed *Send* and waited another eternity for the confirmatory *whoosh*.

He dialed Wetzel, the cruise line's medical director, and she picked up immediately. It had to be 5:30 a.m. in Miami, but she sounded wide awake. "Peter! I hope you're hanging in there. I was just heading out to play tennis."

He pictured her in a white tank top, her thick brown hair secured with a headband. "Sorry to bother you—but check your email, please. I just sent you a video."

"I'm driving. Can it wait?"

"No."

She gave him a few beats—was she hoping to change his mind?—then cleared her throat. "Let me pull over. What's this about?"

"Just watch the whole thing."

"Is it that woman choking her uncle? I'm aware. It's also all over social media."

"No, it's a different problem."

Wetzel went silent for a minute, then: "That looks like Elizabeth Hartley."

"I think it's encephalitis."

He explained the events of the past few days, from the disappearance of Calvin's mom to having his nose broken by a raging detainee. "I think the early symptoms and the extreme behavior are connected. I think they're having hallucinations, but I can't prove it. But it's obvious they have no impulse control."

"Does Dr. Hartley have a headache or fever?"

"I don't know about the headache. She didn't have a fever."

"Seizures?"

"Not that I know of." He drew a shaky breath. These were questions he'd be asking if the tables were turned.

"You think it's encephalitis, Peter? How can I support you?"

Wetzel had emailed him after the kid jumped to his death on the deck. *Just put it behind you. It will get better from here. Call if you need anything.* Well, he needed her now. He wanted to say that he regretted signing up for this job, that things were worse than Houston. The thin veneer of social graces had melted off the face of humanity on this ship, revealing a rotten, maggoty core.

"How can I set her up with testing?" he asked.

"If she truly isn't competent—"

"She's not."

"Then only the captain can force her. Did she know you were recording?"

"Maybe." Hartley either hadn't noticed or didn't care. The stomach-churning thing was that she'd displayed no modesty or self-consciousness. It was pure, undiluted Hartley, raw and uncut.

"Hold on," Wetzel said. "You know what they say. When you hear hoofbeats—"

"Think horses, not zebras. I've been looking for horses." He explained why he couldn't test her for drugs thanks to the missing kits. "She didn't budge with Narcan though."

Wetzel sighed. "This is a house of cards."

"What should I do?"

"Go to Captain Forster. I'll back you up."

"So you agree."

Silence.

"What is it?" Peter asked.

"Do it. I'm just thinking of Martina."

Martina Jacobs, the doctor he'd replaced and whose

stethoscope was now draped around his neck. The rubber tubing of the instrument was an iron chain binding him to her.

"She left in Barcelona and never came back," Wetzel said.

"So this is a cursed job." He pulled the stethoscope off and dangled it from his fingers. They were all pigs charging off the deep end.

"There were rumors she got involved with a performer. A dancer or someone like that."

"She didn't talk with you?"

"Unfortunately not. How long are you in Edinburgh?"

He checked his watch. "Only a few more hours. I'd better go talk to the captain."

What an ordeal tracking down the captain on a shore day. Peter finally caught up with him on the bridge with ninety minutes to spare. Forster jinked his head toward the adjacent chair, but Peter remained standing with one hip braced against a navigation console. He'd take any advantage in this negotiation.

"Captain, we need to disembark Dr. Hartley from the ship," he began. "She's sick, she's delirious, we can't test for drugs, and I think it's encephalitis, which—"

"Your track record is abysmal, Paul."

Ugh. "It's Peter."

Forster rocked back in his chair and checked his fingernails.

"My name's Peter."

"That's what I said." Forster's lips curled with disdain.

Now wasn't the time to nitpick. He needed Forster to authorize this transfer. "They can scan her brain at the hospital and run some tests. I hope they do that for the passengers Harrington's handing over to the police."

"That Indian guy, now her. Can't you tend to your own?"

"Once they're off, we'll be clear."

"Of what?"

This was the sticking point. Peter explained his theory about viral encephalitis.

"How sure are you about this? Scale of one to ten."

That was a tough one. Ten would sound overconfident, cocky. "Seven."

Forster guffawed. "You want to remove the senior doctor on the basis of a seven."

He fought to keep the anger from his voice. "With all due respect, you told me to be ready for anything. And here it is." He pulled out his phone and showed him the video of Hartley muttering and farting in her cabin. Even now, he could hardly bear to watch it. The footage had to be enough justification to remove her, for her own sake and the safety of the ship.

"Are you?" asked Forster.

"Am I what?"

That sneer again. "Ready."

A lump mushroomed in Peter's throat. "Let's—if we get her and the others to the hospital and put all this behind us, yes, I'm ready to take care of the other passengers. Dr. Wetzel is with me on this."

"Who?"

"Nora Wetzel, the medical director of the whole cruise line."

"Scale of one to ten," Forster barked.

Fine, he could play it this way. "Eight."

"If you're wrong, they'll sue your ass to the moon and back. I've never been sued. Not once. Have you?"

Peter shook his head.

"My record is unblemished. I'm the only captain to win the Compass Star Award three years in a row."

Peter's hands prickled with pins and needles. He'd experienced this grandiose aura before, radiating from one of his med school professors—a real hotshot, the sun around whom all others orbited. A little stroking was in order here. "I heard about that."

Forster lit up. "Oh yeah? Where?"

Careful now, careful. "Wetzel mentioned it." Another lie.

"Wetzel … yes, I do remember her." A wolfish grin crawled across Forster's face. "Mmm. Scrumptious."

Peter hated to sacrifice her good name, but he had to keep spreading it on thick. "She speaks very highly of you."

Forster snapped his fingers. "Fine, Pedro, do whatever."

"Okay, so—"

"Yeah, do your little thing." With a flick of his hand, he dismissed the matter, like sweeping crumbs off the table. "That old bitch is past her expiration date."

Peter opened his mouth to defend Hartley—she was still a human being—then snapped it shut. He'd take this victory and proceed. There was no time to psychoanalyze a captain who was untethered to reality.

––––––––––––

"You sure about this, Doctor?" the guard said, glancing down at Hartley.

The breeze from the dock did little to mask the funky odors wafting off the train of gurneys at the head of the unloading ramp.

Peter met Hartley's accusing stare as she bucked against

the restraints on her gurney, the last in line. Spittle flew from her lips. "Go to hell, you pile of bollocks!"

Peter covered his mouth and turned to the guard. "If you came in sick to the clinic, would you want her treating you?"

"Not a chance." The guard lifted his chin toward the crew members who'd been press-ganged into disembarkation duty. "Let's roll it out!"

The train started moving. Halfway down the line, Lamai the Scratcher was moaning and jerking her head around. Just ahead of her, Muller the Wife Beater squawked, "Sayonara suckers! See you on the other side!"

If everything worked out just right, Peter would get his answer from the hospital in Scotland. As to what that answer meant—one step at a time. He marched behind the guard. With each gurney that rolled down the ramp and onto dry land, he breathed a little easier. This must be what it felt like to excise a tumor. Get the bad stuff outta here, off the ship.

Only now it was *his* ship.

9

PETER SWUNG HIS feet off the bed and onto the gritty carpet. Supposedly God said it was all good and rested on the seventh day. But no day off for Peter; he was the only doctor on board. They'd left Edinburgh yesterday, and the gentle rocking of the ship and the warmth of the comforter last night had brought him all the way back to the womb. He lay curled up and could've done so for a hundred years were it not for the breaking dawn casting a pale border around the window curtains.

The real comfort was the knowledge that a dozen sick individuals were now off the ship. A haggard-sounding doctor at the Royal Infirmary had promised to bring the resources of the National Health Service to bear, but confessed they were struggling with a nursing shortage.

Peter stretched, inhaled, and let out his breath through pursed lips. A new day, a fresh start, full speed ahead to New York. This nightmare was over.

He lumbered over to the bathroom and scrubbed his face and beard, avoiding his devastated nose. Reaching for a towel, he spotted a single white tablet on the countertop. The surface of the tablet had gone mealy with moisture, but the *10* stamped on one side and the groove down the middle on the other were still visible. He didn't know whether to laugh or cry. In the mundane rearrangement of bathroom sundries by him and the cabin steward, somehow this lone Lexapro had escaped notice.

He searched the countertop and floor. Nope, this was the last known survivor. He rinsed it under the tap and popped it in his mouth, biting down hard and grinding it into a bitter chalk before washing it down. *There.* He'd get a jump start on absorption rather than waiting on gastric acid to do its job. But, truth be told, one tablet would not make a difference.

He drifted back out and plunked down on the edge of the bed. The cabin steward, that little bald guy who could've been from anywhere, kept leaving folded-towel creatures on his bed. Last night's elephant looked amazingly real. The steward had also placed a bottle of hand sanitizer on the desk and chocolates on Peter's pillow.

Breakfast in the officer's lounge was a tragedy of wasted potential. The signals from Peter's taste buds were lost in translation en route to his brain. The buttery Belgian waffle registered as Styrofoam, topped off with maple syrup manifesting as Vaseline. The coffee was terrible by any measure.

He reported to work. Mandy was kneeling on the floor in the waiting area outside the clinic, unpacking a carton by the vending machine. The glass door of the machine was open.

"Need a hand?" he asked.

"I got it."

"Okay." He leaned back a bit on his heels and watched her load packets of medications into the horizontal trays of the machine. "If I was a little short yesterday, I'm sorry. It's been stressful."

"Yep."

"You're doing a great job, by the way."

"Am I?" Her expression and tone were flat. "Thanks for the performance review."

There was nowhere to hide from her chill. Somebody had vandalized the sign with the clinic's operating hours, incorporating the *8* into a crude cartoon of genitals. A lewd joke was scribbled at the bottom. "Geez, did you see this? It's like elementary school."

She ignored him. She filled the last column in the top tray, pushed it into the machine, and started on the middle tray.

"Pretty neat idea," Peter said. "They can get over-the-counter meds here instead of waiting for us."

She finished loading the machine and pushed it closed. The front panel had a key card scanner like the one he used to enter his cabin. He followed her into the clinic, where she continued to give off icy vibes as she went about her administrative tasks.

Luisa was bleary-eyed, having spent the night on a cot next to Calvin's gurney. "Oh my goodness," she moaned as she worked out a kink in her neck. "This is killing me."

The teen was curled on his side like a shrimp, snoring softly. Luisa had done a good job arranging pillows under his limbs and head, and the baclofen seemed to be helping. But the clinic was no place to hang out. Maybe Nali and Agus could take him to a movie as a respite from day care.

The first patient of the day was a young Egyptian guy with a headache—no fever or hallucinations, thankfully. After Peter discharged him, Mandy wanted to talk. She pulled him into the pharmacy.

"You should've asked us first," she said in a hushed tone, "before you got her off the ship."

He had to tread carefully here. "I thought we talked about encephalitis."

"I've worked with Dr. Hartley for a long time. A few years ago, she lost her husband in an accident. He was working on their farm and fell off his tractor. It ran him over."

"That's terrible." He swallowed hard.

"It was totally random. She used to do six months on, six months off. But after the accident, she signed up for back-to-back stints and just stayed on indefinitely."

Everybody was running from something.

She continued with a sad smile. "She seemed to like it, for the most part. We got to know each other. You might not believe it, but she has a good heart."

"I don't think I've seen a healthy, normal Dr. Hartley."

"You haven't. This time of year is the anniversary of her husband's death. She gets like this."

"You think she was just depressed? I wish I could agree— that would sure be better than the alternative we're facing now."

"You should've asked. You just better be right about all this." She set her mouth in a grim line and spun away.

He sagged against the counter. Actually, it would be better if was wrong. If he was right, it opened up a whole stinking mess of questions.

––––––––––––

Peter questioned himself at every turn for the rest of the morning. Minor symptoms became harbingers of doom. The Canadian woman with abdominal cramping probably had ovarian cancer. The drummer hadn't slipped because the stage was wet but because he likely had Parkinson's disease. It took every ounce of dwindling reserves to return to a reasonable set of diagnoses.

At least he recognized his own debility. What about Lamai, Muller, Stevenson, and Hartley? The light of self-awareness had gone out in their eyes. Had the teen launched headfirst into a pool that existed only in his own diseased brain?

They know not what they do. That's what the preacher man said.

Peter was reconciling medication records with Luisa in the pharmacy when static blasted from the overhead speakers. A rattle of hard objects, a pause, and then someone cleared their throat. Just a hum of static now, followed by a guttural moan. "Oh no, no." The voice was low-pitched and pained. There was a slow exhalation like gale winds from the ceiling, another burst of static, then silence.

What the hell was that? Luisa shot him a glance and shrugged.

Peter retreated to the office and called Scotland. The operator patched the call through to the Royal Infirmary of Edinburgh, some four hundred miles in the ship's wake.

Dr. Banerjee's Indian accent was thick but his message clear. "Muller, Raymond—he was passenger, correct?"

"Yes."

"It took a while to get consent, you know, we had to talk to his wife. All lab tests are unremarkable, and drug tests are negative. But…"

Peter's pulse quickened.

"His MRI showed T2 hyperintensity and a few scattered petechial hemorrhages."

He knew it. "Where?"

"There was diffuse involvement in several areas of the parenchyma but mostly in the frontal lobes."

Decimation of the area of the brain that gives humans reasoning, judgment, and impulse control. He gripped the handset and swallowed a thick lump. Confirmation was cold comfort. It had never felt so bad to be proved right. He asked about the others.

Another passenger, a woman who'd also been detained in the brig, had similar MRI findings, Banerjee said. "The sample from both of their lumbar punctures had high lymphocytes and protein."

Needles pricked Peter's arms. More evidence.

Banerjee was waiting on results for Hartley, Lamai, and three others, and he promised to call with an update. Peter gave him his email address in case he couldn't pick up the phone.

"But hold on," Peter said. "What do you think about all this? Have you seen it before?"

"I have seen couple of cases of encephalitis in my village back home, but not like this. They had dengue fever or CMV. Frontal lobe I have seen with herpes, but it's odd, you know? Did any of these people have headaches or seizures on the ship?"

"Headaches, yes. Seizures, not that I know of."

"Very atypical," Banerjee murmured.

Great. Typical meant standard, as in, *we can deal with it.* Atypical meant a lot of trial and error. "So how are you going to treat them?"

"Acyclovir for now, but I'm not pinning my hopes on it. We're waiting on recommendations from the infectious disease chief. But the thing is, she just got back from maternity leave and has got to catch the train from Inverness. Good job, by the way. This is quite a lot to deal with."

"But now what? Is the ship safe?" As soon as Peter asked, he realized Banerjee would not have the answers. If there were more infected people on the ship, the only way to find out would be to apply the most frustrating test of all: the test of time.

"Oh, that I don't know, Dr. Peter. You'll have to keep a close eye on things."

He hung up feeling more than a little uneasy. He suspected any congratulations were premature.

———————

Evening clinic was winding down. Nobody had come in delirious or swinging fists. It was busy but a good busy, with routine work. Best not to dwell on the diagnostic results from Scotland.

Peter consulted the laminated infection-control sheet taped to the inside of the check-in counter. Somebody had drawn a frowny face in the corner with a blue Sharpie. Outbreak Prevention Plan 1 was the status quo, with hand sanitation highly encouraged in dining areas and high-traffic junctions. OPP2 would be triggered if six passengers fell ill within six hours from a known or suspected pathogen. Hand sanitation would be enforced, and all infected passengers and crew would be isolated. At OPP3, self-service at buffets would be prohibited. All linens from cabins and dining areas would be put in biohazard bags and laundered in a dedicated facility. Ships worldwide had reached OPP3 at the height of Covid.

He checked email and reread the guidance from Wetzel: *Wait for Scotland micro results. You can't start OPP2 without an organism and the required density of cases.* The attached PDF listed the same criteria as the laminated sheet, no matter how many times he closed and reopened the file.

He cleared his throat, trying to sound casual. "There's a big gap between OPP One and Two."

Luisa hissed and crossed herself.

Mandy shuddered as if a ghost had passed through her. "Think positive."

"Six patients in six hours is a lot," he continued. "Do you count the time they show up in clinic, or when their symptoms start?"

Mandy punched his shoulder.

Maybe the number of cases they'd experienced before Scotland had been a glitch, just as Wetzel had wanted him to believe after the teen jumper's death—an anomaly that some academic might write up as a case study. That would be just fine. Time to return to ordinary labor. Sun up, sun down, repeat. There was peace in that rhythm.

Peter knew Mandy was right: He should've talked with the nurses more, included them in the decision-making. They were veterans of this strange world.

"Let's go to dinner together when we're done, just the medical staff," he said. Odd that they hadn't yet shared a meal after six days of working together.

"We could hit the café on Deck Four," Luisa said. "They have great salads, but you can get other stuff too."

They locked up and agreed to meet there in fifteen minutes. It would be good to change out of his scrubs.

The steward was just leaving his cabin as Peter arrived, letting the door close with a soft click. "Oh, sorry." He rolled his supply cart out of the way, unlocked the door, and held it open. "I finish freshening your room. Everything okay,

Doctor?" The little man, whose name tag pinned to his vest read *Yuli*, had fine wrinkles around his eyes when he smiled.

Peter smiled back. It couldn't have been easy to spend months at sea in this kind of grinding job. Maybe he had mouths to feed back home. Lamai and Agus—did they have families too? "I'm okay, thanks."

"What happen on your face?"

Peter eased past the cart and into the room. "Just clumsy. I slipped on a wet spot."

"Pardon me, but can I ask question?"

He turned to Yuli still in the corridor. "Sure."

"What is happening here? We hear many rumors."

Peter stiffened. "What are you hearing?"

Yuli looked down at the carpet. "So many people fighting and things."

"I'm just the doctor, so I don't really know everything that's going on." He laughed weakly. Man, that sounded lame.

"Some of the crew, they post on internet." Yuli pulled out his phone and showed Peter a clip of a shoving match between two women in a dimly lit club. Their shrieks rose above the thumping music. There were already 589 comments on the video.

"When was that?"

"Few days ago."

How much should he reveal? Was this fellow a talker? "They just had a bit too much to drink—you know how it goes."

Yuli's phone came alive with the sound of crickets chirping. "Probably you are right, Doctor. Forgive me, I take up too much time." He glanced at his phone, tucked it into his pocket and, with a quick duck of his head, went on his way pushing his supply cart.

Mandy and Luisa were already at the table when Peter arrived at the café off the grand atrium. The decor featured thick bamboo canes in stone planters filled with smooth black rocks. A nice place, designed to soothe rather than stimulate. Just what he needed to avoid thinking about what might be out there circulating among passengers and crew. He ordered a cup of French onion soup and a lobster roll.

Mandy let out a long breath. "It's been quite a few days."

"I actually may need a drink." Luisa was looking to hail the server. "But it almost feels calm now."

Mandy glared at her. "Don't jinx us."

Luisa gave the slightest of eye rolls, but Mandy seemed to take no offense.

They chatted amiably until their food came. Peter watched them dive into their salads while he feigned interest in his sandwich.

Mandy asked Peter about the prospects of a full recovery for the patients with encephalitis.

"They have a chance. If you assume it's herpes, you give IV acyclovir. Then you change treatment if the results come back different." He described the challenge of diagnosing encephalitis, even in the best of hospitals. There were dozens of viruses and other causes to investigate. Teasing it all out could take days or weeks. "What bothers me is that nobody on the ship had the classic pattern with severe headaches and seizures."

"At least not that we know of," Luisa said.

He laid out his logic. Some patients with hallucinations or shocking behavior had sought care for mild symptoms, like sniffles, cough, fever, headache. Some, but not all. "Maybe they got cough and cold meds from the vending machine in the waiting area."

"Somebody's buying them, that's for sure," Mandy said.

"Motrin, I can see." Luisa shook her head. "But Robitussin? Lugging around a whole bottle? I doubt it."

"Well, there's no luggage limit. People can bring anything." Except he'd forgotten his own stethoscope. Huh. "Anyway, it's clear that a lot of people are having mild symptoms of something. What if we're only seeing the tip of the iceberg?"

Mandy shushed him. "What's wrong with you? It's bad luck to mention that on a ship."

He gave her a distracted smile. What he needed to do was link the upper respiratory symptoms to the encephalitis.

"We've had only a handful of positive Covid tests," Luisa said. "I think the last one was just after we left Lisbon. I checked on her a few days ago, and she's fine."

"It's not Covid or the flu," Peter agreed. That doctor in Scotland had better come through.

They moved on to other topics. Mandy wanted to catch the new James Bond movie in the main theater. She had a thing for the chiseled-jawed actor who played the villain.

Luisa missed her dog. "My sister's taking care of him now. When I'm done with all this, I'm taking him on the Appalachian Trail."

This lady was amazing. "You go big."

"Not the whole thing." She let out a laugh. "Just the part from Pennsylvania to Maine."

"Oh, just that part." It was something Elena would've wanted to do. He'd refused to join her on that prolonged RV trip, claiming his patients needed him. But now he'd fled to the other side of the world.

He pushed a soggy crouton around the bottom of his soup mug as Mandy and Luisa chattered over the reggae music wafting in from the atrium.

Mandy patted his arm. "You still queasy? I hardly see you eat anything."

"It's not that bad. I just don't have much of an appetite." He set his spoon on the table. "Funny, with all this food everywhere."

"What do you like?"

He shrugged. "I'm spoiled. Houston has a bit of everything. You name it: Asian, Tex-Mex, Southern, barbecue—"

"Wait," Mandy said, "aren't Southern and barbecue the same?"

He let out a low whistle. "Pretending I didn't hear that."

"I had fajitas at the Dallas airport once. They were pretty good."

He picked up a knife and feigned stabbing himself through the heart. "You're killing me."

They laughed.

"Ninfa's in Houston is where it all started." His stomach rumbled, reminding him of alternatives to this no-appetite nonsense. "Their fajitas. Oh my God, you haven't lived."

"I'll have to check that out sometime." Mandy narrowed her eyes at him in mock scrutiny. "Anyway, I must've gained twenty pounds when I first started working on ships."

Luisa sighed. "Yeah, my ass got huge. But what are you gonna do?"

"Speaking of which, boot camp versus walking club?"

"Huh?"

Turned out Mandy was cooking up a wellness program for crew members. "They're unbelievably stressed and overworked. And the food that's available—sure, it's all-you-can-eat, but it's just not healthy day in and day out. If we can get them moving, they'd fare a whole lot better."

"Aren't they already moving around all the time?" Peter

asked. His mother must've burned thousands of calories every day cleaning offices.

"Not the same."

He had to give her credit, going above and beyond her call of duty as a nurse. Back in Houston, he'd buckled under the pressure of getting too involved in patients' daily lives. He just wasn't cut out for it.

His phone buzzed with a photo from Nali: her dining with Calvin and Agus outside somewhere. Calvin's face was contorted in mid-chew, and she was lifting a tall black can with a shit-eating grin. Her text read, *Agus coffee!* What a motley crew they made. All hands on deck for Calvin, but their collective effort was no substitute for his own mother.

He finished half his sandwich before the exhaustion hit, as deep as those post-call days in residency.

Mandy snapped her fingers. "Hey sleepyhead, it's only eight thirty. You want a coffee? A Red Bull?"

"I just gotta go to bed." He begged off and shuffled out of the restaurant, drooping under a blanket of fatigue.

The balcony offered a majestic view of the atrium below. This was the centerpiece of the ship, with crystal chandeliers, plush couches, and a gracefully curving staircase connecting three levels. He paused and peered over the iron railing. The drummer down there was working a nice groove with the cowbell and snare, and merrymakers milled about, drinks in hand, laughing and dancing.

These were the people under his charge. He was responsible for their health and well-being. How many had boarded in Edinburgh to join those who'd begun from earlier ports of call? New York was only a week out now, followed by the Bahamas and Miami.

He leaned forward against the railing. The gyrations of

revelers held him captive. He couldn't pull away. Time became meaningless. His head, heavy and dense, bent like an overripe tomato on its stalk. Passengers looked up at him with laughing faces, happy smiles, sharp smiles with gleaming—*Sharp?* He blinked a few times and refocused. The upturned faces were rictus snarls, gaping maws ringed with pointed little teeth.

He drew back in horror. What the hell?

He tightened his grip on the railing and peered down again. Something about the faces. They were all familiar. Shit. They were all the face of his brother, with his serious eyes and trimmed goatee.

Blood pounded and roared in his head. This could not be happening. There were hundreds of Felipes down there, everywhere, their mouths opening and closing like fish out of water, gulping in vain. Suffocating in the oxygen-rich air.

They were thanking him.

They were begging and accusing him.

10

GUZZLING HIS SECOND coffee while plodding along I-95, Peter's left eyelid twitched and fluttered at random. He stopped to lean against the wall, pretending to check his phone. Hallucinations like he'd had last night—all those Felipe fish, no other word for it—might appear for several reasons. The most obvious culprit was his conscience; his brother's ghost had finally caught up with him. How foolish to think that physical distance from Houston could separate them. Even death couldn't undo their bond.

But depression might also make him see weird things. Modern medicine sought to codify all the pathologies of the human experience, and a quick Google search confirmed Peter's diagnostic code: F33.3, depression with psychotic features. He could get it inked on his forehead as a warning to the world.

The third alternative was the worst, the one he didn't want to think about: that he now suffered the same encephalitis that had sent a healthy teenage boy leaping to his death, drove

Lamai to scrape "paint" off her arms, and unleashed a primal howl from Hartley.

He tucked his phone into his scrubs pocket and arrived at work with modest goals: Don't make any mistakes, and no more hallucinations.

Luisa looked refreshed, her hair glossy and tied back as she teed up the waiting patients in her usual efficient fashion. He worked through the first two in a light daze.

The third was Emma, a fifteen-year-old German girl with a bloody washcloth dangling from her mouth. Both parents seemed shell-shocked, but at least mom was verbal. Dad hung back in silence.

"Show the doctor," she urged her daughter.

Emma reluctantly removed the soggy wad from her mouth and handed it to Luisa. Thick beads of blood clung to the corners of her lips. There were no bruises on her face, but her eyes were reddened from crying.

What on earth? Peter nodded encouragingly. "Can you let me take a look?"

She opened her mouth just a crack at first, then wider. Peter winced when his penlight revealed the extent of the damage. Three molars were missing, two on the bottom and one on top. The holes in her gums had congealed with blood.

"Tell him what happened," mom said.

The girl closed her mouth.

"Say it," she commanded.

Dad, tall and slump-shouldered, produced a tool from the breast pocket of his vest, one of those folding multitools that would never have cleared security on a plane but was permitted on the cruise. He opened it to show the pliers and held it steady before his haunted eyes.

"She pulled them out," the woman said, her voice finally breaking.

The muscles in Peter's back knotted. He kept his voice low. "Is that true?"

Emma's breathing accelerated. Fresh tears welled up in her eyes, and she leaned toward her mom. They embraced, murmuring in German.

Peter swallowed a lump in his throat. He had to focus on her for now; couldn't think about what this meant for the ship. "Where are the teeth? Did you save them?" Maybe they could find a dentist on board.

"We think she flushed them down the toilet." Dad pursed his lips.

The girl sniffled and nodded.

With gloved hands, Luisa disposed of the bloody washcloth and brought her a roll of gauze. "You can bite down on that to stop the bleeding. Does it hurt? Do you want some medicine for that?"

Emma shook her head and bit down on the gauze.

Peter tried to think of a joke, like the good-natured ribbing he'd given Nali when she got braces in middle school, but nothing came to mind. There was no way to spin this. Dad signaled for a private conversation, and he led the way out, leaving Luisa to console the teenager and her mom.

"She's a little bit sensitive about her weight," the man said. "Many of her friends are more athletic."

"Okay."

"She used to go on these binges where she eats a lot. She then feels very bad about it."

"I see."

He struggled to continue. "Maybe that's why she did it."

"When did this happen?" Peter asked.

The parents had attended a pottery class that morning, with the understanding that Emma would be at the teen club, playing video games and such. When they returned to their suite, their daughter was crying hysterically in the bathroom with blood dripping down her chin. "She must have found the tool in my carry-on." His face twisted in pain. "Have you seen this before, Doctor?"

Peter met the man's eyes. It was hard to imagine the girl's desperation and utter commitment to her act of self-dentistry: Pull out one tooth, see the results; pull out another; then another. Gentle questioning yielded no history of mental illness or drug use, and her saliva swab, performed with their newly restocked kits, was negative for any drugs.

Panic uncoiled like a snake in his belly. This was supposed to be over. They had taken such pains to disembark every passenger and crew who had displayed neuropsychiatric behavior, but it had been a fool's errand. He should've known there was no way they could identify everybody inflicted; there were bound to be people like Emma for whom the initial signs were just beginning to show.

He labored to bring his focus back to her father. "Has she been seeing or hearing things?"

"Ah, you mean things that aren't there?"

Peter scrubbed a hand over his face—sure, like the face of a dead brother in a crowd. "Yes."

The man's eyes darkened. "She was talking about a little bird that was following her around."

"When was this?"

"When we stopped in Norway. I thought she must be seeing a real bird out there."

Hallucinations as a harbinger, delusions followed by delirium—a most unwelcome pattern. The family left, but Peter was sure he'd be seeing them again if Emma followed the same path as the others.

And how many others were there now?

There was no lunch break. Morning session bled into afternoon. He stitched up the hand of a guy who'd punched a wall in a violent outburst. Peter and Mandy spent a good fifteen minutes trying to convince one of the lounge singers that there were no chimpanzees slinging oranges at her onstage. He sent her out with some Xanax but suspected she'd be back, at which point she'd earn a checked box on a form: *Not Fit for Duty*.

He finally took a breather to text Nali. *If Agus has good coffee, I need it now.* The standard coffee on the ship was falling short.

It's amazing, she replied. *I'll try to get you some.*

A call came through from the Edinburgh hospital.

"I'm afraid I have troubling news," Dr. Banerjee began.

Mandy must've seen the look on his face, because she pulled Luisa into the office with him and shut the door. She slapped the back of his shoulder then gently pushed him toward his desk, mouthing, *Speakerphone*.

"There was a delay, but now we have the MRIs back on Ms. Lamai and Dr. Hartley. They show the same findings that we saw on Mr. Muller with involvement of the frontal area."

"Not surprising," Peter muttered.

"But here is something surprising," Banerjee continued. "The scans showed extensive encephalomalacia. Check your email. One must wonder what this means for the rest of the ship. I've got to go, but we can talk later."

Peter's mouth tasted like bile as they ended the call. One must wonder indeed.

Mandy was biting her fist. "Is that as bad as it sounds?"

He clicked open his email on the computer, the others

gathering around for a look. The message from Banerjee simply read, *For your reference. Would be interested in writing this up.* He clicked on the attachment, and the high-res image filled in from the top down.

Halfway through loading, it was already evident what great devastation had been wrought. The sagittal slice of Hartley's brain on her MRI showed her head and face in recognizable profile—her nose and fleshy chin, the round back of her head. Her brain, with all its grooves and bulges, appeared gray, bathed in dark cerebrospinal fluid all around. In the center of her frontal lobe, spanning both sides, lurked an ominous crater. Roughly half of her frontal lobe had been obliterated.

The meteorite had landed, and they were now dealing with the fallout. Any remaining shred of denial was blown away. This changed everything, everywhere, forever.

"*Encephalomalacia* means the brain tissue is necrotic," Peter said softly. "Gooey, like cream cheese."

Out of the corner of his eye, he saw Luisa shudder.

"I think I know, but what is the frontal lobe supposed to do?" Mandy asked in a small, tremulous voice.

"A lot." He lifted a hand to tick off the tasks on his fingers. "Thinking, attention span, memory. Language, social interactions." He glanced at the fluid-filled chasm in Hartley's brain. "Self-control."

Luisa was staring at him.

"Without it, we're animals. Or worse." He gripped the edge of the desk.

No more guesswork about the chaos on the ship. Sighting down the line for this kind of frontal lobe damage gave them a bird's-eye view of hell on earth—and they were an ocean away from help.

"What happened to you?" Captain Forster lounged in an off-white recliner in the living area of his apartment. The size of the place put Hartley's cabin to shame. It was tastefully appointed with the sleek curves of contemporary furniture. A cylindrical fish tank the width of a tractor tire occupied the center of the room.

Peter had taken to wearing a mask everywhere to forestall questions from passengers, but there was no point in concealing the bruising and swelling from Forster. "A passenger punched me. That's what I'm here to talk about."

"I'm all natural. No surgery." Forster slowly turned his head from side to side to showcase his unremarkable nose. No signs of prior fracture. No tufts of nostril hair sticking out.

What a weird thing to say, but not so out of character. Back home, the chief of cardiac surgery at TexMedCare had gorgeous nurses following him around and parked his Bentley across four slots designated for *other* surgeons, but even he had nothing on Forster's ego.

"It looks good," said Peter.

"It's perfect. My hair's all natural too. No Rogaine or whatever." Forster ran a hand through his full, dark locks, although the silver at his temples gave him away. "My father was bald at thirty, so it's not genes. You were saying?"

Peter sat bolt upright on the edge of a club chair beside Forster. It took every fiber of willpower to resist sinking into the velvety cushions. He couldn't afford to come here with softness. He gestured at his mask. "I'm not just wearing this to cover my nose." He told Forster about being kicked by Muller and the latest news from Banerjee, carefully laying out his case for instituting OPP2.

"No matter how tragic the situation is with a few individuals, there's no use in overreacting. I run a tight ship." Forster paused for effect. "Get it?"

Something about him froze Peter's marrow. It was a bad idea crossing a man with this kind of hubris—especially one most likely well into his own descent into viral delirium—but he couldn't stop now. He pulled up a clip of the club brawl that Yuli had shown him and presented his phone to Forster. The comments and views had multiplied tenfold.

Forster's lips flattened. "It's not a problem. I'll take care of it."

A surge of hope rushed through Peter's chest. "How?"

Forster waved him off like a little puppy, tossing the phone back into his lap.

Maybe another visual would seal the deal. He pulled up the email from Banerjee and showed Hartley's MRI. "This is—was—your senior physician. A large part of her frontal lobe is now Jell-O. Without a healthy frontal lobe, all sorts of bad stuff happens—impulses, urges, things better left unsaid. It's like when you mow your grass too short and the weeds take over."

Forster's expression was stony. "I haven't had a lawn in twenty years. You have A and you have B. You don't know what A is, and you don't know that A caused B."

"But I do! A is a virus."

He pulled out the stack of index cards that now functioned as a catalog of devastation on the *Paradise*. Some cards had names and symptoms. Others told of behaviors he had observed, like those of the prisoners in Harrington's brig. A few cards had dates, but none contained the precise timestamps he needed to put together a solid chronology. If he were an attorney bringing this to court, the judge would toss him out on the street.

"We have the records in the computer, but I just wanted to show you." Peter flipped through the victims, starting from Claudia Stevenson, his first patient.

"So on the basis of your little pile of cards, you want to isolate people who have the sniffles. Do you *want* a riot on your hands? How dare you bring that weak sauce to my table."

The ice in Peter's marrow splintered. He gathered the cards and stuffed them into his pocket as he rose. No conviction could survive in the presence of a captain who styled himself as a god.

11

HE'D EXPLAINED IT as making a strong move to the basket but getting rejected at the rim, like so many fools who'd attempted to score against Olajuwon back in the nineties. But Captain Forster's slap-down of Peter's request for OPP2 made him feel like he didn't even belong in the game.

"I don't get it," said Mandy. "What does our situation have to do with basketball?"

Peter straightened his clutch of cards, which he'd been sorting through one more time. "Never mind. Point is, he said no."

"I'd always heard he was a reasonable man."

"I don't have that kind of baseline to compare it with my experience, but I'll take your word for it. And even though he sounded logical, I can't shake the feeling that there's something wrong with him."

Her eyes went wide. "Like what? He didn't get violent with you, did he?"

"Ever met a narcissist?"

She smirked. "I work with doctors."

"I mean a real, pathological narcissist," he said. "On the level of personality disorder. That's what it's like talking with him. Everything is about how it affects him and his reputation, like he couldn't care less about the passengers or crew."

She looked past him for a moment as if lost in thought. "I never got that impression, but I don't know him."

Peter cradled his head in his hands. "I was so sure we could get a handle on all this. Now I don't even know what's real. Maybe I'm just imagining everything."

Her hands closed around his. "I trust you. You've seen all of… all of this. Yeah, I'm with you. Something's wrong."

He straightened. "So let's do it ourselves."

"Do… what?"

"It starts right here. We spread the word. Everybody washes hands religiously. They wear masks. They stay in their rooms."

Her eyebrows lifted. "Good luck."

"Are you on board?"

"It doesn't work like that. It has to start from the top."

He groaned. She was right. "I might still try it."

Before he dove into the next round of patients, he checked email on his phone. He'd sent another urgent message to Wetzel, pleading for permission to go above the captain's head to institute OPP. Nothing.

He emailed Dr. Banerjee in Scotland: *Any ID of the pathogen? We really need that to start isolation and quarantine on the ship. Please reply ASAP. Thx.*

Patients crashed upon them like waves on a beach. A handful had high blood pressure or high blood sugar. A young Japanese woman had an earache, and an old Greek guy was fighting laryngitis, his voice raspy and tortured. Even workaday issues like these were burying Peter now that he was the only doctor covering the entire ship.

Then there was the Jamaican sous chef complaining about noises in his head. "It's killing me, Doc. It's louder than those pots and pans."

Peter prescribed a short course of prednisone, a medication overprescribed for any malady thought to be caused by inflammation. He once would've scoffed at the old timers who gave it out like candy in contradiction to evidence-based guidelines. But there were no guidelines for times like this.

"Inflammation? That's what's causing all these noises?" The patient frowned but accepted the packet of tablets and shuffled out. Another *Not Fit for Duty.*

Peter dispensed prednisone to two more patients, but his supply was dwindling. He urged them to wear masks and stay in their rooms, but their reactions proved Mandy right. Covid and flu were distant concerns to passengers on a summer cruise. Some openly scoffed or looked at him like he was unbalanced. He couldn't argue against the latter. It took all his strength to avoid blurting *There's something going around that ruins your frontal lobe. You're liable to jump off the balcony or choke someone.* Instead, he offered a generic warning about how you could never be too careful.

During a brief respite in the office, he spread his index cards across the desk and clicked through records of recent patients. He also pulled up records for the detainees on Harrington's list. But the data points were too scattered and disjointed.

The AI panel hovered in the corner of the screen. *I hope you're adjusting well to your new position, Dr. Palma. How may I help?*

What the hell, there was nothing to lose. He entered a query. *Show all patients with respiratory symptoms, including headache or fever, with dates and times.*

The AI responded instantly, filling the panel with names,

cabin numbers, and stats. Peter scrolled through. Lamai, Stevenson, and others were there, along with many more he'd seen in the past week. He was in no shape to remember all of them.

He slammed his hand on the desk. There were too many threads, and he couldn't figure out how to tie them together— plus he didn't have the time to play around with it. The frustration brought him back to his residency, when each day brought logistical quandaries and nothing came easy. How could he wait for the plumber when he had to report to the ICU?

A name caught his eye: Amanda Burchins, Calvin's mother. She'd come in for a scratchy throat and cough. Now Nali was tending to her son when she should've been at home fiddling with software. But she was here. Hmm.

Nali was still being cagey about why she'd joined the cruise, but that was of little consequence now. He texted and asked her to come to the clinic.

Luisa knocked hard on the office door. "Doctor! There's a lady who needs to talk with you."

"Just triage her. I'll be right out."

"She won't come in."

He strode to the door. No lady in sight. "Uh…"

"She's out in the stairwell."

Great. More secrets. "What does she want?"

"She won't say. She's a server."

———

The server was waiting half a flight up, as if she dared not descend to the level of the clinic. He recognized her blonde ponytail and prominent forehead. She was the one who'd spilled coffee on his eggs before asking for a private consultation. And now she was wearing a surgical mask, a rarity among crew members.

She glanced up and down the connecting stairs. "Doctor, we must talk. Please, I am afraid for the ship."

"What do you want?" It came out blunter than he intended.

"My English is not so good." She gripped his forearm for just a moment. "You cannot tell anybody this."

Never a good start to a conversation.

"I had to take the test kits." She squeezed her eyes shut. "I am so sorry, but I had to."

His throat tightened. "What! Why?"

"There is someone bad. I don't exactly know what, but he is doing something. I think it's causing all this madness. How do you say—mayhem?"

His vision grayed out and his mind split off in a hundred directions. "Hold on, what are you talking about?"

A torrent of words spilled out of her mouth, half English, half something else. He urged her to slow down.

She took a deep breath. "There is a man, he wants to know what is happening everywhere, including in medical center. He paid me to do it. Then we hear about you want to start infection control plan, it makes me afraid. So I don't know what to do! I am so sorry. I didn't want to do it, but—" She slapped her forehead three times. "My father, he is sick, and we need the money. Health care in Poland is not so good for this."

Peter backed up against the paneled wall of the landing. "This is... I don't even know. Come with me." The clinic offered more privacy. Out here, they were exposed.

"I cannot! I—I will show you." Fine blue veins snaked across her pale forehead. "How does pirate buy corn? No, I mean, how much does pirate pay for corn? Then you say, a buccaneer."

His bowels turned to water. "What did you just say?"

She showed him the SeaText app on her phone. "He make me get access." She shoved the screen in his face. There it was, Nali's corny joke. She scrolled down to show him the latest exchange, when he'd asked Nali to come to the clinic just a few minutes ago.

"Something else." She clicked on another app. "That is medical center right now."

Shot from up high with a wide-angle lens, the footage was distorted at the edges but the resolution was sharp, so there was no doubt what he was looking at. There was Luisa giving a nebulizer treatment to a staff member, Mandy sorting supplies in the back office. This was live. This was happening right now.

"How… How are you getting this?"

"Wait. I show you more." She clicked around and loaded a video. Sure enough, it was Peter talking with that kind pastor from Tennessee, the one who'd said *They know not what they do*. "That is you, no?"

"Who are you?" he asked, reading her name tag: *Chessa*.

Her eyes skittered over his shoulder like a rabbit on the lookout for wolves. She was about to cry. "I'm just a server."

"Come inside," he insisted. "We'll talk."

"No, he will see. The cameras! I just showed you."

An icy finger traced down his spine. "Who? Who will see?" He was tired of asking so many questions.

"The man who pay me. I'm so sorry."

"Who's paying you?"

A pitiful moan came from deep in her throat, behind closed lips.

It was a hallucination. All this had to be a detailed auditory and visual hallucination. Or he was sleep-deprived. Or his neurons were starved for serotonin. He snorted at himself. Forget the or's; it was all three at once.

He pulled out his phone. "What's your ID on SeaText? I'll message you and— Wait, don't tell me. We're already connected."

"We cannot do text. He is reading messages." She looked him straight in the eye, as if explaining something to a child. "Do you understand?"

Perfectly. It was as clear as the muddy bottom of the ocean. He tried to keep calm, return to a fetal position in the sand as the tsunami bore down, like when patients back home laid their innumerable maladies at his feet. He needed to reset, figure out a starting point. Redirect, focus.

"Please, I warn you." Her voice shook. "But I can't say too much. My father, his lungs are so weak. He has too much pride, and he would be so angry if he know I am doing this. For him." She tapped her phone and showed Peter a frail old man in a faded robe slumped in a recliner, tethered by the nose to an ancient green oxygen tank.

He held his breath for a count of three, then let it out. "You're doing this for him."

She nodded with reddened eyes. "I am his daughter. He has nobody else."

"And what exactly do you want me to do? Listen, I'm sorry he's sick. I'm a doctor, but I'm not your dad's doctor."

Light footfalls came from the upper stairs, then Nali appeared with a plate of food. Why wasn't she wearing a mask? Hadn't she seen his text? Her manner was easy and relaxed. Perhaps a weight had been lifted now that she didn't have to babysit Calvin. It pissed him off as much as her stupid black

T-shirt of an anime girl with fox ears protruding from a mess of spiky orange hair.

"Greek nachos and Mediterranean sushi." She bit into a seaweed-wrapped roll. "Hummus and peppers—sooo good. Want some? Oh," she said, noticing Chessa. "Sorry to interrupt."

The trio stood awkwardly staring at one another.

"This is her?" Chessa asked.

He clamped his lips shut, as if there was any jot of information he could still hold back to his advantage.

"Who are you?" Nali's voice carried more curiosity than irritation.

Chessa turned a hard gaze at Peter. "Do you believe me?" Without waiting for an answer, she pulled a wad of paper from inside her vest, pressed it into his hand, and ran down the stairs. She turned the corner into the corridor connected to I-95.

Nali tipped her head. "She's pretty, but not your type."

"Forget it. Come here." He pocketed Chessa's note and nudged Nali down the stairs and into the anteroom in front of the clinic. His little sister could be of some help here. She'd already done enough looking after Calvin, but he needed her now more than ever. Even though she still should've stayed home.

"Whew, it's so loud up there." Nali twirled a smooth hand at the ceiling, dipped a pita into hummus, and popped it into her mouth.

"See that vending machine?"

"Yeah."

"I've got a project for you."

"You think I'm going to steal—"

"Come on. I need you. You're good at hacking and all that."

She narrowed her eyes. He outlined a scheme involving the vending machine, electronic health records, and a sprinkle of pixie dust, then finished with "And I'll write a letter of recommendation."

"Lame. That doesn't count—you're my brother. Plus, I already have a job."

"Didn't stop you from asking me before."

Her cheeks flushed. "What's in it for me?"

"You might just save us all."

———

Peter was just about to snip the camera cable in the office when Luisa burst through the door. "What the hell are you doing? And what is *she* doing?"

He had to admit it didn't look good. He severed the cable with scissors and stepped down from the stool. Nali pulled her fingers from the computer keyboard and leaned back in the rolling chair.

"There's someone watching us," he said.

When Luisa and Nali clamored for an explanation, he told them about Chessa showing him the videos and texts.

Nali scrutinized her own phone, her fingers flashing across the screen. "So she has *everything*?"

"I don't know," he said. "At least some of the conversations."

Luisa shot him a stern look. "This is not funny."

"Am I laughing?"

Earlier, after setting up Nali on the computer—and convincing her to put on a mask—he'd read Chessa's note. The message was scrawled on a plain sheet of paper with a shaky hand in blue ink, her written English echoing the way she spoke. She claimed she was being forced to monitor the medical team for a man she only knew by the handle *Gatobi9*. She confessed to convincing a technician to hack the security cameras and the text messages, and she admitted sneaking into the clinic to steal the drug kits. In turn, Gatobi9 kept enough cryptocurrency flowing into her account to pay for her father's medications.

Finally, lobbing a grenade that Peter tried to wish away, she questioned whether this had anything to do with the rash of unnerving behavior around the ship.

There was no signature. He'd pressed the note against the glass of the porthole window, but the pale North Atlantic sun had failed to illuminate any hidden text. This was no *Scooby Doo* episode.

"Regardless," Luisa was saying now, "it's just a security camera. Are you afraid they're gonna catch you smoking in here? Or is it more like you want to hide whatever she's doing?" She jabbed a finger at Nali. "No offense. You did great with Calvin, but the computer's for official medical business only."

Peter laid the scissors on the desk. "She's helping us out. I'll explain, but first…" He handed Chessa's note to Luisa.

Squinting, she read the missive. "You believe this?"

He slapped a hand against the metal filing cabinet. He wasn't sure what to believe anymore.

Luisa leaned in to view what Nali was working on. "You're in a patient record. That's a HIPAA violation." She whirled around to face him. "Peter, come on. Enough."

"I haven't done anything yet," Nali said. "I'm not even sure what it is you want me to do."

He ignored Luisa's reddening face. "Chart the symptoms

of everybody who's been in clinic for the past four weeks—no, better make it six weeks."

"Peter," said Luisa.

"See if they came back with weird behavior. Then cross-check it against this." He texted Nali the picture of Harrington's list. "Those are passengers who ended up in that jail down in security. Also, I need to know who bought cough meds from the vending machine."

Nali peered at her phone, then at him. "That's it?"

"Can you do it?"

"Say it."

Little sis was really going to milk it, and he didn't blame her. "Fine. I need you."

Luisa cursed in what sounded like Italian. "I don't have time for this. And you don't either."

"That's my point," he said. "She does this while I see patients."

"Are you going to get back to work or not?"

"I'll be right there."

He stared at the frayed end of the camera wire. Chessa might be the best bullshitter on the planet, but he couldn't deny that she wasn't supposed to have access to the video feeds. What would anybody do with that, anyway?

12

PETER WAS THE only one with a mask in the officer's dining room. He pulled it down to savor his chai spiced waffles and his second cup of coffee, but the caffeine barely took the edge off the mounting pressure in his forehead. Of course, because this wasn't just any ol' headache, but an encephalitis headache.

The overhead speakers emitted a series of chimes.

"Good morning, good morning!" The captain's sonorous voice filled the space like a fog. "This, of course, is Lysander G. Forster the First, your captain, who is pleased to provide a *very* reassuring update on the status of our lovely home on the seas."

None of the other officers made eye contact with anyone else.

"Some of you may have heard about a few irregularities in our operations, but I say to you: Concern yourself not with these matters, for they're but a distraction. Merely base rumors. Remember that your captain, your chief and commander, is in control."

A pair of young officers in the corner rose with nervous

grins and made for the door. It was painful enough to witness the man losing his grip on reality but downright terrifying to realize this was his captain. Peter group-messaged the nurses: *Did you hear that?*

Scary, came Luisa's reply.

Was Chessa spying on their messages? Was her extortionist, this Gatobi9? Peter had to assume so.

At a nearby table, First Officer Kinnard clasped her hands around the back of her neck. Gradually the other officers congregated around her, shifting from foot to foot or pulling up chairs.

Another female officer remained alone at a far table. She looked mid-forties, but her appetite belonged to a high school football player. Piles of bacon and cinnamon rolls disappeared between her glistening lips. Peter, mouth agape, watched as she hunched and licked the plate with broad strokes of her thick tongue, orange yolk dribbling off her chin. She pushed back and unleashed a thunderous burp that turned half the heads in the room.

Peter dug into his soggy, cold waffles before anyone could meet his gaze. He didn't want to connect the dots. The bigger picture might emerge, and it wasn't looking good. But the dots were right there, glowing like the eyes of rats in a cave. He could almost hear the chattering of their little teeth.

What he needed now was a pocket MRI machine. Point and scan. *Just hold still while I scan your brain. Yep, your frontal lobe is mush.* What would he find in his own skull? Better not to know. Oh, but he knew.

He approached Kinnard after the other officers departed. "I need your help." He told her about the recent illnesses and how the captain rejected his request to institute the OPP. "As you can see, it's getting out of control."

She nodded. "You've got your hands full. I'm sorry about Elizabeth Hartley. And your nose."

He was being too tentative. "The thing is—dammit, can't believe I'm saying this—we aren't going to make it to New York this way. We need to keep the passengers in their cabins. We can't keep charging forward while this, this…"

"The general would have to approve a retreat." She resumed eating.

"It's not a retreat. It's falling back to a strategic defensive position." Peter used to sit into the wee hours listening to Felipe relate battle stories and explain maneuvers. He'd seen some ugly action, even as a welder.

"I can't override the captain," she said with a mouthful of food.

"I see."

"I can't go over his head."

"But he's— Has he always been like this?" He gestured at the speakers that had transmitted Forster's bombastic announcement.

"He's not commanding this ship by accident. He rose through the ranks."

He still wasn't getting through. "I thought he was supposed to prioritize safety."

Kinnard took a minuscule bite of her churro French toast and chewed way too long. "I appreciate your concern. I'll take it into consideration."

That was an administrator for you, kicking the can down the road. "We don't have time."

"Your sister's a badass, you know that?"

"Excuse me?"

"The way she is with that kid is impressive. How old is she?"

"Too young—and that's the whole problem. Nobody on this ship, no matter what age, should have to deal with something like that."

"Who? Your sister, or the kid?"

Unbelievable. "It's not fair to either of them."

"I suppose not," Kinnard said.

Peter looked from face to face. Were they all infected? Why was there no sense of urgency here? He pulled out his stack of index cards. He ought to make a card for the captain. And that officer in the corner still stuffing her face like it was her last meal before the firing squad—her too.

The recessed light above Kinnard started flickering, throwing eerie gray shadows across the contours of her face. She looked up at it, annoyed. "I don't understand why they can't get that thing fixed. Do you have much trouble down in the clinic, Doctor? Maintenance around here has really fallen off."

Peter connected with Wetzel in between patients. Her voice was crisp and clear despite the transatlantic span. "NHS is working with CDC and WHO. They sent samples to Brussels for sequencing."

"They couldn't do it in Edinburgh?" he asked.

"Not even London. The preliminary result was so atypical that they want confirmation."

Not a good sign at all.

"Even with Covid, the sequencing was straightforward," she continued. "It was a variant of a known family. This one, whatever it is, doesn't fit into a known taxonomy."

He fought down a rising wave of bile. "So we don't have a diagnosis yet."

"Hang tight, Peter. How's the OPP going?"

"It's not." Mandy poked her head into the office, took one look at his face, and ducked back out. "The captain's in denial, and the second-in-command won't step up."

Wetzel was silent.

"What am I supposed to do? We tell everybody to wear masks, wash their hands, and stay in their rooms. But mostly they ignore us."

"I was hoping it wouldn't come to this, because it's an extremely rare circumstance. You need to gather as many officers as possible and get everyone to sign a petition to remove him from command." She let out a barking laugh. "God, if this call is recorded…"

Her counsel wasn't surprising, but it was hard to accept. If he was wrong about all this, he'd hang from the gallows. But if he was right and he did nothing, the ship would be ravaged before they reached New York. The seams were already splitting.

"I'll get legal involved," she said.

"I suppose there's some form on the intranet—what, Notification of Intent to Stage a Mutiny?"

She laughed. "I can't believe we're having this conversation."

"Welcome to my world."

"I think you just draft a letter with the details and leave room for signatures. It would need the endorsement of two physicians to declare the captain medically unfit for duty."

"But I'm the only doctor here. Can't you sign as the other one?"

"I'm not on the ship. You'll have to find another."

Dammit, he didn't know anyone here. "Like a passenger?"

"I suppose so."

He picked up the photo of the younger Hartley with her

husband in the pub. Those days were over. "How is Hartley anyway?"

"I'll be your contact from now on," Wetzel said. "They're running the info through Miami."

"And Hartley?"

There was such a long pause, he wondered if he'd lost the connection. "She's not doing well."

No matter what he thought of the Hartley he'd seen, there had to be a version of her who deserved a quiet, dignified retirement—working in her garden, enjoying local theater, whatever. Not farting and howling in a haze of confusion.

The Alpha Alpha Alpha broadcast jolted Peter as he sutured a laceration on a man's neck. An inch higher and the guy would've bled out from his jugular. His slack-faced wife claimed to have slipped on the wet bathroom floor while handing him a straight-edge razor.

Luisa stayed to hold pressure on the half-sewn wound, freeing Peter and Mandy to respond to the emergency summons. Good thing the grand atrium was only one level up. Still, a single flight of stairs shouldn't have exhausted him so much. When was that special coffee coming?

"I have a bad feeling about this," Mandy said as they burst out of the stairwell into the atrium.

Chaos ruled supreme. Two days ago, he'd watched the revelers here mutate into Felipe fish. Today it was a good old-fashioned mob. Passengers and crew alike swarmed to the center of the room to get in on the action.

Peter and Mandy worked through the crowd until they reached a red-faced Harrington doing furious chest compressions on a security guard. Harrington had good technique: arms locked, palms on the man's sternum, kneeling directly above him. He kept a good pace too, jackhammering at a tempo approximating "Stayin' Alive" by the Bee Gees. The guard's arms and legs jerked like a rag doll with each compression.

Peter kneeled across from Harrington. "What happened?"

Sweat dripped off Harrington's face. "Stabbed." He nodded to a slit in the guard's black uniform just under the sternum. A thick blob of blood bulged and subsided from the wound with each compression. There was another stab wound just above his belly button. "C'mon, Jamie, don't fucking die on me!"

"I'll take a turn." Peter mustered any last scraps of energy and moved into position. At least two ribs on the man's left side were broken, either from the assault or Harrington's compressions. The guard's thick mutton chops looked familiar, but the face underneath was pale and slack. This was the guard who'd burst into Harrington's office that day with the Zulu alert. Now he was the victim of the crime.

Peter paused to let Mandy deliver two rescue breaths with the Ambu bag. Another round of compressions, and Harrington took over. Peter sliced open the guard's shirt with a pair of trauma shears. There were multiple bruises and stab wounds on his torso, unimpressive from the outside—mere inch-wide gashes with clean edges. Clearly most of the hemorrhage was internal, accumulating in the space between his lungs and chest wall. A hemothorax could hold a liter of blood. They propped his beefy legs on an ottoman, harnessing gravity to retain blood in his central circulation.

Peter unpacked the defibrillator and slapped the paddles on the man's chest. The screen showed asystole, a flat line indicating no electrical activity in the heart. There was no ventricular fibrillation that could be shocked into a normal rhythm.

A bystander joined the compression rotation as Peter checked again for a pulse. Nothing. The screen still showed asystole.

"Any chance you can get an IV?" he asked.

Mandy moved to the supply bag. "Doubt it, but I'll try."

She couldn't get the IV going. Peter failed as well. Chest compressions weren't generating enough pressure to circulate whatever scant volume of blood remained in the man's cardiovascular system. They had epinephrine but no way to administer it. But even if they did, what outcome could they expect? Jump-start his heart for a few minutes after he'd been dead for who knows how long?

Bystanders stepped up for compressions, expanding the resuscitation team to seven. Peter rocked back on his heels. The guard was still flatlined. They could've lined up the population of China and it wouldn't have made a damn bit of difference, not unless one of them could turn back time. They continued CPR for what might've been twenty minutes, might've been a month.

The guard's pupils were now dilated and unresponsive to light, obscuring all but the thinnest rim of hazel iris. Harrington was back on compressions, weeping and cursing. The guard's devastated ribcage creaked with each compression. The crowd murmured, dozens of phones trained on the action.

Peter moved to check his watch. Harrington grabbed his wrist. Mandy tried to pull him away, but he shrugged her off then resumed pumping.

"Harrington," Peter said, "it's over. I'm calling it."

Harrington continued to pound up and down, even as the

crowd began to drift away. Beyond the ring of people, Nali stood on a couch, face buried in her hands.

This virus touched all ranks and quarters. None were beyond its reach.

Nobody could escape.

13

OFFICER JAMIE CARSON had played Division 2 football in Virginia, according to Harrington, so it was no mean feat to hoist his body into the refrigerated drawer. Peter rolled it shut with a metallic thud.

"His wife's pregnant." Harrington's voice was raw. "He was supposed to finish out his contract here next month."

They secured the morgue, and Mandy verified the temperature-control backup. Now two of the three drawers were occupied. The body in the first drawer—Rickey Turner, the teen who'd jumped to his death—was destined for Michigan.

Peter sequestered himself in the office but found no comfort. Everything out the window was ashen gray—the sky, the sea, even the sunlight. Luisa reminded him there were patients waiting. Her fortitude was something to behold. When the world went to shit, she'd be the one sorting canned food into proteins and carbs.

He returned to duty in a haze. Every patient was a victim of assault or abuse of some form. The perpetrators must be filling up Harrington's brig. Discharging victims from the clinic was like tossing bunnies into a lion's den. If things continued this way, the bunnies would all *become* lions.

Peter sagged against the counter. Wouldn't it be awesome to listen to someone complain about fatigue from dialysis, or to bicker with an insurance rep over some crucial medication? All the burdens from Houston felt like easy lifting now.

His cell rang—Wetzel in Miami. "Peter, what the hell?"

"Excuse me?"

"Stop playing dumb. I'm looking at it right here. When did you record this? Was it right before I gave you the update on the virus, or after?"

It was hard not to get defensive. "Tell me what I did."

Her voice tightened. "This thing is everywhere—everywhere, Peter! Shit, if you're not just yanking my chain, do a search for cruise ship and drugs, or something like that. It's not hard to find."

He entered the search terms, and all the social media venues and news sites lit up. Hell, that was his face—it was a video! One post was tagged "Dr. Peter Palma on the Paradise Cruise Ship." He hunched over his phone. The clip showed him sitting in the back office of the clinic, looking somber and exhausted, his eyes glassy. The edge of his surgical mask was indenting the swollen bridge of his busted nose.

The skin on Peter's arms prickled as he watched himself talk: "We haven't found any evidence of an infectious outbreak. Sure, a few people have upper respiratory symptoms, but on a ship this size, that's bound to happen. What's going on is rampant drug use. Stimulants, hallucinogens, narcotics, you name it. The good people of the *Paradise* are partaking in it all."

Only he'd never done that. Never said that. He replayed the video. Was this an AI doppelgänger? His evil twin? This was him, right down to the last detail. His voice, his face, his index cards and pen protruding from the pocket of his ship-branded scrubs. He glanced down. Just like now. Just like real time.

His monologue continued: "It's serious but not completely shocking in this day and age. The ship has pretty tight security, but with dozens of ports of call throughout Europe, it's impossible to prevent all drugs from coming on board."

How had this come to pass?

Maybe he'd posted it in a moment of delirium. He hadn't been himself in months. But if it looked like a duck and quacked like a duck, then it was a duck, and this looked like him. He clicked on the same video on another site. Still him—a celebrity for all the wrong reasons.

He lifted the phone back to his ear. "I'm here."

"What exactly are you trying to do?" Wetzel barked. "You're sabotaging everything we're working on."

He tried to talk but could only spit out nonsense syllables. Where was he? Most importantly, who was he?

Peter sat slack-jawed in the office. The voices around him were muffled and distant. His eyes traced the wire he'd severed in response to Chessa's claims. He couldn't unsee the desperation in her face as she'd shown him the photos of her ailing father sinking into his recliner somewhere in Poland. She'd do anything for him. Anything.

So she'd stolen drug kits and tapped into communications and surveillance systems for this mysterious benefactor, this Gatobi9. What kind of name was that? Whoever he was, he'd gathered and manipulated footage of Peter to create an incriminating deepfake. And now Peter's face was all over the internet discrediting concerns about an infectious outbreak, claiming it was all drugs.

Nali popped her head into the office. "Coffee time! From Agus, with love."

He accepted a slender can, pressing it to the crook of his neck, the cylinder cold against his skin. This felt real enough. He was definitely here, right now, and this version of him took a swallow of thick, sweet liquid. The elixir fired up his neurons like a Christmas tree, bathing his brain and muscles in pure energy. What was this stuff? He half expected to find cocaine listed in the ingredients but couldn't decipher the foreign characters.

His focus suddenly bounced around the tiny room, chasing a massive flow of sensory input. He was blasting into kingdom come. Damn, he needed this.

Ride with it, Peter. Hang on.

Focus. Breathe.

Mandy took a chug of her own can and admired it at arm's length. "Holy smokes, this is incredible. Agus, he's incredible." She did a couple of deep knee bends, adding little kicks like a Russian folk dancer.

Peter grinned. He felt it too and swung his arms in circles. "I gotta get outta here."

He moved for the exit, ignoring Luisa's protests. He needed to get to higher ground. This ship was a tomb. The elevator would be faster, but who knew what fiends lurked within. No way was he putting himself into an enclosed space with another Muller. Besides, this "coffee" had suffused his legs with arcane power.

He took the stairs.

Nali trailed behind, panting. "Where are you going?"

He stopped at a landing. "Just get a bunch of food from the buffet and take it back to your room. Lock the door and don't come out until we reach New York."

"What? What the fuck, Peter?"

As he walked, she continued behind him like when she used to follow him and Felipe to the Stop-N-Go. Those were good times. At least he still had those old memories. What other things had he done recently with no recollection?

The top deck was darker and colder than he'd expected. Only a sliver of moon shone through the foggy gloom. He headed to the section close to where Rickey had jumped. The area was flanked by industrial columns and service equipment. The ship carved through the immeasurable ocean with a low hum.

The sheer vastness reduced Peter to a mere atom. He'd once seen a YouTube video comparing the sizes of objects, starting with a sesame seed and progressing to an apple, an elephant, a T-rex, the Eiffel Tower, and Mount Everest, all the way up to planets, stars, and galaxies of unimaginable scale. The dimensions weren't comprehensible by the human mind.

And this ship, with its thousands of inhabitants, amounted to nothing in comparison.

The reflex was to find dignity in smallness, to cling to the goodness of the human heart as the source of meaning in an infinite cosmos. But where was goodness when a mother abandoned her child or when a husband assaulted his wife? Where was dignity when people tore flesh like animals? The milk of human kindness had spoiled.

Nali's voice pierced the shroud. "Can we talk?"

Half of her soft face was hidden in shadow. She should've been out drinking with her friends in Houston, but she was here in the middle of a storm that had yet to be named.

Coffee and grief swirled in a Lexapro-shaped hole, and it bubbled out to scour away the membranes that had obscured the truth. It was obvious now. All his efforts had been in vain. What a fool he'd been—the same malady that had eaten Hartley's frontal lobe and was turning people into beasts would overtake him too. He hadn't helped a single soul with this encephalitis. He'd been nothing but a witness to its brutality.

"Fine," Nali said into the silence. "I'll go first."

He leaned over the thick railing and let the salt air condense on his skin.

"After this, my job," she said. "It's not in Houston."

"Oh."

"It's at a lab in Nevada, not NASA."

"Okay."

She joined him at the rail, gazing down into the same somber void. "It's actually not, uh, not a job. It's an unpaid internship."

Whatever.

"I had to beg them. I turned down a tech support job because I thought I was better than that, so now I'll be working my ass off for free."

He shrugged.

"Don't tell Mom."

He swung around to face her. "I won't."

"'Cause you know she'll sell her car for me. I'm an idiot."

"So how are you going to pay rent? Come to think of it, how'd you pay for this?" He pointed to the deck. The friends-and-family benefit offered a good discount, but it still wasn't free.

She blushed. "I put it on my credit card."

"Nali."

"I'm getting two percent back, though."

"Right." Such a kid. Fresh like this ocean breeze—no, scratch that. This mist was clammy and impersonal. She still trusted people and systems in a way that he and Felipe had long since relinquished.

She stiffened and turned to face the water. "I thought you were sailing away and never coming back. Like going around the world again and again."

"I thought about it," he said with a tiny smile. "If I could, I'd get on a chopper right now and fly back to Houston."

"I wouldn't blame you. I just... I didn't want to miss the chance to talk with you about him." She craned her neck to gaze into the darkness, as if straining a few extra inches toward infinity would unlock a great mystery. "There. I said it."

He shifted his feet. It was damn cold out here.

"What happened?" she asked.

Better for her to delay the adult stuff as long as she could. And yet... There might come a day when he wanted to fess up but wouldn't be able to. He should just tell her now.

"I prescribed him narcotics." Incision made. Now he had to squeeze all the pus out and it was going to hurt like hell. "At first I was pissed. I wanted to punch him. Like how could he put me in that position? He was supposed to be in rehab."

Felipe's tour of duty in Afghanistan had wrecked him. Nobody went through that and came out the same. The mangled arm was one thing, but the all-consuming pursuit of painkillers and benzos spoke of wounds beyond the reach of modern medicine, afflictions of the soul.

"It was Christmas," he said. "I knew he was going to ask."

Felipe with the pinpoint pupils. The slow, tortuous entreaty on Mom's front porch as a stray dog loped past the rusty chain-link fence. His request triggering a primal reaction in Peter, like a porcupine raising its quills.

"Why didn't you just say no?" Nali said, her voice thin and meek.

He'd asked himself the same thing a million times. He'd only prescribed twelve tablets, enough to get Felipe through the holiday weekend. Told him not to drink or mix it with other drugs—made him promise on Dad's grave. Now Felipe was buried next to that grave.

And Peter had planned on dying with this secret.

"I thought it was better to take hydrocodone than get shit off the streets. They use these pill presses to lace fentanyl or xylazine into tablets that look like prescription drugs." Her eyes welled with tears, but he continued. "I keep trying to believe," he rasped, "that it wasn't my stuff he OD'ed on. Like when everybody on the firing squad thinks they fired the blank."

Nali shifted sideways, her shoulders quaking. He'd lost her. What had he expected—that she'd understand, it would be okay, and everything was going to be fine?

"I was just trying to help." The words dissolved in the thick night as soon as they left his mouth. "I didn't see another way."

Back then, he'd been too tired of all the ways the world declared there were no solutions, only trade-offs. He wanted a solution for Felipe—and oh, he'd given him one, all right. A permanent one.

Peter slammed his fists on the implacable steel railing.

After a thousand years, Nali shuffled closer, eyes downcast, and leaned in for a tentative hug. A formality. "I'm going to bed," she whispered. Her flip-flops scraped along the decking as she departed.

Not so long ago, he'd wondered what it would be like to fall asleep and not wake up. The sky darkened as the crescent moon slipped behind clouds. He looked over his right shoulder, back east toward Scotland, where scientists in the Old World were scrambling to decipher the genetic code of the pathogen turning people into beasts. He turned to the west, the direction the ship was moving toward. Somewhere in the distance was New York, America, and a continent waiting to receive the vomitus of this sick, sick whale.

He drew a long, juddering breath. Being a good doctor wasn't enough. Applying knowledge, sacrificing sleep, and looking out for the interests of others wasn't enough. It hadn't worked in Houston, it hadn't worked with Felipe, and it certainly hadn't worked here on the ship. Not when the virus dissolving frontal lobes was unclassified.

The deep groans of the ship's engines crept into his ears. He'd lost track of time in the blackness. He needed sleep, but the magic coffee wouldn't loosen its grip. Every detail chewed at him. The security camera in the office. He'd snipped the wire; he could practically feel how it had given way under the sharp blades of the scissors. Gatobi9 eavesdropping, wanting to pull the veil over the world's eyes. But why?

He pulled up the video on social media and watched the impostor version of himself denying rumors of a viral outbreak, claiming it was all drugs. And here was the thing: Nobody would bother making and disseminating a video like that without a sinister plan.

So there had to be something to Chessa's claims about Gatobi9. Yep, Gatobi9 was a subtle shadow on a CT scan—easy or convenient to dismiss at first but would resurface ten times bigger and meaner.

If even half of what she said was right, the *Paradise* was bound for ruin. Rickey caving in his own head. Muller pummeling his wife. Some asshole stabbing Harrington's security officer. All that multiplied by hundreds, thousands ... even more. New York didn't stand a chance. There was no police force on earth that could extinguish this kind of anarchy.

He shuddered against the icy flutter spreading through his chest. The worst part was observing his own submission to the virus, an inevitable slow-motion descent into the void. Worse than a slow death—worse than death itself.

He had to do something now, while he still could. There was no one else on this ship with the will to see it through, nor the knowledge of all the moving parts. And he was, after all, their medical officer. He was responsible for their well-being.

The fact that Nali hadn't kicked him in the nuts had to count for something. Yes, his choices had led to Felipe's death, but that didn't make him completely depraved. At least not yet. He actually had a chance to turn things around here, not just for himself but for everybody vulnerable to this virus. Finding the cause of all this was a mere glimmer in the forest—but maybe, just maybe, a path out of the darkness, a flame that might save them.

Or it might consume them. This pursuit might very well leave Nali down one more brother. Still, he had to push toward it: Gatobi9. If he didn't try, this floating city would be a ghost town before long.

14

THE THIRD AND last drawer in the morgue was claimed by a sixty-two-year-old man who died in his sleep. His wife told Peter he'd stopped taking his aspirin and blood pressure meds a week ago. "He didn't care anymore." Her face looked drawn and distant in the fluorescent lighting of the hallway outside their cabin. "I was begging him."

And yes, she confirmed, her husband had complained of a cough and headache before he began acting strangely.

This quiet demise was even more disturbing to Peter than the violent deaths of Rickey Turner and Officer Jamie Carson. All this man had to do was keep taking his meds. Besides suppressing inappropriate behavior, the frontal lobe was supposed to allow people to make decisions and anticipate consequences. So it wasn't just violence; they were in for all sorts of fun and games.

Oh, well. Since the morgue was full, the game was over and everybody got to go home now. See you next year, and thanks for playing. Only they were in the middle of the Atlantic, and this was no game. More deaths would be forthcoming.

Peter sent a quick text to Nali: *You ok?*

He stared at his lame overture and started to compose another, but nothing better came to mind. Maybe she was still asleep this early in the morning. If so, lucky her. In his dreams last night, a pale version of Felipe's face had drifted across a windless, ashen sky.

Fueled by Agus's coffee, Peter tended to seven patients before standard opening time. All the passengers wore masks, as did he and the nurses. Luisa was wound up tight, snapping at him for asking where the sterile saline was kept. Mandy conducted business in a monotone that thickened the mood. Things were different now.

A line cook was gazing at his bandaged hand in bewilderment, struggling to understand why he hadn't noticed his hand on the stove until his coworkers smelled burning flesh. "I don't get it. I felt no pain."

"This is a second-degree burn," Peter said. "So I agree, it should've hurt. In any case, burns are prone to getting infected, so come back tomorrow so we can check, and we'll change the bandage."

"I must have been in la-la-land or something," the cook said. "I actually don't even remember anything about it."

"Are you having trouble concentrating? Seeing or hearing weird things?"

The cook blushed and started to say something but stopped.

"What?"

"Nothing. Well… I did hear some wild-ass rumor about how the military's gonna do something."

Peter played it cool. Rumors were just rumors until they came true. The early days of Covid in China had seen crews in white hazmat suits fumigating entire city blocks—all for nothing, as it turned out. "Like spray it down with disinfectant?"

"Yeah, that's probably it. Man, this shit's unbelievable."

After discharging him, Peter informed the nurses he was ducking out for a quick errand.

"Where are you going?" Luisa asked.

He turned back with his hand on the door. "Looking for Chessa."

"You're obsessed." She planted her hand on her hip. "You're not thinking straight."

"I have to find her." To get to Gatobi9.

He sensed something was wrong before he turned the corner to the main buffet. Flanking the glass doors were crew members offering squirts of hand sanitizer. Many passengers ignored them, pushing and shoving in line. The dull roar from inside was punctuated by sharp clanks.

Peter stopped short as soon as he entered. Uniformed guards trotted around the edges of the mob like sheepdogs, with little success at controlling the mayhem. Martial law was needed; the US Marines would've nipped this in the bud. A metal platter clanged to the floor, sending sushi everywhere. Peter recoiled as a young woman dropped to all fours and slurped the raw fish right off the grimy tile.

He winced as one guy smashed a white plate over the head of a teenager. He could only pray there would be no laceration. The clinic was running low on staples and stitches. Halfway down the line at the carving station, a pack of retirees squabbled over the prime rib. A lady darted in to grab the bloody chunk of meat, only to be slapped away by an older man.

Peter wedged through the crowd to the canister of steak knives by the cutting board. He grabbed four of them and four sets of utensils rolled up in cloth napkins. Dodging sharp elbows, he stumbled clear of the throng and dumped his loot on a nearby table. He emptied the cloth napkins and brushed the forks and spoons aside, then rolled a serrated knife inside each napkin and slipped them into the waistband of his scrubs, two on each side—armed for combat.

Chessa was nowhere to be found. He even stood on a chair to scan behind the buffet counter. Maybe she was a figment of his imagination, a ghost. He patted his breast pocket, feeling the outline of his index cards. Tucked behind the cards was the folded note she'd given him. It was real, a physical thing. She was out there somewhere.

He hightailed it out of the buffet and settled behind a fake plant in a nearby lounge. He pulled out his phone to text her but instead wound up flicking through messages and emails. They were the top story on all the news sites. CNN was calling it a "mysterious illness." The BBC interviewed some group who wanted to divert the ship to Greenland and create a new penal colony, like Australia in the 1700s. Peter's buddy Jared had reached out: *Dude, is that you?* Even Elena had sent a note of concern.

He needed to stop doomscrolling and get back to business. He willed himself to pull up a group text Chessa had been monitoring. He needed a clever message to lure her out of hiding, without alerting Gatobi9 that he was on the hunt, but nothing came to mind. Still running on fumes. If he could get some solid hours of sleep, get back on the Lexapro, and rid himself of this virus, maybe he'd have a chance, but there were no prospects for any of that, and the magic coffee had almost completely worn off.

He defaulted to a brutal, direct approach.

What's your game? he typed, then hovered his finger over the screen. He held his breath and pressed *Send.*

Peter met up with Harrington in a dim alcove just off I-95. The corridor teemed with crew members as usual, but their energy seemed tinged with caution.

Harrington creased his forehead as he studied Chessa's note. His blue gloves flattened dark curls of hair against his skin. "Who the hell is this Gatobi9, some kind of ninja?"

"It's what she calls him," Peter said. "I have no idea why." He described how Chessa had accessed the camera feeds and SeaText messages and how she'd confessed to stealing the test kits. "Can you help me find her?"

"I'd bring her down, but there's no room at the inn. My office is the booking cell now. We had to commandeer a section of crew quarters for the overflow. And let me tell you, they are *not* happy, the displaced crew or the detainees. We're doing double overtime. With Jamie gone"—Harrington's voice cracked—"it's even tougher."

"I'm not asking you to take her into custody. Just help me find her and figure out what's going on. Can't you track her key card swipes?"

"That only gets you so far."

"And the guy who's behind it—we need to find him too, Gatobi9. He must've used the video feeds to create that fake."

"It's not that hard with AI. But what's the point? He wants to get you fired?"

Peter scrubbed a hand over his forehead. That wouldn't be such a terrible outcome. "To sow misinformation and obscure the truth."

Harrington snorted. "What *is* the truth?"

Good question. It had to be connected with the virus

somehow. "Wetzel said they're still working on sequencing the virus."

"God," Harrington muttered, shaking his head.

"Whatever his intent, it'll hurt us."

"Are you sure it's a he?"

Peter crossed his arms. "It doesn't matter. By the time we arrive in New York, we'll need all the help we can get from the authorities. Including the CDC."

"So why no OPP yet?"

The damn captain couldn't see past his own nose. "Forster didn't—he isn't... I bet he had the infection at some point. You must have heard his announcement."

Harrington waved a hand. "He's lost it. So we just have to hold on. We're not gonna solve this without support from up top."

Harrington—bless his grieving heart—seemed like a realist. If they could just get Forster out of the way, there was a good chance Harrington could help get the place back under control before it was too late.

"I'm working on something," said Peter.

"Yeah?"

"Be ready. You'll hear about it from First Officer Kinnard."

Harrington nodded slowly. "Ten-four. Do what you have to do. I'll figure out what I can do. Let's see if we get some traction."

A gaggle of crew members plodded along I-95 in front of Peter in a trance. Evidence of their dereliction abounded. Entire sections of the corridor were steeped in shadow under broken lights. He recoiled from the stench of rotting meat and fruit emanating from an unattended kitchen cart and stumbled into a hamper of dirty laundry reeking of semen, blood, and urine.

He groped for his index cards. Scary how porous his memory had become lately. The to-do list on the top card had little square checkboxes next to each task he'd assigned himself, like back in residency when he was running around the hospital talking with consultants and the family members of patients. It was his attempt to manifest the illusion of control amid the maelstrom: Do a thing, check off a box. Do the next thing, check another box.

The key was to break up large goals like *Save the ship* into manageable tasks. He checked off *Tell H about Chessa* and *Get H buy-in on OPP*. The next item was to talk with the passenger First Officer Kinnard had identified as a doctor. Maybe then ousting Forster would be possible.

The back wall of the elevator at midships was a massive plexiglass panel bowing out over the grand atrium below. He had a panoramic view as the elevator began its slow ascent. A bitter taste pooled in the back of his mouth as he witnessed the mayhem below. Fists swinging and objects hurled. Mouths wide in animal snarls. A mix of passengers, crew, and a few white-clad officers—all ages and nationalities. Everyone was swept up. He shrank back. What was worse, the bedlam roiling the atrium now or his hallucination of the Felipe fish calling out for his blood?

The plexiglass shook, and he scurried away as it shattered into a thousand pieces, leaving him open and vulnerable above the writhing mob.

He touched his palms to the elevator's side wall and jerked back to reality. He whipped around to the buttons. There should've been one for eject. He would burst through the ceiling, soaring into the gray sky to land in a waiting helicopter and leave this ship of fools behind. This cruise was supposed to be his escape from the real world. Until only a few days ago, that had still seemed possible. But who was he kidding? The *Paradise* was some lower level of hell, and there was no eject button anywhere.

The elevator stopped on the sixth floor. A half-naked man stumbled in, sweat glistening on his pale chest, followed by two girls pawing at him and each other. The door closed behind them, hemming Peter in. One girl raked a glance over him. He recognized her from clinic last week, that green peacock tattoo on her neck when he was listening to her lungs. Back then, she'd been just another patient with mild respiratory symptoms. Now she was both victim and perpetrator.

"I'm just a retired anesthesiologist," Dr. Abassi protested. The heavyset Iranian blinked rapidly behind his glasses. "My patients were asleep, ideally."

Peter slid the page across the card table. The gaming parlor wasn't the ideal place to conduct a conversation about mutiny. He tried to ignore the teenage girl muttering in the corner.

"I'm not asking for your help in clinic, although I wouldn't turn it down. I'm asking if you'd be willing to affirm that he's not competent."

"Ah, just that." Abassi gave a wry smile.

"You must be aware of what's going on." Peter pointed to a double column of signatures scrawled below the declaration drafted by Kinnard. "The other officers agree he's not competent to make decisions." He pointed to his own name at the bottom. "I've signed as one doctor."

Dr. Abassi made no move for the pen.

Come on, come on. "You must've had a patient who needed emergency surgery but was incompetent to consent."

Abassi rubbed his chin. "There's a conflict of interest in putting someone like that to sleep. But even if I were allowed to declare them incompetent, it would be one patient with one aneurysm. What you're talking about is the captain of a ship with thousands of passengers."

Peter tapped the form on the table. "That makes it more urgent. Imagine three thousand aneurysms rupturing—that's what it'll be like if we don't get ahead of this outbreak."

"Will it work?"

It had to. "Just sign right here." Peter jabbed his finger at the line designated for a second doctor. "It's clear that he can't lead us."

Abassi's looked to the page then back up at Peter. "How old are you?"

Peter shot up from his chair, fighting the urge to reach over and strangle the guy. "What the—"

"Dr. Palma."

Peter plopped back down and cradled his head in his hands. What had gotten into him? He couldn't do this. "Why can't just one thing work?"

The long silence was broken only by the girl snickering at the other end of the parlor.

"Wait," Abassi said. "I will sign."

Peter's head snapped up.

Abassi seemed to focus far away from this room, this situation. "Then I am going to play a nice game of rummy with my wife. We are going to make love, if she will have me. She almost died of Covid, you know. The days are long, and who knows how many we have left."

Movement in the corner of the room caught Peter's eye.

A koala-sized creature with purple scales slick with mucus was dangling above the teenager, clacking its multi-jointed appendages. That thing had too many fucking knees or elbows, or whatever. A long gob of spittle hung from its puckered orifice. The unholy fiend scuttled down the wall, but the teenager, with her hoodie pulled low, paid no attention to it.

"Hey, watch it, heads up!" Peter pointed.

She raised her middle finger.

He fought back a wave of nausea. Didn't she see it? This is how it would all end: spider food.

With one barbed appendage the monstrosity slipped the girl's hood back; with the other, it stabbed out her left eye. She smirked as inky blood pooled in her empty socket. The spider thing raised the glistening eyeball, trailing tendrils of muscle and mucus, and sucked it into its orifice.

The girl pointed to her right eye. "Want this one? Tastes like chicken."

Peter whipped his head around. Dr. Abassi was saying something, but he couldn't understand the words. He stared at the parquet floor, gasping for air. Had to count to ten. One, two, three, don't look. Count to ten. One, two—

"Are you okay?" Dr. Abassi asked.

Peter gawped. He didn't see it? Nobody saw it. The girl had fallen back into her sullen demeanor. Peter looked again. She had both eyes.

There was no purple spider thing.

This was how the illness progressed, headaches followed by hallucinations. He should've started himself on prednisone to tamp down the inflammation, but each tablet would've meant one less for the passengers and crew. And now it might be too late. Prednisone did nothing for necrosis, and his brain was already rotting.

"On second thought," Dr. Abassi was saying, "I recommend that you seek help for yourself." He excused himself, leaving the declaration unsigned on the table.

Peter dropped his chin to his chest. He couldn't catch a break. He'd have to start over. He stared at the blank signature line on the form.

Well, there was one way he could get the thing completed. He'd be crossing a line, and it was probably a felony. But what did that matter if civil order had evaporated anyway?

———————————

Peter had to give credit to First Officer Kinnard. She was ready to roll when he delivered the signed declaration. She barely glanced at the bold, sprawling *A* leaning into a *b* before trailing into an illegible scribble, and she gave no sign of suspecting malfeasance. If they ever got off this ship alive, he'd send Dr. Abassi a card: *Apologies for forging your signature. I hope you and your wife had a wonderful cruise.*

The coup happened quickly in the background. Captain Forster wasn't forced to walk the gangplank, as far as Peter could tell. All he saw was a simple text from Kinnard: *Done.*

Peter was picking tiny shards of glass out of a Nigerian woman's dainty foot when Kinnard's OPP announcement came overhead. In a crisp monotone, she laid down the law on social distancing, masking, and hand sanitizing. Movies and shows were suspended. The pool was closed. Buffets were shut down. Seating assignments in the formal dining rooms were rearranged to accommodate social distancing. "Most importantly," she concluded, "those with upper respiratory symptoms are required to isolate in their cabins. The crew and staff will provide room service for quarantined passengers."

Was he imagining things, or did the entire ship just collectively groan? It was the whole enchilada, a return to Covid-era authoritarianism.

"Now what, Doctor?" the Nigerian lady asked. She'd stepped on the broken pieces of a glass serving bowl during yet another scuffle. "I'm scared to go out."

"Well, you need to stay off this foot anyway. I think I got all the pieces out, but I'm not a hundred percent sure. Some were lodged in there pretty deep."

He shuffled back to the office. Nali looked up from the computer, her face blank. "Your fly's open."

Fine, he'd take that one. His confession last night about Felipe had been a lot to process, if that was even the right word. You didn't *process* your brother's death; it was a wound that never healed.

She showed him a graph with a line shooting up and to the right. There was no undulation or fluctuation; it was a clear trend, an increasing number of symptomatic patients each week. She flipped to a new graph. "And here's the projection if you layer in the potential infections of everybody who's accessed the vending machine."

The line warped upward, predicting exponentially greater rates of infection in the coming days. Even considering the range of uncertainty stipulated by the AI, things were looking very, very... bad.

"Is this legit?" she asked.

"Only time will tell." He turned to the window, but dense fog obscured the view. "Thanks."

"Don't say it."

"What?"

"I should've stayed home," she said.

"Too late. We're too late." When the CT showed spots

everywhere—lungs, liver, and brain—they hadn't suddenly appeared. You were just seeing them for the first time.

"Might as well go get laid."

Now, why'd she have to say that? But she had a point. "Is there any pattern? Age, gender, when they got on board."

"A lot of them are crew, like Agus. Don't they work here like forever?"

"Keep looking." As long as he could keep her here in the office, she wasn't out there in the wild. Getting laid wouldn't be the worst part. She was an adult. It was that the adults on this ship were destroying one another.

Nali rose and stretched. "I have to go pick up Calvin. Day care's shutting down."

"Hold on, don't go yet."

She sighed heavily but stayed put. He summoned Mandy and Luisa to the office.

"Compliments of the chef." He handed each a napkin roll but kept his own tucked in.

After opening hers, Luisa cleaved the air with her blade, wearing a devilish grin. "It's go time now."

"You never know," he said.

Mandy dangled her knife from her fingertips at arm's length. "What am I supposed to do with this?"

Nali plunked hers on the desk. "I'm a lover, not a fighter."

Peter snorted. Apparently all the Palma siblings were confused about their respective identities. Nali was no lover, no matter what she claimed. Felipe had been no kind of a fighter, despite his battle wounds, and Peter's identity was very much under dispute.

His next order of business would be to clear that up. He adjusted the steak knife in his waistband.

15

THANK GOODNESS WETZEL had finally believed him once they connected by phone late that afternoon. She'd made him swear it three times: *I didn't make that video. It's not me.*

It must've been lunchtime in Miami. He sat on the desk next to the computer, eyes fixed on a pile of paper trash in the corner of the office as Wetzel continued her update. "I'll get legal to work on court orders for the search engines, but it's going to be a long process to track down all the sites. That clip is everywhere. It's like a virus—once it starts circulating, it never goes away completely."

The irony stung. "And what about the actual virus? Did they find out what it is?"

"Yes and no," she said. "They think it's a chimera."

"A chimera?"

"Greek mythology. A creature with a lion's head and a goat's body."

So not a mutation of a known virus, but two viruses mashed into one, a most unholy union. "That doesn't sound good."

"Preliminary data suggests it's an enveloped virus plus a nonenveloped virus."

Microbiology 101: Some viruses had an outer membrane made of lipids, while others didn't. Why all viruses didn't have this protective envelope was a matter that the more practical concerns of primary care had pushed aside.

"Are they talking about genetic engineering?" He rubbed an ache in his neck. "Please say no."

"All the intelligence agencies are involved in the investigation, plus the NHS, the CDC, and WHO."

"It all fits."

"What does?"

"Genetic engineering to create—"

"I said they're still investigating."

"Nothing about this sounds natural, especially when someone is propagating it on purpose."

"What are you talking about, Peter?"

She seemed to trust him again, so now it was *his* turn to talk about outlandish things. He told her about Chessa and Gatobi9. "This mastermind, whoever it is, needed the camera feeds to create the fake video."

"Connect the dots. How does this person benefit from creating a video of the ship's doctor discrediting rumors of a virus?"

The reasoning was thin, for sure, but the evidence of something sinister was clear. He knew that much. "If the doctor claims it's all just drugs, everybody lets down their guard. And people are willing to believe it, because nobody wants to hear about another Covid."

"But it's not working," she said. "The real story is out. Peter, you need to focus on your job. You can't control the outside world."

They wouldn't make it back to the outside world, at this rate. "And what is my job now?"

"Take it one day at a time—one hour at a time, if you need to. Eventually you'll get to New York."

And bring absolute ruin upon the city and beyond, if he couldn't neutralize Gatobi9. He took a deep breath. "So, what… I just treat the encephalitis? We don't have much prednisone, and I'm not sure it's going to make a difference in the long run. It's like spitting on a forest fire."

"Peter—"

"Hold on, hold on. Am I supposed to keep people from killing each other?"

"That's security—"

"We're running out of splints. We have four more suture kits. If anything worse happens, well, I'm not a trauma surgeon." The only saving grace was that guns were banned on cruise ships. One infected guy with an assault rifle would be the end of everybody.

Ice clinked in her glass on the other end of the call. "I know you're stressed. Lean on your people. How are they doing?"

Luisa had responded to the most recent group text with a series of curse words directed at nobody in particular. "I'm worried about Luisa. She's trying to play by the rules, but I don't know how long she can handle it."

Wetzel said something about adjusting shift hours, but that wasn't the point. He'd had no reply from Chessa, and Gatobi9 wasn't taking the bait. Everything was slipping through his fingers.

"Can you throw me anything?" he said. "Harrington has his hands full."

"I'll see what I can do."

"Can't you call the military or the government?" His voice

rose in pitch and volume. "There has to be some kind of agency for these situations."

"Peter, we have to see if—"

"So you're completely worthless."

The open line hummed between them.

"Sorry, I did not mean that." Oh, but he did, even if it wasn't fair to her. That nasty part of him that lived in the primitive core of his brain was no longer shackled. The virus had loosened its chains.

"I'm just going to ignore that, Peter. But I won't ignore the predicament that you and everybody else are in. Just give me some time."

He mumbled more apologies and ended the call.

During his first days on the *Paradise*, he'd witnessed an unfiltered Hartley. Now the world was going to see him—and everybody else on this ship—in the same light. Snapping at each other would be the least of their sins.

Regretful things would be said and done that would destroy lives.

Peter was tallying the total milligrams of prednisone in the pharmacy when Kinnard summoned him. How was he supposed to juggle all this? He asked Mandy to keep counting. "And look for any little bottles that might've fallen into the corners."

When he arrived in the boardroom, Kinnard glanced over her mask at the bloodstains on his scrubs. That teenager had needed staples after all—no surprise, given how heavily scalp lacerations tended to bleed. Peter slid into a seat at the opposite end of the massive oval table where Harrington had shown the replay of Rickey Turner's suicide. Arrayed between them was a collection of clear plastic cylinders the size of prescription bottles, each containing a swab with a sponge on the end. The seals over the lids had been broken, but the lids were closed.

The missing drug test kits.

"Take a look." She did *not* seem happy.

The pattern of red lines in the first kit indicated a positive test for meth. The others were also positive, a regular junkie's smorgasbord: cocaine, benzos, oxycodone, fentanyl, and more meth. He recognized the names on most of the kits: Claudia Stevenson, Rickey Turner, Intira Lamai, Raymond Muller.

"Where did you find these?" he said breathlessly. None of these individuals had been tested.

She folded her arms. "Dr. Palma, this is your chance to come clean. Because right now, I'm not sure what to make of you. You insist that the video is fake, but then these positive drug tests show up. And you said these patients were never tested, so these kits shouldn't even exist."

He could no better explain the existence of these tests than he could the Loch Ness Monster. But Kinnard's accusation hung in the air.

His hand drifted to the steak knife tucked in his waist-band. With the table shielding him from view, he shook the knife free from the cloth napkin and grasped the cold, solid haft. He eyed her across the expanse of polished wood. They were alone, and the door was shut. He'd have to close the gap in a hurry, but a single slash across her jugular would end all this questioning.

Heat tingled from his neck to the tips of his fingers. Whoa, there. He slipped the knife back under his waistband and balled his fists on the table, his breath coming in ragged gasps.

He'd almost murdered the first officer. Better to grapple with the purple spider than wrestle with urges like these.

Kinnard slid into the next seat and leaned in close enough for him to notice the little arterioles in the corners of her eyes. "Time to start talking."

"I don't know anything about them. We didn't even perform tests on these patients. I swear."

Kinnard turned toward the fish tank in the corner, and he could tell she was struggling whether to engage as an ally or an adversary. He didn't blame her.

"They were in the captain's apartment," she finally said.

Forster. The man had indeed been compromised. "So what did he have to say about them?"

"His testimony is not reliable." She hadn't yet explained what had happened to the captain after the mutiny. "We're investigating the matter now. But the fact remains that this OPP is coming at a great price. Is it even justified?"

Good question. He was a fool who'd built his house on a foundation of sand. If all this was caused by drugs, he'd led everybody in the wrong direction. All that time wasted, all those lives destroyed. The ice-cold air in the room made it hard to breathe. Peter laid his head on the table and closed his eyes.

Occam's razor suggested one explanation. A virus and drugs, however, made two. Both at the same time? Not impossible, but not likely. He couldn't let go yet. Had to dig deeper.

He raised his head. "It's not drugs. All tests since Scotland have been negative. The labs are sequencing the virus from the samples of people with encephalitis and brain necrosis. That explains their behavior." And his own. The virus rampaging through his frontal lobe was causing headaches, hallucinations, and inappropriate impulses.

He told her about Chessa stealing the drug kits for Gatobi9 and showed her the note.

"Why would she steal the unused kits?"

"It's farfetched, but it fits. They must have doctored the results to make them positive."

"I don't know if that's possible, Peter, but—"

"It's probably not that hard."

She sat back. "Fine, theoretically, let's just say that all this is true. How did they end up in the captain's apartment?"

"Check the security cameras." This theme was getting old—too many cameras, too much scrutiny, not enough trust or peace.

"We already have. The key card swipes too. There's nothing out of the ordinary, just routine housekeeping activity. No dining servers."

"No overnight guests?"

"Excuse me?"

He smirked. "Captain of the ship with hair like that? I'd assume he would have plenty of opportunities. Especially now, with nothing holding him back."

She shook her head vigorously. "Nothing like that."

Peter had never romantically pursued a nurse, at least not while they were working at the same place. That kind of move seemed stereotypical, an abuse of power. But Mandy? Damn, that ass, those hips—it was getting hard to resist. He'd have to clean up his cabin first though.

Kinnard was rapping her fingers on the table. "You still with me?"

He blinked. "What? Yes." Back to business.

"I want you to start doing telemedicine consultations," she said. "We need to limit unnecessary clinic visits, right? We'll provide webcams that plug right into the TVs in the cabins. Passengers can request appointments on the intranet."

On paper it sounded like a good idea, the next logical step. But telemedicine would only go so far, making it easier for him and the nurses to witness the depravity of humankind without offering any solutions.

16

An urgent knocking awakened Peter while it was still dark outside. His eleventh day on the ship. He squinted through the peephole.

Of course it wasn't Mandy with freshly washed hair, smelling divine from a hot shower. He opened the door.

Yuli's eyes were wide and urgent above his mask. "Come quickly, Doctor."

Peter stepped into the hall and promptly tripped over a tray of half-eaten food. Mandatory room service was in full swing.

Yuli maneuvered around his cart of toiletries then down I-95. "This way."

Peter tried to shake off the grogginess that enshrouded him like a lead blanket. "What happened?"

"They found a woman," Yuli called out over his shoulder.

Damn, the little guy sure moved fast.

It better not be Chessa. She still hadn't responded to the group text, most certainly trying to lie low. Gatobi9 hadn't responded either but had to be monitoring the messages.

They turned off I-95 at midships into a dense warren of narrow corridors with no carpet or paneling, only endless gray linoleum lit unevenly by plain bulbs in wire cages. A low-pitched droning swelled and subsided in a regular rhythm, seemingly from all directions, punctuated by sharp, metallic bangs that echoed along the halls at random intervals. A dark, ancient place where bad things happened.

A series of turns carried them deeper into the crew quarters than seemed logically possible. Peter had long since lost track of their location; the geometry didn't make sense here. This could've been anywhere in the world. They eventually arrived at an unmarked steel door guarded by a staff member pinching her nose over her mask. She nodded and shambled off.

The tiny room had no window. A rancid odor filtered through Peter's mask, faint but pervasive. Dry heaves hit him hard, forcing him to steady himself with one hand on a wall slick with cold moisture. The place needed ventilation.

He groped for a light switch. Yuli pressed something on the wall, but nothing happened. The ceiling light must be dead.

When the nausea passed, he crouched next to a shadowy form on the floor covered with bed sheets. Next to it lay a small, mottled lump. He reached back and nudged the door wider. Faint light from the hallway spilled across the little lump, a floral fanny pack he'd seen before. His stomach lurched again, and he peeled back the sheets from the larger mass.

Calvin's mother, Amanda Burchins, naked. Body number four.

———————

The security guard who arrived was the same one who'd brought in Sharma. Wiry and agitated, Mauricio's eyes darted between Peter and Burchins' body. The woman's face was frozen in a delicate smile, and there were mottled bruises on her thighs, ligature marks around her wrists.

"This is bullshit," Mauricio muttered, his hand brushing the wad of blue gloves sprouting from his back pocket. "I mean, give me a break. I ain't CSI, or FBI, or whatnot."

Felipe had posted similar sentiments on social media. As a welder, he hadn't been trained to pick up that M4 carbine or drag mangled corpses out of a burning bunker. No big leap to surmise that Mauricio's irritation masked an accumulation of mental wounds that would evolve into PTSD. Hell, when all this ended, half the ship would need therapy.

"Who found her?" Mauricio asked.

Peter pulled the sheets over Burchins and gave Yuli a questioning look. A ship this size, you could live on it for months and explore every crook and cranny without discovering all the places where bodies could be hidden.

Yuli glanced away. "A girl ran to me and said they found…"

"She's been missing for more than a week," said Peter.

Until now, he had harbored a flicker of hope that she would turn up, ready to reclaim her son. Perhaps a dissociative fugue had drawn her away, but now she was back and so sorry—oh, and did Calvin want to get some ice cream? Now a different pathway for Calvin shifted from possibility to reality. Orphaned and forsaken in a world already harsh for those with disabilities.

"Fuck," Mauricio said. "Say, uh, shouldn't we be wearing hazmats? You think the mask is enough?"

"We make do with what we have," Peter said.

Platitudes and banalities—little comfort in a time like this. Even as they attempted to play catch-up with hygiene, sanitation, and isolation measures, they were stuck in a vicious cycle. The victims infected with this chimeric virus couldn't think straight and weren't keen on complying with the Outbreak Prevention Plan.

Mauricio did a passable job for not being CSI, FBI, or whatnot. He uncovered the body, took photos, and covered her again. He snapped on a pair of gloves and examined the floral fanny pack. Inside was her phone, which he pocketed as evidence, a packet of tissues, and one of those fidget spinner toys.

Peter pointed to the tri-lobed fidget spinner. "You mind if I take that? Her son would like it back, I'm sure." He imagined Calvin's mother handing it to him when he got agitated, and Calvin working the spinner with his good hand.

Mauricio hesitated.

"Do you really think it's evidence?"

Mauricio shrugged and handed the toy over. "Poor kid. So what's your take?"

"I'm not a pathologist," Peter said. "But I think she's been dead at least a day."

"Was she murdered?" Yuli's face was solemn.

"That's my assumption. Would you know anything about... Well, one of the nurses said she heard some passengers had a huge orgy."

Yuli's face tightened into an uneasy frown. "I don't know. They talk about all these kinds of things, but I don't pay attention."

"It's all talk." Mauricio opened and closed his hand like a sock puppet.

From a physical standpoint, the two of them couldn't have been more different: Yuli, small and bland enough to blend in anywhere, and Mauricio, taut and whiplike.

Peter muttered something about giving Calvin's mother a burial at sea, which he regretted immediately. But they had to put her somewhere. The refrigerated drawers in the morgue could only accommodate one body each. After a series of phone calls with Kinnard and one of the engineering officers, the executive chef agreed to relinquish a somewhat isolated cooling unit behind the pool bar, used for overstock.

They wrestled her into the body bag and zipped it up. The staff was already carting food away for immediate preparation when they arrived at the cooler with the body. The brave people of the *Paradise* would be feasting in their cabins tonight on salmon and pasta salad.

Peter dialed the cooler down to 36 degrees Fahrenheit, matching the morgue settings, and sealed the door with duct tape that Yuli retrieved. For good measure, they dragged a towel cabinet in front of the door and tipped a table sideways against it.

Peter turned to Yuli. "You wouldn't happen to know a server named Chessa?"

"Sorry, Doctor." The phone in Yuli's pocket chirped again with the sound of crickets.

Peter smiled. That soothing symphony of trills was one of his favorite memories of nights spent tucked into the RV with Elena, a sound that must have filled the most ancient nights, lulling his ancestors to sleep under their animal skin blankets.

Back in the clinic, Peter fist-bumped Calvin but said nothing about his mom. Eventually he would perceive the absence of her love. Whatever grieving process was in store for him, there was little point in accelerating it.

But the news cast a pall over the nurses and Nali.

"At least we know. That's something." Nali dabbed tears from her eyes in the office. "What's going to happen to him when we get to New York?"

Peter rested a hand on her shoulder. "We'll deal with it."

She looked at the nurses, but neither of them offered answers. "I'm gonna take him to get a soda." And she walked out of the office.

"Was it murder?" Mandy asked quietly.

The marks on Mrs. Burchins' body told him all he wanted to know. Whether she was a victim or a willing participant in twisted perversion mattered little. "I'm not sure. The virus made her take the first step away from her son. And now she's dead, and he's…" He dropped his head and closed his eyes.

"Maybe Rickey Turner's mother can adopt him," Luisa said flatly.

Mandy tittered.

"Sorry, that wasn't funny," Luisa muttered. "Can't believe I said that. It's just, I've had it up to—" She quickstepped out of the office, her foam clogs squeaking on the tile.

"Hey, are you serious?" Mandy called after her and glanced at Peter. "Unbelievable!"

He raised an eyebrow. "What?"

"I was afraid of this. She's been talking about quitting."

"We're in the middle of nowhere." Last time Peter had looked, the little triangle on the map was south of Newfoundland off Canada's Atlantic coast, which put them past the midpoint, but it still felt like nowhere. The panic that had sent Luisa fleeing—yeah, he could definitely relate. But her sense of duty would win over. That's who Luisa was. "She'll be back. Don't worry."

At some point, a tiny worm of acceptance had burrowed

into his conscience. Things were going to get even tougher—
no way around it—so he might as well stop feeling sorry for
himself. He had to stop walking back into the tunnel, gazing
at an idealized version of earlier days that had never existed.
Moving forward was the only way out, even if that meant
crawling through the darkness.

The next patient was a forty-nine-year-old man from
Oregon, rocking back and forth on the exam table. He
searched Peter's face with sea-green eyes. "Tell me straight up.
What the hell are we doing? They're not gonna let us get to
New York. No way."

Oh, boy. "Who's they?"

"Our president won't allow that to happen. I didn't vote
for him, but he's one tough you-know-what. He'll protect
that city." With a long whistle, the man traced a shallow arc
through the air ending in an explosion.

The ship was a problem, and there were some who called
for the ultimate solution. Peter had seen the online rumors and
dismissed them as hogwash, but after Covid, the authorities
would consider all options.

"How can I help you?"

"I really need something for my back."

"What happened?"

"I dropped my shades. I reached down for them like
this." He demonstrated with a tentative bending and twisting
motion. "All of sudden this sharp pain came on—bam. Out
of the blue."

"You've never had anything like this before?"

"They said I have a slipped disc, L2 or L3. It flares up once
in a while, but this time it's really bad."

Peter tapped all the way down the man's spine. No big
reaction there. He pressed on the muscles alongside the spine,

eliciting a wince when he got to the lower right side. He laid the man back on the exam table. When Peter lifted the right leg about forty-five degrees, the man screwed up his face.

"How far does the pain go down?"

"All the way," he said, pointing to his calf.

"Looks like that disc is acting up again. You also have muscle strain and some spasm."

"So now what?"

Peter helped him back up and recommended ibuprofen.

The man shook his head vigorously. "Oh no, I can't take anti-inflammatories. They tear up my stomach."

Of course. He could have seen it a mile way. "Try some Tylenol, and you can borrow a heating pad."

"Those don't work for me."

"Then a muscle relaxant might help."

"I've tried those."

Echoes of Felipe. It was a familiar script. "So what does work?"

"If we're all gonna die anyway, can't I just get a little relief? My primary back home gives me oxycodone." He rubbed his lower back gingerly.

"I'm sorry, we can't give narcotics here."

"You can't, or you won't?"

Peter tried to keep the irritation out of his voice. "We don't have them. I recommend the anti-inflammatories. I can give you some antacids to protect your stomach."

"I know my body. The only thing that works is oxy."

Cold hostility unfurled from the deepest recesses of Peter's brain, way out of proportion to the situation. "This isn't a pill mill."

The man lowered his chin. "I'm not some drug-seeker, okay? I'm in real pain."

"You think we just hand them out, even if we stocked them?" His voice was rising despite his best efforts.

"What if your own mother was suffering like this? What kind of treatment would you want her to get?"

This guy was smooth, using that old line. Peter would've used it himself if necessary. "Like I said, we don't stock narcotics. I know you're in pain. I can't promise complete relief, but I'll work with you. Hopefully it'll be better than nothing."

The man went silent, nodding at the floor as he contemplated his options. "You know what? I'm not going to say fuck you, you and everybody else on this ship, even though that's the first thing that comes to mind."

Peter asked Mandy to inject thirty milligrams of ketorolac into the patient's glute, which brought some relief within minutes. Armed with a box of antacids and a handout on lumbar stretches, the man limped out with a breezy salute.

Peter retreated to the office and slumped into a chair.

Mandy followed him in and plunked down beside him, folding her hands in her lap beneath her precious bottle of sanitizer. "You okay?"

"I went overboard on that one. I've, uh... I've had some bad experiences with narcotics." That didn't sound right. "With my brother."

"I see."

"How're you holding up?"

She tapped the handle of the steak knife protruding from her waistband. "Ready to rock."

He chuckled and clicked on the virtual waiting room for the telemedicine appointments. "Funny—when I gave that thing to you, you held it out like it was a dead rat."

She laughed. "Weird times, I guess." Her eyes fell. "I'm worried about Luisa though."

Without Luisa, there were fewer hands on deck to handle the escalating workload. His pulse climbed as the system loaded fifteen patients already waiting in the queue, each listed with their age, reason for visit, and a little icon that looked like the outline of a camera. It also included each patient's cabin number and country of origin.

The first patient had a low-grade fever, headache, and cough. The virus, almost certainly. Peter prescribed ibuprofen and the last of the prednisone. A crew member would pick up the meds and hand them off to the patient's cabin steward, who would deliver them directly to the cabin—first-class service in the name of social distancing. Wetzel and her team had done well setting this up a few years ago as the world battled with Covid.

The videoconferencing platform, however, was glitchy as hell. At one point, he accidentally popped open two patients simultaneously. On the left, a sharply dressed older man paced as if waiting for his wife to get dressed for a formal dinner; on the right, a teenager with baggy eyes cradled her chin in her hands. Peter managed to bump the teen back into the queue before the gentleman ever noticed.

A look into his patients' cabins put class inequality on full display. The living quarters of the chief purser dwarfed the cabin with four crew members in bunk beds. One thing he was sure of: Once somebody became infected, everyone in their cabin would contract the virus too, no matter their privileges or the lack thereof. Their only hope was to mask 24/7, wash their hands religiously, and make use of every last drop of hand sanitizer.

Once he'd cleared the initial queue, Mandy brought him iced tea and a soft pretzel.

He nodded a thanks and took a sip of tea, working out a

crick in his neck with this free hand. "Anybody waiting out there now?"

"Nope, I just checked." Her warm touch on his shoulder soothed and electrified him at the same time. How was that possible? Mandy, Mandy, Mandy—she almost made this chaos worth enduring.

The next telemedicine patient's ills were emotional, not physical, but he didn't know who else to call. The young man pounded the desk. "She said she only married me because she thought I'd be more like my brother. Why would she say something like that?"

Physical wounds were one thing, but the lawless behavior unleashed by this virus could also shatter lives. The encounters drifted deeper into bizarre territory. A saxophonist in the jazz band insisted that the mother of "that one in the wheelchair" had been killed by a roving band of monkeys. "I can hear them chittering. They're right outside." He cocked his head toward the door of his cabin. "You probably can't hear them, but I can. Those beasts are coming for me now. You think they can smell me? I've taken three showers today…"

On and on it went. Their theories about the virus echoed those floating around the internet. The virus had escaped from a capsule that NASA retrieved from a giant asteroid, or it had emerged when a patch of ancient Siberian permafrost melted last year. Truth be told, none of them were completely out-landish explanations.

"Ethnic cleansing," said a fifty-three-year-old man with impossibly black eyebrows. "Total erasure."

Peter was about to ask which group was being targeted when he noticed a woman sitting on the floor in the back-ground. She was caught in the throes of intense pain or pleasure, judging by the way she was moaning in rhythm with her heaving shoulders.

"Is she okay?"

The patient swiveled the webcam away from her. "Ah, never mind her. She's just getting the kinks out."

After powering through nineteen patients—four more had signed up after they started—Peter scrolled back through the queue. He clicked on the age column and sorted it in ascending order. The youngest patient was fourteen and the oldest eighty-three. He sorted again by cabin number.

"Huh, that's interesting."

Mandy leaned over his shoulder, her hair brushing against his ear. "What?"

It was hard to focus with her this close. He highlighted three consecutive rows. "Their cabins are all next to each other."

"That's how it spreads, right? People in close quarters."

It was more than that. There was another cluster of four cabins. "But do they actually come in close contact? Maybe passing each other in the hallways..."

"To me, the movie theater or the dining rooms should be the worst," Mandy said. "That's where they spend the most time packed together."

He tapped the calendar icon, widened the date criteria to the past thirty days, and refreshed the view. Then he sorted once more by cabin number. There it was again: more clusters but even larger—groups of eleven, eight, and nine.

The right-hand column listed the reason for each visit—headache, cough, confusion. He opened the charts for those patients. The presumptive diagnoses given by him or Hartley, depending on the date, included nonspecific upper respiratory tract illness, delirium, mental status changes, and encephalitis.

All were variations on the same theme, with the encephalitis label appearing only after MRI results of the first victims had come back from Scotland.

The hairs on his arms stood on end. The clusters included Intira Lamai, Claudia Stevenson, and Rickey Turner. The Muller family was in room 9183.

He jotted the room numbers down on an index card. There was definitely a pattern underneath all this data. Now it was a matter of puzzling out what it meant.

17

MORNING TRAFFIC WAS sparse on I-95, mostly masked and gloved crew members pushing carts of covered breakfast plates. There were no entertainers or shopkeepers in sight. A dozen lights flickered, casting dancing shadows across the murky tile.

For the first time in days, the waiting area was empty. Peter set a cardboard holder of steaming coffees and a bag of pastries on the counter, and Mandy pounced. She had stayed the night with Calvin.

"We're over the hump." Mandy brandished a sausage kolache, its savory scent spreading through the little office. "The OPP is working."

Or it was only an artifact of converting visits to telemedicine. Peter scanned the clinic for lurking horrors, but the only atypical occupant was Calvin, still snoring on the cot in one of the exam rooms.

"It was like the creepiest reality show ever, don't you think?" Peter asked. "This musician was hallucinating about monkeys. And another woman was getting herself off. They're all just holed up in there."

Mandy, having finished her kolache, began surveying the donut holes. "Yeah, remember how everybody stayed home during Covid? That put a lot of stress on relationships."

"If a couple barely tolerated each other when they were spending the whole workday apart, lock them up together a few months..."

She nodded, mouth full.

That's what they had here. The passengers were all stuck in their cabins. "If someone's infected and the virus destroys their impulse control? Not good at all."

"Ideally, everyone needs to be in solitary confinement."

"And that's impossible." He set down his coffee. "Speaking of which, where's Luisa?"

"You had to ask."

"Shall we go knock on her door?"

They stared at each other, motionless.

"I'll do it," she said. "You stay here."

She folded a few donut holes into her napkin and headed out. Taking advantage of the quiet, he drained his coffee and logged into the system. He pulled up the AI panel.

Peter: *How many patients have encephalitis symptoms?*

AI: *Please clarify the time frame.*

Peter: *Past 30 days.*

AI: *Using data drawn only from the EHR, I estimate 215 individuals have displayed signs and symptoms that could be consistent with encephalitis. The margin of error is approximately 8 percent. Keep in mind that I cannot assess individuals whose information is not included in the EHR. Therefore, actual figures may be higher.*

Peter: *Cross-check against security cameras.*

AI: *I'm sorry, I don't have access to footage from security cameras.*

Peter: *Try their social media accounts.*

AI: *I'm sorry, I'm not permitted to link information from the EHR to outside data.*

Peter: *Cross-reference from the ship's manifest.*

AI: *I'm sorry, I don't have permission to access the manifest.*

What a ridiculous game of cat-and-mouse. Surely the AI had more oomph than this. Nali had worked it like clay.

Peter: *Map out the temporal and spatial patterns.*

AI: *I'm sorry, I don't have access to geospatial data related to your inquiry, but here's a temporal representation.*

The AI produced a litany of graphs depicting the known cases, parsed out among passengers, crew, staff, and officers. The avalanche of data was suffocating. Was there a pattern here, or was this just random noise? Working through it would require time and clarity of mind, but those were in short supply.

When Chessa had first approached him at the buffet, he'd written her off as a skittish, overworked server. Her confession about the text messages and video cameras, however, had been impossible to ignore. Gatobi9 was driving things somehow. The deepfake video and recovered drug tests made it clear—something was going on here that was important to hide.

Finding Gatobi9 was the key.

He spun around and gazed out the porthole. Nothing but ocean. Was he just chasing the wind? There had to be a logical pattern in the data, but he wasn't seeing it. By this point, he should've known that nobody on this ship could be trusted 100 percent, himself included.

Mandy returned with an update. "Luisa's calling in sick."

When it rained, it poured.

"Did you hear me?"

He was barely keeping his own bizarre urges at bay,

swinging his torch at the beasts encircling him in the darkness. With Hartley long gone, they couldn't afford to lose Luisa.

"Do you think she has it?" he asked.

"I don't want to think about it."

There was a hardness in Mandy's face that he hadn't seen before, as if she were absorbing energy from her absent colleague. Mandy alone seemed to remain healthy, peppy, and sane. If she got sick now—perish the thought.

———

An unidentified male voice crackled over the speakers: "Oscar, Oscar, Oscar."

Then Kinnard jumped on. "Ladies and gentlemen, this is your first officer speaking. We are initiating a search-and-rescue operation for a passenger we have reason to believe has gone overboard. Please be reminded that the Outbreak Prevention Protocol is still in place. Please stay calm and remain in your current location. Avoid common areas. Your cooperation is critical. We prioritize safety and are working diligently to address the situation. Further updates will be provided. Thank you for your understanding and cooperation."

Peter texted Nali. *You ok?*

He stared at his phone, willing her to reply. What were the odds that Nali was the one? Roughly one in three thousand. Yet he imagined long ropes and orange lifesaver rings flung from the balcony, searchlights sweeping over the waves and missing her by inches. Their old neighborhood didn't have a public pool, although she might've mentioned taking swimming lessons in high school. Or maybe it was woodworking. He'd been too busy to notice.

He stood up and squinted out the window. The sea and

sky blurred into an indistinguishable haze. Finding anybody out there would be impossible. He had to step back from the daylight spearing his eyeballs. "What happens now?"

"They'll search," Mandy said. "We have warming blankets."

"I guess it's cold out there even though it's summer?"

"The water, for sure. It'll probably get down to forty tonight, this far north."

The ship's momentum shifted subtly under Peter's feet. "We're already slowing down."

"Silly goose—they started that way before the announcement. It's all about the controlled release of messages."

Kinnard came on again. "The missing passenger's name is Samuel Okafor. Please take the time to check the ship's intranet home page and view his photo. If you've seen Mr. Okafor within the last twenty-four hours, please notify any crew member or officer. O-K-A-F-O-R."

A long sigh of relief. It wasn't her. He looked up the pic of the missing man—a familiar face. The guy was the partner of somebody who'd come in delirious and angry.

Rumors were already sprouting on the intranet and social media, conflicting eyewitness accounts. The scuttlebutt from one group was that Okafor had leaped overboard after a series of devastating rounds at the slot machines. Peter doubted that. The casino was supposed to be closed. But who knew?

The assistant hotel director was the first victim of collateral damage. He came in pressing a thick white towel against his wrist. "I thought it would stop bleeding, but as you can see, it hasn't." He peeled back the bloodied towel to reveal a short gash two inches below his wrist.

"Ooh, Salim, what on earth?" Mandy pulled open the cabinet. "Let me get some supplies."

Peter applied pressure to the laceration with a wad of

gauze. As the bleeding slowed, he examined the extent of the damage until more blood welled up from the bottom of the wound. Back to the gauze, then inspect again.

"It's mayhem out there." Salim looked past Peter's shoulder. "As soon as she made that announcement, it was like OPP went out the door."

It was happening. Peter swallowed hard. "Where were you…"

"This was from a champagne glass, I think. I was trying to—" Salim raised his other arm, demonstrating how he defended himself against blows.

Mandy set up a suture kit on a stainless steel table and rolled it close. She leaned over and spoke softly into Peter's ear. "This is the last one."

Of course it was. He glanced at the red biowaste bag in the corner, bulging with soiled surgical drapes and bloody gauze pads. The sharps container was filled too, jammed with used scalpels and needles.

He irrigated Salim's wound with sterile saline and cleansed the surrounding skin with a Betadine swab. He filled the syringe with lidocaine. "You got lucky. An inch to the left and it would've sliced open your radial artery."

"Is that just something you doctors always say? An inch to the left." He winced as Peter injected the anesthetic. "Kinnard should've known. Even in the best of times, they hate it when the ship stops."

No going back now. Lifting the edges of the gash with forceps, Peter pierced the skin with a curved needle attached to the 5-0 nylon. In and out one edge, across the wound, up from the bottom, and out the other side. Tie the knot and snip the excess suture. The first stitch looked good.

The patient's arm twitched. "Wait, you're the one who talked with Kinnard. About the captain."

Peter focused on his suturing.

"Salim, please try to hold still for the doctor," Mandy said.

"That was something else," Salim said. "A lot of the officers were tied to Forster. His fate affects their careers."

Another knot, snip the excess. "I guess I made some more enemies."

Salim clucked his tongue. "I signed that paper too. I knew there was something wrong with him. What is it you called it, elephantitis? Wasn't there a movie about that?"

Peter outlined the symptoms of encephalitis and how a virus could create the initial insult. "Unfortunately, the effects on the brain persist beyond the infectious period."

"Seriously?"

Even though Hartley had stopped coughing well before her MRI, her frontal lobe was pudding.

"You have to get your staff to protect themselves. Masks and hand sanitizer."

Salim groaned. "Honest truth? After the pandemic, we're all done with that stuff."

The edges of the wound were now neatly aligned by six sutures. Peter rolled backward on his stool. "How long will the search take?"

Salim studied Peter's handiwork. "Who knows? Sometimes a few hours, sometimes a whole day. Depends on the weather, the circumstances. It's different each time."

Once Mandy escorted Salim out, the realization hit Peter harder than Muller's haymaker: *Man overboard* meant the ship had stopped, maybe even backtracked. And that meant a delay in reaching New York. He'd been counting the minutes till the end of the line, when the ship would finally disgorge its charges into a real health care system. But with dwindling supplies, a corpse—the first of many—stored in a food-service cooler, and an actual epidemic on his hands, a positive outcome seemed unlikely.

Because New York City wasn't just the relief valve for Peter. It was also the fuse to a bomb. Lit by their arrival, this bomb could destroy the country. The OPP was too little, too late.

Silly of him to board this vessel dreaming of providing straightforward medical care to happy, grateful vacationers. That notion had burned away like a morning fog. It had been a selfish indulgence anyway. That wasn't how life worked, because complications weren't the exception; they were the rule.

He swiveled his chair to the window, searching the inscrutable ocean. The waves writhed and churned, beholden to meteorologic forces beyond his reckoning, but the overall view always stayed the same. What lay behind the reflex to always look out there? The seascape offered no solutions for the problems in here.

"This chimera has never been documented in the wild," Wetzel said over speakerphone. Her voice sounded tinny in Kinnard's windowless office. "Phylogenetic network analyses are pending but so far it looks like Nipah virus plus a nonenveloped virus."

Kinnard twisted the octagonal speaker on her desk, as if to fine-tune Wetzel's meaning. "I don't like the sound of that."

Ditto times a hundred. The office lurched as the ship plowed over a crest. How could the officers up here get anything done?

"We're looking at a brand-new virus," Wetzel said. "It's not just a mutation or a rare strain."

"Nipah virus plus a nonenveloped…" said Peter, sitting opposite Kinnard. "I'm afraid to ask." Strange how the calmness in his voice hid the queasiness in his belly. "Is it a bioweapon?"

Silence.

Kinnard met Peter's eyes. "Is this a bioweapon?"

"They can't rule it out," Wetzel finally said. "Manipulation is the assumption here, given the specific combination of those viral genomes. The security agencies are running the scenarios."

Kinnard cocked her head to the side. "China?"

A knee-jerk reaction after Covid, but not unreasonable.

"Three confirmed and nine probable cases have been identified in cities where the ship has docked in the past four weeks. Many of them have been detained in jail."

Peter winced. They were just starting to peel the layers off this onion. "So did it start here on the ship, or did we pick it up from one of the ports?"

"We don't know," Wetzel said.

Either way, they must've made the deepfake to draw attention away from the ship. The casual remark by the man with back pain about a preemptive military strike rang in Peter's head. How far would the president go? Would he press the red button? They'd all go up in smoke, only to be memorialized in a Wikipedia entry.

Kinnard scowled and drummed her fingers on the desk.

"We scheduled a video conference for nine a.m. with Athens, Barcelona, and Lisbon to discuss cases," said Wetzel. "Scotland will be there also. Try to join if you can. I'll send you the link."

He pounded the desk. "Hold on, a video conference?

What am I supposed to do now to keep everything together?"
Maybe it was too late. Gatobi9 was going to win.

"I'm not sure how much I can say."

"Say it."

"The authorities are working on an experimental treatment."

"I'm talking about right here, right now." He blew out his cheeks and glared at Kinnard. "Harrington should have been here. He's the muscle, the enforcer."

Kinnard's thin lips twitched. "He was too busy to come."

Shit.

The meeting concluded, but Peter felt himself at loose ends. New York seemed so far away. Was there any light at the end of this tunnel? Maybe that's what he needed, some fresh air and light.

He drifted through the corridors to the upper deck to watch the rescue effort. Passengers gathered at the railing, some pointing and shouting, others watching calmly. He followed their lines of sight to a bright orange boat darting across the ocean in cryptic patterns. Someone nearby called it a MOB boat—Man Overboard Boat. So women were out of luck?

He grimaced. The ocean was far too large for a search like this.

His phone buzzed in his pocket.
Clinic 911.

Mandy appeared frozen at the computer when Peter skidded into the clinic office, her face ashen. Never had he seen her so rattled, not even when Sharma crashed. It would be so easy to cop a feel right now.

Ugh, he was losing all self-control.

He hustled around the desk to see what was on the screen. The telemedicine window showed a view of a mid-tier passenger cabin. A female crew member lay spread eagle on the bed, her wrists and ankles tied to the corners. She was clothed in trousers, white shirt, and vest. Her eyes bulged above a makeshift gag as she strained against her bonds.

"What's happening?" Peter rasped.

"He said he's coming back." Mandy's voice was low and tense. "Watch."

Sure enough, the screen abruptly filled with a masked face. "Can you see this?" the man asked them and backed up just a bit to display a straight-edge razor, twisting and turning it for their appreciation. Held so close to the webcam, details were blurry but the message was clear.

Peter's stomach dropped.

Mandy groaned. "No, no, no."

The man then held up a sheet of paper and sliced it in half with the razor. Clean and sharp. His eyebrows shot up toward the camera—oh yes, he most certainly had Peter's attention. But he turned his back to his audience and took a knee beside his hostage. The woman bucked and writhed. He hovered the razor above her neck.

Mandy leaped from her chair and stumbled back.

"Stop!" Peter bellowed. "Stop now!"

The man looked slowly, almost casually, over his shoulder to the camera. "I'll do it. I swear I'll slice her fucking neck open."

"Call security," Peter whispered to Mandy without moving his head. He had to stay composed. Had to appear respectful. "What do you want, sir?"

The man swaggered back to the camera. "Keep the ship moving, or I'll kill her."

"Okay, keep it moving. To where?"

"Stop the search. Go on to New York."

"I get it. Is that it? Keep moving?" He itched to click over to the EHR and check if an occupant from that room had been in clinic, but he couldn't risk losing the connection by accident. He imagined the headline: *Clumsy Doctor Clicks Wrong Button, Hostage Murdered.*

"I need to get off this ship." The man tore off his surgical mask, revealing a beard encrusted with blood and snot. "We all do. It's killing us. You're the doctor?"

"I am."

"You know this better than anybody. No delay is worth saving that moron that went overboard." He waved the razor toward the window. "We're eating each other alive here, don't you get it?"

He got it, all right. The chimeric virus had indeed laid bare the worst parts of humanity. It revealed who we all could be, if not for the continually firing neurons suppressing our inner beasts. Even now, with the life of this woman hanging in the balance, he wanted Mandy to come back so he could bend her over the desk, slide her pants down, and do bad things to her. With her. Whatever.

Peter's breath came in ragged heaves, and he grabbed fistfuls of his hair.

"You okay?" Mandy asked from behind him.

"Yes. No!" He wanted—needed—to take her. Right now. He'd been battling these thoughts for too long. He swiveled around. God, she looked *ripe.*

"Peter?" She backed away with eyes wide. "What are—"

The clomp of boots in the outer office snapped him back.

The door burst open, and Harrington charged in, nostrils flaring. "What's going on?"

Mandy cautiously sidestepped around Peter and showed Harrington the computer screen. "He's holding her hostage."

The man was shouting at the camera. "New York! New York!"

"What room is he in?" Harrington demanded.

"Don't go barging in there," she said. "He'll kill her."

Harrington shifted sideways, out of view of the camera, and lowered his voice to a hiss. "We have the master key. Tell me the room number."

Hands low in his lap, Peter wrote the room number on an index card and slipped it to him.

"I'll text you." Harrington rushed out.

"I don't think he's the negotiating type." Peter avoided eye contact with Mandy.

"The guy, or Mr. Harrington?"

The guy in the room had been watching with twitchy eyes. "Don't think I won't do it."

"Sir, I feel you," Peter said, heart thudding in his chest. In the movies, the negotiator always tried to establish a personal connection with the hostage-taker. "I get it. What's your name?"

The woman on the bed started wriggling again when the man set the razor down and rubbed his face. "The things I've seen. I won't allow myself to become one of those animals."

Peter himself had been seconds away from slashing Kinnard's neck with a steak knife. And just now, with Mandy… "Then let her go. Don't hurt her. Don't give in."

"He's infected." Mandy whispered.

"Infected and not thinking straight," Peter said, "or desperate to avoid infection. Either way's bad."

His phone buzzed. He rubbed the back of his neck to steal a glance. It was Harrington. *here. what is he doing.*

He shoved the phone into Mandy's hand and maintained eye contact with the guy. He could hear Mandy tapping out a reply.

"Let me get in contact with the captain, and I'll ask him to keep heading to New York," Peter said. "Just give me some time."

"Tick-tock. Her blood is on your hands." The guy slid back over to the bed and lifted the razor.

A muffled thud in the cabin issued from off camera. The guy's head whipped around, and he leaped up with a grunt. Someone bellowed incoherently, and the screen went dark.

"No!" Peter slammed his palms on the desk.

Mandy thrust a bag of supplies at him. "Go, Peter! Just go!"

―――――――――

Peter bullied his way through the rubberneckers clotted around room 2498 and stepped over the upended plates and utensils near the door. The abductor lay moaning on the carpet between the bed and closet.

"Switch." Harrington was hunched over the bed, holding pressure on the victim's neck.

Her eyelids fluttered, and her breath came in shallow rasps. Her wrists and ankles were still tied down. Jesus.

Peter emptied his supply bag onto the blood-striped bed, wadded up a large gauze pad, and pressed it over Harrington's gloved hands. "I got it."

Harrington slipped out from underneath, and Peter pressed down hard. The gauze reddened under his bare hands in seconds. He peered cautiously under one edge. A squirt of blood dotted his scrubs. A truckload of bandages wouldn't save her. If it was her arm or leg, he could've stanched the flow with a tourniquet. What he needed was a hemostat, an operating room, and a decade of vascular surgery experience. He grabbed more gauze and reapplied pressure.

Harrington was now straddling the man, and he cinched him up with black zip ties, and went about the business of securing a crime scene. He slammed the door shut and radioed for backup. He dangled the bloodied straight-edge razor from gloved fingers. "This thing's just under the legal limit."

Maintaining pressure on her neck wound with one hand, Peter fumbled for her bonds with the other. The black webbing around her wrists appeared to have been yanked from a life vest, and her ankles were hitched to the legs of the bed with clothesline.

Harrington finished the job of untying her. He shucked off his gloves and pulled out his phone. "Mandy texted this guy was at the desk, but when I unlocked the door he was waiting for me. I barely got my stun gun out to fry the sonofabitch."

All the gauze was saturated. Peter looked around for a suitable substitute. Apparently this murderer had a soft spot for the towel animals the cabin stewards created, because a terrycloth swan sat in tranquil repose on the nightstand. He shook it out and pressed it against her wound, even as the arterial pulsations diminished in vigor and tempo. Her eyelids were half open, and the tip of her tongue protruded through cracked lips. He flattened the fold of her vest that obscured her name tag: *Sunila Tharanga, Sri Lanka*. She couldn't have been more than twenty-two. She deserved even Peter's most futile gesture. Dignity, if there was any left to be salvaged, would keep his hand on her wound until her last heartbeat.

He sat on the edge of the bed, one hand on her neck, the other smoothing her hair back from her forehead. He'd never met this woman before, but he leaned in and whispered, "I'm sorry. I love you." It made no sense—she had nothing in common with him, nothing in common with Felipe—but he kept repeating it. "I'm sorry. I love you."

The man on the floor grunted and coughed. "Just kill me."

Harrington climbed from the love seat and nudged him with his boot. "I guarantee you this, if we were on a deserted island, I'd take you out right now."

"Do it." The man lifted his head from the carpet and said to Peter, "You won't tell, right? It's about mercy."

"Shut up," Harrington said.

"Don't let me become one of them. Please."

Every nook and cranny of the cabin bore witness to the OPP. The wastebasket overflowed with paper plates and wadded tissues. Bottles of hand sanitizer lay about. The guy had even sealed off the ventilation grate in the ceiling with duct tape.

"Why'd you close off the duct?" Peter demanded, his hand still on Sunila's neck.

But the guy had already gone back to moaning and muttering. Finally he said, "You're all screwed."

Maybe the duct thing wasn't so outrageous after all. Maybe this guy was a genius.

18

As Peter slogged back down to the clinic, Kinnard announced over the PA system the end of the search for the man overboard, considering the "local conditions, uncertainty of the circumstances, and rapidly diminishing chances of a successful operation, weighed against other factors."

Other factors.

Like the fact that Sunila had bled out like a sacrificial lamb, slain for the sins of many, yet there wasn't enough blood in the entire world to appease the demons that had been released. Well, if it hastened their arrival in New York, maybe her death would count for something in the end. For now, her body was enshrined next to Calvin's mom at 36 degrees in the cooler.

Whatever hope had bloomed after resuming their journey, it was quashed by the second half of Kinnard's announcement—an unprecedented level of OPP, total lockdown. All passengers were required to remain in their cabins for the remainder of the cruise, as were nonessential staff. Designated crew members would deliver food and drink.

Fine, but Gatobi9 was still out there.

At the clinic, Mandy returned his phone with an out-stretched quivering arm and blank eyes. "Don't worry, I didn't peek at your messages."

There was no wink, no flirty suggestion that she was interested in his private life. She simply turned heel and left. Thinking about the way he'd loomed over her, he understood. He still couldn't believe he'd thought...

Since nobody was allowed into Calvin's original cabin, Nali had decked him out in one of her anime T-shirts, showing a one-eyed wizard wielding a blazing staff. "I assume this lockdown means day care is shut down, so who else is going to watch him all day?"

"Puh-puh-pah," Calvin chanted, nodding in rhythm. "Pee-Pee-Peeeeter." That crooked smile again—Harrison Ford had nothing on this guy.

She patted his leg. "And who am I? What's my name?"

"Nuh-nuh, Nah-dee."

She laughed softly. "Yes. He has trouble with his *L*s."

Calvin picked up the fidget toy from his lap and banged it on the edge of his armrest, setting the gadget spinning. *Whirrr.* Peter touched the back of Calvin's neck. So much loss amongst the three of them.

"Are we okay?" Peter asked Nali.

She glanced away, caught his gaze again, and turned to brush a wayward lock of hair from Calvin's forehead.

"So—I'm sorry for ghosting everybody," Peter said. "I couldn't even look at you all without feeling sick to my stomach. I was pretending it never happened, like I wasn't attached to anybody, but—"

"Shut up. Did you eat yet?" she asked with a determined smile.

Thank goodness for her willingness to move on, at least for

now. His baby sister rocked. "Come help me with something. Please."

In the office, he pulled up the EHR and the AI. His conversation from the prior session was still open.

She parked Calvin nearby. "What are you trying to get it to do?"

"Too many threads I'm trying to tie together. Maybe it's all just random noise. I don't know."

He asked the AI to show the pattern of encephalitis symptoms according to cabin location. Its response was just as cluttered and no more helpful than yesterday's.

"Copy and paste the link to the map," she said.

"I tried that. It doesn't have access."

"It's all on the same server."

"The systems don't talk to each other." A familiar refrain in the over-siloed health care field.

"What's the point anyway?"

Ah, the point. Good medicine wasn't just about getting the diagnosis right the first time but about being willing to poke around and try again. Weigh the evidence, and lacking any, make an educated guess. Leave no stone unturned. He'd been avoiding stones for too long now. And there was one stone he did not want to pick up, but he had to.

In the early days of Covid, everybody had become obsessed with decontaminating their environment. Clorox wipes flew off the shelves. Facilities managers installed HEPA filters in their ventilation systems. Sunila's executioner had taped up the ventilation duct in the ceiling. Peter hated to take cues from a murderer, but he couldn't afford to ignore this one. He'd buried Chessa's claims like bones in the yard, but the dogs kept digging them up.

"What if the virus isn't just spreading person to person?" It sounded ridiculous.

"What do you mean?"

"The ventilation system."

Nali looked up at the ceiling. "Like that?"

The metal grill was a rectangular plate with two sections of vertical slits flanking horizontal slits—just like in an apartment or house, as if the shipbuilders had picked them up at Home Depot.

He climbed on a stool. A stream of cool air tickled his fingertips, and he actually laughed for the first time in what felt like months.

"What?"

"Ever heard of Legionnaires' disease?"

A puzzled look washed over her face.

"Back in the seventies or eighties, there was a convention for the American Legion at a hotel. A bunch of attendees died. The CDC traced it back to the hotel air-conditioning. It was contaminated with a bacteria they later named Legionella."

"My roommate has an air purifier." Her eyes narrowed. "Can't they regulate the flow or suck it all out or something?"

"Fresh air has to get in somehow." An image popped into his head of a guy in a hazmat suit swirling chemicals in a vial and decanting the solution into a cartoonish vaporizer device. Lord, he really was losing his mind.

When working up an illness, he liked to keep two lists. The first had the most probable causes of the symptoms. The second list detailed the most lethal possibilities, which he didn't want to miss. Multiple public health agencies had already raised the specter of bioterrorism, so it made sense to keep pulling on that thread.

"There has to be a schematic of the ventilation system somewhere."

She slapped the desk next to the mouse pad. "Agus!"

His jangled nerves twitched, but his mind wasn't keeping up.

"The maintenance guy," she said.

Ah, the coffee guy. "Yeah, and he helped you with Calvin. What would we do without him?" She nodded excitedly, and he studied her smooth face. It wasn't right to rope her into all this, but they were knee-deep in it now.

She pulled out her phone. "I'll message him."

"Wait!" He stuck his hand over her screen. "What if it's him?"

She snorted. "Agus? He's— Oh my God, you're kidding me. You think he started all this?"

He crossed his arms and looked out the window but quickly turned back. No rescue was coming from out there. "Who knows? We can't rule it out."

She chewed on her lower lip. "Scoot over. Let me give it a shot."

"Don't mess up any of the records."

"I'm just going to see if I can link up everything to the AI."

"You know how to do that?"

She shrugged. "I built an AI for class. It's not a big deal. You have to train it on the data models." She settled into the chair. "Otherwise, it's pretty stupid."

Weird to ask his little sis about stuff. It wasn't like he was some old guy getting frustrated over his TV remote, but she really had skills. This was... big.

"Keep me updated, then." He stood up.

"Where you going?"

"Time for a reality check."

———————

It was a matter of trust. Peter had no problem with giving Nali his login to poke around the computer systems. There had to be something with the clustering of cabins. But digital representations weren't enough. He needed to see and touch the evidence—if not to convince others, at least to reassure himself that he wasn't going completely mad.

The map posted near the midship elevators matched the online diagram. So far so good, but not enough detail. It only showed colored sections without individual numbers.

He started at the top, just like hospital rounds. The clear wall of the elevator afforded an unobstructed view of the grand atrium. People had gathered below in scattered pockets. This could go in any direction. Either the laggards would dutifully report to their rooms for lockdown, or the whole place would erupt in rebellion.

Remnants of room service cluttered the corridors on level nine—paper plates, plastic utensils, and empty water bottles. Behind a service cart, a cabin steward sat slumped against the wall, eyes closed and head between her knees. He bent down to check her breathing and heard soft snores.

Farther down, another steward was embroiled in a heated conversation with the unseen occupants of another cabin. Hands flew out and flung him against the opposite wall. A pair of passengers, man and woman, barged out of the cabin. Peter flattened himself against the wall just as they hurtled by. Judging by the trailing cloud of funk, they hadn't showered in days.

The victimized cabin steward was none other than his own attendant, Yuli. It was strange to see him way up here on the ninth level, attending to other rooms. Like when he found out his seventh-grade teacher had a boyfriend—that irrational twang of betrayal followed by embarrassment at such a silly crush. But it only made sense that stewards would be assigned to multiple blocks of rooms.

Yuli was shaken but not seriously hurt. His assailants had burst out of cabin 9176, embossed in black on a round plaque of frosted glass just below the peephole. 9176. Wasn't that...?

He double-checked the room number against his index cards. Sure enough, he'd found the spot. Six cabins in a row, all with ocean views, all even numbers: 9176, 9178, 9180, 9182, 9184, 9186. Across the hall, five consecutive interior cabins, all odd numbers: 9177, 9179, 9181, 9183, 9185. Eleven cabins in proximity, housing passengers with signs and symptoms of this diabolical illness. They weren't the only cabins on the ninth level with infected patients, but none of the others were clustered like this.

"Are these all yours?" Peter asked Yuli.

"I take care of them." Yuli's eyes wrinkled above his mask. "I don't know why they do that. Maybe they have *magwala* virus."

"Magwala?"

"My Filipino friends call it like that. No control, act wild." He made a slashing motion across his own neck with a gloved hand. "Did he really cut her head off?"

Peter shook his head. "He just cut the carotid artery." As if that made it any better.

"She was friend of my cousin."

He frowned. "I'm so sorry." He gestured to the six ocean-view cabins. "Are any of these linked in any way? Are there connecting doors between them?"

"All my cabins are separate."

"What about the ventilation ducts? Are they connected?"

Yuli shrugged in a way that made his head seem too big for his body, as if he might have great ideas but would struggle to put them into practice.

This was like pulling teeth. "I need to check something related to the outbreak. Would you mind letting me in?"

Yuli eyed him with caution.

"It's important."

"Look from the hallway, but you cannot go in. I would get in trouble."

Rules and regulations would matter little if the virus continued to spread unchecked. Following Yuli as he unlocked each cabin, Peter poked his head into all eleven. Most were in a severe state of neglect: clothes strewn everywhere, TVs blaring, and the stench of rotten food. They were on full lockdown now. Where were the passengers?

Yuli's chin hung low. "It is hard to keep up. The sick ones make so much mess." The black bag on his cart bulged with refuse. Bins on top of the cart contained little bottles of shampoo and packets of soap. "Can I ask you question?"

Peter nodded.

"What happen when we get to New York?"

"The CDC's working on a plan. That's the public health agency."

"Why you ask about the rooms?"

Good question. Entertaining the prospect of bioterrorism and chasing down patterns felt like stretching a thick rubber band inside his brain. It required a strange level of physical and mental energy to maintain the effort. It wasn't just fighting against fatigue—more like pretending to be someone else, and as soon as he let his guard down, he'd snap back to his true self. That would be perfect. Then he could curl up in a ball somewhere, rising only for food. Or self-defense.

He had to keep moving. He thanked the steward and descended to the fifth level, swimming upstream in the carpeted corridor against passengers making haste for the lobby. He opened his mouth to remind them about lockdown but shut it promptly. No sense getting mashed to a pulp. One woman called out over her shoulder as she passed, "Hey, they got a fire going."

There were indeed eight ocean-view cabins on the fifth level corresponding to the numbers on his card, but no interior rooms in this cluster. Across from these quarters were a few unmarked doors and long spans of blank wall.

On his way to the final cluster, he passed Calvin's room, still bearing the trappings of tragedy. Yellow tape that had once spanned the doorjamb had been torn and now hung from both sides. A clear plexiglass plate had been installed over the entire lock mechanism, blocking the key-card slot and fixing the door handle in a horizontal position. A thick padlock secured the plate. No entry.

The corridor on the third level was partially blocked by a dead body. Peter was surprised at how calmly he mentally cataloged the discovery: No biggie, another one for the cooler. The passengers scurrying out simply stepped over it.

He texted Harrington: *FYI another dead body on your ship.*

So it had come to this. His shoulders ached. His palms were slick with sweat. He'd begun this gig excited to treat minor maladies, and now he was stepping over corpses in hallways. Funny how standards eroded in the face of devastation.

The thing he couldn't figure out was why the outbreaks occurred in blocks of cabins. Basic epidemiologic principles, confirmed in brutal fashion by Covid, dictated that a respiratory infection would spread in communal areas such as restaurants and theaters. It made little sense for so many cases to be concentrated within a few groups of adjacent cabins.

He pulled out his cards and pen. Theory A: The virus spread through the ventilation ducts. He would need a maintenance guy to investigate it. Agus was their man.

Theory B: The occupants knew each other and mingled outside the cabins. Maybe a large family had booked those rooms on level nine, another on the fifth level, and yet another on the third. That would be easy enough to confirm, if Nali was as good as she claimed.

Time to head back to the clinic to test theory B.

But stairwells and elevator lobbies were filling with passengers and crew, all streaming toward a common destination. The thrust swept toward the front of the ship. The atmosphere was electric—festive, even, like a crowd headed to a Mardi Gras parade.

He willed himself to turn away. Had to get back to the clinic.

One enterprising guy pushing a rolling chair was hollering about letting it all burn. Other folks carried rolls of toilet paper. Must be that fire the woman had mentioned.

Peter hugged himself, rubbing some warmth into his biceps. He needed to do something but couldn't quite remember… Might as well go with the flow. He plodded along behind the masses toward the fire.

———————

The intoxicating sense of freedom grew with each whiff of smoke Peter inhaled. This was the perfect place for a bonfire, centered on the giant white *H* of the helipad on the snout of the ship. The *Paradise* plowed through the sea in the twilight, nose aglow like that famous reindeer. Whether they'd chosen this location by democratic vote—doubtful—or whether one person started it and others followed, it mattered little now.

The crackling flames illuminated their capering, half-naked bodies, the evening chill bringing them close to the fire's edge. People ripped off their clothing as fuel, right along with splintered pieces of chairs and pool towels. Anything flammable was fair game. Toilet paper seemed to be the kindling of choice, given its wide availability, at least for now. But what would they use to wipe their asses?

Peter giggled. Silly question. Throw off the shackles of consequences and long-term planning, give in to your own true nature. Become who you were always meant to be. Toilet paper would take you there.

Bare-chested young men and women twirled and cavorted in tight circles around the fire. The older among them lurched and shuffled—like that old geezer with a walker over there. Passengers, crew members, staff, and officers were amassing here as equals, streaming in from all quarters like congregants late to church.

Peter threw his head back and let out a guttural whoop. Damn, that was good. He did it again. He hadn't felt this liberated since he'd relinquished his pager on the last day of residency.

He turned slowly in circles, taking in everything around him. Amazing how the ship could be so big, yet so small. Faces that were at first distorted by the flickering flames became known to him. He recognized people from clinic visits, and there was the young woman who ran the self-service coffee kiosk. He loved them all. They were freeing themselves together.

The disgraced former captain was impossible to miss, even in plain clothes and a coarse beard. If anything, Forster's swagger had intensified during his exile. He took a long swill from a familiar crystal decanter, held it aloft, and poured liquid over the head of the young woman. She squealed with delight, sticking out her tongue for more. Forster ignored her and tossed the rest into the fire. Now *that* was an alpha dog.

It was time to let it all go. Only the here and now counted. Peter whipped the stethoscope from his neck and tossed it into the fire. As revelers danced around him, he crouched and watched the long rubber tubing melt with a *hissss*. The serpent had met its fate in Hades.

He stood up and patted his pockets. Oh yes, the cheap plastic pen and index cards. Stupid things. He couldn't remember why he'd written notes, and he didn't care to keep them. He dealt them one by one into the fire, like playing cards, a full deck. Their edges curled and blackened as the flames devoured his last great ideas. He tossed the pen in for good measure.

"Ow!" A small object had bounced off his chest and clattered at his feet: a cell phone.

A woman laughed from the other side. "I missed!"

He kicked the phone into the fire.

And then Chessa appeared next to him, her eyes glimmering in the firelight. Her flushed face bore none of the stress and anxiety of their previous encounters. She'd found freedom too. She gave him a mischievous smile. All their transgressions dissolved in her glow.

He needed her. Sweat glistened on her slender neck, and her long hair was caught up in a wild tangle. He grabbed her waist. She raised her toned arms above her head, then blew him a kiss.

"I'm so glad I found you," he said into her hair. He'd once

sought something from her, but nothing mattered except right here, right now.

She rewarded him with a warm, fervent kiss. They stumbled sideways, somehow avoiding the fire, then regained their balance.

"Let's go." She took him by the hand and led him through the carousers and around a scuffle, ducking errant fists. It wasn't one big happy family, for sure.

Somebody blocked their way.

"Come with me," Mauricio said to her. The security guard.

A wicked grin slid across Chessa's face. She grabbed Mauricio's hand too, forming a trio.

Mauricio yanked hard and pulled her away, out of Peter's grip. "Just you."

She looked at Peter, her expression full of wonder, as she disappeared into the flickering shadows with Mauricio.

19

Shortly after Felipe's overdose, Peter had sought refuge in a YouTube sage who said you can't control what happens to you, but you can control how you react to it. Nothing new at all, but the guy presented it in such a compelling, believable package.

But that was pretty much bullshit once encephalitis had started nibbling away at your frontal lobe. Not much control there. He was past the infectious stage—no cough—but the damage had been done.

He'd blown it last night, slinking back to his room after the bonfire. What a bonehead. Sitting on the side of his bed, with the scent of ashes in his hair, he scrolled through all the messages he'd sent to Mandy, Luisa, and Hartley since he boarded the ship, now knowing that Chessa—and Gatobi9—had had access to them. No response from Gatobi9 though.

He'd had a chance last night to make up ground with Chessa. He scrubbed his eyes, annoyed by the aftereffects of the smoke and ashes. It was too late. Mauricio had her now.

The navigation map on his TV showed their little triangle

cruising south of Nantucket. It zoomed out to show the eastern coastline of Long Island on the left side of the screen. The next refresh brought the great city of New York into view, marked by a black star. No more than a few hours away. The end was in sight. But what kind of end was it? And if Gatobi9 remained free…

He jammed a fresh stack of index cards into his pocket and reported to clinic. He had patients to see if he was going to jump on that conference call Wetzel had set up.

Mandy greeted him with a strange smile. He'd have to figure that out later.

Calvin was getting some good mileage out of the fidget spinner. The metallic pen from Felipe had been demoted. "Puh-Peeeter."

Peter dug around in the satchel hanging from the back of Calvin's wheelchair until he felt the pen. *Ta-tick, ta-tack.* It was good to have it back. He stuck it in the breast pocket of his scrubs alongside the cards.

"How was the party?" Mandy asked, all innocent and sweet.

Oh, but she knew. Heat rose in his cheeks as he turned away. Of course people had seen him, gyrating with Chessa and surely performing other deeds he couldn't remember.

"Is Luisa still out?" he asked.

"As good as gone. I saw the room service tray by her door, untouched."

Chalk up another loss. They started working through the aftermath of last night's revelry: burns, bruises, a broken wrist.

In between patients, he texted Nali: *Coming down here?*

Each time he checked and saw no response, the knots in his shoulders tightened. Finally, she breezed through the front area straight to the office. He shucked off his gloves and followed her in.

She was already tapping on the keyboard. "Remember Mother's Day at Discovery Green?"

He sat down next to her.

"I was so obsessed with Rocky, and thrilled they allowed me to keep him at the dorm."

The bearded dragon. What a thing to be thinking of at a time like this. "I was annoyed that bucket of fried chicken didn't have enough dark meat."

She smiled, but her eyes were sad. "And he was actually excited about something."

He—this was about their brother. Felipe's foray into ambient music, composing with a synthesizer, had surprised everybody. But then he'd played them a clip on his phone, bobbing and weaving like Stevie Wonder, and the air felt lighter. Peter told him he would learn the guitar and they'd form a duo.

"He was pretty good on that keyboard. That was the last time we were…"

"All together." Nali slapped her thighs and nodded at the computer. "Anyway, this AI, it can tell it's not you by the way I enter the prompts. What are we working on today?"

Peter outlined theories about the clustered cabins he wanted her to test. She prompted the AI. In seconds, it produced a table with the names, addresses, and phone numbers of the cabin cluster on level nine. He saw no pattern that suggested these people had known each other before boarding the ship. Same for the clusters on levels five and three.

"It doesn't look like it's a family thing," Nali said.

"What about friends?"

She rolled her eyes. "You're pushing it."

"Check. Please?" He chewed his lip, watching her work the AI, cajoling, challenging it.

"It's checking their socials."

Based on IP addresses, geocodes, profile information, friends, likes, chats, and other data, here are the probabilities that any given occupant in each cabin was connected to any occupant in another cabin before embarking.

There were 119 unique pairings, but the probabilities of significant social interaction were low, on the order of 0.4 to 2.9 percent.

Theory B was out.

"What about the ventilation ducts?"

"I already asked Agus. He said he'll look into the duct system later, something about missing keys."

"We don't have time for later."

Mandy cracked the door open and pointed over her shoulder. "This patient originally signed up for a telemedicine visit. She said she had swelling, so I thought you should check it out in person."

The woman said she started puffing up yesterday. Peter's thumb left indentations on the top of her feet when he pressed down hard—edema from the prednisone he'd prescribed earlier for her encephalitis headache.

She fiddled with her necklace and searched his face. "Should I keep taking it? What happens if I stop? Will I go crazy too?"

Their depleted supply of prednisone was the only weapon they had against inflammation induced by the virus. "How many tablets do you have left?"

"You only gave me ten."

His strategy had been to prioritize patients with early, unequivocal symptoms of encephalitis, but as more patients came in, he'd had to lower their doses. It was a fixed-sum game. There'd never been enough to go around.

"Have you had any urges to hurt anybody?"

She stiffened, looking offended, but shook her head.

"Or hurt yourself?"

Another shake.

"Do anything that you might regret later?"

Her gaze dropped to the floor.

"Well, just keep taking your medication," Peter said. "And elevate your feet whenever you can."

He checked in with Nali. "Can you combine all the vending machine data with the patients seen in clinic and telemedicine? Then get the percentage of sick patients registered to the clustered cabins."

She side-eyed him but didn't object.

"Also, the timing. Cross-reference the date of symptom onset."

"You toss around *cross-reference* like it's so easy to do, but you don't even know what it means."

"But you can do it." He mimicked quick typing.

"Dates of what? When they came into the clinic?"

"Yep. For the vending machine, all we have is the date of purchase. For the clinic and telemedicine patients, you can look at the notes." He showed her the section for History of Present Illness and hoped that Hartley and Martina Jacobs had done a decent job with their descriptions. His weren't perfect either.

"Where's Agus?"

"I just texted him," she said.

He needed to ask him about that ventilation system, but for all he knew, Agus might be dead somewhere, that's how bad things had gotten. Don't answer a text, that means you're dead.

"One more thing. Look at the correlation between—"

"Nope." She held up her hand. "That's enough for now. Go back to being a doctor."

He let out a bark of laughter and couldn't stop. She'd nailed the crux of the matter. His responsibility as a doctor had morphed in ways that made his head spin. Spinning and spinning, just like this uncontrollable laughter.

When he returned after the next batch of patients, Nali was proud of the answers she'd coaxed out of the AI. "I can't do a time lapse, but just imagine it. I'll click through as fast as I can."

She started with Deck 9. While the ship was in the Mediterranean, the infections were rare and sparse, indicated by red dots in each affected cabin. As the days progressed leading up to Copenhagen, dots began appearing in the cabin blocks he visited yesterday.

"That's the first outbreak," he whispered.

The cluster grew, with sporadic cases popping up in more distant cabins on the same level. The pattern repeated itself on levels five and three, gaining a foothold in a cluster of cabins before appearing elsewhere.

As he struggled to wrap his head around this, Agus knocked on the open door. "Are you okay?"

Peter laughed bitterly. "Perfect. What's the situation?"

"The air ducts are normal," Agus said. "We use fiberoptic camera to check all through the ventilation ducts in the sections that Nali said, but we found nothing strange. No tampering or messing with."

Peter rubbed the back of his neck.

"I'm so sorry, Doctor—or maybe, it's good?" Agus offered

a sad smile along with a can of his magic coffee, which Peter accepted and quaffed immediately.

His eyes widened. "Move over," he said to Nali, then jumped on the computer and queried the AI about enveloped versus nonenveloped viruses.

The envelope of a virus is an outer lipid membrane that helps the virus enter and exit host cells. Examples of enveloped viruses include influenza, HIV, and human coronaviruses. Viruses without an envelope rely on other mechanisms for cell entry. Nonenveloped viruses are typically more resistant to environmental factors. Notable examples are adenoviruses and noroviruses.

Host cells—that was us.

Peter: *Expound on environmental factors.*

The AI listed temperature, humidity, pH levels, ultraviolet radiation, surface materials, and chemical disinfectants.

Peter's scalp prickled, and he shifted in the chair. What could somebody control on the ship if they were trying to manipulate an environment to foster viral growth? Temperature and humidity maybe. But the air felt normal, except that room where Mrs. Burchins was found dead.

This had to be something chemical.

Chemicals were the building blocks for molecules, which made up everything inside us, even viruses. The ability to manipulate molecules unlocked everything. This virus was a chimera, a combination—the kind of work that happened in a laboratory, not a cruise ship.

Chemicals could destroy viruses, but perhaps not all of them.

Peter: *More on chemical disinfectants.*

The AI enumerated the various applications of bleach, quaternary ammonium compounds, alcohol, and hydrogen peroxide as disinfectants.

An idea was there, but he couldn't grasp it. The damn virus was pushing his brain through a sieve. The pieces came out the other side like miniature squares of gelatin jiggling on a cutting board. The contour looked like the original, but the pieces didn't stick together.

He needed a change of scenery to clear his mind. The waiting area outside the clinic was deserted, save for a rolling cart with breakfast left by the crew. The food was portioned out in mass quantities instead of individual meals: a plate stacked high with syrup-soaked pancakes, another with sausage and hash browns. Everything was covered with plastic lids, which made the food soggy. The crew must've left it here hours ago, on one of their endless rotations through the ship.

He slumped against the wall, chest heaving, eyes darting everywhere. Agus's magic coffee had opened a million pores and let all the devastation seep in. The scales had fallen from his eyes. All he saw was ruin and decay. Any semblance of order in the universe had been shattered.

Cruises were supposed to help people unwind, not harbor a deadly infection. Nali should have been getting ready for some crappy job, not querying an AI on viral outbreaks. Nieces weren't supposed to strangle their uncles. What was supposed to help could also harm.

And steroids were supposed to tamp down inflammation, yet prednisone had side effects.

What was designed to help could also harm.

He'd given Felipe a temporary reprieve from the fiends that had plagued him since the war. That was supposed to bring peace, not send him to his destruction.

Side effects. Adverse events. People in your corner who could hurt you. Unintended consequences. Different labels for the same thing.

That which was supposed to help could also harm.

Agus shuffled by on his way out, giving Peter a little nod and a smile.

"So you didn't find *anything* unusual?" Peter called out. One last shot.

"Well…" Agus paused. "Never mind. It's nothing."

"What? Say it."

"I already told your sister."

"Tell me, Agus. Come on!"

"Some things have gone missing."

"So what's missing?" Peter asked as they climbed the stairs to Deck 2.

"I couldn't find my keys for the storage closets," Agus was saying over his shoulder. "I had to get new ones made. Then I check inside, just to make sure nothing is gone."

"And?"

"I couldn't find them, but now it seems okay." He gave a tiny shrug. "Maybe…"

Peter took his time drawing in a hearty breath. This virus had stripped whatever remnant of fitness he'd possessed before boarding. "What's missing, Agus?"

"Things for hygiene. In one of the closets."

Storage closet. Hygiene. Chemicals. "Can you show me?"

Agus stopped at a narrow, nondescript door that blended in with the wall paneling. There was no sign on or near it. He pulled a key from a retractable reel on his lanyard, unlocked the closet, and flicked on the light.

Peter blinked against the sudden illumination. The closet was roughly the size of the room where Calvin's mother had been found. Sturdy metal shelving held toilet paper, tissues, and other basic supplies.

The door snicked shut. Agus waited patiently behind him in the quiet space, raising the hackles on Peter's neck—Agus, always in the background yet always ready to help, exactly the type of person who society overlooked. Was he…? Peter shifted sideways to create space and stole a glance over his shoulder. Agus's round face glowed like a moon in the darkness, still and watching.

"So what was missing?" Peter's voice cracked.

Agus pointed to a shelf at knee height. "Hand sanitizer. But now it's back."

The overhead light cast a shadow over the front half of the shelf. It looked empty.

Peter tensed his legs, anticipating a sudden move from Agus. When the moment passed, he released a breath and crouched to inspect the shelf.

There in the back were a dozen cylindrical bottles arranged neatly in rows. He picked one up then stood to examine it more closely. It was soft plastic, the kind you turn upside down and squeeze, with a plain white label written in English, French, Spanish, Arabic, and some Asian language he guessed was Chinese. *Kills 99.9% of illness-causing germs. Rub hands together briskly to cover all surfaces of hands until dry.* The active ingredient was 70 percent ethyl alcohol.

He flipped open the cap and gave it a gentle squeeze, feeling resistance as the gel bulged against the top of the bottle. Nothing came out. He twisted off the cap. The mouth of the bottle was covered with a plastic seal to keep the gel from drying out and to prevent contamination. Not that any microbes would survive in the alcohol anyway. That was the whole point.

He pinched the tab and pulled off the seal. No resistance, no sucking sound of a vacuum seal being broken. It had been compromised.

Hmm. Not good.

Peter tore his mask off and squeezed the bottle under his nose: a mild bite of alcohol. But thanks to Muller, his nose wasn't completely trustworthy. He handed the bottle to Agus. "Smell it? Just a little whiff."

Agus did so and shrugged.

"What's it smell like?"

"A little like flowers, I think."

"Do you smell alcohol?"

Agus furrowed his brow, and he took another whiff. "I guess so. Normal for this stuff, right?"

Normal? Of course. What had he been thinking? He slumped. "I thought it—never mind."

"Okay, Doctor. Ready to go?"

Not yet. The seal on the bottle had been compromised. "Hold on."

Peter reached for another bottle, a fresh one, and twisted off the cap. He examined the plastic seal, but the storage room was too dim. "Do you have a flashlight?"

Agus pulled out his phone.

"Point it here." Peter indicated the top of the bottle.

The brilliant white light revealed an irregularity near the edge of the plastic film. Peter ran his finger over the spot. It was a tiny hole no bigger than a pinprick. He held his finger just above the hole and squeezed. A needle-thin whisper of air puffed against his skin.

Needle-thin. Air came out.

Needle-thin. To get stuff in.

A virus living inside a container of hand sanitizer was like a mouse thriving inside a cage of hungry cats. It just wouldn't happen. The gel was supposed to kill everything—at least 99.9 percent. But what about the remaining fraction, the one out of a thousand?

Hand sanitizer, hand sanitizer… What could be different about this sanitizer? Mandy used her own boutique brand, and her hands were smooth and soft because hers didn't contain alcohol, which dried out your skin. Mandy didn't seem to be affected by the virus.

Alcohol killed microbes, but not all of them, not non-enveloped viruses like adenovirus. And adenovirus caused a cough but didn't cause encephalitis. Nipah virus did.

It looks like Nipah virus plus a nonenveloped virus, Wetzel had said.

Nipah virus plus adenovirus—a combination not yet encountered in the natural world.

Oh, fuck.

Mandy wasn't sick yet. She was healthy. And that made sense, because Mandy wore masks, and she didn't use *this* hand sanitizer, from this closet, distributed around the ship, even in his own cabin.

He snatched up another bottle for a sanity check, praying he was wrong. Nope, this bottle also had a tiny hole in the seal.

Peter sucked in a breath and his veins froze. The needle hole wasn't an accident. None of this was an accident. These bottles of hand sanitizer were the seeds of the pestilence, conveyed throughout the ship by the very routines and behaviors that were supposed to protect everybody.

He turned to Agus, shaking a bottle in his face. "This is what they're using. This is the delivery system."

Agus blinked a couple times. "What, Doctor?"

"The virus is in here. It survives in hand sanitizer. They

engineered it that way." He mimed the action of squeezing gel onto his hands then set the bottle on the shelf and rubbed his hands together. "It's all over our hands, see?" He wiped at his nose—casual, automatic. "Then we touch our face without even thinking. It's a bad habit."

Agus's eyes were wide as saucers.

"We have to secure these." Peter started gathering up the bottles. "We have to bring these back to the clinic. Nobody can open them. They're contaminated."

No, contamination can be accidental. This was intentional tampering. The work of Gatobi9.

Agus pulled a white trash bag from a carton and held it open as Peter dumped all the squeeze bottles inside. That sieve feeling came back again, his brain pushing through a grate. He grabbed his pen and an index card then scribbled frantically, racing against his waning faculties. For insurance, he sent a quick text to Mandy: *Coming with hand sanitizer. Do not open!*

A faint chime sounded just outside the door, making Peter flinch. Was Mandy out there? Was that her phone? "Mandy?"

He stumbled out of the closet but heard only a faint rustle fading around the corner.

Peter and Agus proceeded directly through the waiting area, past the exam rooms, and into the office.

"You've been here the whole time?" Peter asked as he passed Mandy.

"Yeah. Where have *you* been?" She followed him to the doorway.

He dropped the trash bag by the desk. "Close the door."

She did so.

He pointed to the bottle dangling from her lanyard. "That's the key. Your stuff is good. That's why you never got sick." It was impossible to concentrate with the glimmers of purple flickering across the floor.

"What are you talking about?" she demanded.

He inhaled slowly. Had to focus. He dug into the trash bag and retrieved a contaminated bottle as he explained. Her eyes darted between him and Agus, who shrugged and held his hands up.

Mandy asked him something else, but that giant purple spider was back—that horror—dancing across the floor on clacking legs. He staggered backward, wheezing for breath. The spider thing trained its slavering orifice at him and spit.

"Aie!" Hot white mucus splattered on his chest. He dropped the bottle and wiped furiously at his scrubs, flinging off globules of the secretions with his hands.

Couldn't get it off, couldn't get it off, couldn't—

He bolted from the clinic and booked down I-95 between gangs of hooting crew members. Get it off, get it off. Shower. Must get to shower. Each frantic breath sucked needles into his lungs. The needles circulated and pricked every cell in his body.

He pulled up short at the rolling cart of supplies in front of his cabin.

"Doctor, you okay?" said Yuli.

Peter bent over with his hands on his knees, panting. One of the little needles popped something inside his head. Dammit, that hurt.

"I will just clean bathroom," Yuli said. "Sorry I am late, so busy."

Peter dragged a palm over his chest, patted his scrubs. They were dry. No mucus. "All right, yeah." He stood up straight and blew air out of his cheeks, then opened the door for Yuli.

Once Yuli slipped past him into the bathroom, he took off his scrub shirt. The mucus had been another hallucination, but it still felt better to change into fresh clothes. He transferred his index cards and metallic pen to the pocket of his new shirt.

From the bathroom came the sounds of domestic banality. The spritz of a spray bottle, soft humming, the shower curtain skittering across the rod.

Peter took an aimless step around the bed. Wait, he was supposed to be working on something. What was it? His phone buzzed—and simultaneously, a chorus of crickets sang out in the bathroom.

He shook his head. The hallucinations still held their grip. It sounded like a message on his phone had sent crickets chirping in the bathroom, but that's where Yuli was.

Yuli—whose jurisdiction included the cabins clustered on the ninth floor.

Peter's legs gave out, and he barely caught himself on the wall. He tottered over to the bed, rubbing his temples.

Yuli, his cabin steward. A cart full of supplies. Chirping crickets whenever Yuli got a message—whenever Peter or Mandy *sent* a message.

Could it really be him?

Heart thudding in his chest, he read the text from Mandy. *Hand sanitizer?!*

His thumbs stiffened with adrenaline. If Yuli had really just received the same message, he needed to convince Yuli that Mandy wasn't a liability. He needed to send some subtle, clever message that would throw him off her scent. But he was at a loss.

Run and hide. Take bag. Bring sis and kid.

No crickets from the bathroom this time, but a faint buzz confirmed everything. That treacherous bastard!

Peter snatched the hand sanitizer from the nightstand and shook it, feeling the blob of gel shake against the inner surface.

Yuli emerged from the bathroom, slight of frame but surely cooking up big ideas. "Peter," he said with a gentle smile.

Peter leveled the bottle at the little shit, pointing it like a gun. He was a healer and had taken an oath to do no harm, but a homicidal urge burned inside him. "I know what you're up to. You're Gatobi9. You started it all."

Yuli's smile slid right off his ethnically vague, utterly forgettable face. He blew out a long breath through a scowl. "All right." The edge in his voice, the lift of his chin—gone was the humble cabin steward.

Peter hurled the bottle.

Yuli ducked, and it bounced harmlessly off the wall. The cabin door clicked open.

Mauricio burst in and slammed the door behind him, chest heaving.

"Get him!" Yuli barked.

Peter lunged at Yuli, but Mauricio intercepted, tackling Peter and pinning him to the bed face up. What the—

He slammed his fists on Mauricio's back, but the security guard maintained his bear hug, shoulder digging into Peter's ribs. Peter groped for the napkin-wrapped steak knife in his waistband, but he could only reach in so far and he couldn't get around the bulk of Mauricio's torso.

Snick. Yuli had popped open a folding knife next to Peter's cheek. This was no gentleman's Swiss Army knife—more like the stuff Felipe used to mess around with before the war: short, wide, and definitely not kosher on this ship.

"Let him go," Yuli said.

Mauricio rolled off, yanked the steak knife from Peter's waistband, and tucked it under his belt with a sneer. "Planning some surgery, Doc?"

"Your phone," Yuli continued, heat in his voice.

Peter sat up on the bed and glared at Mauricio. "What did you do with Chessa?"

"Phone," Yuli repeated.

"Did you kill her?"

Mauricio unholstered his stun gun and produced a bouquet of long black zip ties from his pocket. "Do what he says."

They flanked him now, Yuli on the left and Mauricio on the right, both meaning him harm. The three men occupied all the space in the tiny quarters. Peter fished out his phone and dropped it on the carpet.

Yuli picked it up and shoved the screen in Peter's face. "Unlock it."

Peter squeezed his eyes shut.

"Open your eyes, Peter. Unlock it."

They'd have to pry them open. Even if he was being childish, a little control was worth something here. The longer he held out—

A cracking pop exploded and lightning shot through his side. Searing convulsions ripped through his body, head to toe. He collapsed back onto the bed, head juddering. After a thousand years of pain, a scream of agony finally tore out of his throat.

At some point, chest heaving, he rolled to one side. Grumbling and moaning, gasping for air.

Yuli jabbed the point of the knife under his chin. "Do not move."

As if he could. All strength had drained from his limbs.

Rough hands wrenched his arms behind his back and

bound his wrists with zip ties. His ankles were next. Funny how a couple of plastic pieces worth less than a cent changed everything. It was a different game now. Yuli was in full control. He had been from the very beginning.

"Now, unlock it." Mauricio pressed the stun gun to Peter's hip.

Defeated, he opened his eyes.

Yuli brought the phone up close until the facial ID unlocked it. He pecked on the screen and started scrolling. Peter watched the little weasel's eyes. If Yuli was looking for something, he either found it quickly or gave up, because he clicked the side button to lock the screen again.

"What's the lock code?" Yuli asked.

No way could Peter withstand another electro-hit. He spat out the six-digit code.

Yuli tested it and, apparently finding it satisfactory, slipped the phone into his vest pocket.

"If you're monitoring all our texts," Peter muttered, "why do you need my phone?" The realization struck home as the words left his mouth—Yuli could now assume his identity in all texts and emails.

Yuli whispered something to Mauricio.

Mauricio hesitated. "You sure?"

"Go now."

Mauricio left promptly.

Peter closed his eyes and dug his chin into the bed. They were going after Mandy. Nali and Calvin were in their sights as well. And it didn't look like he was going anywhere or warning anybody soon.

20

Yuli slid into the little chair and brought his knee up to his chest. "Mr. Peter, let's talk." His English was smooth and confident. Everything before had been a charade.

"Who are you?" Peter demanded, lying bound on his side on the bed.

"How much does Nora Wetzel know?"

"You're a murderer."

"That's not very nice." Yuli retrieved a bottle of Lexapro from his pocket. "This was in the trash." When he flicked it with a fingernail, Peter heard nothing; it was empty. "Did you think this would help? It's no better than a placebo. Haven't you read the trials?"

Peter searched for a snappy response, but nothing surfaced. The antidepressant had been a crutch, for better or for worse, but now the virus had taken over anyway. And the stun-gunning sure hadn't helped.

"You American doctors." Yuli's lips curled into a sneer. "You think you can save the world."

Ouch. Peter hadn't even been able to help his patients back

home, at least not the way he'd wanted to. He hadn't been able to help his own brother.

Yuli stood and whisked the window curtains open. Peter winced against the pale daylight slanting across the room. Sensitivity to light was yet another sign of the illness.

"You're just like everybody else," Yuli said. "Straining, striving. Do you really think any of it makes a difference?"

"She knows it's a chimeric virus." Yuli couldn't possibly reach Wetzel in Miami, not immediately. "They're tracking it in Europe too. They're going to stop it."

Yuli snatched the bottle of hand sanitizer from the floor and pocketed it.

"They all know about that too." Peter licked his lips. "A lot of people know."

His eyes drilled into Peter's. "Only you and the nurse do. Isn't that right?"

And Agus. He glanced away. Shit, maybe a few more bodies would be nothing for this monster.

Yuli was staring at him when he looked up again. "You're a little different from Martina and Elizabeth."

How dare he use their names so casually. Peter flexed helplessly against the zip ties.

"Martina, she was randy as a goat," Yuli continued. "She went all out, right there in that bed. You should've seen the sheets. Elizabeth though, she's had real pain—so in that way, a little like you and me. But your pain seems more raw. I remember that time, the first few years after my residency."

A sour taste gathered in the back of his throat. It couldn't be.

"The real world can be quite jarring."

Peter swallowed hard. "You can't be a doctor."

Yuli rubbed the smooth crown of his head and sighed.

"There are many ways to help the world, but maybe we have the best way. The pain all around you—not here on the ship, these are the necessary pains—but everywhere else. Why does it exist? Why do people suffer?"

"Because of people like you."

"It's our own doing. We reach too far. We grasp forbidden fruit. All our efforts to build and develop and optimize, they only lead to disappointment in the end. Why can't we be content with living in the moment and just *being*?"

Well, that much was valid. Peter's therapist had encouraged him to let go of the past and stop worrying about the future—generic advice, difficult to apply, yet based in truth. It was one reason he'd taken this gig in the first place.

Yuli pulled out a phone and scrolled. "This was a few weeks ago after we left Barcelona." He showed Peter a broad-chested man wearing a T-shirt with four words in large block letters: EAT. SLEEP. MATE. REPEAT. Life boiled down to its essentials.

"If it could only be." Yuli shook the bottle of hand sanitizer. "Then none of this would be necessary."

A chill swept down Peter's arms and legs. So that was Yuli's plan, a virus targeting the frontal lobe to take everybody back to the Stone Age—no, farther. Even cavemen had aspirations.

"All the woes of the world will be gone," Yuli continued. "All the things that divide us will be gone—nationalism, politics, religion. Think about it. No more racism, no more inequality, no more stepping on each other to get to the top."

"You're demented." His shoulder was starting to ache from lying on his side, wrists and ankles bound.

Yuli snorted. "You see it. You just won't admit it."

"How do you think it's working out? What about that kid who dove into the pool deck? The woman who strangled her uncle? All because of you. Now there's a boy with cerebral palsy out there who doesn't have a mother. Is that the world you want?"

Yuli shrugged. "Collateral damage."

"And now you're going to kill me too. Isn't that the plan?"

Yuli stiffened. "I told you, I'm not a killer."

"You're the very definition of one."

"These are birthing pains, nothing more. When we all become our true selves, the suffering will be no more."

There was nothing true or right about this. "It's all suffering now."

Yuli clucked his tongue. "Pain and suffering are different. When Mauricio hit you with the stun gun, it hurt, but that's not the same as prolonged emotional suffering."

"Gee, thanks for understanding."

"We must become more like animals. Don't you see? Animals are not burdened by guilt. They don't waste away, brooding over missed opportunities or lamenting their mistakes. They don't have PTSD." Yuli spat the four letters like a bitter concoction. "Regret? They don't even know the word."

It was hard to admit, but there was a cold seed of truth buried in the man's rhetoric. Law of the jungle, kill or be killed. Brutality was part of the thread of existence for wild animals, whether they were predator or prey. There were no wounded feelings, no fog of despair.

But it wasn't that simple. In the weeks after Felipe's overdose, the simple life of a dog had held a certain appeal—eating and sleeping and mating, just like the shirt said. But even a dog's life consisted of more than primal acts and reflexive satisfaction of bodily needs. The bond between dogs and humans ran deep. Maybe their brains operated on different levels, but their spirits meshed. Love thrived there, and separation caused pain.

Peter closed his eyes. He didn't have all the answers, but Yuli sure as hell didn't either.

The air congealed around him. All doubt was gone. He was right about Yuli and the hand sanitizer. Yuli was remaking humankind according to his own twisted gospel, a truly visionary quest. Though small of stature, Yuli wielded the power of a black hole. It was horrifyingly clear.

Yet surely he couldn't have engineered all this alone. "How did you create the virus?"

"As much as I'd like to, I can't take full credit." Yuli smirked. "We are everywhere now. We—"

A message buzzed on Peter's phone and chirped on Yuli's.

Yuli looked between both devices. "Your sister."

Peter's tongue stuck to the roof of his mouth. Everything looked wavy and shimmery. He twisted to look at Yuli. "Leave her. Leave us. We don't— You can't…"

He let his eyes droop. His head was so heavy. He needed a nap. If only this kind person would just untie him, please.

———

He awakened in darkness, sucking air through ruined nostrils. Something thick and dry in his mouth. Still curled on his left side, wrists and ankles bound. Shoulder throbbing hard now. He squinted into the dimness but could make out only shadows. The world swayed and churned, prompting a wave of nausea. A low-frequency groan emanated from somewhere, barely above the threshold of aural detection. It welled up from his surroundings—he was within the groaning. He felt it as much as he heard it.

Peter shuddered. He was inside something, a living thing. He'd been swallowed by a leviathan.

His fate was inevitable. Glands would secrete acid and enzymes that broke down his flesh. Bile and pancreatic juice would baste muscle and sinew. Peristalsis would push his mutilated form along coils of intestine, where more enzymes would render him into smaller and smaller chunks. The large intestine would extract any remaining water from the remnants of his tissues. The human body was 60 percent water, not 99 percent, as others claimed—he knew his stuff. He was a doctor. All his medical training had prepared him for this. Once the bowel had harvested all useful nutrients, the waste particles would be molded and expelled as a piece of shit to sink down into the abyss, where the bottom-feeders would slurp him up.

He drew a shaky breath. Some infinitesimal kernel of himself—his nuclear, elemental self—would find a more dignified resting place: He would be metabolized and assimilated into the beast's ponderous beating heart.

———————

Digestion?

Fuck that shit.

He needed to induce vomiting. Peter lifted his head off the bed and looked around. A red eye glowed just beyond his bound feet: round, inert, and unblinking.

Huh. A flashlight maybe, once owned by the leviathan's previous meal.

He craned his neck. A faint strip of light glowed somewhere below him—a lightsaber. The whale had swallowed a Jedi. But the lightsaber should have cut through the tender inner lining of the stomach, eliciting an inflammatory reaction.

Staring at the light made his head hurt. He closed his eyes, counted to an eternal ten, and opened them again. The light shone through a linear, straight-edged gap. He'd seen that before, in his previous days. Before he'd become fish food.

A door. The light was coming from beneath a door. He was inside a room.

Something sharp and unforgiving bit into his wrists and ankles when he tried to move. He dug his chin into the mattress—that's what it was, a bed, not the rugae of gastric lining—but the position put direct pressure on his tender nose and pushed his gag deeper into his mouth. He swung his bound ankles over the side of the bed and wrenched himself up. With his head reeling, he fell backward.

He tried again. He planted his shoes on the floor, lurched forward, and pushed through his heels. His starting position was too low.

Again. He leaned forward to situate his center of gravity over his heels. The movement seemed familiar, not muscle memory but something else. He remembered teaching frail, elderly patients in his clinic back home how to do this. Rising from a chair without using your arms was a test of leg strength and vitality. Chair squats helped maintain muscle mass and agility.

Peter scooted to the edge of the bed and leaned forward until his backside lifted off the mattress. Drove down through his heels. Up, now!

He collapsed back onto the bed. Not enough momentum. He tried again.

Up... and... success!

He hopped toward the closet and chinned on the light switch, blinking against the instant illumination. His next stop was the bathroom, where the mirror revealed a sorry-ass sight: eyes bleary, nose wrecked, and mouth muzzled with duct tape. He pivoted to examine his wrists, then scanned the countertop. His electric shaver was no use. In the mirror, he spotted Felipe's metallic pen in his breast pocket. A viable tool, perhaps.

He craned his neck and scrunched his abs tight, trying to grab it with his teeth. Off by inches. He crouched at an awkward angle and torqued his head to the side, puffed out his chest, and lowered himself until the nib of the pen caught on the countertop. The pen lifted out of his pocket and clattered into the sink.

He turned and grasped the pen behind his back. The thick, knurled barrel made for good ergonomics. *Ta-tick, ta-tack, ta-tick.* With the writing tip retracted, the business end of the pen was a crown of three teeth—not sharp enough to cause inadvertent injury but prominent enough to catch against the smooth edge of a zip tie. He mouthed a silent thanks to Felipe.

But he couldn't angle the pen up toward his wrists and apply enough force to slice through a wet Kleenex. He needed to anchor the pen to something and rake the zip tie across the teeth.

Every hop to his nightstand made his head pound. He gave himself a count of ten to recover, opened the drawer behind his back, slid the pen into the gap with the teeth pointing up, and shoved the drawer shut with his hip. The only way he could get his wrists to the pen was to kneel and bend forward at the waist, as if waiting for the axman to lop off his head. He lowered the zip tie, hoping for a bull's-eye with the teeth of the pen.

Thunk. The pen slipped into the drawer. He bit down on the gag and repeated the sequence, this time using his thumbs to hold the drawer shut around the pen. Ah, that was the trick. He sawed the zip tie back and forth, again and again. An infinitesimal loosening of his bonds confirmed the process was working. The polymer was slowly thinning and stretching.

And then it snapped in two.

He gently peeled back the duct tape and tore the gag from his mouth—a washcloth—then sat on the bed, taking greedy breaths. He used the tip of the pen to saw through the zip tie around his ankles.

Freedom!

His wrists were crisscrossed with angry, blood-beaded fissures. Something was scribbled on his left hand in black ink: *Yuli*. He didn't remember writing it, but who else would've done it? He'd probably used Felipe's pen for that too.

Hell of a thing, trying to remember whether you'd forgotten something. But there was no denying that he'd been having spells where his mind went blank, and the episodes were growing in frequency and duration. He shuddered to guess at the misdeeds he might've carried out in such a state. *Regretful things.*

Still, this message had to be something important, something vital to his current predicament. He couldn't afford to assume it was the random output of a feverish delusion. Whatever *Yuli* meant, its explanation had to be out there, not in here.

Dusk darkened the edges of the curtains. No voices or footfalls came from outside the cabin.

Time to get out of here.

He pushed the door lever down and was met with solid resistance and a clacking sound. The door wouldn't budge.

They'd locked him in.

21

AT SOME POINT, the night had lightened to pale dawn. Peter traced a swollen finger down a seam of the bedspread. His throat was hoarse from yelling for help, and his hands ached from pounding on the door. The lock was supposed to keep people out, not seal him in.

The holes in his memory were filling in like groundwater welling up in the paw prints of a rabid raccoon. Muddy and random.

This was his cabin on the ship. Yes, his toiletries in the bathroom and his suitcase in the closet. Yet this was no vacation, as evidenced by his scrubs and dim recollections of treating patients in a place of stainless steel and off-white panels. He was working as a physician here. That's who he was.

His cell phone was gone. The desk phone was missing too. The gray cord snaked out from the wall and ended in a curl on the desk. Surviving a thirty-second wait for the elevator was nothing compared to this phoneless solitude.

But why would he have written *Yuli* on his hand? Of all

body parts, the hands were the most likely to be washed. If the word was so important, he shouldn't have risked erasure.

Hands washed, hands cleansed. Something important there.

Hands sanitized.

Yuli, hand sanitizer. Yuli, washcloth, towel animals, gag.

Yes, that was it.

"Thank you," he whispered to whoever was listening. He clicked his pen open and wrote high on his forearm: *Yuli hand sanitizer virus.* Pressed down and retraced the letters, carving depressions into his epidermis. These words were the rope dangling into the pit, a lifeline.

It was coming back to him now. There were two potential explanations: Yuli had pulled this off independently, making the man some kind of demigod, or he had the backing of an organization. Neither alternative seemed better than the other. Regardless, Yuli was the cornerstone of the whole wicked scheme.

That thick and foggy feeling... He couldn't afford to give in again. He rubbed his tender nose hard and pulled his hair. The pain brought clarity.

Yuli was a devil who aimed to turn the people here into beasts—and not just the *Paradise* but New York, the whole of America, and beyond. This contagion would not respect political boundaries. And if this was the destiny of humankind, what was the point of stopping it? He might as well give in, go with the flow. Eat, sleep, mate. Not such a bad life.

A knock on the door.

"Peter?" A woman's voice, muffled but tense.

He scrambled to his feet and squinted through the peephole at a haunted, disheveled woman with twitchy eyes, her face huge and distorted by the fisheye lens. He'd never seen Luisa like this.

He rattled the handle. "Let me out!"

"They're coming, Peter. Let me in!"

The door jangled with their concurrent beatings, their contrary ambitions blocked by the same slab of laminated steel.

"Wait, wait. I'm giving you the key." He tried to shove his key card under the door, but it was obstructed by some kind of immovable lip. "I can't... It won't—"

"It won't work anyway," Luisa said. "It has a big plate, and there's a huge lock across the handle. Yellow tape too."

It had to be one of those plexiglass contraptions with the padlock he'd seen at Calvin's cabin. No key card would work. Only someone with a metal key could set him free—someone like Mauricio, who'd put him here in the first place. He frowned. She should've immediately understood that he was trapped inside and she was locked outside. If she was only now seeing this, she must be delusional like him or hopelessly desperate. Probably both.

"Our cabin steward did this," he said. "Yuli. Watch out for him."

"Who?" She pounded again on the door.

"The little guy who cleans your room."

"I don't know who you're talking about."

It was no use. Direct commands were his only hope. "Go get Harrington."

"They're coming already." She let out a high-pitched whimper. "They're gonna take us all out."

He pressed his forehead against the door. Talking with her was painful. There was no telling whether her next sentence would be tainted by illness.

"The little things," she continued. "I saw them outside. They're gonna shoot us up."

Despite knowing her testimony was suspect, he couldn't afford to ignore even the most bizarre warnings. He rushed to the window and flung the curtains wide. The sudden intrusion of daylight from the overcast, mottled sky jabbed like a spear into his brain. He recoiled and squeezed his eyes shut.

Blinking and squinting, he searched the seascape for any hint of marauders. The rolling swells could be hiding pirate ships in their troughs. But there were no vessels out there, no squid monsters, only the soupy sea under a drab, misty sky. Nothing to see.

He was about to pull the curtains shut when a bird caught his eye, a seagull skimming in from the left. They must be closer to land than he thought. Sleek and slender, it was a regal thing, gliding in a perfectly horizontal plane—a little too perfect. That was no seagull. A dragon had come to belch hellfire upon the ship, delivering the ruination of the *Paradise*.

But that didn't seem—No, dragons didn't exist. This must be another hallucination. He shut the curtains, caught himself, and threw them open again to consider the impossibly long, unmoving wings and precise, inorganic maneuvers of the flying thing.

This was a drone, no doubt.

It panned across the sky with its nose facing the ship, pausing several times to hover before curling up and out of view.

Whereas Felipe had worked on the ancient, steel-hulled tanks, these carbon-fiber drones were the future—or, apparently, the present. Peter tugged the curtains closed again. The ship's destruction, and the security of America, would be wrought not by huge nuclear warheads but by a barrage of missiles fired by drones.

The harsh glare of the TV screen was almost unbearable for Peter's sensitive eyes. He fumbled with the remote until he found the brightness setting and turned it halfway down. The navigation animation showed the little triangle chugging toward the black star of New York, which was closer than ever.

It didn't take long to find a CNN segment covering the story. The anchor was interviewing a medical correspondent from Emory and some dour-faced professor from Cornell about the new chimeric virus. They argued about the various manifestations of encephalitis, with the prevalence of seizures their main point of contention. A 3D rendering of a human brain rotated slowly in one corner of the screen. Peter watched, mesmerized, as the frontal lobe darkened under a cloud of viral particles until the tissue disintegrated. The brain reappeared intact as the animation repeated, the whole cycle taking about five seconds. Brain good, brain bad—the lives of victims encapsulated in less time than it took to tie your shoes.

There was no mention of where the virus had come from or why. So far, Peter appeared to be the only one who knew. He alone stood between Yuli and freedom, between Yuli and worldwide dissemination of the virus. Nobody would suspect contaminated hand sanitizer as the seed. They could obliterate the ship if they wanted to, but if Yuli still had repositories of hand sanitizer elsewhere…

It all came back to Yuli.

Peter flipped through the channels in search of more news. His throat tightened at a familiar face, with bright eyes and a golden tan. Nora Wetzel, dressed in a serious blazer, was on the BBC, looking out of sorts, speaking stoically about standard procedures for removing the captain of a cruise ship from command. Forster's photo was displayed in the adjacent panel.

The panel shifted to social media clips from passengers and crew: scenes of chaos and torment. Fistfights and chairs thrown. Primitives frolicking around a bonfire. Peter winced but didn't spot his face in the semidarkness around the flames. Each clip was accompanied by a box at the bottom: *Verified* with a green checkmark, or *Unverified* with blue.

"On the topic of videos," the anchor said, "we haven't been able to verify the authenticity of the video of the ship's physician, Peter Palma. He claimed that anarchy on the ship was due to drug use. Can you offer any perspective on that?"

"Absolutely," Wetzel said. "That was a deepfake, as I've mentioned before, confirmed with state-of-the-art analytic techniques. I've had conversations with Dr. Palma since that video surfaced."

"When was the last time you talked with him?"

"You know, with cruise ships, sometimes the signal is spotty, even with modern satellites." A nervous smile flashed across her face. "We do have an ongoing dialogue."

His stomach dropped. Yuli had Peter's phone, unlock code, and identity. Wetzel would have no idea it wasn't him.

Yuli was in complete and utter control.

"Don't believe him!" Peter bellowed at the screen. He swung a fist downward, punching nothing but air. "He has my phone!"

"How about other communications with Dr. Palma or the medical staff?" the anchor continued. "What are they saying about conditions on the ship? Is it true that the number of deaths has exceeded the capacity of the morgue and that bodies are being stored in a freezer?"

Wetzel's voice came out jittery. "Norton, excuse me. As

you know, this is an evolving situation and we need to make sure details are verified."

"Then perhaps you can shed light on the deepfake video," he said. "The critical question is why. Who would have created and posted a deepfake, and to what end?"

"My cabin steward did," Peter muttered. "He made me towel animals."

"We don't know yet," Wetzel replied. "That's under active investigation by intelligence agencies."

It was too much. He snapped the TV off and dug in his suitcase for his sunglasses. Forget the pool deck—he now needed shades just to look out the window.

The drone had reappeared, panning left and right, nose once more trained on the ship. What was it looking for? Bodies, maybe, dead or alive. Signs of unrest, no doubt. Justification for a permanent solution.

The pad of ship's stationery in the desk was about half the size of a regular sheet of paper. Peter tore off a sheet and printed in block letters: *SOS HELP!* He slapped it against the glass and pointed to it, willing the drone operator to take notice. The drone slid to the right. It would soon disappear from view entirely, and it might circle back again or might not. He was losing time.

He scrambled back to the closet and pulled down the orange life vest. He pressed it against the window, a fluorescent flag of distress, leaving just enough room for his face and the note.

Oh no, it was happening again, that fogginess. He was slipping into that zone, that pool of warm water from which unpredictable deeds sprang up.

Not now. He needed to focus—no, he needed to *act*.

He dropped the life vest and untied the drawstring of his

scrub pants. Hooked his thumbs under the elastic band of his boxers and yanked them down. He stumbled across the room, pants around his ankles, and dragged the desk chair back to the window. If Mandy could see him now...

The window was cold and real against his bare buttocks. He grinned into his empty cabin. He had no shame at all. If this didn't show the world the state of affairs on the *Paradise*, nothing would.

———————

Peter's chest was as hollow as a gourd. So many times over these past weeks, he'd fought the temptation to lock himself here and succumb to the overwhelming futility. Now he was fighting to get out.

The all-nighters of med school during preclinical years had been followed by more all-nighters on hospital rotations. Residency had kept him juggling critically ill patients on every shift, pushing IVs, reading EKGs, and draining abscesses. Joining the clinic in Houston had offered a brief honeymoon, when it had felt good to help people as their doctor. But the health care system had gradually ensnared him in its quagmire of inefficiency. Most of all, he'd struggled to balance the weight of duty and expectations. It added up to an immense burden.

Then Felipe's request, uttered in a moment of agony after years of torment, had flattened him completely.

All that was a cakewalk compared to what was happening now. The Peter of Houston was a stranger, no more resembling the current version of himself than Queen Elizabeth did. The virus had exposed his true self. His primal urges defined the core, unchanging essence of his being. It would be easier to welcome this degeneration if it made him some flawed, tortured hero. But nothing was romantic here, trapped in his cabin without his pants on. Random neuronal destruction would determine his final state.

He crawled into bed. It wouldn't be so bad to just go with the flow. Give up the fight. It was time to let go.

He pulled the sentiment over him like a wool blanket and sank into a welcoming slumber.

Dull percussions enveloped him. The marching band had come out to play. They must've set up the RV too close to the stadium. The beat swelled in pitch and volume and finally resolved into the window-shaking *thup-thup-thup* of a helicopter.

Peter came to and clambered out of bed, threw on his sunglasses, and tore the curtains aside. A massive twin-rotor chopper veered toward the front of the ship, pummeling and misting the waves below. US Army, according to the yellow block letters on the bottom of its fuselage.

The Bridge Cam channel on TV showed the hazy smudge of Manhattan in the distance. The black helicopter whizzed through the sky, mother eagle to the little scout drones. Its rotors scattered the burned-out remnants of the bonfire from the center of the helipad.

What a damn fine sight to see.

The military was here to help, not to blast them out of the water. A swell of patriotism filled his empty chest, pride not just for America but for humankind.

He had to be ready for them. He didn't want to look like a scrub or be wearing scrubs. He peeled his shirt off, pulled his boxers on, and reached for the formal white officer uniform he hadn't worn since the first day.

A glint in the narrow gap between the chest of drawers and the closet caught his eye. Probably a reflection of the light from the bathroom across the way, but he crouched for a closer look. He stretched one arm into the gap, groping, almost there...

He knew as soon as his fingers closed around the round head of the stethoscope that it was his missing 3M Littmann Cardiology IV. He dangled it in front of his face like a dead snake. It must've fallen into the crack when he was stuffing things into drawers while Luisa was waiting for him.

It had been here all this time.

Urgent pounding on the door. "Hey, hey! Anybody in there?"

Peter pressed his eye to the peephole. It was a man with cropped gray hair in an N95 respirator mask and a transparent full-face shield. "It's me! Let me out!"

The man turned to confer with someone out of view, then spoke to the door again. "US Army. Identify yourself."

"Doctor Peter Palma." The cavalry was here, the cavalry was here.

"Is anybody else in there with you?"

"No." He slapped the door and rattled the handle. His eyes fell on the note on his forearm. Yuli. "He locked me in. I've been here for..." He didn't know how long. "I need to find him!"

"Date of birth, please."

He normally didn't furnish that kind of information to anyone who asked, but he couldn't blurt it out fast enough now. Social security, driver's license—nothing was sacred after mooning a drone.

A sharp crack, pop, and click issued from the door. "Go ahead, sir," came a female voice.

Peter yanked the door open, dragging in torn yellow ribbon from the doorjamb. His rescuers wore black fatigues and gloves, but they might as well have had wings and halos. The man carried a tablet computer and the woman, a foot-long bolt cutter. She had the same mask and face shield as the man.

"Major Elbourne," the man said, adding something like *you sam rid.* "US Army Medical Research Institute of Infectious Diseases. We're coordinating with CDC and WHO, and we're taking the lead on the AECT."

Peter gaped at him.

"Aeromedical Evacuation Control Team," he said.

The woman with bolt cutters introduced herself as Gajwani, sergeant first class. Her gaze swept over his shattered nose and scabbed wrists. "Are you okay?"

He motioned them inside. He could've kissed them. "How did you know I was here?"

Gajwani squinted. "Your little display there"—she pointed over his shoulder at the window—"it worked."

Oh, yeah, his ass prints. Finally a win, if he could call it that.

"Hold still." Elbourne pointed the camera of the tablet at Peter's face until it beeped. He scrolled and tapped on the screen. "Clear." He handed Peter a surgical mask. "Put this on."

He did so.

"You should see a doctor about that nose." Gajwani nodded up at him. "It's probably broken."

The army pair seemed relaxed yet alert, but they'd casually

drawn closer, surrounding him much like Yuli and Mauricio had.

"We need to find my cabin steward," Peter said. "He's behind all this."

The soldiers looked at each other.

"Your part is over, sir," Elbourne said. "She'll show you the way."

Gajwani stepped back into the hallway. "Come with me."

Peter threw up his hands. "No, no! He put the virus inside the bottles of hand sanitizer. It's a combination of Nipah virus and I'm guessing adenovirus. It causes frontal encephalitis."

"We know about the virus." Gajwani glanced at Elbourne.

Peter pointed to his forehead. "Don't you see? That's what's making us act up."

Elbourne just kept scrolling on his tablet. They were only there to rescue him and they thought he was deranged. Well, there was some truth in that. But he alone knew the truth that superseded everything. He checked the writing on his arm just to make sure.

Yes.

He clasped his hands in front of his face. "I'm grateful beyond words, I am. My brother was in the army"—his voice cracked—"but we really need to find Yuli. A nurse, Mandy Chin, is also in danger. And my sister. She's watching over this kid in a wheelchair. And the other nurse—I don't think Yuli sees her as a threat, but she's a danger to herself."

Gajwani took a step closer, reaching for something in her back pocket. He twisted sideways to slip between them, but Elbourne caught him by the elbow. "Not so fast, Doctor."

"At least let me go back to the clinic. I can show you what I'm talking about."

22

THE ARMY HAD turned the clinic into command central. Mandy, Nali, and Calvin were nowhere in sight. Severe-looking men and women in dark fatigues moved with efficiency. A few of them had handguns holstered at the hip, including Elbourne and Gajwani, which Peter hadn't noticed till now. Black duffels lined the waiting area, and soldiers were unpacking monitors, IV bags, and cartons of white plastic bottles from rugged green crates.

"Please tell me you brought steroids," Peter said.

Elbourne grinned. "We have enough prednisone to eradicate lupus from Earth. More efficient than starting IVs on everyone. But it's only part of the plan."

Plan?

Center stage in the critical care bay, they'd brought in a sleek gurney mounted off-center on thick pedestal. A soldier busied himself at a touchscreen in front of what looked like two large drums, one atop the other. The upper drum was open on each end, allowing the special gurney to pass through. An articulating arm arched over the gurney, with a thick, curved plate on the end—a dentist's chair from hell.

"You all setting up to fill cavities?" He was only partially joking. That young girl Emma could've used a dentist after she pulled her own teeth out.

Gajwani appeared by his side. "Relax, Dr. Palma. You've done a remarkable job. We'll take it from here."

The chilly serenity in her voice unnerved him. "What is all this?"

"Ever heard of transcranial magnetic stimulation?" Elbourne asked.

"Of course. But that's for depression and OCD."

Peter had once tried to get a patient approved for TMS, detailing how she continued to suffer from depression despite three medications and endless rounds of counseling. She was petrified by the idea of electroconvulsive therapy, so TMS seemed promising. Magnetic pulses directed at the brain would alter the firing patterns of neurons, a potential game changer, but insurance denied her repeatedly. And he had even looked into TMS for himself at one point, when the convergence of stress and grief from Felipe had buried him in a pitch-black hole.

"This is a portable MRI-TMS machine," Elbourne said. "A one-stop shop. The MRI identifies the inflamed area of the brain, and the TMS targets it."

"Give it a try," said the soldier setting up the machine. "A little zap'll do ya."

Peter frowned, rallying his wavering focus. Encephalitis wasn't the same as depression, at least not in the early stages. What were they up to here?

"Encephalitis boils down to inflammation and necrosis," Elbourne said. "Do you agree?"

He nodded cautiously.

"Well, this is a no-brainer, then." Elbourne cracked a tiny smile.

"Preliminary studies suggest that TMS can modulate the immune response via novel pathways," Gajwani added. "We can't reverse the encephalitis, but we might be able to halt it and allow the brain to heal itself."

So this was just a theory. "How preliminary are these studies?"

She looked at Elbourne.

"What did the trials show?" Peter repeated.

"This *is* the trial," Elbourne said.

Peter tilted his head.

"Did you know that one of the very first clinical trials was conducted at sea?" Gajwani said. "James Lind, Royal College of Physicians, 1747, on board the *Salisbury*. He fed twelve sailors with scurvy different diets. Guess which one worked the best?"

He gave her a flat look. "Citrus."

"That's right. Oranges and lemons."

"Things have changed since then," Peter said. "There are rules for research."

Elbourne pulled up a PDF on his tablet and pointed to a highlighted paragraph. He blathered on about United Nations law of the sea, part this, section that, saying that a country's territorial waters extend up to twelve nautical miles from the coastline. He snapped the tablet shut. "Anything beyond that is international waters."

Heat climbed up Peter's neck. They weren't continuing to New York—not yet. The ship was in no-man's-land, the gray zone where anything goes. "This has never been tried in people with encephalitis?"

"All participants will get standard of care, which at this point is steroids." Elbourne tapped his tablet. "Steroids with or without TMS. Who fares better? Wouldn't you agree it's a worthwhile question, especially with so many lives at stake?"

The MRI-TMS was clicking and beeping as the soldier continued the setup.

"By definition, if they're infected and delusional," Peter said. "They can't weigh the pros and cons."

"What about you?" asked Elbourne. "You seem to harbor a healthy skepticism about this, despite your infection."

He folded his arms. "Maybe the virus has made me paranoid."

"So you're the perfect candidate. Or you can turn it down. Anybody is free to decline."

The perverted logic made his head hurt, like that *Catch-22* novel from high school. What was it about the military that produced such impossible dilemmas? "Who authorized this?"

"The president is aware," Elbourne said, "as are the UN General Assembly and Security Council."

"What about the World Health Organization?"

"Them too."

There was no higher authority for these matters.

"One zap, that's all." Elbourne held up a fat, scarred finger.

"I thought you needed dozens of sessions for TMS."

Gajwani jinked her head toward the machine, which now filled the cramped space with ravenous thrumming. "Not for our program. Like he said, one round."

The amount of coordination and planning they'd managed was stunning. USAMRIID must've had everything ready to go before the ship neared the East Coast. No doubt years of preparation had led to this moment—tax dollars at work.

"I get it, I understand." Elbourne clasped his hands behind

his back and studied the floor. "You've been the man for what, ten or eleven days now? This is all pretty sudden for you."

The arrogant little... "How are you deciding who to use it on? I bet hundreds of people are infected but haven't shown symptoms yet."

Elbourne shrugged. "True, there's no rapid test for this virus yet. But we'll take nasal swabs and blood samples. They'll go to the biobank for future testing."

An icy finger ran down Peter's spine. "You're trying to enroll *everybody*?"

Him, Yuli. If they both went into that TMS machine, memories might be erased. The truth would never come out.

Elbourne merely blinked and worked his mouth.

They were being cordial now but would bring hard pressure soon enough. Peter gave a nod of what he hoped looked like acknowledgment, then slowly backed away before they could "strongly encourage" him to "volunteer" for TMS.

The words on his forearm caught his eye: *Yuli hand sanitizer virus.*

Shit! The bottles. Mandy must've stashed them somewhere safe like the pharmacy. He glanced around at the commotion in the little clinic. Nope, they wouldn't be there. Maybe the office.

The daylight streaming in through the office window burned mercilessly. He shut the curtains halfway, shrouding the room in dimness. He must've forgotten his sunglasses in his cabin. His legs slackened and he stumbled, catching himself with a hand on the wall. He lowered himself into the chair and hunched over his knees.

Head so heavy. Eyelids so heavy. He'd come here to find something. What was it?

"Are you all right?" The firm voice of Elbourne. "Dr. Palma."

After a few seconds—or a few years, he wasn't sure—the fog dissipated enough for him to look up. This was his future: spells of clarity and confusion, jockeying for supremacy. Squinting in the half-light. The swelling and bruising in his nose would eventually improve, and his aching muscles would recover, but his mind? All bets were off.

"I know you don't believe me." Peter grasped at an important idea, but it slipped away. Maybe Elbourne was right; he should just strap himself in that gurney and let it rip. The magnetic waves would reboot his brain back to system settings. "Will I remember anything afterward if I get it done?"

"That's something we're very interested in finding out," Elbourne said. "We'll conduct a battery of tests."

They had no clue. But it wouldn't be so bad to not remember anything. People spent a lot of time and energy trying to forget.

Elbourne pulled up a chair next to him. "I'm glad you came in here, actually. We need access to the EHR. We need to cross-reference medical records with our trial data."

Alarms sounded in Peter's brain. There was something… There was a leverage point here. "Then help me find Yuli."

"After your TMS you'll feel right as rain, and you'll be able look for anyone you—"

Peter shook his head. "You don't know shit about how the brain responds to TMS in this situation, with encephalitis. That's why it's a trial."

Elbourne clenched his jaw.

"I need to find Yuli first. Before I get TMS." Peter swallowed hard. "Before I give you access to the EHR."

"Sir, are you negotiating after we just liberated your ass?"

"These are private records."

"We're here to help."

"Private records."

Peter drew a deep breath. Now the thread was coming back: He had to stop Yuli from escaping, from getting away with this—but he lacked the willpower to filter his words and they came tumbling out. "Mandy, my God, her smile makes me tingle, but she probably thinks I'm a loser. Nali, I could kill her—not really, she's my sister. She's too smart for her own good. I gotta give her credit though. She took it pretty hard when I told her about Felipe, and I think she might've known. Yeah, somehow, she already knew what I did."

Elbourne shifted uncomfortably.

"Calvin." Peter emitted a shrill giggle. "What a tragedy. His mom, I guess she couldn't take it anymore. She's dead now. There's no winner here." He slapped the desk and surged from the chair. "That's who I'm looking for—not Calvin's mom, not her. Yuli. That bastard's going to continue this thing and—" He stopped cold, feeling completely hollowed out, even emptier than when he'd learned of Felipe's overdose.

Elbourne stood and clapped a huge hand on Peter's shoulder. "This is how it goes. Those in the study, they get TMS or sham, followed by observation for seventy-two hours. Then we let them go with wrist trackers. Those who decline to enroll, we route to quarantine. Location TBD, duration TBD. But before we start, we need access to the ship's EHR."

No way, no how. He shook off Elbourne's hand and glared at him.

"We have international support," Elbourne said. "The public is terrified."

They couldn't force him. They couldn't force anyone. "You and Gajwani and ten or eleven soldiers are going to make this happen?"

Elbourne strode to the window and pulled the curtains back. "Look out there."

Peter cowered from the sunlight. Peering through his fingers, he saw the city as a silver smear in the distance. He couldn't see the Statue of Liberty. She'd probably taken a leave of absence; she wouldn't welcome these huddled masses yearning to breathe free, lest the whale disgorge its bile on her coppery-green feet.

He followed Elbourne's finger off to the left, where a half dozen dark humps were approaching. They were coming, first the drone, then the chopper, and now a whole fleet converging on the *Paradise* like a pod of orcas.

But none of them were listening.

———

When the most recent hurricane had swept through Houston, Elena had confessed to Peter that her main concern was the fate of the zoo animals. *Who's going to take care of them? What if they escape?* They joked about baboons terrorizing the streets only to meet their demise in the jaws of alligators rising on the bloated Buffalo Bayou.

Here on the fifth-level balcony overlooking the grand atrium were baboons and alligators aplenty. Peter fought his way through, dodging random scuffles and stepping over a fornicating threesome. Squeals echoed through the magnificent chamber—ecstasy or terror, it was hard to tell. Human animals with no moral compass writhed and thrashed. A smattering of security guards fought the good fight, but they were badly outnumbered. They'd already lost Jamie Carson to violence and Mauricio to corruption.

Yuli was nowhere to be seen.

The crush had thinned out along the outer rim, where the ravaged eyes of the infected were battered by sunlight. Peter squinted and pressed forward. Relief came only when he plucked a pair of sunglasses off the floor seconds before they would have been squashed under boots.

He donned the shades. Ahh, so much better.

Good thing he'd ditched Elbourne by saying he needed to take a dump. Now if only he could find that devil who'd started all this.

"Yuli!" he cried for the hundredth time. "Yuli!" He'd developed a slight hitch in his step at some point, an overcompensation for the lack of phone weight in his empty pocket. All he needed now was an ax and he'd be a dead ringer for that Jack fellow in *The Shining*, lurching around the frozen maze and yelling for his son.

A series of sharp tones blasted from the overhead speakers, stunning the rabble-rousers into a pause. It was short-lived. By the time Kinnard called "Attention, attention," the mob had already resumed doing mob things—bashing and smashing, mostly.

Peter barely avoided trampling a toddler with a tear-smeared face who bumbled into his path. A silent cry froze the little girl's mouth. Seeing no adult searching for her, Peter hoisted her onto his hip. "Where's your mom or dad?"

She erupted into a full-throated bawl.

"Okay, I got you. It's okay," he sang, pinballing through the horde. It was too chaotic here. One slip and the savages would trample them. He had to get this child to safety.

Straining on tiptoe to locate the stairwell, he spotted a black-fatigued soldier on the sixth-level balcony, a position of relative security: surrounded by comrades, armed with a rifle, relaxed and ready. Peter's innards turned to ice. Rubber bullets—please let there be only rubber bullets. What crime would meet the threshold for such an extreme intervention? Their backups were sure to arrive soon.

Someone jostled him from behind and wrested the girl from his grip. He whirled around, fist cocked, but stopped short when she buried her head into the weeping man's neck.

Tears did not hide the man's anger. "What the fu— What are you doing with my daughter?"

Peter backed away, hands open. "I was just trying to get her to safety."

The man's nostrils flared. Confusion in his eyes gave way to desperation. "You're the doctor."

Peter nodded.

The man tucked the girl into his shoulder. "What's the army doing here? Did they bring medicine?"

He had no time or easy way to explain the army's plan. The zoo animals had busted out of their enclosures, and Yuli could be anywhere by now.

———————

A pungent scent lingered in the damp air of Harrington's office, and wads of tissue had spilled from the trash can onto the floor. Sitting behind his desk, he licked his lips, his eyes unfocused. "So what you're telling me is that fairies hide in flowers, and if I'm super quiet, I might hear them."

Shit, so it was down to this. Fairies.

Peter shook his head. "I said my cabin steward is working with Mauricio to spread a bioengineered virus designed to destroy society, and they're doing it with hand sanitizer."

Harrington chuckled, light and easy. "Oh, I'm sorry, don't get mad. Let me get this straight. You want to have a tea party."

Should he force the issue or just try to wait out the spell? Peter glanced down, nudging the tissues away from his chair with one foot.

A huge smile cracked Harrington's face but his brow furrowed, as if demons were fighting for jurisdiction over his psyche. "Ha ha, yeah, I'm just kidding." He puffed his cheeks out for a second. "Okay, tell me again."

"Mauricio's working with the man who unleashed the virus on this ship." Peter lifted his shirt to expose the two small welts. "That's where he got me."

Harrington unholstered his own stun gun and abutted the business end of it to Peter's wounds. The span between contact points matched exactly. "So someone zapped you."

"Mauricio."

"Who?"

He could do this. He could. "He reports directly to you. You're his boss."

Harrington shrugged and pouted like a child.

Even if Harrington's brain was Swiss cheese, he should still have a few functioning clusters of neurons. "Can you search the system for Yuli?"

"Huh?"

Peter slapped the desk. "Search the system for Yuli."

Harrington snapped to attention, serious now. He jiggled the mouse.

"Y-U-L-I," Peter said.

Harrington tapped on the keyboard, clicked, tapped again. "He's not here. You sure you got the spelling right?" He swiveled the screen around. They tried some alternate spellings, but nothing came up.

Peter checked his arm again. *Y-u-l-i*. That was the spelling. Either he had it right, or he'd hallucinated the whole thing and

Yuli was a figment of his diseased brain. *Yuli hand sanitizer virus*. No, Yuli was not a figment of his imagination, but the name was probably fake. If Yuli or whatever his real name was could create a deepfake video, pinning a phony name tag on an employee vest would be nothing.

Harrington was still clacking away at the keyboard. "What's he look like?"

"Kind of on the smaller side—not thin, not thick. Bald. Could be from anywhere. What's the most secure place on the ship that a cabin steward could access?"

This question seemed to greatly disturb Harrington.

Peter moved around the desk to Harrington's side and reached for the mouse. This window of clarity might close at any moment—time to squeeze the orange before it spoiled. "May I?"

Harrington sat back as Peter leaned over and unpaused the video he'd been watching earlier. A weak smile played across Harrington's face. "You won't tell?"

"It's none of my business," Peter said. "But you can't do this when you're on duty, right? That would be breaking the rules."

Harrington nodded slowly. "Rules."

"We don't want to break the rules."

"Don't break the rules."

Now, to see what he could shake loose. "I have an idea."

"Idea?" Harrington's face lit up.

"When you're on duty, you need all your stuff. But when you're not on duty, you don't."

"Stuff, yeah. Stuff."

"So let me just hold on to some of that for you." He pointed to something on Harrington's belt. "The stuff you don't need. I'll keep it safe, I promise."

Harrington reached down. "I don't need this?"

"No."

"Okay." He handed it to Peter.

"And that too. You won't need that now."

Harrington agreed and gave him the second thing.

"Just one more." He pointed to the last thing. This was pushing it, and a sneer darkened Harrington's face. He was coming out of it. Peter jiggled the mouse and motioned to the screen with his head. Harrington's jaw slackened, and the tip of his thick tongue slid out like a turtle's head.

There we go. Peter lifted the third thing—easy does it. He patted Harrington's shoulder. Poor bastard. They were both in the same boat. The only way forward was to take turns rowing, and it was Peter's turn now.

23

AT LEAST THREE rooms should've been sealed, but Yuli would have access to all of them. Peter wrote them on his arm: *Cal mom dead, Cal mom cabin, hostage.* The script was sprawling and uneven, but he couldn't afford to lose this train of thought. Harrington was halfway to Hartleyland, Yuli owned Mauricio, and the army had their own agenda.

Peter was on his own.

First and easiest to find was the fifth-floor cabin where Calvin and his mom had stayed. The room was still sealed with a plexiglass plate and padlock, but the yellow tape had been torn off and lay in shreds by the door. The fourth key on Harrington's ring worked. The lock popped open, and he tossed the plate aside, inserted the key card he'd lifted from Harrington, and held his breath. A soft click and a little green light confirmed it was indeed a master key card.

Nobody was inside.

On to room 2498 on the second floor, where Sunila had been slashed. Same sequence: Key open the padlock, remove the plastic plate, unlock the door. This time, a dull rustling from inside raised the hairs on Peter's neck. He held his breath and flung the door open.

Calvin sat bound and gagged in his own wheelchair by the sliding balcony door. The gag in his mouth muffled a soft whimper. Mandy sat similarly restrained in the desk chair, eyes wild. Nausea coiled in Peter's belly when he saw the bed which bore witness to the earlier sacrifice—pillow and sheets encrusted with blood, clothesline and webbing dangling from the corners.

He was about to rush for Calvin when Mauricio leapt up from behind the bed and closed in fast, lunging for Peter's throat.

But Peter, still near the threshold, gripped the steel door and yanked it back with all his weight, feeling a sharp stretch in his shoulder as he hurtled out of the cabin. Mauricio gripped the edge of the door. Momentum carried through, and the door slammed shut on Mauricio's fingers with a crunch. Peter landed on his ass in the hallway. Hot pain shot up from his tailbone, and his teeth snapped closed on his bottom lip.

Ka-plink, ka-plunk: Peter's howl of agony was cut short as two thimble-size chunks ricocheted off his chest and tumbled to the floor. The bone protruding from the severed fingertips looked like snake eyes on dice.

Behind the door, Mauricio bayed and cursed.

Dammit, that animal was still in there with Mandy and Calvin.

Peter clambered up and flattened himself against the wall beside the door, out of view. He unhooked Harrington's stun gun and curled his finger around the trigger. When Mauricio burst out seconds later, he jammed the weapon into his abs, pulled the trigger, and sent the scumbag into electroconvulsive agony.

Mauricio spasmed and groaned on the floor. The stumps of his fingers pulsed and squirted thin ribbons of blood onto the carpet. Under different circumstances, Peter would've wrapped the fingertips in a moist cloth and put them in a plastic bag on ice to preserve them for surgical reattachment. But as a— Well, whatever he was now, he'd just as soon shove the flesh-nubbins down Mauricio's throat.

A few zip ties from Mauricio's own stock rendered him immobile. Peter patted him down and found that nasty knife with the charcoal blade. "I'm keeping the door open. Make a move, and I'll hit you again."

"You're too late," Mauricio muttered with a demented grimace.

Peter used the charcoal knife to release Mandy, who sputtered and wiped saliva from her mouth, and they both rushed to free Calvin. Mandy worked on his towel gag while Peter sliced the layers of duct tape wrapped around Calvin's upper body and wheelchair. That asshole must've used a whole roll.

"Pee-pee," Calvin said when his mouth was finally unfettered. "Pee-pee."

Affection swelled in Peter's chest. "Yeah, I'm here, buddy. I'm so sorry this happened to you."

Calvin shook his head and pointed at the plastic urinal on the floor.

Peter snorted a laugh. "I thought he was saying my name."

Mandy grabbed the urinal and levered Calvin up. "Get something to cover him. He can do the rest."

Peter took a blanket from the top shelf of the closet and tossed it over the teen's lap. Calvin used his good hand to position everything, and within seconds relief washed over his face as the stream pelted the inside of the plastic container.

All this time, Peter hadn't thought much about how Calvin

navigated these daily necessities. He'd only had the vague sense that people were around to help.

Mandy eyed his white uniform. "You changed. Are you… okay?"

Maybe he could force the universe into a show of symmetry. He'd worn the uniform his first day on the ship, and wouldn't it be grand if wearing it now meant he'd get off this forsaken vessel today? "Where's Nali?"

"She took off just before he barged into clinic." She nodded toward Mauricio, who was still supine in the hallway.

"Where'd she go?" Maybe she'd simply decided to get a soda at just the right time. Or maybe Yuli had her and… He put that thought away. "Have you heard from her?"

"No." She handed him the urinal, which was now full, heavy, and warm. "Dump that in the toilet while I get him settled."

He stopped short at the sight that greeted him in the bathroom. The bathtub was piled high with bottles of hand sanitizer, all the same size as those in Agus's closet—the mother lode. He picked one up. Empty. He set it aside and picked up another. Empty again. He shoved his hand into the pile, searching for any bottle still containing virus-infused gel, like one of those ball pits little kids jump into. All the bottles were empty.

He unscrewed the lid of a random bottle, held his breath, and peeked inside. A scant few drops of water rolled around inside but no gel. Yuli had done a primo job of discarding evidence. The drainpipe under the sink ran at an acute angle into the wall, with no P-trap or bend in the pipe that might have retained the last known evidence.

He hurled the bottle against the tile backing of the bathtub. "Dammit!"

"Peter?" Mandy called.

"There's nothing here." Nothing but a pile of empty bottles.

"Pe—" Mandy's call broke off abruptly.

Peter whirled around.

"There you are," Yuli said. He must have simply stepped over Mauricio's writhing body. He kicked the steel door shut behind him and sank into a crouch, rocking on his heels and brandishing a steak knife.

Peter straightened up, closed his fingers around the stun gun, and sidestepped out of the bathroom to face Yuli. He'd tied the score with Mauricio, and now he had a chance to go one up.

He surged forward, but immediately Yuli slashed at his face, and Peter jumped back, tumbled onto the bed, and somersaulted over the other side, crashing into the nightstand.

Mandy huddled over Calvin, who was yelling in staccato bursts. Beautiful, sweet Mandy.

Yuli was advancing towards her, that piece of shit, and Peter scrambled up and jabbed forward with the stun gun, animal rage burning in his gut. "She my woman!" he roared.

Yuli flinched.

Peter charged, backing Yuli against the desk. Thrust, another thrust, a short arc. Yuli parried with a raised knee and slashed with the blade, splitting the hem of Peter's sleeve and opening a gash along his upper arm. He yelped and dropped the stun gun.

Yuli lunged for it, but Mandy kicked it away.

Howling, Peter whipped the pen out of his pocket and drove down hard into the base of Yuli's neck, just above his left collarbone. A tiny pop of released tension signaled entry into the pleural space, and he yanked the pen free.

Yuli crumpled into the corner where the door met the

floor, slapping at his chest as if to work it like a bellows. The neck wound emitted a high-pitched whistle with each labored breath. He pitched forward onto his belly, head twisted to one side, as he scrabbled at the seashells and crab designs woven into the carpet.

Peter grabbed him by his vest, slammed him onto his back, and planted a knee on his chest. He fished inside Yuli's vest, recovered his own cell phone, and eased back on his heels.

Yuli's eyes bulged and his tongue flickered in and out of his mouth with each breath.

Die. Fucking die.

"Is he dead?" Mandy asked meekly.

Time to finish the job. Peter was a protector of life, after all. If he couldn't stop the virus from dissolving the brains of his patients, he would stop the contagion at its source.

"Not yet."

He grabbed the pillow stained with Sunila's blood; now it would receive Yuli's death rattle. He straddled Yuli, pinning his arms with both knees, and pressed the pillow over his face. Yuli's hands and feet drummed the floor. Killing Yuli would save others; plus, it felt *so damn good*. He leaned into the pillow as if to cram all the vices and sorrows of the world back into Pandora's box.

Somewhere, someone was calling his name. He shut his eyes and fought back a wave of nausea.

It kept going, the bucking and kicking. This guy was a fighter.

A hand on his shoulder—Mandy's hand. He had to protect Mandy.

He put all his weight into it.

Suddenly the fight was over. The kicking and spasming had

stopped. He pulled the pillow away and stared at the slack and completely unremarkable face of the devil.

Yuli's mouth extruded a gray, slimy foam of bubbles.

"Peter!"

Forever silenced. Yuli would never infect another innocent, never take that insolent tone with anyone to explain—

Oh, no. A vise clamped around Peter's chest and squeezed the air from his lungs.

Oh, no. No, no, no.

He needed Yuli alive and talking. Yuli and the hand sanitizer were the only evidence that would allow the authorities to trace this outbreak and keep the world from crumbling into chaos. There had to be others behind the plot, not just Mauricio—maybe a shadowy ringleader in a bunker with a satellite phone, or a slick-haired gent in a penthouse—but without evidence, no one would go looking.

His frantic fingers found Yuli's phone.

"Peter?"

He unlocked it with Yuli's limp fingertip and turned up the volume, then held Yuli's phone in his right hand and his own phone in his left.

"Text me," he said to Mandy.

She did.

Yuli's phone chirped with crickets as his own device buzzed. Mandy's message—*What's going on?*—glowed on both screens.

Mandy's mouth formed an *O* as Peter jammed his own phone back into his pocket. "Yes! I wasn't just hearing things."

A quick search through Yuli's phone revealed another messaging app with the Gatobi9 handle. There had to be more, but he had trouble making sense of it, especially with Mandy's soft hand on his knee. Of course it was complicated. The law of entropy declared that the universe runs to disorder and chaos, and he'd been fighting against it this whole time. But now it was time to turn things around, to make sure that Yuli's plan never came to fruition. The world needed people like him to counteract people like Yuli.

His breath came rushing back in bursts. He had just punctured Yuli's lung and nearly suffocated him. In a real city, Yuli would've been whisked away to a real emergency room, where a real surgeon would've inserted a chest tube. Here, the clinic was on the other side of the ship, co-opted by the army, and everyone there thought Peter had lost his mind.

"I screwed up," he said, gasping. "I need to save him."

Silhouetted against the glass balcony doors, Mandy's scent was the only pure thing in this room. Sweet and fresh, like her. She leaned down and grabbed his shoulders. "You can do it."

Calvin punched his fist in the air. "Go, Peter!"

Peter shivered. It was the first full sentence he'd ever heard him say.

Peter clambered to his feet, scowling at the lingering ache from the stun gun. He couldn't call 911—he *was* 911. "Yeah, but I'm sorry, buddy. I'm going to need that wheelchair."

Mandy cracked a clean blanket from the closet over the bloodstained bed, and they transferred Calvin from the wheelchair.

"I'll send someone for you all, I promise," Peter said. Calvin gave them a thumbs-up and a crooked smile.

Peter hooked his hands under Yuli's armpits, and Mandy grabbed his feet. Together they hoisted Yuli, limp and moaning, into the wheelchair. He slumped forward and nearly toppled out before Peter caught him.

Mandy snatched a towel penguin from the bedside table, shook it out, and wrapped it around Peter's upper arm to cover the laceration. She pressed his elbow to his side. "I think it'll stay if you keep holding pressure." She propped the door open. "You better get moving."

He nudged the wheelchair into the hallway. The movement loosened the towel, and it dropped to the carpet.

Mandy bent to pick it up.

"Forget it!" Peter growled. "I need to go!"

"Fine." Her face screwed up tight. "Wait." She stuck her hand into the V-neck of her scrubs and came out with a bottle of hand sanitizer. "He missed this one."

Peter grabbed the bottle, still warm from her skin but containing a world-ending virus. "I could kiss you right now."

The corners of her eyes crinkled. "Save it."

24

Either Yuli had swallowed rocks or the hubs on Calvin's wheelchair needed some grease. It shouldn't have been this hard to push a small man down these corridors. Gripping the plastic handles hard enough to maneuver around obstacles required constant flexing and contracting of his hands, which widened the knife wound on Peter's arm.

Basic geometry also conspired against them. This staff hallway was barely wide enough for two-way foot traffic in civil times. Add in carousers and brawlers, and every inch of progress was hard earned.

Yuli's smooth head lolled back, not with the purposeful roll of Calvin, the rightful occupant of the wheelchair, but a signal of his dwindling strength.

"Hey, stay with me!" Peter stopped, leaned over Yuli from behind, and dug his knuckles into his sternum. Yuli's mouth popped open, and his jaw worked up and down. All the color had drained from his face.

Peter resumed their battle forward, his feet moving automatically. She'd told him to save it. Save the kiss or save the hand sanitizer? Both would do, thank you very much. He paused to remember which way to turn next.

He could have hustled Mandy and Calvin to safety first. If he had, Yuli would be dead by now—the simplest of all solutions. But simple wasn't always better. Withdrawing didn't make the problem go away. He'd come halfway around the world to escape his problems, and how was that working out? Letting Yuli die would make him no better than Yuli himself.

Another ten feet of headway, and he paused again to gather his strength. He leaned on the wheelchair as much for support as for momentum. His patients back home with spinal stenosis did the same with their shopping carts at the grocery store.

Ahead, a group of revelers poured out of the elevator. Stairs would be impossible, even one flight down. He had no choice but to take the elevator and hope they didn't get trapped inside with someone deranged, but it was empty—a stroke of good luck. He glided in, pressed the button, and tightened his grip on the handles of the wheelchair.

They emerged unscathed. Before them, two moving columns of troopers in black helmets disappeared up I-95 in the opposite direction. Reinforcements had arrived. The first dozen rows carried rectangular riot shields.

"Need some help, Doctor?" A nearby soldier eyed the oozing wound on Peter's arm.

He nodded. "Clinic."

"You heard him." The soldier gestured with two fingers and, just like that, a trooper commandeered the wheelchair and started trucking Yuli down I-95. Another soldier jogged ahead to clear the way.

They quickly outdistanced Peter, rounding the corner in front of the clinic. The sign that had promised Peter the

comfort of banker's hours had been covered with a plain placard that read *US ARMY*.

When Peter hobbled in, he saw a dozen passengers and
crew had wedged into the little waiting area. A rapid sequence
of clicks behind the curtain of the first bay signaled that the
TMS trial had already begun.

"Where do you want him?" asked the soldier. They had
already lifted Yuli onto a gurney.

The question sent Peter hurtling into outer space. No
foothold, no lifeline. He was supposed to check something,
a reminder. He patted his breast pocket and felt the outline
of a cylindrical bottle. One hip pocket held his phone, which
he opened, but the little square icons meant nothing to him.
Another phone bulged in his other hip pocket. Blank and
locked. Equally useless.

"Well…" He rubbed his temples and steadied himself
against the check-in counter. "Yeah, hold on."

"Your patient's not looking so good. What's the plan?" The
soldier leaned in and got a good look at Yuli. "Ah, this guy
needs medical attention, stat. Is there a doctor here? I mean,
besides you?"

Peter leaned both elbows on the counter. The floor seemed
to slip and slide under his feet. He closed his eyes and took
slow, deep breaths.

A hand on his shoulder brought him back. "We're putting
him in bay number two over there and getting him hooked
up."

"I'll be right there." He gathered the bits and pieces of
himself and forced his eyes open. Behind the counter sat a tall
black can of Agus's coffee.

That fucking coffee.

He cracked it open and let the infernal potion do its work.

Warmth infused every cell of his body. The laceration on his arm sizzled with fiery agony. His head throbbed, but everything held together through the pain, and he could see and think again. At the end of all this, if the world was still spinning, Agus deserved a Nobel Prize for all the ways he'd shifted the course of events.

"Take the wheelchair back to 2498." That was the right room number, he was sure of it. "There's a boy there who needs it, and a nurse who's watching over him." He warned them that they'd find Mauricio bound in the hallway outside. "He's a security guard who was working with this guy here."

The soldiers stepped back in deference. "You got it, sir," one said.

Yuli was limp and restless at the same time. Gajwani appeared and hooked him up to the monitor. A web of creases spread across Yuli's face with each shallow breath. His oxygen read 88, heart rate 120s.

Peter listened to his chest. The right side was clear, but no breath sounds came from the left—a tension pneumothorax. With each breath, the negative pressure in his chest cavity would suck air in through the hole Peter had made with the pen. The jagged wound was a one-way valve, letting air in but not letting it out. The air pressure building between his ribcage and lung was surpassing the pressure inside the lung, squeezing it smaller and smaller.

Peter lowered his head as a wave of dizziness swept over him.

"Are you all right?" Gajwani asked. "I'm here for you. What do you need?"

"Chest tube kit." He yanked open the steel drawers in search of a proper needle.

She called over her shoulder for the kit, setting off a flurry of activity. Cabinets banged open and closed, open and closed. "What else?"

"Cut his shirt off."

She did so.

A lone 14-gauge catheter needle was tucked in the back of a plastic bin behind rolls of gauze and IV tubing. Yuli's head had dropped to the side, and his O2 sat was plummeting. He couldn't have weighed more than a buck fifty, so it was easy to feel the curve of each rib. Peter slid the needle into the flesh just above the second rib.

A whoosh of air from the needle confirmed he'd successfully entered and decompressed the pleural space. He fed the catheter over the needle and withdrew the needle, leaving the catheter in place to act as a port. Only then did Peter let out a breath.

And Yuli's breathing started to ease.

"Lift your arm, Dr. Palma." Gajwani stretched out a length of gauze and gestured at his arm with her chin. "I need to get a dressing on that."

Peter obeyed with one eye on Yuli. As soon as Gajwani began wrapping Peter's wound, Yuli's oxygen cratered. His heart rate shot up, and a thin bubble of blood ballooned from the catheter Peter had just inserted into his chest.

Peter brushed Gajwani off. "He's crashing!"

He tore open the chest tube kit. The tray inside included catheters, tubes, and stylets as well as a scalpel.

He painted the skin between Yuli's fourth and fifth rib with Betadine. Yuli didn't deserve topical anesthetic—a little pain wouldn't even begin to even the scales—but now that Peter's fog had lifted, at least temporarily, he would do the right thing. He drew a generous two milliliters of lidocaine into the syringe.

The last time he'd put in a chest tube was as a medical student on a mission trip to Nicaragua. The patient, a young woman who'd fallen off a small cliff, had wanted Peter to stick around because he spoke Spanish. With a retired surgeon guiding him through the procedure, Peter had inserted the tube, allowing her lung to expand to its normal size. That was years ago, back when Felipe was still in the service.

And here he was again—only this time, he was saving someone who'd tried to launch a pandemic. He made the incision in Yuli's chest and worked a gloved finger over the rib, probing by feel. Yuli groaned and held on tight to Gajwani's outstretched hand. There was no way to make the procedure completely painless. Peter punctured the pleural membrane with a pair of surgical clamps. A puff of air and a squirt of pink fluid confirmed he had reached the pleural space that was squeezing Yuli's lung. Once inside, he opened the tips of the clamp to widen the hole.

And then chaos erupted.

———————

Hemopneumothorax—blood and air flooding into Yuli's chest cavity.

Peter fed the tube into the space, angling the tip toward the top of the chest. He connected the tube to a sterile plastic box on the floor, and the box to the wall suction port. The box began filling with blood. He sutured the incision around the tube.

It was an ugly job. The old surgeon in Nicaragua would have docked him a few points.

Yuli's eyes remained closed, but his chest expanded further with each breath as his left lung filled with oxygen. His heart rate slowed, and his oxygen saturation climbed. Peter ripped off his bloody gloves and slumped onto a stool. Yuli mumbled and whimpered, but nothing more could be done for him on the ship.

Elbourne had swapped places with Gajwani during all the commotion. Peter let him wrap his arm with gauze and secure it.

"He doesn't look good," Elbourne said.

"I must've nicked a branch of the subclavian when I stabbed him," Peter said. The blood filling up the chest tube box had to be coming from somewhere. They had to get him off the ship before he hemorrhaged out. He needed a card-carrying vascular surgeon.

Elbourne's eyes bulged at the blood rising in the box. "You did that?"

"We need to get him to a hospital." Peter rose from his stool and gripped the railing of Yuli's gurney.

Elbourne checked his watch. "We could take one more on the bird, but it's leaving in four minutes."

Peter's heart leaped. "Let's go."

Elbourne hesitated.

"C'mon!"

Elbourne jerked a thumb over his shoulder. "We have another critical patient, and you don't look so hot either. You sure this guy takes the last spot?"

Peter whisked the curtain back and balanced the chest tube box on the gurney. "He is the most important man in the world right now. He holds the key."

"What does that— Okay, I'll play along for now, Dr. Palma, but you'd better explain." Elbourne grabbed the other end of the gurney and nodded at the soldiers jammed into the bay.

The soldiers parted before them like the Red Sea, and they raced down I-95, Peter pushing and Elbourne pulling.

Peter corralled his wits. "He's been spreading the virus that caused all this."

Elbourne snorted. "So he's coughing on everyone?"

"I thought it was the air ducts, but it's not. It's the little bottles of hand sanitizer, like the one in my pocket. They designed the virus to thrive in it. Squirt it on your hands, because that's what you're supposed to do, then rub your face without thinking. It gets into your nose, into your system—and boom, into your brain. It's damn perfect."

Elbourne braced hard and squelched their forward momentum. "You know how loony you sound?"

Peter leaned into the gurney. "Don't stop!"

Elbourne stepped back and opened his mouth.

Peter held up a hand. "If you say 'One zap'll do you...'"

They locked eyes over the husk of Yuli's hemorrhaging body. Peter's teeth all but ground to dust under the force of his tension, and a hot flush rose to his face.

Elbourne nodded, pivoted, and yanked the gurney hard. They continued onward. Peter let out a whoosh of relief.

They passed a caravan of white body bags. Four blue-clad servicemen handled each bag, one at each corner. Gurneys were reserved for the living.

"Did I mention the coolers?" Peter said. "There are more bodies in there."

Elbourne cursed and squawked a command into his radio.

They passed the loading bay where he and Luisa had unloaded Sharma a thousand years ago. At the bottom, connected by a ramp, a sleek black boat was floating, a hearse for Yuli's victims.

The chopper's twin rotors pummeled the air on the helipad. Helmeted troopers loaded Yuli, chest tube and all, into the last bay alongside other wounded and ill. Wincing against the daylight, Peter saw a young woman vomiting and a disheveled man staring with raccoon eyes. The troopers collapsed Yuli's gurney, buckled it to the floor, and moved to shut the door.

"Wait! Hold on!" Peter yelled. His words disintegrated in the roar, but he blocked the door with his lacerated arm, hissing against the pain. He plucked an index card from his pocket, scribbled on it with stiff and sore fingers, and tucked it in the pocket of Yuli's pants.

Elbourne tapped his wristwatch and pounded the fuselage's belly.

Peter felt for the bottle of sanitizer. Just a few ounces of clear gel. Yuli plus the hand sanitizer. The authorities needed both. He extended the bottle to the soldiers.

A metallic screech pierced through the roar of the rotors, shifting the soldiers' attention to the side of the *Paradise*. He followed their stares to the orange boat dangling in the air—the MOB boat.

Peter jammed the bottle back into his pocket. He couldn't put all his eggs in one basket. The chopper might crash into the sea and all would be lost. Or his note and the bottle would get cast aside during surgical prep. He had to get this proof into the hands of someone who would believe him—and he had to do it before his brain turned to oatmeal.

That MOB boat was his ticket to New York City.

25

THE ORANGE MOB boat hung from stout arms extending from midships, the same boat that had been deployed to search for Calvin's mom and the man who jumped overboard. The open vessel was the size of a Chevy Suburban, sleek and built for speed.

Shouts rose as a figure in white climbed over the railing into the MOB boat. Another man stood ready at the control box, ready to winch it into the water. Peter leaned over the railing and squinted. Those were officers' uniforms. Didn't he know those men?

Captain Forster looked up from the bright orange boat and met Peter with a jittery stare. He'd kept his stubble, and his uniform wasn't all white after all; a dark splotch bore witness to some foul deed. Peter froze. He had instigated the coup to remove the proud captain from command. The last time he'd seen him, the captain had been dancing around the bonfire in street clothes.

"Forster!" someone shouted. "Stop where you are!"

Forster spoke, but the chopper drowned him out as it

lifted off. He pointed to the man at the controls. The MOB boat jolted and began descending on a thick steel cable over the side of the ship.

No time to waste by asking permission. This little boat was Peter's only hope. He clambered over the railing and tumbled in next to Forster, sending it seesawing wildly. He covered his head and braced for blows. Instead, a hand closed around one of his.

Forster pulled him up and encircled him in a bear hug. Peter winced at the pressure on his arm, but he grinned and thumped Forster's back. No time to look this gift horse in the mouth. He'd take it.

The moment the boat splashed into the water, Forster unhooked the cable and took the helm near the outboard motor at the rear. Peter parked himself on a padded bench in front as the motor guttered to life. The boat squirted out from the *Paradise*'s side like a jet of pus from a lanced boil. They bounced hard on waves as Forster cut through the wake of the cruise ship.

Shielding his eyes from the sun's glare, Peter twisted left and right to search for signs of pursuit. Good thing the army transport boats were huddled on the other side of the ship. If the helicopter pilot had any intention of intercepting, the time would be now. But the chopper continued toward the city.

His shoulders tightened. That's where he needed to go too. What if Forster steered for the Bahamas instead? With a brain as riddled by the virus as Forster's, anything was possible. Not that his own was much better. They were cut from the same cloth, one covered in blood and one— Come to think of it, Peter's own uniform wasn't exactly pristine either, stained with the blood of Yuli and Mauricio.

His cramped muscles unwound as the little vessel turned

for the coast. It was rough going until they achieved critical speed, after which the boat skimmed over the waves effortlessly. Forster looked like a kid with his wide grin and the wind whipping through his glorious hair.

Peter looked back at the ship, a beast bloated with purulence. Nali was still there. She'd better be holed up somewhere safe—Mandy and Calvin, too. Blood had seeped through the gauze wrapped around Peter's arm. Yuli was somewhere in the air above them. He forced himself to turn around and fix his eyes on the horizon, where New York City waited for him. He just needed to hang on.

The salt spray stung his face. They were probably getting close to the territorial waters of the United States, where Elbourne's TMS trial would not be condoned. He glanced back at Forster. Territorial waters would be little comfort if the ex-captain suddenly decided to toss him overboard.

Each mile closer to shore also meant a better cell signal. He dialed Wetzel and jammed the phone against his ear. It rang and rang until a faint, crackly voice answered.

"Peter, oh my gosh, is it you? You're all over the news!"

That wasn't Wetzel. Dammit, he'd dialed Wendy. He didn't even remember who she was and why he'd saved her number or how long ago. He hung up. Battery life was down to 8 percent.

He tried Wetzel again, and thank God she answered.

"Where are you?" he shouted over the motor and stinging spray.

"In the city. Just getting out of LaGuardia. Where are you?"

He grinned. "Heading there too. I'm in a little orange boat with the former captain."

"You're what? Peter, I don't know—"

"They're airlifting Yuli to the hospital." This was it—he could offload all the details.

"What?"

"I have the hand sanitizer!"

"What are you talking about?"

He clenched his jaw. Of course she was clueless. Once he'd recovered his phone from Yuli, there'd been no time to reach out and explain. With his battery about to die, he blurted out the story, aiming to balance clarity and speed.

Near the end of his rant, a winged woman speared out of the water. He nearly dropped the phone into the waves as she hovered above the MOB boat, transfixing him with eyes burning gold and purple. The anthem of the heavens poured from her mouth, and she beckoned him with graceful fingers tipped with glittering claws.

Her song filled his head with the light of Earth's first morning. He rose shakily and tottered to the edge of the boat. She was calling him home. She would lift him into the primordial plasma that held everything together. All the little particles he was made of would lose their cohesion, and the form of him would be forever gone. What a relief.

The boat lurched and slammed down on the waves. He fell to his knees, sputtering and choking on salt water. Where did she go? He searched in all directions, but the angel was gone. He slapped his face and beat his chest and let out a scream.

Forster yowled back in glee.

"Peter! Can you hear me?" Wetzel's voice squeaked out from the phone somehow still in his grip.

"I'm here. I just got— I have to give you the bottle. It has the virus in it!" A message in a bottle.

The signal cut out. When it came back, she was saying something about bowling.

"—me at the bowling bull, and we'll—"

More crackles, then silence. His phone was dead.

His vision darkened, and he lowered his head between his knees. Humanity would end because he'd forgotten to charge his phone last night.

He suddenly sat up and whipped around to Forster. "Lemme borrow your phone."

This phase of post-viral degeneration had rendered Forster agreeable and disoriented, yet apparently still able to pilot a boat, like a happy drunk. He tossed Peter his phone.

Peter gaped at it blankly. The device was no more useful to him than a brick because he didn't have Wetzel's number memorized. He waved to Forster and lobbed it back to him, then dug Yuli's phone out of his pocket, but it was still locked, still useless.

———————

The city blossomed before them like a bouquet of crystal reeds, the city of cities, a world in itself. Forget the bouquet; this was a hulking riot of steel and flesh. The spire of the Empire State Building glowed like a sword of flame. A taller, newer building soared near where the Twin Towers must have once stood. The Statue of Liberty waited patiently to the left, her torch held aloft. She hadn't trotted off after all.

The MOB boat joined vessels of all sizes in the bay—sleek yachts, workhorse tugboats, and a ferry named *Skyline Explorer*. The whole way in, Peter kept muttering Wetzel's last words so he wouldn't forget: "Bowling bull, bowling bull, bowling bull." Now if he could only figure out what they meant.

Gigantic bridges with their towers and cables spanned the waterways, carrying the nations to and from the city. Peter imagined movie mobsters dumping bodies into the river. These waters would be choked with bloated corpses if he failed to prove that the plague bearing down on New York was driven by terrorists.

A terrorist. That's what Yuli was.

The MOB boat slowed as Forster scanned bulkheads and rocky beaches in search of a place to land. A patch of greenery appeared at the foot of Manhattan. They pulled up alongside a narrow slip, and Forster cut the engine. Peter rose carefully to his feet and nearly lost his balance as the boat rocked on the rolling tide. He lunged for a thick wooden post jutting from the dock and wrapped his arms around it, restoking the embers of pain.

He scrabbled and pushed with his legs, but the effort only shoved the boat back. The vessel slid out from beneath his feet. He plunged knee-deep into the water, still clinging to the post but with a weakening grip.

Someone above grabbed hold of his arms. "Holy smokes, man, what are you doing?"

Peter was pulled high enough to clamber around the post and over a steel railing. He planted his soaked shoes on concrete stamped in the pattern of hexagons—his first dry land since Mioven, Norway, where he'd evacuated the strangled Sharma.

Forster gunned the engine and pulled away from the dock, whooping like a savage. He pumped his fist at Peter and sped off to continue his world tour, captain of his own ship again.

"Are you okay?" The man who'd hoisted him up regarded him with caution, scanning him up and down. His shorts and the bottom of his Hofstra sweatshirt were soaked.

Peter didn't blame him for his wariness. A guy in a bloodied white officer's uniform with a busted nose and poorly bandaged arm, climbing out of the sea like Godzilla's quarry—not your average waterside encounter. Once again, however, he had to convince someone to make sense of details that made no sense to him at all.

Peter figured Wetzel must've said bowling *ball*, because *bowling bull* didn't mean anything. "Is there a bowling alley around here?"

"You should see a doctor," Hofstra muttered. He backed away and turned tail.

Peter staggered up a shallow flight of granite steps to a lush park filled with trees and shrubs. He dodged pedestrians and electric scooters, young and old. A gap-toothed woman with a stroller, a grizzled old man in an impeccable pin-striped suit. Peter could only keep moving forward, his shoes squishing and sloshing with every step.

"Where's the bowling alley?" he demanded of a woman on a bench.

She looked up lazily from her book. "You mean Bowling *Green*? With the big bull?"

The bull! He nodded.

She pointed toward the far edge of the park, where it met bustling streets. "That way."

He lurched along manicured pathways. There was a glass building shaped like a snail and a circular fortress of old brick. A dozen monuments and statues. A food truck selling cookies and boba tea. Leaning against the back of the truck was a young man with tan, wiry arms crossed over his chest, head bobbing and earbuds dangling. As Peter drew near, the man raised his head.

Felipe's eyes bore straight into Peter—his nose, a smooth ball of flesh without nostrils. His lips, charred like sausages. Felipe in degenerate, inhuman form.

Peter stumbled sideways and landed hard on the warm concrete. Felipe opened his ruined mouth and blew out a giant bubble that hovered in the summer heat. Deep within the bubble floated a small, round object: a tablet of hydrocodone.

Peter scrambled backward on his hands and feet. The narco-bubble expanded until Felipe was completely obscured. Peter bumped up against a bike rack then used it to pull himself to his feet.

When he looked again, the bubble had popped, and his brother was gone too. He tiptoed to where Felipe had been standing and he peered at the ground. There were cigarette butts and candy wrappers but no hydrocodone.

Peter continued forward. After a few steps, he found himself listing toward a woman in black yoga pants. Damn, what magnificent hips she had—perfect for mating. He clamped a hand briefly on her marvelous ass as he tottered past. She launched into a much-deserved tirade as he continued on his way toward the ball. Or the bull.

He patted the hand sanitizer in his pocket and willed himself to put one foot in front of the other. He had to keep moving. Earlier he'd almost knifed Kinnard, first officer turned captain of a cruise ship. In the clinic, he'd advanced on Mandy like a wolf. He'd smashed a pillow into Yuli's face in a full-on murderous rage. What else had he done?

Eat, sleep, mate, repeat. Make like a beast, Pete.

It would be easy to let it all go and unleash the animal. In this city, of all places, he could indulge himself in anonymity. The damage had already been done. Better to embrace the carnal life than long for a state of innocence that was gone forever.

He emerged on Broadway and continued in the direction the bench lady had pointed. Walking ahead of him, a young woman in shorts captured his attention.

She probably smelled like—

Focus! He tore his eyes away.

He passed under the shadow of regal, ornate buildings of granite and glass. Moving, moving, always moving, straight ahead. Finally he broke out into a plaza in the rough shape of a triangle. His destination? He looked around for a bull. Or a ball. Or a lady. Wasn't he here to meet a lady?

Squinting against the light, he made his way toward a cluster of tourists. Maybe there would be some benches here, and he could rest at last. He pushed through the group and emerged at a bronze statue of a bull about the size of a UPS truck.

A bull—*the* bull.

He stared at the beast with muscles like boulders, flared nostrils, and wicked horns. A world-ending scrotum hung between colossal haunches. It was the paragon of brutality and rage, just like Peter.

This is where he belonged.

Peter shoved his way through a knot of people snapping photos, crouched low, and crawled under the beast's belly. He curled up on the cobblestone and laid his head down. It was finally time to let it all go.

———

Something was jabbing him in the ribs.

"Hey, buddy!" Rough hands tugged Peter out from under the bull and pulled him to his feet. A male police officer in navy-blue gave him the once-over. "No loitering. But do you know the other reason I'd like to talk with you? Any idea?"

Peter rubbed his face and tried to blink away the grogginess.

The officer shifted his gaze to a group of onlookers. There

in front was a woman in yoga pants. She nodded briefly at the policeman and faded back into the crowd.

"Seen her before?" he asked Peter.

She did look familiar—Shit! "I didn't mean it. I couldn't help it because her ass—"

A black SUV screeched to a halt at the curb. A tall, trim woman in a charcoal suit climbed out from the passenger side and hustled over to them. She shot Peter a quick glance and turned to the officer. "It's okay, he's with us."

She continued talking with the officer in clipped, urgent tones. Something about national security and bioterrorism. She pulled out some papers, but the man wasn't budging.

He turned back to Peter. "Hey, you know her?"

The tall woman opened her mouth, but the officer put up a hand to shush her. Peter tried to shake the webs from his brain.

"Peter!"

Something about her voice.

"No idea?" The officer looked to her, who glared at Peter.

Peter swayed on his feet and leaned against the bull. Wait a minute, he did know her. The voice on the phone all this time. She was the medical director from Florida. Nelly Williams, or something. No, that wasn't it. It was—

"You're Wetzel. Nora Wetzel," Peter said. "I was trying to meet with you."

She let out a massive sigh of relief and turned to the officer again, negotiating fiercely, handed him a card, and ended the discussion with her arms crossed.

"You." The officer crooked a finger at him. "Keep your grubby hands to yourself, and don't show your face around here again." The officer departed the scene, muttering, and the crowd that had gathered dispersed as well.

Wetzel turned to appraise him. "Goodness, what a sight, Peter."

She wasn't wrong. But one thing stood out among the bruises and blood: the scribble on his forearm—*Yuli hand sanitizer virus*. That was the key, the only thing that mattered.

He pulled out the bottle of hand sanitizer and Yuli's phone. "You understand what these are, don't you?"

"I have a pretty good idea."

Handing her the two small objects felt like dumping sandbags off his shoulders. He rested his palm on the bull's flank, the bronze warmed by the summer sun shining on the city, the same sun that smiled upon all creatures roaming the earth. He squinted through the strident light—everything hurt, but he didn't need to run from it anymore.

"We're taking you to the hospital," Wetzel said. "You look terrible."

26

THE FBI AND CIA extracted their pound of flesh while Peter received IV steroids at New York Presbyterian. The card he'd placed in Yuli's pocket before the airlift, Yuli's phone—all of it entered the official record.

But it really came down to that one little bottle.

The corroboratory call from Wetzel came through just as Peter and Nali stepped off the plane in Houston. "They confirmed the hand sanitizer as the reservoir of the infection."

Peter froze in front of the duty-free shop and touched Nali's shoulder. He released a long, slow breath.

"Nipadenovirus," Wetzel continued. "A mashup of Nipah and adenovirus. That's what WHO is calling it."

Hot damn, a novel virus—he'd nailed it. The Nipah virus attacked the brain, while adenovirus was resistant to alcohol. The combination formed a brain-chewing menace spread by the antiseptic substance that was supposed to protect everybody.

"It's genius, when you think about it," Wetzel continued in his ear. "It was only a matter of time before a few bad actors did something like this. It's pretty darn perfect—except they failed to plan for one crucial thing."

"What's that?" His gaze swept across the travelers crowded at the gates. The moms, the dads, the kids—harried and stressed, but not bashing each other's heads in. This was the peace that Yuli had almost destroyed.

"Some punk named Peter Palma."

A flush rose in his neck as the implication sunk in. His name would be forever attached to this saga, so he might as well start getting used to it.

All told, according to Wetzel, some one-third of the passengers and crew had shown signs of encephalitis. Ninety-eight had received MRIs on board, and all but five showed frontal lobe damage and neuropsychiatric symptoms. Results of the TMS trial were pending. Similar cases of encephalitis had been confirmed in numerous port cities.

"Is Yuli… Did he make it?" he asked.

"He's alive."

"Is he talking?"

"He is. They worked his Gatobi9 handle and traced his communications all the way back. That network is deep and wide."

He caught Nali's eye and tilted his head toward the escalator at the end of the terminal. They rolled their suitcases along as he finished the call. It was too easy to remember how seductive Yuli's dream had been. Eat. Sleep. Mate. Repeat. Who wouldn't want that kind of life?

But he'd nabbed the bad guy in the end. Felipe would never come back, but countless would-be victims were still alive because Peter had thwarted Yuli's plan.

———

Wetzel's updates continued after he settled into a new condo. Chessa was recuperating in Florida on the cruise line's dime from the fractures and lacerations dealt by Mauricio. She was week-to-week until cleared to fly back to Poland, and she'd been awarded compensation that would cover her father's meds, at least for a while.

Calvin faced an unclear future. His estranged father had turned out to be a complete flake, and Child Protective Services was vetting candidates to foster Calvin.

Nali wanted to visit Calvin on Labor Day weekend. "We should take a road trip up there. Just think of it—the mountains! And no ocean in sight."

It would be good to see the guy, but even Colorado seemed too far. Peter needed to stay home for a while. "Besides, I'm not sure they'd let us visit him. That kind of situation can be tricky."

For that matter, so was his own. Mood swings, fatigue, fogginess—some days were worse than others. A decent night's sleep was the only thing that seemed to tamp down the urges and hallucinations. His MRI in New York had shown hyperintensity on T2-weighted images in the frontal lobe—the "mark of the beast," according to certain pundits. At least the edema and punctate hemorrhages were receding on serial scans now. One spot would never improve, though: a walnut-sized focus of necrosis, the ultimate souvenir from the *Paradise*. The hole from which purple spiders crawled out—only now he knew they weren't real.

Pastor Burkett kept his word and visited from Tennessee. They met for beer and enchiladas, and Burkett told him he'd come out of retirement. People needed a message of hope and truth, and who was to say he was done?

"But how can you parse it out?" Peter asked. "How can

you tell if someone's mentally ill or if they're struggling with impulse control … or they're just plain evil?"

Burkett sipped from his mug. "The Apostle Paul was tormented by his own base nature. He said, 'The evil I do not want is what I keep on doing.'"

"I bet he was a hoot at parties."

"Peter, there's only one way to make peace with the beast, and it isn't the way of that guy on the ship."

He'd have to think about that. Maybe the virus didn't create murderous urges, but it had unleashed them in a way never seen before. Some were calling it "the regression strain." Fully realized, Yuli's vision would've ravaged the entire human population, as with a snap of a demigod's fingers.

Peter's therapist preached patience and grace. "You didn't get away scot-free." That sounded right. He'd been torn down to the studs, and rebuilding was tough work. He picked up an acoustic Yamaha guitar and discovered he wasn't terrible. Maybe he and Felipe would've made a decent duo.

And a local clinic was hiring. He said he'd consider it, which he did for a while, and then woke up one Friday ready to take the job. It was time to dive back in. It wasn't about figuring everything out, but more about adapting and persevering. No more retreating. The important thing was to do the good thing, even if the outcome was uncertain. *Especially* when the outcome was uncertain.

Plus, seeing patients again would distract him from the hole that bothered him the most—not the hole in his brain, but the lack of a single photo of Mandy. He hadn't even taken a selfie with her smiling in the background.

The week before Halloween, Peter eased his Outback down Harborside Drive in Galveston, just south of Houston. A cloudy day, but he still needed sunglasses. Nali rode shotgun, nursing an extra-large Dr Pepper and texting friends the whole time, squealing and groaning. It was good to see her acting silly. Silly but resilient, and making bank at a cybersecurity firm.

The *Paradise* towered above the cruise terminal, a floating city gleaming white and blue against the Gulf Coast sky. His throat tightened. Geez, the ship was even larger than he remembered. Maybe it had grown fat on the pain and suffering it had once contained.

He parked on the street, and they waited inside a café on the ground floor of a renovated warehouse in the historic Strand District. It was a perfect place for a reunion—rustic tables, casual vibe—but the dispenser of hand sanitizer up front? No thanks. He steered way clear of that.

Mandy arrived in shorts and a T-shirt, duffel bag on her shoulder, no mask. His pulse quickened. Her hair was longer now, her face aglow, and she looked even better than he'd remembered. They hugged, first all jangled, then settled, her cheeks brushing his and sending electric shivers down his spine, and she smelled *so good*, a tropical breeze.

They ordered cake.

"That healed up well." Mandy pointed to his nose with her fork.

He had relived the gentle pain of her ministrations a thousand times. They had all come a long way. "Your Steri-Strips must have done the trick. How was your last contract?"

"Interesting. The other nurses were fun, and the doctors were chill."

"And Luisa? Is she still…"

Her eyes dropped. "She tried to make that Appalachian trip, but she had to stop in the middle. Some crisis, I think. She doesn't post very often, and she's not answering my texts." But her face brightened as she went on to describe the progress of her wellness program. "I finally got them to bring in new equipment for the crew gym."

He gave her a thumbs up. "Way to go."

"And we started the peer counseling program. Even the small stuff adds up."

"That's not small—that's huge!" A grin spread across his face. She was hitting her stride. Good for her. "What's next?"

She shrugged. "My next contract doesn't start till February. I'm heading back to Portland for a while."

"Oh." She was just touching down, then off again. Of course. They were all moving on. "When's your flight?"

"At three. I'll call for a ride."

Nali stiffened and kicked him under the table.

"Nonsense." Peter wiped his mouth and dropped the napkin on his empty plate. "We'll take you."

An hour later, they were cruising up I-45 toward the airport, Mandy up front, Nali in the back. He mentioned the clinic where he'd started working. "The patients and their families, the cards are stacked against them."

She turned to study him. "Sounds tough. Are you…"

"It's okay." He glanced over. "It feels right."

She nodded. "Then I'm happy for you, Peter."

They traded stories about recent patients, but at some point he wanted to stop talking shop. Their worlds didn't intersect anymore—he doubted he'd ever set foot on a cruise ship again—so he had to make today count.

"Wait, I almost forgot." She reached into her bag under the seat and retrieved a familiar can of iced coffee.

He let out a yelp—the wicked stuff.

She grinned back. "Need a shot? Agus brings these by all the time now."

Nali said no thanks, she was still working on her soda, but he got Mandy to crack open a can for him. The first gulp brought back that unforgettable adrenaline zoom, as well as an important question he'd almost forgotten to ask. "That last bottle of hand sanitizer—the one you saved—how exactly did you end up with it?"

"Yeah, about that." She folded her arms. "The security guard dragged me and Calvin up to that horrible room at knifepoint. He snatched the bag of bottles that you had saved, and Yuli sent him out to get more. At that point, something clicked. I knew they were trying to get rid of the evidence, but I didn't understand what it all meant. So I was like"—she mimed slipping the bottle down her shirt—"'In you go.'"

Brilliant. She was absolutely brilliant. And kind, and brave, and sitting right next to him.

She cocked her head. "Remember what you said when Yuli tried to get me? Right before he cut your arm?"

Oh, no. It was safe to assume that encephalitis-induced delirium had spurred him on to a number of regretful deeds. There were many things he couldn't recall, and it was probably best that nobody remembered them. "I'm afraid to ask."

Her laugh brought him back to that first day on the ship before everything went to hell. "You said I was your woman."

Oh yeah, that was it.

Nali perked up in the back. "Hold on—what?"

"Actually," Mandy said, "it was more like, 'She my woman!'" It was impossible for her to sound Neanderthalic, but he gave her an A for effort.

"Geez." He shook his head. "I wasn't myself. You know, encephalitis and all. I'm sorry." But if the virus had uncovered his truest, deepest instincts, then—

"You're sorry?" She stared down at her hands.

Damn, there was no right answer. "I mean, I must've meant it. At the time."

"But now?" Nali prodded from the back.

"Now I'm not delirious," he said.

"That's good to hear," Mandy said.

"And I'm not your supervisor anymore."

"Thank goodness."

"So we can do whatever we want, right?"

Nali's big goofy smile lit up the rearview mirror. The only sounds were the purr of the air conditioner and the seams of the freeway thudding beneath his tires. He glanced at Mandy, then back at the road. She reached over and rested her hand on his shoulder. He leaned into it.

They passed dozens of strip malls and billboards, Mandy beside him and Nali in back, iced coffee flowing in his veins. Nothing better than this. A sign announced that the airport exit was half a mile ahead.

He had a chance here, maybe. A detour. "I don't know if I mentioned it, but they have great Chinese food in Houston."

Mandy adjusted the vent on her side. "Oh yeah?"

It was do or die now. "Are you up for it? I know you have a flight but…"

She paused for what felt like forever. "What about those fajitas you were talking about?"

"I know just the place."

"Your condo doesn't count."

Nali sputtered on her soda. "Hah! He can barely turn on the stove!"

He chuckled and settled into his seat. Mandy was smiling right at him, her eyes shining just like when they'd laughed together behind masks at the clinic. "No, this place, when they bring it out, it's all sizzling on a cast-iron platter. You smell it before you see it."

"Mmm." Mandy rubbed her hands together. "That sounds incredible."

A warm tingle swept through him from head to toe. Anything, anywhere with her would be incredible. He cleared his throat and mimicked holding up a microphone. "Attention all passengers, this is your captain here. There's been a change in the itinerary and—"

Mandy laughed and batted his hand down. Their palms met across the seats and their fingers intertwined. As to whether their futures would do the same, he'd take that one step at a time.

LETTER TO READERS

Thanks for reading. I hope you enjoyed the story!

May I prevail on you again? Please consider leaving a review on Amazon and/or Goodreads. Reviews help other readers discover the book.

Visit me at **KevinHwang.com** for more info about forthcoming books and to sign up for my newsletter.

ABOUT THE AUTHOR

I'm a father, husband, and internal medicine physician in the Houston area.

Some of my favorite things are:

- Index cards
- Frito pie
- Appropriately sized packaging
- The guitar intro to "Where the Streets Have No Name"
- Plugging in my phone after the battery plummets below 80%
- Hakeem's dream shake
- An accurate blood pressure measurement
- Chicken enchiladas
- Aragorn telling the hobbits, "My friends, you bow to no one" – chills every time

ACKNOWLEDGEMENTS

It takes a village. I'm so thankful to everyone who has nurtured the book along the way.

To Lisa Poisso, for coaching, editing, and challenging me to keep working on the story through multiple drafts. Her notes are a fount of wisdom.

To Lisa Kaitz for copyediting and Elizabeth Thurmond for proofreading.

To Pritha Bhattacharyya and Nathan Carlin of the McGovern Center for Humanities and Ethics as well as my colleagues in the Center's inaugural class of Writing Fellows. Those Tuesday night sessions got me going after I'd almost shelved the novel for good.

To those who gave feedback on early drafts and sections: Eric Thomas, Lilit Sargsyan, Bonnie Chan, Michael Lee, Mary Pinkowish, Rachel Froelich, Christopher Ryan, and James Morgan.

To Norty Cohen, Shanon Hunt, and B.R. Keid for feedback on the cover and a few key scenes.

Finally, to my wife Florence for her gentle spirit and sharp eye. It was only after she proclaimed a draft was "a good story" that I had the courage to proceed with (another) tortuous round of revision.